The Shipbuilder's Daughter

Virginia M. Lofft

The author is deeply grateful for the encouragement and suggestions of Claire L. Jurkowski, Robbie Dunlap, Beth Crymes, S. Roxandich and mentors and fellow students at Vermont College of Fine Arts and Thomas Edison State University

Hoorn — 1628

. *"They were most happy while they were out of their wits."*

In Praise of Folly by Desiderius Erasmus (Classics Club edition)

CHAPTER 1—MAAGDA

A GRUELING DAY OF CHARCOAL STUBS, SMUDGED work and soiled hands, of redrawing lines here, angles there. Cramps splayed my fingers into odd shapes when I tried to knead the kinks in my shoulders after hours over the drafting board. I wanted to rest, let my mind wander. My eyes caught tiny motes of dust drifting idly in the still air, their slow moves calming my jumbled thoughts, until a sudden draft from the door stirred their fragile dance. I looked up, and grabbed for the corners of my drafting table. Willie van Pelt! What brought that odious creature to our boat yard, and him walking directly to Papa.

"Good morning, Maagda," he grinned, the crevices in his teeth caked with the cheese he sold on Hoorn's main road. Crumbs of yellow Edam trembled on the edge of his chin hairs. He reached to stroke my face, but I pushed back beyond his hand. The mere thought of his touch iced my blood. I'd cringed at the sight of him since childhood, our days in primary when he sneezed and snorted through numbers and history. He was a man now, but that suspect shine still glistened on his sleeve. And didn't I still have the odd apron or two spotted with the ink he would flick at me from his dripping nib.

Papa's chair scuffed the wide oak floorboards as he rose to greet Willie.

"Ah, Boscher." Willie walked toward Papa's desk. Calling Papa by his last name. No Lars. No Mr. Boscher. What gall, elevating himself to Papa's level. Willie extended his hand and nodded in my direction. "I see our little girl is here to tidy up for you."

Our little girl! At 24 and working in this Yard since my thirteenth birthday. I was about to protest, when Papa took Willie's hand and said, "No tidying up for Maagda. She pens our design drafts, knows the business as well as I do." He pointed to the detailed plan of our new fluytship on the wall behind my table. "That's her work. And she can tame a decent bargain out of any supplier whether for the best timber or a delivery date."

Willie smirked and seated himself in the wobbly cane-back chair beside Papa's desk where he had a broad view of two hulls under construction in the Yard, and to the East, the sun shot waters of the Zuider Zee.

Willie might know his cheeses, but he wouldn't know a spar from a spanner, so what brought him here this day. I didn't like it. The thought gnawed, ate at me.

"Maagda, might you take these papers out to Freddie. He's working with the oakum crew on the hull in the north cradle. He reached for the iron bar on the floor near his chair. "And this rave hook as well. Ask the blacksmith to sharpen the angle."

I frowned at Papa, but he turned his eyes away. He rarely sent me on such errands in the Yard, especially where the crews pounded oakum and hemp into the hull seams. Dirty work and staring eyes.

So. I was not to hear his conversation with Willie.

"And, Maagda. Go on home. You've had a full day."

My head snapped back. A full day? Papa's treasured lantern clock had just struck three. We never left before six, except in the deepest winter. I caught Willie's smug glance, his lips tight, no doubt to hold back his laughter. What were these two about? The question shot a tremor down from my neck along my arms. Clutching the rave hook and the sheaf of papers, I quickened to the door and the safety of the steps before anger-fed watery eyes betrayed me.

Freddie, Papa's Yard manager, stood on a crate, calling names of workers for the two oakum crews. He waved when he saw me skirting round the stacks of wood and pots of tar and oakum that blocked my passage.

"My nephew, Pier, visited yesterday. He asked after you."

A swell raced to my throat. Pier, the dashing ginger-haired diamond man from Amsterdam. After but a single meeting at our home, my thoughts buzzed with plans to meet him again. When our hands touched at the table that day my whole body answered with a heat so searing, I feared I brushed a burning candle. In these weeks since, that warmth sweeps over me at the mere mention of his name.

"Was that young van Pelt I saw climbing up to the nest?" Freddie tilted his head in the direction of the office.

I nodded. All the men called Papa's office the crow's nest. It was built on stilts, offering a view of the entire Yard, and sheltered storage for our lumber supplies.

Freddie laughed. "Maybe he wants to peddle his cheeses to the men at mealtime."

I couldn't return Freddie's banter, my thoughts and heartbeats still frozen in the mystery of Willie's visit. Even his mention of Pier failed to budge my anxiety.

My walk home through the salt grass on the dunes was a weary trudge, urging each heavy foot forward, wondering what news Papa would bring to the supper table.

A trade issue perhaps, but surely, the van Pelt cheese exports were not so big they needed their own ship. Or maybe Willie bargained for better shipping rates now that the competition from the expanding boatyard in Amsterdam promised a cut in price. The Boscher Boatyard was primarily a shipbuilding business, but Papa did accept trade shipments from local merchants on our finished vessels when they were to be delivered to nearby ports. But such trips were months apart, surely not something of importance to Willie.

Sweet figs. Oh, sweet figs. How blind of me. The thought assailed me with such force, I crumbled onto the damp dune. Did Willie come to Papa to barter his mother, to arrange a union between my widowed father and his widowed parent? The thought, repulsive in every hue, hit me as hard and brittle as the oyster shells biting through my skirt.

Dear, dear god. Was there any thought more disgusting, more repulsive. Bile lodged in my throat. Madam van Pelt, a woman so tart of tongue, so, so… I couldn't allow myself to finish the wicked words that begged to trip from my lips. Willie was his mother's son.

The evening ahead loomed a stormy shadow even though the sun had yet to spray its final colors over the waters beyond me.

Papa unlocked the mystery the moment he swept in from his day at the Yard. He took his seat in the reading chair by the canal window and bade me take mother's old floral padded chair facing him.

"Close the door, Maagda. No need for your sister or Sophie in the scullery to listen in."

Beads of moisture ran in rivulets beneath my collar. "Miekke shouldn't be here?"

"No. This discussion concerns you and me, not your sister."

If Papa thought of remarriage all these years after Mama's passing, it most certainly would involve Miekke. I was about to protest when he reached for my hands.

My palms dampened and a frightening dread prickled my skin.

He looked into my eyes, then away through the window and out across the canal waters. "You've known that it is your lot to marry and produce an heir for the Hoorn Trust, the legacy that keeps our Yard and our town alive."

My fingers went limp in his hands. I lowered my head, unable to look at him, trying not to hear his voice.

"And Maagda, you've entered your marriageable years. Early, yes, but I think you ready nonetheless." He cleared his throat. "The Widow van Pelt has proposed an alliance and her son, Willie, agrees. It would be a fine match. Good local people."

Papa's words knocked the breath out of me. A betrayal, and from the man I most loved in this life.

For twenty-four years I'd been the dutiful daughter, but this, this, sparked a rebellion in me so foreign, I shuddered at my own thoughts. A demon seized my speech. Never had I said no to Papa, harangued him, no less. But I did and my words, flung hard and biting, left me quaking in spirit. How could I not have thought of this, instead, conjuring a wedding for Papa?

"No, no, no, a fleet of no's," I cried, shaken that my own father should countenance so base a proposal. Me marry the loathsome Willie van Pelt? I jumped from the chair and paced the room, fifteen steps corner to corner, my limbs shivering, but still I managed to unearth every affront about Willie I might give tongue to.

"Maagda, you shake loose my moorings. I can't fathom why you object."

"He's callow. Loathsome."

"But you've known him for years. He's bred a Hoorn man, and from a decent merchant family."

"He reeks of overripe Gouda." I wasn't to be silenced, spewing word upon word to cover the fear creeping over me, the very space around me tasting strange to my shattered senses. "I could not allow myself near him to create an heir."

"Speech from the docks, not from a daughter, not from my daughter." Papa dug the heel of his boot into the curved edge of the hooked rug, shoving it left, then right. "I can't believe you so suddenly shallow, you my child of keen mind. The man has good qualities and he's been reared to understand trade." He inhaled a sweep of air. "There are other issues here, and well you know them."

I firmed my quivering lips and pulled my skirts tight around my legs to still the trembling in my knees. I couldn't fathom which the more bitter dose, Willie or the thought that Papa would give me so easily. And to add to my misery, a squeak of the floorboards told me my sister, Miekke, savored every word in her hiding place near the door.

"I will not," I said, mustering some newly found strength and mouthing every word in a slow cadence, "marry *him*. You think only of the Hoorn Trust."

Papa's head reared back, nostrils wide as a lashed colt. I'd stabbed the sore spot and with purpose. Yes, I know well my duty to mother an heir for the Hoorn legacy. Hadn't I heard it on every birthday since my tenth year? "My glory in life," Mother had called it. Did she die trying, I wondered, only to birth two girls and a third that went to the ground with her?

"You will not defy me." Papa balled his hands into fists and pounded them against his thighs, flinging motes of dust and wood shavings from his breeches. "This is a father's decision, and I will make that decision before this very week counts its last day."

"*You? You* decide?" I collapsed onto the cushioned window seat, my head against the cool pane, breathing hard, my fingers crushing the jonquils I had rescued moments earlier, a small cluster barely sheltered from the frost in the rear garden. At this moment the same cold frosted my blood, and without the shelter I'd always expected in my life, my father's protection and love.

"Why, Papa. Why?"

"Why?" His lower lip quivered. "Because you know nothing of men."

"You are the one who knows nothing." I pressed my palm against the cold glass, a vain effort to cool my anger and my fear.

Papa moved to grab my wrist. He was a patient man, not without a streak of temper, but he controlled himself and looked at me, eyes mere slits.

"Take hold of yourself. You shout like a cod hawker on the wharf." He shook his head, sighed and slumped again into his reading chair by the window, his favorite view overlooking a canal still rimmed with thin bits of ice. I saw how the veins in his neck throbbed, and I choked a wisp of regret for my anger.

"I've been too soft," his tone spoke a volume of self-doubt, "giving you higher learning and work at the boat yard. But now, Maagda Boscher, you go too far. Where is my daughter of yesterday, my temperate daughter?"

The room stilled, quiet enough to catch the faint echo of Miekke's snicker and the pecking of sparrows on the window ledge where I'd scattered crumbs of bread. I stepped forward to face him, wanting him to see my pain.

Papa reached for me. His calloused palm closed around my free hand, my fingers still grimy with streaks of charcoal. He hesitated, turning my hand over in his. "My years race to a finish. I crave the promise of a grandson, and your sister is too frail for the task. Willie would be a good caretaker at your side until a son is readied. Haven't I trained you for just that day, teaching you every step, every move at the Yard?"

"I know. I know my duty. But please, not with him, not Willie."

How to tell him I wanted the stranger, Pier Veerbeck. Images of his ginger crowned face taunted many waking thoughts since that Sunday six weeks ago when his uncle brought Pier to our Sunday table.

To argue more was useless. I ran toward my bedroom, hobbled by long skirt and petticoats, and paused on the landing in the light of the transom. Papa stood below, his hand gripping the newel knob, me above, my back wedged against the ridged paneling, a brace for my ire.

"You no longer love me, Papa, to give me so easily." I hurled the words with all the bravado my halting breaths would allow, and heard them bounce and echo from wall to steps.

He shook his head, waves of white hair tumbling across his brow. "It's because I love you that I think of your future, our future." He stomped toward the scullery, but turned back to look up to where I held my rigid pose.

"I could have taken you to the Weight House where a broker matched you with an eligible burgher, though with that damned war between the French and German princes there are few worthy men around."

"Am I but a piece of scale and bone to be bartered on the quay for a handful of stuivers?"

"A few stuivers? Ha! You carry a handsome dowry." His voice burned with an edge that told me *argue more at your own peril.*

Sweet figs, to be a woman with both a duty and a price. I said as much.

"By god, you've become a defiant one on this day, miss. No man wants that in a wife."

I slammed the door to my room. The quality of a wife indeed. How had our poet Father Cats phrased it in his writings? "A true woman, she has the spirit of Sarah, the virtue of Ruth and the humility of Abigail."

Perhaps that's the way a poet fancied women. But I'd yet to meet a Dutch wife with an aura, and I foresaw none in my future. I thought myself an honest woman, a good woman, but certainly not one of biblical virtue, nor did I aspire to such virtue.

I locked my bedroom door, knowing my sister, having heard everything, would stop to torment me. And no sooner had the thought escaped me when Miekke came by to pound on the thick oak. Her voice seeped through the solid barrier. *Wil... lie, Wil... lie,* she chanted.

"Go away. Go a...way."

I skipped dinner so they'd know how badly I suffered, and awoke after midnight, realizing as I rubbed my eyes that my earlier tears of frustration and anger had sealed them shut. The house was quiet except for the occasional moan and creak of a cold night settling in its joints, and my room black, not a flicker of light. But no need for a candle. My nightdress hung at hand on the bedpost, and I welcomed the dark, wrapping it round me like a cloak to hem my fear close. Angry though I was, my fear was far more potent, binding me in a quivering chill, my arms and legs no life of their own. I lay awake, sifting thoughts, plans, and far-fetched ramblings, but a saving grace was as distant as the dawn.

I sought to soothe my spinning head with thoughts of the man I wanted to know more of. Where did Pier Veerbeck rest his head this night? As a boarder in some burgher's home, at an inn, perhaps rooms of his own? I knew so little of him--who could resist a bit of mystery-- yet he filled my head with rich imaginings. How, I wondered, could a man so foreign to my safe little world of Hoorn come to fill it like no other man, save Papa. And I felt in my innermost heart that a man of business experience in a thriving city like Amsterdam would welcome a woman like me, a woman with her own vision, a woman who ached to seize the helm of an enterprise she's known her entire life.

My head rumbled while I dug back into the evening, the words flung between Papa and me. And there in the pitch of night, it stole upon me that I liked, even savored, the bittersweet taste of speaking my mind about the heart of me. Papa insisted I parry and thrust my thoughts when he read Erasmus to me, or sought my view of local feuds, or one vendor over another at the Yard. He urged me to speak my mind then, but never, never, about what lay inside me. Now this threat of so distasteful a marriage reached a core I'd not realized dwelled within me. So tight, so confined my world, I'd never considered, save in my dreams, there might be more to my being than the quotidian Maagda, the daughter of duty and drafting table. Might there be a Maagda who explored, tested? Clutching that thought, I drifted into a troubled slumber and turbulent dreams.

When a streak of morning sunlight forced my eyes open, my first thought was Papa and how I might face him this day. My nerves stretched taut. I lay, vexed still, and yet, awed that I'd refused him. The stones of apprehension, the knowledge that my future would not be of my making, crushed the air from me.

I dressed slowly, measuring words, sentences that I might use to bring Papa around. I slipped two fresh sticks of charcoal and emery into my apron pocket. Papa's agitation after last night would surely make him fuss over my drawings today. My lines must be sharp, clear, though I feared the tremor of my mood would reach my fingertips. I never transferred the sketches to ink and nib until Papa approved. Still I couldn't bring myself to face him.

I slumped onto the green cushion on mother's chestnut rocker. Father had placed it by my window after she died, calling it the proper chair for lullabies when I gave the Hoorn Trust its heir. I ran my fingers along the smooth knobs worn to a shine by her hands, a reminder of the touch I missed so. Did Mama spend her brief life waiting, existing only to produce a son? How disappointing I must have been when a boy was sorely needed. But I could not accept the accident of my birth as reason to tie my life to a man with all the redeeming qualities of rotting cod.

Papa's old readings came back to me. Am I, I wondered, to be no more than a Petrarch, my passions awakened, my dreams hopeless? I shook loose from such thinking and roused myself to walk down the stairs one practiced step at a time, lightly, making little sound, prolonging the short trip to the kitchen, my kitten Folly tripping round my feet, jumping at the hem of my skirt.

Papa was there, ready for the Yard in a leather apron and an old frayed tunic well past any known color, perhaps blue before its hundredth soak in the tub. He warmed his hands over the peat fire. I watched his back, ready to mention Willie without meeting his eyes, but Papa, alert to my footfall, turned and walked toward the oak trestle table set with pewter mugs and plates. My plate had a fading M scratched in the center. I'd dug it there when I was eight, incensed that Mother had me scrub the dishes to "learn a woman's way."

Papa chafed to begin his day. "Sophie, can you hurry please," he called toward the scullery, puffing his cheeks impatiently. The yeasty invitation of warm bread laced the air. He sat preoccupied, as if yesterday never happened, a page missing from the book of our days on Oosten Kanaal steeg. My plight lay in some distant reach of his mind, his thoughts, it seemed, on the day's work only. He wasn't a vain man, but I know he harbored a fathom of pride that our Hoorn boat yard still outranked Amsterdam. How I wanted to change his channel of thought, how to mention Pier.

"You'll finish the draft for the deck storage corner by nightfall? That Cologne merchant sails in Tuesday next to inspect our work. You know he'll look every peg, every line ten times over."

Before I could answer, Sophie walked in carrying a tray with buttermilk and honey for me, ale for Papa and a wedge of hard, nutty Gouda and dark bread. Yesterday's anger curbed my usual morning hunger even though I'd had no meal last night. I took nothing but a small nibble of cheese. Papa on the other hand ate with relish. He slathered a heavy slice of Gouda onto the bread, squashed the pulp of a ripe fig over the cheese, and devoured almost half the serving in one bite. Our row hadn't dulled his appetite. Did our quarrel even cross his mind?

"Papa, about yesterday, about Willie…"

He frowned. "Stop. Not one more word. I told you to think on it." He took a swallow of his ale and looked at me over the rim of the tankard. "We'll speak of marriage when I feel you've cooled yourself, given my words a proper stir through your waking hours." He reached across the table and tapped his fingers on the bare oak mere inches from my plate. "I am a reasonable man, Maagda, and I expect reason from you. Reckon well that I have a duty when it comes to your marriage."

I bit my lips, and pushed my plate away. I knew it useless to speak further.

So unfair. My one swallow of Gouda rose to choke the words in my throat. Papa, I wanted to shout, you remind me that I am to finish the drafts for our new fluytship, yet you do not trust me to name the man I must spend my life with. You deem this reason?

CHAPTER 2—MAAGDA

IT SIMMERED AND SPUTTERED, THIS WARFARE between Papa and me. The more I chewed on our embittered words, the more my bile rose and choked my very air. Fear gave way to a throbbing resentment that I was to have no choice in the most important decisions of my life. But I'd learned that cutting words flung at unhealed wounds were fallow.

And yet I fretted, and cried alone, locking myself in my room, beating my pillow against the bed post, the steam of frustration and hurt inside me so real I thought it might spring forth in a hot cloud at the slightest word. Even Miekke stopped her teasing, kept her distance. And I ached. Oh, how I ached, a pain, a sadness so deep I could not name the place from which it sprang.

But I kept my tears, my bitterness, my fears from Papa's view or hearing. This beloved man was of sudden a stranger to me, much as I had been a stranger to myself in defying him. The man who had soothed my stubbed toe or blistered thumb of childhood, the man who made me laugh at a churlish word or playmate snub, this man was ready to hand me to the most loathsome husband in my small world. I was atwitch, confused with my anger and hurt, foreign to the very skin that held me.

But honoring Papa's order, I kept my counsel that first week, seven tormented days while I toiled at my drafting table, not a pleasantry between us. When I could hold it no longer, I launched my own campaign of small engagements to woo and win him, first teasing with bits of gossip from the Yard, then reminding him of my skills at the drafting table, and finally, turning sweet, loving, the very image of the proper daughter. I helped Sophie prepare his favorite dishes -- Papa relished his salmon stuffed with Gouda and figs – and engaged him in talk about Erasmus and the cleric's friendship with the ill-fated Thomas More. Papa relished Erasmus even more than the salmon, a man of hearty appetite whether the food for his palate or his mind. I abided Erasmus well enough, but I harbored mixed feelings about his friend, Thomas More. I always thought him a dog that reproached all for harboring fleas, except himself.

I kept Pier's name in my heart and each time temptation bade me mention Willie, I locked my lips and swallowed the vile name, worse than a spring dose of stinging nettles. I soothed myself with fancies of Pier and me walking, my arm in his, through the lanes of Hoorn, warming him, perhaps, to a love of my seaside home and quite possibly, me.

We were in the office alone, Papa and me, on Thursday of that week. He sat at his desk, nib to ledger. I blew the charcoal dust from the final stroke of my draft, wondering as always what waters this new ship might ply, what timber, ores or grains it might carry. I took a risk and asked him.

Papa turned toward me, but his eyes found a space just over my head. "Of what consequence is that to you?" He thumped the rave hook he used as a paperweight over a stack of ledgers, and it came to me that, grey hair or no, he was still strong enough to wield that tool on the seams of a ship for its seal of oakum. Still an ijzer mens.

I hesitated. "Because, Papa, I see our ships as the most important link in the chain of trade, especially from The Indies. Is that not so?" I was about to say more, but he went back to his inkpot and papers without another glance or word. I lowered my eyes to my drawing board, smarting to know my impulses had once again betrayed me. But the stir in my heart told me my interest in trade was somehow right. Last night when I paged back through my diary, I realized my nib frequently scribed notions of trade and less frequently, notions of marriage. A startling revelation. I'd not been antiquity's Penelope waiting for the man who never came, each night unraveling the day's weaving. Until Pier.

Papa thawed gradually, and finally, finally, gave way, seeking my company and conversation for more than Yard business. He admitted that perhaps he had rushed me, that I was just at the start of my marriageable years. It was the widow, he said, who pushed for nuptials and that he, Papa, had not yet considered a specific marriage for me, though given his advancing years, sooner was better than not. And, of course, in a town as small as Hoorn, even households beyond Grote Noord heard of the widow's quest from her own wagging tongue. I knew curtains parted each day when I walked Oosten Kanaal, meal kettle in hand, toward the beach path and the Yard. A small town hungers for the tiniest morsel when two of its own are stirred in the gossip pot. I pointedly slowed my usual brisk pace and ambled until beyond prying eyes as if I had not a care.

On the seventh day after Willie's visit to the Yard and our war of words at home, Papa went to the widow van Pelt and told her he would not consider betrothal for me before Christmas, some seven months away. My labored breathing of days past eased, even as my knees went weak with relief. I hugged Papa and kissed him just above his beard on his right cheek. He returned my embrace and almost smiled, his lips still a taut, skeptical line.

I stopped my custom at the van Pelt cheese shop even though Willie was rarely about. He spent his working hours at the family's storage house on the wharf where they loaded their cheese for their export trade. I sent Sophie to the shop in my stead. Cowardly, I admit, but I had no desire to face the widow, or to fan the faintest ember of matchmaking on her part.

I was to learn that the van Pelt woman did more for my cause than my own objections. She had asked, "Maagda has so many suitors?" Papa didn't tell me. Miekke did, adding her own tart imitation of the widow's rasping voice. Waiting near the shop door, she said she watched color race up Papa's face, fearing apoplexy might drop him on the spot. He had to grip the edge of an Edam wheel to steady himself, or as I liked to imagine, to keep from putting his hands to the woman's throat.

"So, Maags, you remain a maiden," Miekke said, taking my hand in hers and swinging it to and fro. We were snipping spent jonquils from the pots that lined our front steps, blooms I had nurtured to early growth in a sheltered shed. Beyond Miekke's shoulder I could see the curtains move in the Eltood house across the lane. She missed nothing, that old woman. I imagined her the courier who took news from each house to other gossiping neighbors.

"Merely a delayed sentence, little sister. But I will make the most of it." I still hadn't told Miekke about Pier and she had never mentioned him after meeting him when he shared a meal at our table in February.

I'd tortured myself through that initial seven-day wait at Papa's behest, but now I had seven months—seven times thirty-plus days. I would sow opportunity everywhere, beginning with Freddy at the Yard. He was, after all, Pier's uncle. A more direct path could not be hoped for. Papa would be the trickier task. It required more than a stiff wind to shift his course. I planned my moves a step at a time, how I'd stage settings of my own design, and plot encounters and less than subtle suggestion if required. I knew Freddy's routine, like the nap he took in a hammock he kept behind the lumber stacks, always after his noon meal. It was a simple matter to connive chance meetings and ask after his nephew. *Did Pier keep good health? I hear Amsterdam considers a diamond guild; does Pier still work in the trade? Might he visit Hoorn soon again?*

Freddy saw through my ruse. He'd known me since I wore a child's ribboned bonnet. But, he and fortune responded. Two Mondays after Papa's trip to the widow, Freddy hailed me descending the stairs to the lumber stores. He'd just risen from his noon slumber and stood rubbing his whiskered jaw, his head barely clearing the low deck that held our office above.

"Pier comes Saturday." He yawned and stretched, suspending me on the news. "Might you show him a young person's Hoorn?" A grin puffed his cheeks.

I shot with warmth from crown to toe at this unexpected change in fortune. Freddy was perhaps only ten years older than Pier, and certainly aware of what little there might be of a young person's Hoorn, other than the annual May festivals where many a courtship was born. "You'll find my nephew a quiet man," Freddy said. "He's had a solitary life. An afternoon in the company of a handsome woman with a lively mind might be the tonic he needs to flood him with the warmth of spring." He hesitated, looked at me. "Pier's had a hard start in life, grown to manhood believing every corner hides an evil hand ready to slam him down."

Freddy's concern for Pier touched me. Early on he had taken it upon himself to be my knight protector, a buffer between me and some of the Yard laborers who were not beyond the unsavory word within my hearing. Shielded me a bit much, I thought, though all in kindness. I had an insatiable curiosity and always wanted to know what was about among the men, but Freddy was worse than my father in maintaining a guard lest I hear a blasphemous word or earthy jest. I'd heard many and my ears had yet to shrivel.

I took Freddy's arm. "I must ask Papa about Saturday, but I'm sure he'll want you and Pier to come to our supper table."

He laughed. "Nice how the flush on your cheeks brings out those golden curls you hide with your cap."

Self-conscious now, I reached up to push stray locks back into the discipline of my plain workaday cap, pulling it snug over my ears.

"I'll arrange it with your father. Let him know Pier's not a bounder nor a dyed-in-the-wool Papist, though he was baptized." He grinned.

Freddy knew Papa had little time for Papists, other than Erasmus. For myself, I cared little what sect Pier claimed. Like Papa I was not one for religious ritual. At the moment, I didn't care. The wonders of Saturday claimed all my thoughts.

My drawings for the remainder of the day were spotted with heavy smudges from daydreams of the ginger-bearded Pier leading my charcoal astray. I was much too excited to concentrate on space and lines, instead doodling images of me in my best dress, linked arm in arm with Mr. Veerbeck of Amsterdam. Would his touch be warm? Might he recite a verse as we strolled? Did he ever relate jovial tales of life in his larger town, his work, his neighbors? Might he have a pet, a friend for my Folly. Nor was my work any the richer when each time Freddy stomped up to the office from the Yard, he'd whisper *Saturday,* and tug the ribbons on my cap.

That evening, with my door locked against an intruding Miekke, I wandered around my bedroom, touching little pieces – Mama's crocheted scarf, my baby teething bone—one keepsake after another, letting my mind go where it may, all the while, tying each piece of my life to Pier. I turned his name around on my tongue sweet as the juice from an August plum. At last in our little Hoorn, a new man, a mystery to be unraveled. Back in February, Pier spoke little of himself, made no boasts, but I sensed an energy there 'neath the quiet guise he wore.

Had Pier sensed some daring in me? I made certain to brush his hand when I passed the platter of carvings from a spring lamb joint, but I kept my eyes lowered, allowing him to accept the gesture, or not. Might I soon know?

"For suppose a man were eating rotten fish, the very smell of it which would choke another, and yet believed it a dish for the Gods, what difference is there to his happiness?"

In Praise of Folly by Desiderius Erasmus (Classics Club edition)

CHAPTER 3—MAAGDA

ON THE APPOINTED DAY, I STATIONED MYSELF IN Papa's reading chair in the front room, feigning interest in one of his books, a political tract of some stripe. When a double rap echoed on the polished oak door, I moved to answer, but hesitated to smooth my hair and my skirts, and in that brief instant, Miekke appeared from nowhere, all giggles, rushing to open the door to a glare of sunlight and Pier's six-foot silhouette. He doffed his hat, reminded her of his name and asked for me. I grabbed her waist and tugged her aside.

He smiled. "Maagda, you are good to take me in hand. I've visited Hoorn often, but my Uncle's had little time to squire me about." He cocked his head and broadened his grin, a schoolboy caught in the cookie jar. "We spend our hours in front of the grate with many a tall ale in hand."

I laughed at his small confession, but noted his quaint word *squire*, a term I thought only the talk of courting couples. He waved his soft felt hat in front of him as if the March afternoon had melted

~ 19 ~

into August heat, though in truth it was unseasonably warm for Hoorn. So, not for him the tall, stiff topper of our burghers. Here was a man with his own mind. I meant to note that bit of independence in my diary. Oh, I was sure I'd have much to pen between those calf-skin covers when light faded from this day. And I'd note, too, that more than one curtain along our steeg fluttered as Pier stood there. Even that infirm Madam Eltood across the lane swept the same spot on the same step with her eyes riveted on the back of Pier's head until she caught my eye.

Before I might utter another word, Miekke smirked, "Pier, you're early. Papa says I'm to walk with you and Maagda this afternoon." She rolled her eyes.

Pier looked startled, his smile thin. Might I blame him? The word sassy tripped on my tongue, but I was not ready to lock horns with Papa again and made no complaint about Miekke's company. I stored each little victory. Apparently, Papa had accepted Freddy's account of his nephew, but knowing Papa, he'd mete out his own precautions.

I'd pondered all week where I might walk with Pier. Instinct told me the sea held men in thrall, but this man worked in a diamond shop in a city, so what might Hoorn offer? Our town was small. Even I could walk it end to end from quay to the tip of Grote Noord in minutes. Not that I'd ever been so quick. I preferred the longer route where I might dally by the Zuider Zee, always something new to discover on the beach. I kept a jar of shells and beach pebbles on my drafting table, a link to pleasant afternoons that relieved the tedium of tiny, precise pen strokes.

I asked Pier what might take his eye.

"I seek little in shops, and I see enough of them in the city," he said. "I'm a countryman at heart. Had a dairy farm before I moved to Amsterdam."

Immediately my mind spun a route to the Weight House. Carts lined up for a mile or more each day bringing edams and goudas to stamp before sale to the market stalls. Not my idea of a courting stroll, but I'd be by Pier's side and little else mattered. I found it rather promising. After all, wasn't one of my favorite afternoons, a stroll through our lanes and along the beach. Already I found common ground with him.

I drew a light shawl of crimson and peach around my shoulders and reached to take Pier's arm. Miekke was there before me. She managed to squeeze between us before we turned the corner to Rode Steen Square, then right to the quay where the curved stone walls of the Weight House glowed in the peaking sun, not more than a hundred yards from a line of berthed ships, many guided to port at the sight of its tall spire. No doubt some of the cheese would find its way aboard more than one vessel bound for Baltic or Mediterranean ports.

The Weigh House swarmed with farmers from the countryside west of Hoorn. Drivers jostled for position, snapping whips or mouthing soothing nonsense to skittish animals. Rumbling baritone voices shouted bids for the lots, their buzz of numbers flitting through the air. Dray horses snorted and pawed the ground in the stalled queue of wagons, their tails swishing flies drawn by the steaming piles in their line.

Pier's eyes darted from dray to hand cart, absorbing the chaos, a smile creasing his cheeks. "The Weigh House wasn't finished when we still worked our plot. My father would drive all the way to Edam. He'd harness up after supper and not get back 'til noon the next day. I saw little of him." His hands stroked the velvet nose of a sorrel, its liquid eyes luminous in gratitude.

"A lonely life for you."

"Much of the time. My father bade me stay behind for schooling and when I was home, we worked different parts of the place, him in the barn with the animals and me in the fields." He straightened up. "Builds a man, strapped to a plow and a good horse."

When he spoke, I noticed how his upper sleeve pulled tight across the muscled arm beneath. A fiery heat rippled down my chest.

I wanted to be close, feel that muscled arm. A voice in head echoed what I feared might slip from my lips: *please like me, Pier. Please, please just like me...for now.*

Pier walked to a wagon and sniffed at the rounds of cheese under the sacking.

"Rich. Fit for the Orange's table."

How might he tell something was of a quality for our prince? The air rolled in waves of strong scent... the nutty, sometimes tangy bite of the cheeses, the effluence from the horses, the sea salt and fish oil from the wharf. His nose was more discerning than mine.

"Really." Miekke tsked and frowned. I knew our stroll among the cheese wagons a blow to her sensibilities. She'd rather browse at the cloth merchant, or linger near Rode Steen Square to watch the young men lolling there. But if she were to be Papa's presence here, today it was cheese or home.

"You don't care for the dairyman's work, Miekke?" Pier moved to the next wagon in line, an open back, canvas tossed loosely over its load. "Too bad. It's said to make young ladies fair of face." He winked at me. "Not that you need to be more fair than you are. Nor you, Maagda."

Miekke reddened, and I sensed a touch of warmth on my own cheeks. We left the dock to start home for our meal. Pier took my hand and slipped my arm through his. I thought him the most engaging of men, his teasing and compliment to Miekke and to me so unexpected. Made a bit of gold glow through his quiet demeanor. Such depths to plumb. I shivered ever so slightly at the feel of the taut muscle 'neath my hand. My cheeks held their flame, but better a blush than a glass to my thoughts.

We crossed Rode Steen, almost home, and I could silence myself no longer. "Might you visit Hoorn again?" I blurted, sure the earlier blush had fired deep scarlet on my cheeks, my voice not without tremor.

He squeezed my arm close to his chest. "The first coach from Amsterdam next Saturday…if I am welcome."

His quick response sealed my lips, no words left in me.

It would be done. Not for Maagda Boscher the old courting rituals of wreaths on the window ledge, notes at the door, or the sudden knock in the night to know a suitor paced near my home.

My days would be endless, heavy with anticipation and on edge for Papa's approval, until Saturday dawned and the coach from Amsterdam rounded the Square.

"Or what should I say of them that hug themselves
with their counterfeit Pardons..."

In Praise of Folly by Desiderius Erasmus (Classics Club edition)

CHAPTER 4—MAAGDA

IN THE ENSUING WEEKS I WALKED OUT EACH
Saturday with my diamond man, Pier Veerbeck from Amsterdam. In
the full glory of lime and gold afternoons, we'd pick our way among
the barrels and ropes on the wharf and watch the traders unload
their ships, or stroll along the shore to watch the sea birds. I'd gather
stalks of sea grass for the jug in my room at home, or we'd make
a game of pitching seashells to lines in the sand, like the teams of
Hoorn men who pitched horseshoes in a pit west of the shore road,
and always with a good supply of ale at hand to sharpen their aim.

There was little else to see in our tiny seaside cluster of homes
and shops, but we were a close community, at ease in each other's
knowing. I felt comfortable, safe, among Hoorn folks, though I knew
curiosity about Pier crossed stoops from the wharf to the shops and
in the homes along many lanes. Why I'd even heard one of the men
at the Yard tell his mate, *Maagda's got herself a young man!* You might
suppose me a maiden preserved under glass!

Only on market days did the stalls on Grote Noord bustle with matrons and their scullery girls, girls younger than Miekke in their plain white caps and aprons, girls toting tub-bottomed baskets for the day's larder. And after looking at cheeses or brooms or knotted rugs at the few shops off Rode Steen Square and an occasional artisan's display, Hoorn had scarce material wares to tempt your eye. I craved nothing more with the harbor and the sea so close, our gateway to the larger world, but I worried my simple pleasures common fare for a man from a bigger town.

I thought to take Pier to the Yard, to show him our newest fluyt, its frame now rising from a cradle of cedar arcs. I wanted him to know my thrall with our burgeoning commerce, and my fancies about the ports our ships would travel, my excitement at being some small part of it all. Might he share it? But I feared the workers would stare and smirk, and come Monday, sly taunts would follow me. Hadn't I already heard one comment? Our knowing was too new, too tender, not yet with a callous of time to ward off the men's mocking. And no need for heckling to reach Papa's ears. I'd heard him more than once question Freddy about Pier's work, whether he might be in debt, and what of his health, and that strange I thought, since Pier is robust, the finest figure of a man.

With all of this, Papa still insisted Miekke tag along on each of Pier's visits, although in daylight and in public view, neighbors would give little thought to our strolling the lanes alone, except perhaps to speculate on when we might take the next step. Not so the van Pelts, of course. I purposely avoided the lane where their cheese shop opened to foot traffic. But I knew other eyes watched us, all of Hoorn hungry for a glimpse of *Maagda's young man*, a *diamond merchant from Amsterdam*. With Pier at my side women who never more than nodded or smiled when I passed by stopped to visit, to ask after Papa, or had I heard from dear old Hannah of late. The solicitations kept a smile on my lips.

On one such afternoon, Anna Pellter who had been a childhood school mate and now a young mother whom I rarely saw, grabbed me by the arm in front of the chemist's shop, exclaiming over the colors in my shawl and telling me I must come meet her two little girls. All the time her eyes roved over Pier who had politely removed his hat. When I introduced her, she let go of me and swallowed his hand in both of hers with such force I thought she might drag him away. Pier disengaged himself and stooped to retrieve an herb packet she had dropped to the cobbles. We bid her a hasty goodday, Miekke laughing aloud, he grinning and remarking how friendly the folks of Hoorn, hardly what he'd expect on the lanes of Amsterdam. He tucked my hand in his where Anna's had gone uninvited. I glowed and yearned for even more of his touch.

Pier said nothing of Miekke's presence on our walks together. She chattered endlessly while he quietly nodded or smiled at her nonsense about Hoorn boys or bolts of the newest fabric she fancied. And like me, she was sure to wear a different frock on each occasion. Both of us tired of the grays and blacks of everyday dresses. I chose plums and mauves, and I'd promised myself that when the time came, I'd marry in a gown of glowing peach that I would fashion and stitch myself.

My friend Ria, whose front steps adjoined ours, inspected me before each of Pier's visits, sharing motherly wisdom, while she fussed with bows, streamers or the tilt of my cap. "Don't be too forward, or too sharp," she cautioned, knowing my penchant for quick retorts. "Draw him out. Urge him to speak of his own doings. That's what men enjoy, the chance to boost." She laughed. I listened. Her marriage seemed pleasant enough, though I know she missed children. Well one day she could find joy in my brood.

After Pier's fifth visit, Miekke chided me. "Maags, I fail to understand what you see in him." We were in my bedroom removing our street dresses and donning aprons for dinner. "Why a cricket's chirp on a hot night is more entertaining. If my Jan were so dull, I'd feed him to the gulls quickly enough."

"Miekke, how could you?" I pursed my lips. "Don't you sense that bite of vitality about him, and how might you expect him to speak when you talk so? He couldn't utter a syllable no matter his wit."

"Vitality? He must whisper it in your ear alone for he doesn't amuse me at all," she pouted and moved to the stairs. "I'd rather walk out with my friends."

"I'd rather you did as well. You're too young to appreciate Pier. Why he bristles when you listen close enough." I told her she might learn his fine points if she paid heed to his eyes, his changes of expression as I did. "Didn't he give you a handsome compliment about your very own glow of face? And I notice you dress for his eye."

"That remark was weeks ago, and you, my sister, see only what you want to see. You may work around men every day, but I think you see them as lifeless as your sticks of charcoal. And now with this man, you draw pictures in your head. He's a diamond grinder, not a grand duke who wears fine jewels. Besides, he's not the only man on Hoorn's lanes that might find a nicely fitted dress worthy of a second glance."

I shook my head at her. Frail, but flirty. I wished I had a bit of that in me. Papa and I tolerated more than a normal dash of vinegar from Miekke, fearing the day when she might decline like Mama whom she so resembled in all but her dark eyes and dark hair. I often wondered had somewhere in years past a conquering Spaniard planted his swarthy seed in our family. Yet her comments left me piqued. I sensed Pier's worth. What could Miekke know? After all, at sixteen she was still a child, though I had to admit, her comment about the men at the Yard had some truth to it. They were fixtures along with the wood and the hemp, no more. I'd never reckoned them as men with wives, or a brood of babies at their hearth. But unless you're a common woman of the taverns how might you know any man save kin?

And what might I say of Pier? I found his quiet demeanor soothing given the usual fray of conversation at home, but Papa, like my
sister, thought it worth marking. "What is the substance of his mind?"
Papa would ask. "The fellow rarely speaks. Though I do fathom he's
an able business man from what Freddy tells me." From Papa such a
comment was akin to accolade.

I noted each of Pier's visits, including this fifth along with
Miekke's unsolicited censure in my diary. Little vixen. I knew future
pages, a growing list of entries, would prove her wrong.

I wrote how we, the three of us, had strolled the dew fresh lanes of
Hoorn, a particularly warm day, with buds breaking on the Lindens
around the square, and buttery jonquils peaking from tubs beside
many doorsteps. I had abandoned my usual shawl, but I noticed that
Pier still wore a heavy winter tunic, the same he had worn on his
previous visits. I decided that I would stitch him a new tunic, a gift,
something in a dark, but brisk shade to bring out the ginger in his
hair and the ruddy tone of his cheeks. I could picture him in a cloth
of dark green, a tone with depth like robust oaks in a dense forest.
Yes, a fine handmade gift. I'd buy cloth next market day, and I'd present it from the Boschers. Much too soon for a personal gift. I under-
scored that last entry.

My diary pages, brief and prosaic so long, now bloomed with
page after page of Pier, how a smile creased just the left side of his
lip, how the sun flamed the ginger in his hair along the edge of his
favorite soft hat, how he turned his head just so to look at me as if no
one else peopled our world. Yes, the calfskin cover creased with signs
of use. I was particularly fond of returning to the page where I noted
the day he placed his arm round my shoulders to steer me away from
a shop sign about to whip free in the wind. His touches were few but
becoming more frequent and tender, and they left a mark of warmth
that I fanned to high heat in my musings.

Thoughts of Pier, I admit it, tuned my body to a vibrant hum.
His quiet, his reserve, so different from the raucous Hoorn boys I'd

known. The best of them had rushed off to fight the German war. But Pier was here in this moment, and he had a way of stealing a glance at me that raised my spirits as if I were one of his rare diamonds. Might a woman need more?

On the very next weekend, his sixth visit in as many weeks, we dallied on the quay, another day of blue sky and a southern breeze chasing up the coast from Edam-way to blow the chill from the air. We idled, watching barrels of haddock off-loaded from a fishing vessel at the far end of the dock, laughing at the seamen who slipped about on the oily boards. We'd been speculating on which ports the fish might be shipped off to when Pier asked Miekke to skip over to the coach depot two lanes north to check the evening schedule. He might, he said, return later than usual.

I caught my breath. He meant to stay on. A bubble of pleasure rose in my throat.

When Miekke walked to a turn at the lane, he took my hand and led me to a stack of boxes that shielded us from the bustle of the seamen. I sat. He stood facing me, his legs firmly planted shoulder width apart, his arms crossed. After clearing his throat a first, then a second time, he said, "I wanted to speak. Alone." His eyes followed Miekke's path. I turned, too, to catch the last glimpse of her rose floral skirt turning the corner.

"You're very fond of her, yes?"

"Fond? Oh, much more. I love her like my other self. I raised her after our Mama died."

"Like me," Pier said. "My mother died when I was born." He leaned forward to take my right hand in both of his, his fingers stained black in little crevices from the stones he ground in his shop, not unlike my own that I scrubbed free of charcoal every evening.

"I don't know fancy words like your father," he began, "and with my mother gone, I've not had much gentling from a woman." Again, jaw pulled tight, his eyes strayed over my shoulder in the direction Miekke had walked. "But I've grown easy with you." He hesitated, pressed his lips tight before he spoke again. "What I mean... I like our time together, like this, you and me." He reached up and softly touched my cheek. I placed my hand over his, hoped to keep it there, but he let go.

I was tempted to laugh and say, you mean you, me and Miekke. But his tone cautioned me that now was not a moment for humor. Pier seldom spoke personal words, but a new tightness in his voice trilled a beat in me. I sank back into the shadows to shield my throbbing head from the sun's heat, afraid to guess what words might tumble next from his tongue.

He released my fingers and pressed his full palm against mine. He parted his lips to speak, but halted, then coughed, a flush rising in his cheeks. "I think... I've arrived at that time in my life when I should," more throat clearing, "when I should acquire a wife."

I stiffened from bonnet to boots. I'd not an inkling, not so much as a sniff, that he might speak so this day. All these weeks of strolling our lanes, quiet times of idle talk, family dinners, but so few personal words between us.

The muscles in his cheeks jumped and tightened, his eyes roving somewhere over my head. "Might you think to marry me?"

My breath caught. I grabbed the edge of the box under me fearing some gust of wind would blow me and the moment into the scoops of clouds above. A proper young woman would have feigned shock, and I was shocked, but without hesitation, my heart whirling like a windsock, "Yes, Pier, oh yes." I returned the squeeze to his hand and leaned forward to kiss his cheek, feeling fire creep across my lips.

He smiled and patted my hand. "I am satisfied."

Satisfied? I soared, my spirits up among the gulls and terns, wheeling and swooping in a mellow late spring sky. Pier Veerbeck drove right to the heart of his desires. I admired such spirit. And Miekke thought him dull.

In my head I stitched that green tunic, but now a wedding gift, each stitch a small act of devotion.

He stepped away from where I sat. "I must speak to your father."

"Papa? Yes, Papa." My joy plummeted, and I was suddenly aware how hard the boxes on which I sat, how noisy the seamen mere yards away. Papa.

"Besides, he (Jupiter) has confined Reason to a narrow corner of the brain, and left all the rest of the body to our Passions."

In Praise of Folly by Desiderius Erasmus (Classics Club edition)

CHAPTER 5—MAAGDA

NOW THAT THE TIME HAD ARRIVED FOR PIER TO speak, Papa would have none of it.

When I broached Pier's impending visit, Papa sprang from his chair as if a hot peat coal had dropped on his breeches. He slammed his book down on the side table, rattling the candleholder and spilling a pile of political tracts to the tiles below.

"A May marriage, Maagda? Never. We still know little of the man." He exhaled a great whoosh of air, a sigh that spoke volumes. "First you reject Willie van Pelt, a lad you've known since childhood, and now you're ready to rush to a stranger."

"Oh, come, Papa. Hardly a stranger. His Uncle Fredrik has worked for you for how many years now?"

"It is not Freddy who seeks your hand."

I wanted to shout that I knew he'd questioned Freddy endlessly about Pier, but this was no moment to set further fuel to his ire.

We had lingered after supper in the sitting room, Papa thumbing through the stack of books he kept beside him, me picking imaginary threads from my apron when I brought up Pier's visit. Candles flickered a mellow glow on the walls, the house still fragrant with the aroma of fennel and poached cod from our supper. Despite the soft light and the lingering scent of finely seasoned food, I harbored not a mellow thought, and I judged from his fidgeting that Papa was not quiet of mind either.

Did I say to him: *I'm a maiden with blood afire?* Who tells her father such a thing? But it was true. The scenes of Pier and me together I'd conjured made me realize my senses languished in a maiden's slumber waiting for a lover's touch. After these last weeks, I knew Pier's touch the one I wanted. And from what Ria confided after I told her of Pier's proposal, I'd need my fire. "Dutch men," she'd said, "are better at commerce than coupling. I'll teach you ways to change his course." Rather Ria than Aunt Loekke, or god forbid, my father. I needed help. All I knew is what went where. Reason alone made it so, but there had to be more.

Papa rose from his horsehair reading chair by the window and stood with his right hand pressed down on the book he had put aside.

"You've caused enough turmoil, rejecting your father's counsel in the matter of marriage." He turned to walk toward the stairs, but spun back round. "Half the fathers in Hoorn hound me now, their daughters ready to defy them. I'm as welcome in the Rode Steen tavern as an empty tankard."

I knew word that I had turned tradition on its head sped around our small seaside town like the might of a North Sea gale. Families might battle and girls might sulk because of it, but in my heart I believed I was right. Some of the arranged marriages I'd seen up close in Hoorn were no livelier than rusted barrel hoops in an alley. Like the Jareeds two doors up. They sit outside on separate hard-backed benches after their supper each spring evening and I'd never heard them exchange a pleasantry. Not one. Husbands and wives who are strangers to each other. I wouldn't have it.

"Papa, you've said yourself it's near time for me to marry and become a mother." Who knew better than Papa my need to bear a child, the Hoorn Trust always first in his thoughts. I didn't doubt that he took the small model ship, *Count of Hoorn,* from it's shelf at least once a week to read the deeds stored inside, deeds that kept the land and the business in our family. Nor did I doubt he could recite the words from memory.

"Your mother was twenty-eight when we wed, Maagda, a proper time in a woman's life. The measure of the man is more important than the when. I know I'm getting on and it's your duty to become a mother, but not in the face of ill reason."

I twisted the muslin apron in my hands. I knew to tread with care because after a dozen years, he still grieved for Mama. But I chanced it, flinging my hurt at him. "And it took how long for babies, me and my sister? I don't want to wait for babies, to wait like you for the boy who was never born." I wanted to bite back the words even as they tumbled off my tongue, knowing the pain he'd suffer. But it made me wonder, too. Was my Papa like the men Ria spoke of, quick with commerce, slow with bed, perhaps why I was born so late in their marriage.

"You've been raised to speak your mind, but at times you try me sore." Papa clamped his lips. His eyes watered. "I want you to find the affectionate companionship of marriage," he hesitated and pressed his lips, "with a man who is worthy."

He prattled on. Companionship. Affection. A unity of wants and needs. "An ox and an ass don't yoke well to the same plow. A good marriage is kindred souls pulling together. Do we know enough of Pier to think him a kindred soul?"

He stopped, looked me full in the face, then with a finger wagging near my nose, "I'll talk with your young man. Mind you, only talk." He pulled at a white hair looping from his ear. "About time I heard *something* from him. The man says little enough to me for all of the time he spends around here."

"Shy, Papa, he's merely shy. And you are such a strong figure of a man, you chase the words from his head." I didn't say I saw a hint of Papa's strength, his mulishness in Pier, both qualities I'd learned to live with. Was that kindred enough?

I hugged Papa, this *izjer* man, this iron builder of ships who was soft as a young lamb at home. I knew Papa teetered on a thin line, between a desire to hold me safe, and his need to see me a mother. I was torn because I wanted to be a good daughter, but I harbored an even deeper urge to be myself. But so many tests of my will.

The day arrived, bright with a high spring sun, bright with prom-ise. Everything seemed so normal, so *quotidian* Papa might say. His new word. After our Sunday readings, usually from Erasmus, Papa insisted we learn a fresh turn of phrase and use it each day for a week. Miekke and I went along because Erasmus wrote with a wit far jollier than our Calvinist predicants. Papa had little time for the pulpit, a taste that suited me.

For Pier's visit today, I'd dressed slowly, with care, in my best vel-vet, a rich plum with a white lace collar that I'd bleached in the sun. I spun to the front, the back, twirled around with my arms overhead, then at my sides. How would Pier first see me today? He was not one for fine phrases, but he had of late said when I'd worn the dress that the color made my cheeks look ripe like autumn apples. I savored such snippets from him, noted each on a fresh page in my diary.

Now I awaited his arrival, my brow and palms wet with expec-tation, and no apron to dab away the moisture. Although Pier told me little of his life in the city, or the small house he had bought, I drew my own pictures of him in my mind. I saw him walking to his work along an Amsterdam canal, whistling perhaps, or biting into a vendor's sausage. Did he smile at the pretty girls or stop to feed the ducks from a bun he'd bought along the way?

No, today was no quotidian day for me.

Papa insisted I stay out of sight, but uttered no word I might not listen. I would hear every syllable, not let my imagination rummage through wild rambling later when I tried to stitch phrases and fragments together. I gathered my skirt close to hide in the cabinet under the stairs, the door ajar less than a hand's width. The cramped closet was my favorite hideaway when Miekke and I played seek and tag as children. It gave a full view of the front rooms. She never ventured here because dark places made her flesh shrivel she told me. But this moment was no such game, and it was my flesh that tingled.

Peeking round the door, I saw Papa in his second best black suit, gray wool stockings below his knees rather than his Sunday white silk. He paced by the windows looking out to the canal, his arms locked across his chest, his neck and face flushed.

I nestled into the heap of old clogs and winter wraps jumbled in the corner now that the cold months gave way to the warm. I wrinkled my nose at the moldy smell of cloaks tossed here still damp, and wiggled around to shake loose from one of Papa's fishing spears that lodged against my ribs.

Only occasional murmurs from the scullery broke the silence that whispered through the rooms. Wisps of honeyed ham curled round the door near me. Dare I invite Pier to share our meal without asking Papa?

I moved close to the opening, just enough to see most of the sitting room. After breakfast I had picked the last of the jonquils from the back garden and arranged them in our best glass. They brightened the table by the far window. The crystal, cut in a pattern of tiny petals, caught rays of low afternoon sun and sent sparks of mellow gold 'round the walls. A good omen I thought, for I sensed my life about to spin dizzy with May a mere thirty-six days away.

Heavy rains during the night, a pelting storm off the North Atlantic, had smashed most of the flowers I hoped to cut this morning. I wondered at nature's perverse ways, coaxing her blooms to ripe beauty only to knock them about in her sudden furies. The thought gave me hope that anything worthwhile had a way to be salvaged.

My reverie fled when a rap sounded from the door, the thump, thump echoing in my chest, halting my breaths.

Papa greeted Pier stiffly with a "Mr. Veerbeck?" and ushered him to the horsehair chairs near the windows. But neither of them sat. Pier removed his hat and ran his fingers through his ginger hair. They faced each other, eye to eye, like preacher and sinner in a church. Pier placed his soft felt hat with its ornate pewter medallion on the side table near the jonquils, almost tipping the glass over. Papa scowled. Pier stood there, his hands behind his back. I saw him tap his fingers together, and I smiled. He was nervous, too.

"You know why I've come, Mr. Boscher?"

Would papa toy with him as he sometimes did with my sister and me? He had a taste for it.

"I do, Pier Veerbeck, but I would like to hear your words." Papa's face was set with every line, every crevice deep in cheerless composure.

"Yes, yes, I see." Pier hesitated, rubbed his palms together. "Well, you understand, Maagda and I want to marry…soon…in early May." He fidgeted. "My employer threatens no more Saturdays from the shop to come courting."

Papa arched his brows like he'd never heard me mention a date. "May? May? That's but weeks hence." His eyes measured Pier from ginger locks to boots dusted with grit from the Amsterdam road.

My father understood a strong work ethic, but I knew Pier would not dent this *ijzer* man with his excuse of little time from his job. Papa never took trifling excuses from Miekke and me. If we wanted something, we knew to go to him with our own plan. And I admit to a disappointment that nibbled at me. Was time off Pier's only desire to marry soon? Might he not say his affection for me sped his desire to marry, or how had he put it...*acquire a wife*? His word *acquire* did nettle, but I put it down to his lack of ease with women.

Papa fixed his gaze on Pier's eyes and gave the man no quarter. " What do you offer my daughter, Mr. Apprentice Diamond Cutter? You have prospects?"

Pier stood rigid. "I've money from the old farm here. I sold it last year. The place killed my father, trying to raise feed crops on worn out soil. Cost him more to run the place than it brought in." He thumbed his chest. "I want decent land for my life and I mean to earn it."

This man of near silence spoke the words in a voice cold and strange, a voice I'd not heard before, but I could see he reached Papa, struck that vein of business that flooded in my father's waking hours and no doubt, his dreams.

"Yes, yes, getting on forces hard choices on a man. I've made sacrifices that cut to the bone when our boat yard faced hard times. I respect a man who weighs facts and makes decisions."

I could almost see Papa's head working. A strong sense of business and the vigor to produce a male heir would mark the measure of a son-in-law for Lars Boscher.

Pier's face relaxed. "I don't expect to work as a diamond cutter all my years. I'm a dairyman, and I'll work in the city no longer than it takes to save money for acreage with good pasture, pasture that'll support a fine herd."

I eased my grip on the door. Those words, I knew, would reach Papa. Here was a hard-working man laying a foundation for his family, our family.

Pier's talk of saving, of the years to come, seemed to engage Papa. They blathered for another fifteen or twenty minutes about the problems of financing ventures – old or new. I sensed Papa warmed to Pier, but I wanted their conversation back on course.

The tiny stair cabinet pressed in on me, and my legs cramped. I could stand it no longer. I burst out of the closet and ran to Pier's side, taking his hand in mine.

"Maagda, what are you doing?"

Papa glared at me. Winter skates wouldn't flake the ice in his "What is this?"

I didn't look at him, but kept my eyes on Pier. "Papa, might we invite Mr. Veerbeck to sit?"

"You, young woman, have no place here." Papa moved toward me, I thought to walk me from the room.

"Oh, Papa, Pier's told the purpose of his visit. Any more is bluster."

My father snorted like a horse about to paw his hooves in the air.

I looked to Pier, his brow trenched in deep lines. I tossed my hand as if it was all nothing and said, "Now, Papa will want to know of your family, your health, your house, all those motes of detail that make little sense inside a marriage."

"All I have every right to know."

"You've known Pier's Uncle Freddy since his boyhood when he came to work at the Yard." Still he glared, lips pursed.

Pier followed my lead. "True, and there is no other family save a cousin on my mother's side who lives over in Edam."

My innards chilled. Not good. I imagined the thoughts colliding in Father's head. *The Veerbecks did not produce heirs.*

Pier's palm was moist in my hand.

Papa relaxed his face. "Maagda, I should order you from this room, but being the head strong woman you are, I know you'd lurk beyond the door. Bad enough I have the ire of every parent in Hoorn because I've let you choose your own course here, but there are some things that *will* be done my way. And one of them is that you will keep your silence."

Papa finally sat and motioned Pier to the facing chair by the front window. I perched on the arm of Pier's chair. Papa narrowed his eyes. He was not pleased.

He looked hard at both our faces. "Marriage is no light step. You make a commitment for life,"

"Of course, Papa. I know how you feel about honor and vows."

I waited for Pier to say he held me in some regard. But no, he kept his quiet.

Papa flicked imaginary dust from his white cuff. "You ask nothing of Maagda's dowry?"

Pier flushed. "Well…I thought…well, there's talk. It is expected."

Papa smirked. "Quotidian, eh?"

"What?" Pier jerked his head up.

Papa tilted his head forward and asked Pier, "What kind of talk?"

Pier's face colored a shade short of sunstroke. He was flummoxed. "You're a businessman. People talk…you…you send your daughters into marriage well provided for."

Papa shook his head. "The gossips miss nothing. Never mind. Yes, a generous dowry would be expected. I've set aside 5,000 florins for each of my girls." He hesitated, and looked at Pier. "But the dowry money given at the wedding is to be considered a dotation, an endowment of sorts, only for my grandchildren's education."

A *dotation*. Papa's words sounded centuries old, along with some of his thinking. Didn't he realize it was 1628? Lord, we'd even earned a mote of respect from the Spanish who tried so long to claim our lives and land.

"My daughters will go to their marriage homes with clothing to last for years, and proper linens, and well made pieces of furniture." Papa ticked the list off on his fingers. "My sister, Loekke, assures me that this is required and proper."

I wondered if next he'd take a paper from his sleeve where the number of petticoats in my cupboard might be noted, but he returned to the dowry.

"It must be understood…" Papa's face tightened. He looked directly into Pier's eyes. "The money which I'll give on Maagda's wedding day is to be put aside for my grandchildren. I expect her husband to provide for her everyday life after the personal goods she brings to the marriage."

Papa reached to the side table, toying with the long stemmed clay pipe he never smoked. "Children concern me. I am told you are a baptized Papist, and I know that sect has strict rules about how children must be churched."

Pier swallowed so hard, he coughed. "Baptized, yes. But it's nothing to me. I had the waters as an infant. My parent's wish, not a choice I would make."

Pier took a cloth from his sleeve and wiped his mouth. The sun had moved lower, directly opposite our windows to cast a searching beam on Pier's face. I watched drops of moisture bead on his forehead and upper lip.

Papa sat quietly, allowing the silence to shroud the air. I wondered did he let Pier squirm on some whim? Finally, he rose from the chair, faced the window, his back to Pier and me and told us he expected my husband to sail under his own wind, make his own living.

Pier sucked his cheeks in and matched Papa's tone. "I have means, sir. There is cash from the sale of our farm west of Hoorn as I told you, and some savings. My recently bought house in Amsterdam, too. Small with work to be done, but enough for a new marriage and a good resale in a few year's time."

"Then what's the rush? Have you...?"

Pier clamped his hands on the chair arms, his face aflame. "No. Good god, no." He almost choked on his words.

I buried my face in my sleeve to stifle my laugh. Neighbors would watch to see how quickly I bulged in the middle. Let them wash their thoughts in a night pot. I would become pregnant quickly. Hadn't I drunk my beer of stinging nettle for weeks? Midwives swore the brew readied you for a baby.

But there must be marriage first. I saw it all in my mind's eye. We'd live frugally in Amsterdam for the year or two that Pier needed to save more money, and then we'd buy the farm of his dreams near

Hoorn. I could continue my work at the Yard, coaching up every few weeks from the city. Papa needed me. I knew the Yard had been thrust upon him as a duty and he worked it with devotion. But I don't believe he was destined to a life of shipbuilding. He was more a dreamer, my Papa, a scholar. Did a builder relax at day's end translating classics from the Latin? Lars Boscher did. I thrived at the Yard, excited to be in the midst of commerce and a future that promised new ventures. Why, I felt I could take it on myself this very moment... well, almost.

Papa stood up. "I will think on it, Mr. Veerbeck...Pier." He reached for Pier's hand, but his lips and the lines in his face remained bowline taut.

Pier smiled. With his head tilted, the sun's late glow fired his ginger beard. He dabbed his lips. I wondered how sweet the taste should they touch mine.

"Come to our Sunday table," Papa said. "Bring your Uncle Freddy. We'll speak of this again, and I'll want to know more of your substance."

Papa locked his hands behind his back. "Much too soon," he muttered more to himself than either Pier or me. "With a ship in the ways ready for delivery and another behind schedule, I don't have time to visit Amsterdam to see what you offer my daughter." He turned to me and put his arm on my shoulder. "Understand, Maagda is my heart."

I squeezed Pier's hand, hoping for some tender word from him, but he said nothing and didn't squeeze my hand in return. When it was apparent that Papa had no intention of leaving us alone, Pier bowed, briefly touched my fingertips to his lips, his eyes on Papa, and hurried to the door, saying he must visit his Uncle Freddy who lived two lanes east, closer to the harbor.

"Nor do I esteem those Wise-men a rush, that call it a foolish and insolent thing to praise one's self."

In Praise of Folly by Desiderius Erasmus (Classics Club edition)

CHAPTER 6—PIER

I SPED FROM MAAGDA'S DOOR AND HURRIED MY step to Rode Steen Square, the houses along Oosten Kanaal steeg blurring into one shapeless churn. I crossed the canal near Freddy's lane. He wasn't expecting me, but I couldn't face the long ride back to Amsterdam with Lars drumming in my head.

Two hours with Lars Boscher sucked the blood from me. I'd wrestle a bull in heat before another such meeting. I worried his every question a trap. And some of his words. What did the man speak of? Quotation. Quotidian, whatever that meant. And that other poser, a dotation? Did he seek only to vex me, or trick me?

I learned one thing. He's not a man who'll easily move off his ideas. Wonder if under her soft talk, Maagda thinks like him. She showed some vinegar this afternoon, defying her father; coming into our talk. Her backbone is good. We'll need that, but I'm glad we'll live in Amsterdam for a bit after the marriage. I couldn't have Lars looking into our lives every day, stirring her up. A wife I might handle; him I was not sure about.

I thirsted for a long pull of ale, hoping Freddy had something in the larder.

My tunic stuck like a damp sheet when I walked, still at a quick pace, down Freddy's lane. His door was ajar and a thin veil of smoke swirled through the opening.

"Freddy, what kind of offal you burning in there? Smells like a cow pen on fire." I heard his laugh before I saw him. He walked toward me covered in a thick apron of some sort, a huge paddle in one hand and a cloth in the other that he mopped across his brow. He kicked the door stop, a molded iron pig, out of his way.

"It's supposed to be gingerbread, but I think I picked up the wrong sack at the millers. I was in a hurry." He slicked his hair back, a mix of black and gray that curled into womanish ringlets from the sweat running off him. "What are you doing here? Thought you'd stay with your woman." He pointed to my tunic. "Looks like you've been in a fire yourself."

"More like some cursed Spanish trial." I slipped into the single stuffed chair that he'd moved away from the grate, swinging my legs over the arm and kicking my boots to the floor.

"Lars?"

"Lars. I think the only question he missed was if I had holes in my hose." I stuck my right foot in the air to show my large toe naked as a baby's arse.

"You do need a woman in your life."

"A woman is easy, not so a wife it seems." I shook my head. "Had no thought that old boy would pry so deep. Even asked about my baptism. Small wonder he didn't ask if I was headed to heaven or hell."

Freddy smacked my stockinged foot with his paddle.

"My fault, I fear."

He admitted that he told both Maagda and her father about my Papist beginnings, my mother's doing, not mine, and then said Lars called him into his office on different days to ask about my work, my health, and especially whether or not I had debt.

Freddy poured me a tankard of ale and pulled a bench close to the fireplace. A kettle hung over the glowing peat and he gave it an occasional stir with the paddle that looked like an old oar, one that'd spent considerable time in the water.

"You can't blame Lars, you know, for wanting to know more about you than our relationship. It's a father's place." He swiped a finger along the edge of the paddle, tasted it and grimaced. "Needs salt." He shook the paddle free of a lump dripping from the edge. "My word holds water with Lars, but it's not enough where Maagda is concerned."

"I know. I know. But he tests me like a stud at auction."

Freddy laughed and gave his kettle another flip with the paddle. I sipped at my ale and watched him fuss with the rank mixture.

"You gonna keep that stuff?"

"Might turn out worth a nibble." He wrinkled his face. "I'm not the cook I'd like to be." Freddy laid the paddle aside and stared at me a second or two, all the time sucking in his lower lip. He leaned toward me.

"You know, Pier," he shoved the paddle against my foot…"would you please move that bare toe of yours from out of my face…if you don't want this marriage, brave up to it now. I've got a lot at stake with Lars, and as much as I'd value being real kin, I'm not ready to risk my place in that family or my work at the Yard."

"It's not the marriage. It's the father." I drained my tankard. "Lars is a nipping sand flea that bites where you can't scratch."

Freddy just shrugged, but told me more about how he'd moved along the idea of my walking out with Maagda, falling in with her little ploys.

"She made it plain that she found you appealing." He tapped the kettle. "Why, I'm not sure."

I tossed my boot at him, but it made me feel good to know Maagda sought my courting. When he'd first suggested I meet her at that dinner back in February, I agreed, and then I whistled back to

Amsterdam pleased with the look of her and the words she spoke. She wouldn't turn all the heads in a line, but there was a spark in her eyes and a warmth in her smile that kindled flame in me. And now that we'd gotten this far, I couldn't falter. I knew there were few chances I'd find such a marriage in Amsterdam. Only Freddy's good will with Lars made this match possible. I couldn't be found wanting.

Tricky, this betrothal business. But she favored me, and I would lay claim to her and her rich dowry. I'd come to next Sunday's dinner so full of business prattle, Lars'll think me the merchant prince of Amsterdam.

*"...the roughness of the Masculine temper is
season'd and sweeten'd by her folly."*

In Praise of Folly by Desiderius Erasmus (Classics Club edition)

CHAPTER 7—MAAGDA

WHEN PIER LEFT US TO SEE FREDDY, I SLIPPED MY arm round Papa's elbow and we walked toward the kitchen. "Oh, Papa, a joyful day." I thought to keep our talk easy, his mood light, not a reflection on Pier's visit. Better to leave small advances without further testing.

"Joyful, eh? Don't get your mind set on this yet." He juiced a breath through his teeth. "Ah, but maybe our poet, Father Cats, has it right when he says a ready maiden is like a chestnut in the fire. She'll explode if not cooled down in marriage." He gave me a playful rap on my shoulder. "Mind you, it's not easy to think such a thing of a daughter, even when it comes from a mind so admired as Cats."

I laughed, but knew it true...I was primed for the heat of marriage.

"I jest, Maagda, but I do want to know more of the stuff of this man, as you should. He says so little of himself. Words must be pried from him."

"Papa, Aunt Loekke always told Miekke and me you'll never know your man until you live with him. Do you want me to be like those girls in the North who let a swollen belly pick their partner?"

"Don't tempt my humor."

"I'm sorry. But you've said many times that you can't trust the manners a man shows in Rode Steen square. It's what he does behind his own door that counts. How can you ever know that before you marry?"

"Fair enough. Still your courtship's been short, but if it pleases my child…."

His face clouded for an instant, mulling some worry or another. "If I didn't know Freddy so well, I would not give such a union another thought, because in my head, I think I place more trust in the haste of this arrangement than a father ought." But the moment passed and he smiled again, sat down and stretched his long legs across the floor, placing one foot in a white tile, the other in a black. He'd taught Miekke and me games with marbles on these very tiles.

"Your young man does have prospects, ties to commerce. I must think more on his future and what it will mean for you and my grandchildren." He drew a strong breath. "Those children of yours to come will mean everything."

Hadn't I heard the tale of the Hoorn legacy on every birthday? It was as much ritual as the tray of caramel waffles in three different sizes Mama prepared for my special treat.

I jigged a step or two. "And how many grandchildren do you expect?"

Papa laughed and clapped his hands to the rhythm of my steps. "I've room for two or three here on my knees." His gaze drifted to the window. "I always thought you'd marry someone from Hoorn, then raise your family here, keep a hand in at the Yard. You have a natural head for business. I know you'll teach my heirs properly." Papa spread his hands in front of him. "I'm only a builder." Rough, brown calluses mottled the joints where his fingers met his palm.

I caught his hand and pressed it to my cheek.

"I've known the young men around here since my school days. To think of them as suitors?" I shook my head. "They've grown into good men, but I've learned their quirks over the years. I need a fresh wind, a new course."

"A new course, is it? You know they jest at the tavern that you hold yourself above our local boys. Men ask how I feel about your marrying an Amsterdam man, with family working for me at that. Maybe I've raised you too much like a son with all of your time at the Yard. Left you little time for the frills a girl should fancy."

"Nonsense." I whipped the bright paisley scarf from my shoulders and twirled it round my head. My kitten, Folly, pounced near my feet, ready for play. "Do I look like a boy? And I doubt the lads who've pursued me at our May First festivities every year thought so either." Though truth be told there were times I dreamt of frills, of whirling in a merry reel with a dashing man. I'd be gowned in layers of chiffon, a bit of lace. Somehow there never seemed a fit time to dance for a woman who spent her days between home and a drafting table in her father's boat yard.

Papa ushered me into the sitting room where he and Pier had talked. We settled on the chairs by the windows, facing each other. The purple of day's end faded in the western sky, leaving the canal waters a deep mauve. I watched two small boys roll their hoops in the shadows of East Bridge. This was my magic hour when the world moved in light and shadow and anything was possible. The stillness, the beauty almost beyond breathing, steadied my tumbled thoughts. I watched, absorbed the last bits of mellow light, the shadows, the muted sounds from children in the lane, and closed my eyes to let the fiber of my world seep deep into my marrow. Papa's voice roused me.

"We must talk of the years to come." He drummed his fingers on the side table. "It's hard, Maagda, no mother here to guide you."

Oh figs. Don't let this be about marriage and intimacy with Pier. I shifted in the chair. Before I could protest, Papa leaned forward to take my left hand. He slid a delicate ring with a square-cut garnet onto my smallest finger.

"This was your mother's." Papa fit the gold band with its blood red stone tight to the base of my finger. "Perhaps the ring will pass her wisdom to you."

He kept my hand locked in his. "You know, Maagda, years ago your Aunt Loekke gave me a tongue lashing because I took you and Miekke on my short voyages. I can still hear her: *Lars, those boats of yours are no place for young girls. They need to grow up like the other lasses in Hoorn.*"

Papa mimicked his older sister's piercing soprano. We both laughed. My dear aunt made *stiff* sound like the fourth Grace.

"I said, Loekke, I want my girls to grow up smart, able to take care of themselves." He squeezed my hand. "That was before we realized Miekke's frailty. The burden is yours now, solely yours."

I tightened my lips.

"That is why your mother's ring. Wear it every day. Look at it and remember who you are, your duty to yourself and to your family.

Papa picked up a book from the side table, his thumb tracing the ridges in its well creased spine. "One last thing." He hunched his shoulders. "Lord I wish your mother was here. A father is poorly skilled to launch a daughter into marriage."

Oh, oh, now comes the bed, the intimacy. Instead, he placed the russet-colored book in my hands. And this man of words, fulsome words, stammered.

"Take this. Read it. Understand what Plutarch relates here. It's a fine translation."

I opened the title page, *Rules for Husbands and Wives*. Relieved that Papa would not be the one to enlighten me, my breath whooshed free.

Papa caught my reaction, furrowed his brow. "You've read this?"

"No, but within the hour I shall know every word, every rule."

"An now, having vindicated to my self the praise of Fortitude and Industry, what think ye if I do the same by that of Prudence?"

In Praise of Folly by Desiderius Erasmus (Classics Club edition)

CHAPTER 8—MAAGDA

THE HOUSE BUSTLED FROM EARLY MORNING UNTIL well after the dinner hour. Although my wedding was still weeks hence, every cranny from the front marble steps to the highest corner under the highest gable at rooftop, an old warren of an attic, had to be dusted, scrubbed, scrubbed yet again and then polished. Young Sophie juggled meals, frazzled with the constant troop of help combing through the house, friends wielding broom, cloth or mop. Bless their help; they had to be nourished twice each day. During my daily absence at the Yard, my dear Ria kept order, a militia commander marshalling a dust-cap army. Our front steps adjoined so it was easy for her to slip home to her own concerns if needed, but I knew she gave the Boschers the fullness of her day.

Miekke helped as best she could, given her frailty. "Why must you be different?" she wailed. "A bride should be taken to her new husband's home for the feast." She flopped into the cushioned chair by the front window where Ria's husband whistled a salty jig while wiping the panes dry.

"We'll be too tired to dance when the day comes." She lifted her legs and crossed her slim ankles on mother's footstool.

"Be reasonable, Miekke. Pier's home is thirty-five miles away in Amsterdam. If we had to travel that distance, we'd be too tired to dance or to eat…or, or anything." I smiled inside.

My work at the Yard kept me busy until at least three each day, but I did don an apron and consult Ria's list of chores when I came home in late afternoon when the sun slanted just enough to send strong light through all our rooms that fronted the canal. I could see well enough to attack a room's hidden crannies. I snatched the later hours in my room to stitch my wedding gown and to jot a note of progress in my diary. And then yesterday, in the midst of this buzzing, Papa casually announced we were to have a dinner guest tonight.

"Papa," I pleaded. "Now? Why now? We'll never have the house restored in time."

"Of course you will. You need not come to the Yard tomorrow. Besides Klemp lives alone. He'll not notice a bit of disorder."

A bit of disorder. Had he gone blind? Boxes and buckets bulged from every nook of space. Divans and chairs stood empty of cushions that were being beaten dust free in the clean spring air. The young lads cherished that chore. They smote the cushions as if George's dragons hid within. More than one cushion came into the house in sore need of stitching repairs.

Lord, now Papa with a guest, and a single day to make the lower rooms presentable. We scurried like blizzard bound squirrels with no acorns laid by, but the house had some semblance of order when the brass knocker pounded promptly at four o'clock. Miekke, totally fatigued, escaped to her room, and Ria hurried out the back door. I gave a quick glance around the sitting room, straightened one pillow, and sighed. It was the best I could do. At least the laurel blooms were fresh from the garden, and a welcome aroma of roasted meat hung in the air.

Papa took our visitor's elbow and guided him to our best chair in the sitting room. Klemp had walked the four cobbled lanes from his wharf quarters. The man wheezed, short of breath. I thought the rigor of four lane crossings beyond the endurance of his too ample frame.

"My daughter, Maagda, Mr. Klemp. She draws the final drafts on that ship of ours that you admire, the fluyt."

"Ah, *the* Maagda Boscher. The taverns buzz with your name, young lady."

He took the chair next to mine by the windows, his boots at ease on mother's rose-embroidered stool. He sat in front of heavy damask drapes that cast deep shadows from a waning sun, hiding the details of his face.

"And why would that be?"

Fire crept up my cheeks, but I held his eye and sat straighter in my chair knowing pepper gathered on my tongue. I saw Papa fidget to adjust the flat white collar that spread across his shoulders. He'd known Klemp for years, but I wondered at his sudden interest in having the man to dinner. I'd never had conversation with Klemp before, merely a nod on his visits to the Yard. The man, I'd been told, lost his wife in the birthing of their first child. He'd lived alone since, Papa said, taking most of his meals in the tavern at Rode Steen.

Klemp leaned into the light. Eyes aglow under a solid bush of white brow, he grinned at me and reached to give Papa, who sat on the edge of his horsehair reading chair, a playful thump on the arm.

"They say you've turned Hoorn on its keel, naming your own husband. Folks been wagering on who might seed the Hoorn legacy." He winked at Papa. "Can't say I haven't put a stuiver down myself, but I truly expected a local man."

I looked at Papa, but addressed Klemp. "Sir, would you allow another to name the meat for your plate at the tavern? I think not, but a small matter beside the weight of how someone is to spend her life."

Papa's eyebrows flew into arcs above his lids, but Klemp laughed. "Very so, very so." He tapped his long clay pipe stem against the soup cup at his side. "A fiery one, heh, but what Hoorn needs if a Boscher heir is to keep this town afloat." He leaned toward my father. "I was across the Channel last month. Those English women don't breathe a word beyond simple dainties, and those behind open fans. Makes me proud our ladies speak their minds."

It never occurred to me now that I was not to say what I thought, and I knew well my duty to birth a child so there'd be no void in the bloodline. I'd little doubt that the longing my ginger-bearded Pier fanned in my belly would find me wanting. But you hardly speak thus. Inside I cringed that Klemp spoke so freely of me, though I'd felt shamed for Papa of late, knowing that many in our town speculated on my future, that my most private life was a thing to be gambled over in the tavern. I sought to turn the conversation elsewhere when Klemp reminded us that the widow had flouted the norm by coming to Papa herself to speak of marriage when she should have sought an older male kin to seek a betrothal. I'd forgotten that custom and Klemp's mentioning it now brought a smile back to my lips. I'd not been so wicked after all.

Sophie came with a soft yellow lamp and whispered to me that dinner waited. The hearty wisps of roast mutton licked round every corner. Twice I'd noticed Klemp sniffing the air and looking toward the back of the house. I played Papa's proper hostess, hooked my arm through Klemp's, and invited him to the table and the cane-backed chair to my father's right. Handing him a pewter mug of ale with a lace of foam on top, I inquired about the East India Company's voyage now in Batavia.

Papa passed the basket of black bread. "I assure you, Klemp, my daughter asks not of the silks and baubles that might return, but of the trade itself."

"What, no interest in female whimsies?" Klemp slathered a layer of salted heavy cream on his bread. The pale yellow spread came from the creamery shortly after daybreak when Sophie and I shopped the markets for tonight's meal.

I turned in my chair to face him full. "Whimsies? Of course," I smiled, "but in their place." The gauzy nightdress I had sewn for my wedding night was whimsy enough for any woman, not that thoughts of whirling to music in a frilled gown with an agreeable male hadn't entered my mind often enough. On Ria's advice I'd spent my evenings sewing gauzy nightdresses, a set of three. "Even new husbands need a bit of enticing," she said.

Klemp opened his mouth to respond, but apparently thought better of it and turned his attention to the steaming joint of mutton in the center of the table. Papa carved and I heaped Klemp's plate with roasted squash and baked figs.

"Enough, enough, Maagda. That prune and pea soup dulled my hunger."

I hardly thought so. During our talk in the sitting room, Klemp has finished two cups of the thick pottage along with several rhoemers of elderberry wine. His bulk spilled over the arms of the chair and his belly lounged through his open tunic, so unlike Papa at the head of the table with knife in hand, hard and lean from hauling hemp and lumber. Klemp asked after Miekke.

Papa nodded toward the empty chair beside mine and explained that Miekke was ailing."

"Like they say," Klemp sighed, palms up, "sickness comes on horseback and departs on foot."

"Too much like her poor mother, I fear," Papa said. "She's resting upstairs so she'd be well for Sunday, when we bless Maagda' marriage."

"So it's all arranged, then," Klemp said. "Bet the Widow van Pelt blows a foul wind. Rumor favored her Willy."

Papa didn't answer. Although he'd known Klemp for more than three decades, long before Klemp became an East India Company governor, I thought Papa reluctant to bare himself to new barbs.

I held my tongue and chose to ignore the subject of Willy van Pelt.

"My Pier comes with his Uncle Fredrick to brave the family gauntlet. Miekke, like Papa, is reluctant to let me go. We've been that close all our lives."

Klemp laughed, dabbing his mouth where bits of mutton hung, ready to tumble to his white tunic. "A gauntlet, is it?"

Papa sucked his lips in. His face tinged with a flush that crept behind his white beard. He glared at me, but turned to Klemp, and spoke of Pier's farming background and his present post.

"Diamonds, eh?" said Klemp. "The coming thing I hear. Even a guild brewing to join them up in Amsterdam. Though can't say I think much of burghers using their investment money on those stones, or in this risky new tulip market, by god."

I sensed Klemp's meaning, but urged him on, a much more fascinating bit of talk than gossip of my marriage. We heard words from all quarters that the VOC, our East India Company, was hard-pressed for investors. Those English traders, and even the Germans, who visited the Yard to inspect our fluyts, talked of the VOC's shrinkage.

Klemp told us that burghers with courage to invest dwindled by the voyage. They feared both the long wait for returns and Spanish piracy blessed by Phillip himself.

Sophie brought a fresh pitcher of ale to the center of the table. She poured and I turned to Klemp and asked him how his VOC might counter the diamonds and the tulips.

Klemp, his own tankard in midair, stared at me. "Lars, perhaps this daughter of yours chose wisely with her diamond man. Much as I loathe even thinking the words, I know it's safer to hold a stone in your hand than the promise of a ship returning with riches."

Klemp admitted that the tulip traffic left him baffled. He told us the State's treasury trembled with speculation rampant, wondering if the VOC would keep its coffers full. "Yet burghers, austere when it's a stuiver's expense, will chase a small brown bulb to their last bag of silver. Can't fathom it myself."

Papa nodded. "I know little of this tulip business, but I am certain the Prince and the States General will be after every town and every business for more money. They've shaken those trees into a leafless December."

So this is why Papa invited Klemp. He worried about our trade. And why not? I saw it now. Since my girlhood I'd traced borders on the map of Europe Papa kept in his office from the cartographer, Blaeu. France and the German provinces bulged like a fist from the center of our near world. Now, dear god, they sought to slaughter each other. Klemp's words brought the war fresh to my mind and made me wonder yet again how long our stadtholders would support the German cause. Papa thought them right, but I could not agree. It would never strike me as right to kill innocents, to burn their fields and their homes. The thought sent shudders through me. And now those families flocked to our country for work and shelter.

I looked to Klemp, not with my anger at the war, but a sudden thought of my own striking a vein I thought more to his line. I reminded him of the inland war between Germany and France and the hordes of people starving for supplies. "Only ships like our fluyts reach their ports. Perhaps your Dutch East India Company needs our fluyts to sail those shallow waters."

I thought Papa about to reprimand, but I caught him biting his lower lip to suppress a smile.

"Hold on, Lars." Klemp rapped the table. "Your daughter astonishes me. Maybe we are like the hungry horse with blinders, can't see another field with better pasture." Klemp winked at me. "You know the Gentlemen XVII, the company board of governors, arrive this week for our month-long meeting. Should I suggest you appear before them to speak of your fluyt?"

I wanted to shout *yes, why not*, but I felt a flush rise from my neck knowing he toyed with me. Klemp reached across the table to take my hand. The edge of his lace cuff dangled just over the gravy bowl. "And what of your young man, Pier? Where will he seek treasure?"

"Here, of course. The war is far from his mind."

Klemp tossed his head back and laughed. "Did a bride ever hold a different thought? All light and rapture 'til the real living sets in."

A jolt, and one unwelcome from a stranger. I didn't respond.

My dreams of Pier brought riches of a different sort to mind. My flesh tingled to think I would soon surrender my maiden's life to him. Yet I warmed, too, at the thought the VOC should be united in a marriage of commerce I had put to Klemp. It did not yet rise to full understanding among the many thoughts whirling in my head, but I sensed our fluyts and the VOC was a future to ponder. Trade, commerce, there lay the challenge of making life happen. And Pier.

"Tell me, I beseech ye, what Man is that would submit his neck to the Noose of Wedlock, if as Wisemen, he did but first truly weight the inconvenience of the thing?"

In *Praise of Folly* by Desiderius Erasmus (Classics Club edition)

CHAPTER 9—PIER

I'D LEFT THE DIAMOND SHOP EARLY YESTERDAY SO I might sleep in Hoorn last night. A joyless trip, but I wanted a solid snore before the marriage. That endless stretch of rutted road left me arse weary and me cranky. After today, the trip would be a torture of the past. No more aching arse for me, no more Hoorn. I'd get Maagda settled in Amsterdam until I made our final move.

Freddy had brushed my jacket and breeches, the only pair of knee breeches I owned. I favored a workingman's baggy pants and loose blouse. We dressed in his bedroom, talking, idling away time since we weren't due at the magistrate's until two hours hence. I was edgy, the talk good for my spirits.

"Damn. Uncle Freddy, can you help?"

"What's wrong?"

"This ruff scratches like chicken claws and it's too fancy. Even a flat collar's too much the burgher for me." I jerked the back of the ruff and pinched the ends between my fingers, no clear look in the glass to see it right or wrong. I whipped it from my neck.

"Here. Let me adjust it," he said. "A man should look a bit dashing for his marriage."

"Including that stiff brimmed hat of yours? If it were left to me, I'd wear my battered old felt." I picked my soft hat up from the bed knob where I'd tossed it last night. "Like the medallion?"

Freddy fingered the hat and held the medallion to the window light for a better look. "Never knew you one to be taken by vanities."

"Not a vanity. That's a rough cast of the new guild symbol. All the diamond men are joining. Have to."

He shrugged and tossed the hat back on the post.

Freddy lived two lanes south of Maagda's home on Oosten Kanaal steeg. I'd stayed the night with him, and we'd sat to the last of the peat's glow drinking ale.

"Good of you to lend me a ruff, Uncle, but I look like something out of that painting." It amused me to call him uncle on occasion to remind him that he was the older, and I could tell it nettled him.

I pointed to the framed picture across the room, the sole spot of color along the whitewashed walls. A troop of men stood around in what I called *church* clothes. Local people seemed to fancy these pictures of militia units. Once we passed our eighteenth birthday all of us had to join up. But to belong cost big stuivers, more than a gem cutter's apprentice could afford. Even at twenty-eight, my year's wages wouldn't buy me a gun or armor. I grinned at the thought of this farm boy on parade with one of those colored chest plates. What would I paint on it, a cow's tits?

"Is that your Unit?" I knew better, but I never missed an opportunity to poke a bit of fun at him. "I have a thirst. Did we drain the bucket last night?"

"Here, have some of my ale you impudent whelp. Lars pays me a good wage at the Yard, but enough for the militia? No, that's a practice piece of sorts by a young artist hereabouts. Name of Baburen.

He's found subjects more to his liking among the serving girls in the Rode Steen Tavern. His new earthy style." Freddy rolled his eyes.

We joked about our ages and the local militias, but if that Spaniard Phillip invaded, or the endless war in Germany moved west, I might yet tramp out of Amsterdam, armor or no. I paid little heed to the war though. Let those German and French kill each other. And little Bohemia wasn't worth a manure heap. My thoughts sailed to a different world. And I knew that Maagda with her strength, and yes, her dowry, could make that voyage real. I ran my finger around the inside rim of the collar and tried to ease its jabs to my skin.

"Rot this thing. It pricks worse than August straw. Can't they make these collars out of something that doesn't jab a man to jitters?"

"My boy, I doubt the heat is from your cambric collar. More likely you sizzle with the anticipation of marriage. Very healthy indeed."

"So you think me new to the ways of women?" I grinned. "I've bounced around in more than one sleeping closet in Hoorn."

"Maagda's?"

"By god, no. She's under lock and key. Lars'd whack off my balls and use 'em for bait."

"Then, I assume the lady's still intact and ready to be initiated into the joys of marriage." Freddy left the small oak chest where he'd leaned and walked over to the one chair in the room, a clunky wing back with a stiff, bristling cover. Suited him, I thought.

"I've always suspected her an innocent. Smart enough, but not carnally aware. Can't imagine that your thoughts never plowed that furrow."

"I'm not a fool. Maagda's a different sort, not like these small town women who don't wed until the seed sprouts."

Freddy lounged in the chair, while I smoothed my wiry hair with a brush. The day ahead promised little for me. New people. Talk. Questions. No joy there.

"Maagda seems hale enough," I said, still thinking of that nuisance sister of hers. "But it's curious, her talk of that fluytship. Even says it could save the VOC?" I laughed. "The VOC yet. Wouldn't do for Maagda to fancy herself more than a wife." I turned to Freddy. "Makes me wonder who readied her for a husband. Certainly not Loekke, that dried up aunt of hers."

Freddy ran his fingers along the arm of the chair. "Maagda's a sound girl, and mark my words, the fluyt has a big future, but she'll know her place when the time comes. She'll make a fine mother,"

"That sly old Lars has our family planned. Tied her dowry to our children's schooling. But he's a long wait ahead. I won't be breeding."

Freddy got up from the chair and turned my shoulder toward him.

"That's a rare thought for a man about to wed. Why marry a fine woman like Maagda if you don't want children?"

"Oh, there'll be babies some day, and plenty of work for that dowry." I busied myself at the small reflecting glass. "But not right off. Babies eat a man's savings. I've broken my back picking rocks out of fields at the farm, and now I squint in lantern light over other men's gems. I want a better life before babies chain me in one place."

Well I knew how children ate at a man's funds. Didn't my own father remind me often enough. Yes, and the hand-me-down breeches that the old man had already worn to nothing, always too big, tunics that hung loose on my bony frame, sleeves rolled to elbows to keep them out of the muck, and didn't he rail about what it cost to keep me in a bit of bacon. By god, that man even resented the price of a candle to read by of an evening, made me stop bothering with books all together. To my father I was just another rake, another hoe to lift some of the work off his own back. No, there would be no children in my marriage until there were stuivers, even florins, to spare.

"Does your bride and her father know you want to delay a family?"

"Soon enough. Maagda had wanted me to read some old wag's book her father had given her about husbands and wives. I've no need for a book. My father left me with one good lesson. He swore a man's right mate is clean, able and bends to a husband's head. That's one place I agree with him."

Freddie laughed. "Such a warm fellow you are. But beware. I don't think many women hold with thoughts like your father's in these times. Dutch women are known to have mind of their own."

"I notice you're still a bachelor." His color rose, but he said nothing.

It occurred to me that my father festered with anger his entire life because mother died too young to work beside him. I didn't want to think it, but there it was. I grabbed a small comb and raked my bristly mustache and short beard, hoping to drive Freddy's talk elsewhere. I wasn't ready to tell anyone, even my favorite relative, where I planned to be in five years. Not bad, I thought, with another look in the glass, not a bad cut of a man at all.

Freddy wouldn't give it up. "Surely Maagda or her father has spoken to you of the Hoorn Trust?"

I thought a minute, judging what to say. "With the dowry tied up in babies and their schooling, they take a family for granted." I didn't meet his eye. "I know there's some old chestnut about a trust, but to me it's buried under a century of dust. No meaning in my times."

"It's risky, Pier. I hope you know what you're doing. Maagda's not to be trifled with. Secrets? No sir, not a good way to start. And I wouldn't want to see any bad will here."

Freddy drew his cheeks tight. "You realize all of Hoorn will be waiting for that first baby? Families here depend on the Yard, that Trust, for a living."

I looked at him. "Hmmm. What's that old saying? …all in the fullness of time."

He didn't smile. "You need some gentling, some softening. Growing up as you did with no mother, a father in the field from sun up, it puts a brittle edge on a man. Not good in a marriage."

"What would you know of starting a marriage?" I poked my uncle's ribs. His work at the Yard left him muscled as the ships he built. "You've never been closer to an *I Do* than the last row in the church. I'm at the age when I need the comforts of a woman. Maagda's easy on the eye and she's a hard worker."

"You court trouble. Girls here wed late. Maagda's a bit younger than many, but she'll be anxious for children. Her father draws breath in hopes of a grandson. You marry her and tell her no family? Bad business. If she's all you say, you may forget that resolve, you know."

"Don't give it a thought." I looked at him square. "My future's tied up in more than a romp on that new bed her father had made for us. Bye the bye, thanks for letting us stay here tonight. I have no taste for spending my wedding night with my father-in-law in the next room."

Freddy laughed and slapped me on the back. "I won't be in the house either. A friend takes me in for the night."

With Freddy, I wondered whether the friend might be a man or a woman. I didn't ask, but I knew that he approached forty still a bachelor and that raised eyebrows in a little town.

Glancing around Freddy's spare bedroom, I hoped the woman wouldn't find it too stark, though I thought to occupy her in other ways, if, I trusted, she was knowing enough not to plan this marriage night at the time of her monthly. I could not abide the bed with a woman in blood.

"I know one…that gave his new married Wife some counterfeit Jewels, and, as he was a pleasant Droll, persuaded her they were not only right, but of an inestimable price…"

In Praise of Folly by Desiderius Erasmus (Classics Club edition)

CHAPTER 10—MAAGDA

I'D AWAKENED WITH A KNOT OF DOUBT AND FRIGHT heavy on my chest. Ria warned me I might feel so. What had I committed myself to? Papa was right. I knew little of this man. I knew little of men. Never even had a brother to show me what lay beneath the street talk, the rough and tumble play. The grown men at the yard seemed of the same cut. What lay ahead, this day, this night, this life, would be as strange to me as all the world outside of my beloved Hoorn. Ria had explained how Pier would approach me, cover me with himself, but reminded me again that some Dutch men needed prodding. She described places I might put my hands on Pier if he seemed to hesitate, and she'd urged me to stitch nightgowns of fine, gauzy fabric. Mine were so frail I could almost put my finger through the cloth. "Just lay still," she urged. "You might even find it pleasant." Might?

I yearned for tomorrow, for the guessing, the worry to be over and thought of all the warmth and passion that would fill my diary's pages.

I tried to swallow my bridal doubts in the excitement of our wedding day. It began with a fierce storm, but by midday, we basked in a bright May sun.

We stepped from the magistrate's office to a canopy of sky bluer than a summer sea, with the earlier rain now sweeping East over the Zuider Zee. Cobbles in the street danced with sunlight on tiny pools of water, and my gown, the color of ripe peaches, blazed like a flint sparking fire. I felt no less aglow and vowed to keep my fright from marring this moment.

I'd fancied that Pier would come to me with a single white rose and a pledge of comfort and affection for all of my days. Yet our brief ceremony had sped by in a babble of words, and it seemed only seconds before we turned to each other bound for life. The ceremony had been simple, following the law. We never considered the ornate papist rites or the cheerless drone of a Calvinist predicant. The simple swearing before the Mayor of Hoorn was enough.

There was no white rose, no special words from Pier, but he smiled a rare smile and held my hand to guide me down the few steps from the magistrate's chamber to the street. The small sapphire ring he had slipped on my index finger moments ago caught the sun.

At the bottom of the steps Pier looked at me. "You belong to me now," he whispered, "my wife."

*Wife.*I tasted word on my tongue and shivered. I didn't know whether in delight or fear, but squeezed his hand while we threaded our way among friends who showered us with kisses and embraces, waiting for us to lead them through the streets of Hoorn to the feast set out at home.

Anna Pellter, my old classmate who had devoured Pier with her eyes weeks ago near the chemist's shop, sprang forward and kissed him on the cheek. "Oh, you most fortunate of women," she mouthed to me. Pier recoiled in surprise, his hat flipping to the cobbles, and I laughed, more at his face than her antics.

Miekke, sing-songing "Maags, Maags," ran ahead with our cousins and tossed buttery jonquil petals over Pier and me.

We promenaded past Hoorn's main gate. Its tawny brick and gray stones glistened from the earlier rain, and the town's symbolic horn shadowed in deep relief atop the arch. So fitting then when music swelled around us, not from a horn, but a fiddle. "Oh, Pier, listen." A jolly string man joined the procession. He lent a lively cadence to our walk, almost a sailor's jig. His music suited the salt tang in the air, a tang that roused my taut spirits.

Neighbors clapped their hands and ran to loft flowers over us. "God bless; God bless, Maagda. Bring us many little ones." Some cheered and fell into our procession.

Pier nodded toward a woman standing in the shadow of her open door. A scowl tightened her lips into dark line. "Who's that sour old tart?"

She held her night pot and made a slight move of tilting it toward the street. Would she dare?

"Old Widow van Pelt. She's tried since school days to push her Willy on me. Now she tells people, 'the shipbuilder's daughter is too good for a Hoorn man.' You'd think I was heiress to a fortune. Such nonsense."

Pier smiled at me. "Your father gives a generous dowry."

"That's for our children." I kissed a little Oosten Kanaal steeg girl who handed me a posy of violets. Her mother waved from the stoop.

Pier looked away for a brief moment, then smiled again, touching the brim of his hat in salute to our well-wishers. I blew tiny kisses with my free hand. Pier held my left hand high as if we were dancing.

Papa, Ria, and the Mayor had hurried home before us. They waited in the gabled shadow of our house with brandy-filled roemers raised in a toast. Ria, forsaking her customary apron, and splendid in a filmy amber frock, gestured to a tray she held with its silver-clad glasses for Pier and me. I knew they brimmed with hippocras, a blend of wine and spices, an old medicinal drink. We must have it now, our first drink, a custom for newlyweds.

Pier whispered to me, "Makes for a lively bedding."

"Probably an old wives' tale." I felt my blush, and a warmth pass between us, and wondered if he'd need the prodding Ria had said I might expect.

"Come, come," she now urged. "A sip of the old hippo starts a healthy marriage." She laughed, as did the others, and insisted on refills. Then she whispered, "I think every young woman in Hoorn tastes freedom today."

"Inside now." My father ushered us past the carved oaken door into the front room. "We must toast you on your wedding thrones." Stems of sea lavender draped the chairs by the front windows. The small candle table between them had been removed and the chairs pushed close together.

Papa lit Pier's marriage pipe. The tobacco had been laced with citron for the special occasion. It added a tangy aroma to the bouquet in the room. Pier coughed, turned scarlet and held the pipe at arm's length.

"I don't...don't smoke," he said in a hoarse whisper.

Papa took the pipe from Pier and slapped him on the back. "Don't worry, young man. It's the trying that counts." Pier managed a smile.

I wondered had Papa grown fond of Pier. He certainly spoke kindly of him since that Sunday dinner when Pier had regaled him with tales of Amsterdam's commerce on the Damrak and trickster antics at the Bourse.

When Pier recovered from his coughing, Miekke reached behind me to remove my cap and place a bridal wreath of woven bayberry on my hair.

"Now, my Maags is truly today's princess," she said.

Pier brushed his lips on my cheek.

Our guests were to arrive within the hour. Papa took Mayor Jessel to the corner where the wine and goblets were laid, and the others drifted from the room for last minute chores in the kitchen.

"Come," Pier said. He took my hand and edged me into a small parlor next to the sitting room.

He shut the door. His hands cupped my bottom and pulled me tight to his thighs. He tilted my head back. "You belong to me now."

My breath flew from me, never an embrace like this during our courtship. Thoughts scattered from my head. A dizzying warmth flooded my belly. So rapt, I didn't hear the door open.

"Ahem..." More throat clearing. "Ahem."

We wrenched apart.

My face heated, I glanced over Pier's shoulder to see Freddy's smirk.

"Your guests arrive." He turned and closed the door behind him.

I fluffed my crushed dress, dazed by such an embrace, such urgency. Pier arranged his tunic and pulled it taut over his breeches.

"Later," his voice a heavy syrup of promise. "Later."

I felt he'd unleashed the tight reins that held him in check these last months. What more lay ahead? Certainly not the restraint Ria had warned of. Would I need the gauzy gown at all?

The house filled to bursting with guests flowing through all of the rooms. Friends and neighbors arrived and piled ribboned parcels on an oak table in the corner of the sitting room. We were gifted with carved wooden paddles and hammered pewter spoons, and sweet Aunt Loekke gave us hand-embroidered linens. I would use all in my first kitchen. There would be no scullery girl like our Sophie here in Hoorn until we were well established.

"Oh, look at this edging, Pier." I held up a linen table cover the tone of winter straw with bright gold and orange stitching. "Have you ever seen anything so delicate? Some day, with good care, these will be heirlooms for our children." He barely nodded and moved away to the wine table. Well, when did household linens excite a man?

Freddy joined me to admire the array of gifts. He fingered the embroidered linens and remarked on the intricate stitches. "I'd guess this to be relaxing work. Wouldn't mind trying it myself," he said, and then he took my hand and pulled me toward the staircase. For a moment, I half expected him to shove me into the under stairs cabinet where I had hid on Pier's visit to Papa.

"I wanted to move away from the dancing, to talk a little." His eyes searched my face. "I've watched you grow up. I know you're a good woman, and today begins big change in your life. For Pier, too." He ran his finger along the cabinet molding. "I hope you'll loosen the straps that bind that nephew of mine. He balls himself tight like he's trying to press inside a small barrel." Freddy hesitated, searching for the right words, I thought. "Pier permits no softness. He needs affection to show him a side of life he's not had." He gripped my hand. "You're a woman who knows challenges, Maagda. Be patient with him, guide him quietly and you'll both be happier for it."

What a strange suggestion and from an old bachelor at that. I was taken aback, but I'd heard the love in Freddy's voice, and, too, I marveled at his wisdom and his courage to come to me. Then I thought of Pier's earlier embrace, hardly the mark of a man who held his passions in check. Kissing Freddy's cheek, I whispered, "I'll do my best to show him how tender life might be." Freddy held his lips tight and nodded, moisture stealing into his eyes. A gentle soul, this Freddy. Pier was fortunate in his affection. We both were.

Klemp from the VOC came by as Freddy left, his words still in the front of my thoughts. "Well, my girl, I see you reeled your fish in, and on your own line, too. Maybe you do have the mettle of commerce in you."

I couldn't respond. These were words I sought, but only on the morrow.

"Where's this young man of yours, Maagda?" He looked 'round the room. "I want to talk to him of diamonds."

"Surely not today, Mr. Klemp." My cheeks grew warm. "I think you'll find his mind not on the business of diamonds."

"And yours?" Klemp guffawed, a deep rumbling laugh that could only rise from a man of his proportions. "Might you honor me with a dance and more words of your wondrous fluytships?"

Even though I'd provoked his joke, and the future of our fluyts niggled the back of my mind at all hours, I chose to ignore his invitation. My thoughts were only of the day and night ahead. "Come," I said, "you must charm my Aunt Loekke. She's quite the stepper."

He took my hand. "Always a monkey at the ready, heh?"

Aunt Loekke sat near the scullery door in animated conversation with Ria's husband. I led Klemp to her and introduced them. His invitation and his extended hand brought a glow seldom seen on her dear face.

Around me rowdy laughter and booming voices all but drowned the tunes of the fiddler who played from a corner of the sitting room. Papa had put a box on top of a small table where the fiddler perched to be seen and heard by all. I'd covered the box with one of my colorful shawls and put a pillow for a seat. He seemed comfortable enough, and our guests let no tune go unstepped.

I noticed that small groups of two or three spilled into the rear garden, the rain gone and the benches dry. Late jonquils and white mayflowers heavy from the earlier downpour brought a delicate scent of late spring drifting through the open doors. I walked from room to room filled with a sudden tenderness to watch our guests enjoy themselves because of my good fortune. I searched for Pier, but he was forever being snatched away by one or two of the men, most likely to the ale barrel in the scullery.

Papa, an exuberant host, laughed and joked, danced with our guests in the space we had cleared from the sitting room to the staircase. He reeled with enthusiasm, but stopped several times to catch his breath. I noticed that raspy breathing of his only yesterday when he and Jan rolled up our hooked rugs to make room for today's dancing, I saw him pause twice to breathe deeply, his face a dark ruby shade.

"Come, come, Loekke." Freddy grabbed my aunt from her dance with Klemp, and whirled her around to the fiddler's tune. She sprang to life like a young girl and smiled even when his missteps stomped her new black slippers. She waved to Klemp behind Freddy's back.

"Here, you take her." Freddy laughed and handed her off to bar-rel-chested Mayor Jessel, a stout stump of a man. "She's too much woman for me." Dear Aunt Loekke beamed like a sixteen year old. Taller than the mayor by a head, her smile an aura just above his bald crown. Freddy walked toward the garden, his arm around the shoulders of a white-haired man I couldn't name.

"Would you look at her, Ria?" I nodded toward my aunt. "She hasn't laughed so much since she tried Papa's new wine last year." I flushed with pleasure to watch her enjoy herself so.

Ria, who'd become more friend than neighbor to me, grinned, and helped herself to a chunk of Gouda from the tray she carried. "You should be out there with some high steps of your own, Maagda. Show off that beautiful dress you've stitched."

I pointed to my battered shoe tops. "I've been. And where were you in the circle swirls?"

Klemp came by again, took the tray from Ria's hands to place it on a side table, and pulled her to the center of the room, stomping to the step of the fiddle.

Sweet Miekke whirled by. She flirted outrageously with every man in the house. Jan, the boy who adored her every move, looked crushed when she passed. She winked and tossed her mop of blue black curls at him, her eyes full of mischief. My little sister would be Hoorn's heartbreaker one day very soon. She pricked me like a rose's thorn at times, as only a younger sister may, but she also gave me a love like no other. I felt blessed that she was well enough to enjoy the day.

And Pier, poor Pier. We managed to greet each individual guest, but when we were about to share a moment of our own, someone pulled him aside for a brandy. I knew that with the brandy came *manly advice*. He'd made several of these excursions to another room. I wondered that he walked. I heard fragments. *"Now, Pier, be sure to..."; or "The best drink for wedding night jitters is ...."; "After the stockings, you should..."*

It was all good-natured, I knew, but I wanted to hear some of their adages myself. There was so much I didn't know about what was to come. Thoughts of the night left me anxious, searching for my next bit of air.

Ria, still panting from her excursion with Klemp, came with wine. "A fill up, Maagda? Relax, enjoy this day."

"Ria," I confided, "I'm nervous enough about this night with Pier. I fear too much wine might make me...well, you know. I wonder how Pier manages."

"You'll do your part." Ria raised her eyebrows. "It comes naturally. Just remember what I've told you. Put on the nighgown and do a little dance of your own for him before you climb into bed." She winked and smoothed down the puffed sleeve at my shoulder.

And what was my part? I could draw the hull of a ship in detail, but an unclothed man. I had only vague notions, mostly from my early teen years when I hid behind the sea grass to watch the boys race bare into the summer sea. Ria and Aunt Loekke gave me only the sparsest accounts. From Aunt Loekke's wisdom, I would be naught but an unclad body, letting Pier do whatever it was he would do. At least from Ria I had a sense that I should take part, help Pier find his way.

Would Papa's heir start on this night? Might a baby start so quickly?

Ria hugged me. "You'll have a lifetime of special nights, memorable nights," she reassured me, then traipsed off to fill other cups.

I smiled to watch Ria move among our guests. She'd covered her fancy gown in her customary white apron and frilled cap. Though a guest, she was happiest in or near a kitchen and today that meant keeping all libated and fed.

A hand tugged at my wrist. "Come. Dance this reel with me."

Pier's cousin, Willem, a merchant lawyer, had traveled from nearby Edam, today our first meeting. He took my arm and pulled me into the circle stomping and twirling around our tiled and planked floors, so much motion the window curtains waved and the chained candle holders danced from the ceiling.

"Now that we're family, we must get to know each other. Pier's a tight-lipped farmboy. He's told us nothing about you."

We dipped and turned and spun. I felt Papa's gift, small sapphire earrings, dance on tiny gold chains against my neck, and my hair brush against Willem's cheek. I thought him half a head taller than me. "What's there to know, cousin? I'm a village girl about to taste the city." The fiddler quickened the beat. Faster and faster. We whirled 'til the room became a blur. I laughed with dizzy breathlessness.

"That's all? Surely," Willem, too, breathed hard, "there's more to Maagda than the places she lives."

"Perhaps." I tossed my head and let my long curls dance with the music. "I promise to reveal all to you tomorrow in the coach." I enjoyed the feel of my hair moving freely, escaped from its workday cap.

He twirled me under his arm. "Your word then? What a fortunate man, our Pier. I had no idea he had the charm to captivate such a woman."

I stopped dancing, steeled myself. "You think so little of Pier, then, Willem? I'm sure we see my husband with different eyes. You would not picture him as I do."

"Whoa, Maagda. No insult. I meant to compliment you."

Did he mock me? The looking glass in my bedroom had confirmed long ago that I was no beauty. I'd been called handsome, whatever that meant. A flush warmed my cheeks. Pier had little family. Could I grow to like his cousin, a man so direct? He was only three or four years older than Pier, but I sensed a settled confidence that allowed him a light spirit and an easy quip. No doubt a man of wit and grace, he teased and shared an effortless mirth. I would trust that he scoffed at Pier good-naturedly.

Willem would ride as far as Edam with us tomorrow. Since Freddy had given us his home for our bridal night, Ria invited Pier's traveling relatives to stay in her home. Even widowed Aunt Loekke had opened her musty home for wedding guests. I knew the party would last long after we'd departed on the morrow, go on as long as there was wine and food to keep spirits high.

My brief reverie ended amid shouts and loud bangs on pots and pans. My ears rang with the clamor. I searched for Pier.

Willem led a noisy parade of guests who drummed soup ladles against pots they wrested from Sophie's scullery. Others clapped hands and sang from throats loosened by rhoemers of wine. I hoped none of the glasses fell from frolicking hands. We'd had to borrow from neighbors to have enough for the day. Someone stomped a reel with heavy wooden shoes that smacked the boards under our feet. The air around me pumped in clouds of sound.

"Papa," I shouted above the clamor. "I think the walls tremble."

He laughed and stomped with the others. "We dance like a galliard, Maagda, like a galliard." Thump. Thump. Thump.

I laughed with him. This raucous roar was hardly anything so musical as that vigorous dance's triple rhythm, but I'd never forget this day's gaiety, or the tightness that gathered in me.

Our guests prepared to escort us to Freddy's home. Papa had arranged with Ria's husband to go ahead. He would make sure the guests stopped at the front door. Wedding parties have been known to carry the fray into the bedchamber. The tales told on market days after some weddings! I remember the story of poor Edda Ressler. She tried to mount her snoring bridegroom to the delight of peeking friends. A far different picture than Ria had painted for me. Perhaps Edda had drank the phelter, the love potion meant for her husband, but Ria had assured me the hippocras was enough for my wedding night.

The longed for moment arrived and my thoughts tumbled in a mix of anxiety and excitement. I twisted my ring, curled and uncurled my toes. My arms and legs danced a galliard of their own. Oh, for tomorrow, the safety and comfort of quiet moments in reflection with my pen and my diary. Would my face fire anew to write of this night?

The men brought Pier to the door. I drew in my breath and laughed for their ears. "Where is my bridegroom?" I joked. "Who is this sad scarecrow, this creature with hair over his eyes and his tunic askew?"

"Maagda?" He croaked like a pond frog. Willem and young Jan propped him up. My new husband slouched, his ruff gone, his tunic open at the neck. Willem plopped Pier's broad-brimmed hat atop his head and half carried, half pushed him into the lane. He slumped to his knees before they lifted him upright to walk.

I swallowed my disappointment, my throat tight to see that Pier's earlier passion drowned now in the day's flow of hippocras and brandy.

"Whereas Women's cheeks are ever plump and smooth, their voices small, their skin soft, as if they imitated a certain kind of perpetual youth…"

In Praise of Folly by Desiderius Erasmus (Classics Club edition)

CHAPTER 11—MAAGDA

WILLEM CLOMPED DOWN THE BARE OAK STEPS. HIS boot-fall bounced from one plastered wall to another, echoing to where I sat on the edge of the rocker by the fire.

"He's undressed down to his linens. His clothes are on the chair by the wardrobe. You might want to keep a candle burning through the night." He turned his head away, clearly embarrassed at such a personal talk. "He'll probably need the nightpot."

He struggled his considerable shoulders into a well-tailored coat. A lesser man might not have managed Pier. "Is there anything else?" He edged toward the door, eager to leave.

"Thank you, no. Go ahead and find your rest."

I closed the door behind him and slipped the latch, sure that no one in Hoorn locked doors. The quiet descended on me like a blanket snuffing my breath. I fought an urge to run after Willem and beg him back to sit with me. He had a quiet strength that I wanted near me at this moment, a strength to ward off the loneliness and yes, the disappointment that dampened my spirit. The noise-makers had wandered off to their own homes. Uncle Freddy's house, shrouded in silence now, bore down on me, empty, cold. I glanced around the sitting room with its bare shuttered windows and blank walls. He lived simply. The room cried out for the soft touches a woman might bring… fabric, ornament, perhaps curtains, a few scenic tiles.

A single painting broke the plainness of the whitewashed wall to the right of the fireplace. In the room's dim light, I judged it a hastily brushed copy of the storied Hoorn sea battles of decades ago. The cannon fire from the ships sparked and jumped to life as the flames from the fireplace flickered to move shadow and light across the embattled ships. How clever of Freddy to capture this play of light in hanging the work.

I wandered round the room, searching out a mote of comfort. Willem's earlier question still lay uneasy on my mind. *Of course I wasn't all right.* Here I sat on my wedding night in a strange house, uneasy at my first time to bed a man. Yet this man I had wed only today felt a total stranger to me. I longed to flee to my home, to burrow into the warm duvet of my own bed, to fling open my window to the reassuring sounds of the sea, the squawk of the gulls. Their raucous chatter annoyed me in the past. Tonight their piercing cries would soothe me.

A light rap at the door startled me. Who would disturb a bridal couple at this hour?

Ria stood on the step with a package in her hands. "You forgot this, Maagda. I know how much your dressing gown means to you. I promised myself I'd rap only if a candle still burned."

She walked into the sparse room, glanced from wall to wall and rolled her eyes. "Plain, eh?" She stroked the sleeve of my wedding dress. "Where's Pier?"

"Upstairs." I shrugged. "Willem put him to bed."

She laid my gown on the chair by the fire. " Most brides spend their wedding night alone with a sick husband. Take it from one who knows." She sighed and wrapped her arms around me. "Look at it this way. Your marriage union is yet to come, and you might find some enjoyment if you're rested." She moved to the door. "I must get back and sort out our guests. You get some sleep, too."

What Ria saw as anger was a wedge of disappointment that grew with each tick of the clock. Her words, *some enjoyment*, needled my thoughts. I had little knowledge of what this night might bring, only remnants from girlish whispers over the years and the few tidbits Ria and Aunt Loekke chose to share. I questioned what was fact, what real. If men felt a duty to 'loosen Pier up' as the mayor quipped earlier today, what about the bride? It wasn't wine I needed, rather, a warm look, a warm touch and the assurance that I had, indeed, married a good man. The heat his kisses had ignited in me this morning cooled to ash now, but I did crave some sign of comfort from him.

To make myself drowsy, I warmed milk and tried to nestle into the stiff covering of the fireside chair, tucking the folds of my wedding dress under my legs. Ria had unbuttoned the back before she left, commenting again on the fineness of the stitches and the inlay of three tapestry strips I had sown vertically down the front of the skirt. I thought to start a small sewing business when we established our home in Amsterdam, a way to add to the funds Pier would save for our future, a step to get us back to our real home in Hoorn. I needed some commerce in my days.

I picked up the dressing gown she placed near the fire and stroked its soft silk, always consoled by the softness of fine fabric on my flesh. Delicate pink and white flower sprigs, a promise of spring against a wintry background of pearl gray, had been screened across the cloth. I brushed the silk against my cheek and my body tingled in response. I felt an urgent need for touch, long languid strokes like those I slipped along my Folly's fur from ears to tail. I thought of how the drapes and folds of the silk clung to me and caressed my breasts and thighs.

I'd played the scene in my head for weeks. First, I caress him, offer the touches Ria told me, then lay my sheer nightdress across the bed where Pier would see it and know I would come to him in my natural state. I would enter, dressed only in the silk wrap, its sleek softness teasing me for the hours ahead. He would slip his arms around me, hold me... I clamped my eyelids shut. Not tonight. I was desperately alone.

The gown slipped through my fingers. Silk was a lavish and rare treat in Hoorn. I remembered my excitement the day I first saw my silk gown and reveled in its caress.

Miekke and I had stomped our feet against the evening chill along the shoreline where we awaited Papa's return from the Yard. We climbed to a high spot among the feathery beach grasses and the lavender blooms of sea rocket to watch the men trudge our way, Papa a giant among them.

On the day of the gowns Miekke ran to him, jabbering about the package he held. Papa scooped her into his right arm and let her ride atop the oilskin parcel. He teased her about what it might contain. He pulled me close with his other arm.

"Hmm." He hesitated. "Perhaps a joint of mutton for Sunday dinner. Would you like that?"

"Well, yes, Papa," she said, her lower lip pushed out in a pout.

When Papa saw the smile fade from her young face, he couldn't tease any longer. "When we get home," he promised. We gathered in the sitting room, and Papa made slow work of peeling away the oilskin wrapper. I lit candles on every table so we might see all.

"Hurry, Papa. Hurry," Miekke pleaded.

My own excitement waxed full. I fidgeted in anticipation, no less anxious than my sister.

Papa slid two lustrous silk dressing gowns from the oilskin.

"They're called kimonos," he said. "This, my darling girl, is for you." He handed me a gown that shimmered in subtle pearl, almost mauve. "And for you, our baby, this." Miekke's kimono was identical to mine, only in tones of blue.

"Papa," I gasped. "So beautiful." I slipped it over my dress and whirled around the room. "It takes my very breath." Silk after our everyday rough muslin or wool, a treasure. I threw my arms around his neck and kissed his cheek.

Papa told us one of the East India Company ships had returned to the harbor laden with cinnamon and nutmeg, bolts of silk and a few precious kimonos.

"Captain van Kerk's a friend. He brought these 'round because he knew I like surprises for my girls."

I sipped the last of my milk and laid the gown aside. No point in wearing it now. Perhaps this time next year I'd loosen the sash and lift my breast to the sucking lips of our first infant. Bumps of delight raised the hair on my arms at the mere thought. A tiny balm for my disappointment this night.

I snuffed the candles and walked to the stairs. Pier's deep gurgling snores bounced through the stairwell. Sleep would not be easy. How long, I wondered, to become accustomed to a man's presence in my bed.

Pier lay sprawled across the duvet, his arms flung wide, legs spread.

I managed to free enough of the duvet to cover him, and found a knitted throw from the chair for myself. I climbed into Uncle Freddy's high, hard bed and moved toward Pier. No eiderdown here.

My eyes had barely closed when I felt him reach for me.

"What foolish discourse and odd gambols pass between a man and his woman, as oft' as he has a mind to be gamesome..."

In Praise of Folly by Desiderius Erasmus (Classics Club edition)

CHAPTER 12—PIER

ACK. SATAN'S PISS, THAT FOUL WINE.

The bed 'neath me rocked like a dory in a storm. And my mouth, a wad of wool dried in sour milk.

Damn the hippo; damn the wine. Surely, god left me for dead.

I forced my eyes open a slit. Somewhere in the room a candle flickered; shadows moved on the wall. The room looked familiar. That big painting on the far wall. The local militia. Uncle Freddy's room where I'd dressed only this morning. How the hell did I get here?

Oh, great mounds of cow shit. The wedding!

I moved my fingers and brushed soft cloth.

Maagda!

Some husband you turned out to be, Pier. Pissed on your wedding night. Laying here like a bull without a bone.

Maagda breathed low, soft. I wondered if she slept.

I forced my head to the side. Ack. A goose egg would crack under the sodden ball of my skull.

She lay on her side with her back toward me. I saw she had loosed her hair. It waved across the pillow.

In the candlelight the curve of her rump took my eye. I wanted to reach for her, slide my hand along her hip, that long thigh. Mine now. My skull thumped. I couldn't believe the stir in me, though a good round rump roused me like nothing else could. And a woman so near to hand. My woman.

Oh, nailed Jesus. My head boomed like the inside of a church bell, but her nearness hardened me. To have a woman in my bed, a woman who belonged to me. Why should I hold back? This day gave me rights.

The swell of her rump tugged at me, and I thought of the curve of her breasts beyond. Better those breasts warmed my hands.

I wanted to press myself against her back, feel her skin that I knew would be smooth as cream just out of the churn.

No seed, Pier. No seed.

I was too full of wine to be sure of what I might do, could do. A crude pig gut sheath lay in the pouch of my breeches, but I had no idea where my breeches were. Not worth the effort. Leaked, likely as not. And blood. Perhaps blood. Couldn't chance blood.

My head splintered, but my need beat the pain down. I reached for her. I slid my hand around to her breasts and pulled her back to me. She stiffened.

"Maagda," I breathed in her ear. "You are a wife now. I take what is mine."

She didn't move. I felt the short, hard puffs of her breathing.

My right hand pulled her gown up to her waist. Now I could stroke her skin, the slope that mounded along her hip. Soft, but firm. She was still. My hands reached for her haunches. In the quiet, I could hear my calloused fingers rasp against her skin. I pulled her hips close to me and with both hands spread her rump wide.

She lurched. "Pier, what do you do?"

I spit on my finger to wet her, and plunged in. She screamed. Her fist beat against my thigh. I feared I'd lose my wood.

"Maagda, Maagda, no more cries." I pinned her squirming body to the bed.

I plunged…bucked…pumped.

"Animal, filthy, filthy animal." She struggled, cursing me. I clamped her against me.

Done, my breath hard, short gulps, I rolled off her and closed my eyes against the murderous throb in my head.

"The only way. No seed."

I sank back into the pillow, my arm still locked across her breast, her wrist in my grip. Her sobs stirred the cover, sending her shivers against my leg.

I drifted, heard a voice. "No seed, Maagda, no seed."

CHAPTER 13—MAAGDA

AIR, I NEEDED AIR. I NEEDED TO BREATHE, TO
unlock myself from his weight. I had to leave this bed, this room,
these four walls that he filled so completely even as he slept. The
room was dim, just one small window on the north wall. I slid from
the hard straw-packed mattress and moved across the cold floor. My
gown tore from my flesh with each step. I reached round to touch the
back of my nightdress. Damp, sticky. Tears of rage stung my eyes. I
was soiled, a bitch used by a back alley cur.

He still sprawled over most of the mattress. My stomach lurched
at the sight of him. I grabbed at a small chest and tried to hold steady,
but my stomach turned, roiled. I lunged for the night pot and retched.
Oh god, how foul.

I slid into the chair, but moved up quickly, fearing my damp
gown would stain the rough brown covering. Pier's fluids, blood?
I bite my lip and wiped my mouth with my hand. Fleeting images
of my mother struggling to give birth, dying, blood-soaked sheets

that Papa tried to hid from me. I stood gripping the chair, repulsed, frightened, burning with anger.

My right wrist still throbbed from the way he pinned me down, kept me locked to him through the night. Why had no one warned me that marriage gave vile rights to my body?

Oh, I longed for the warmth and comfort of my bed, the vision of the budding linden tree from my window, and my sweet Folly nestled in the crook of my knees. I wanted to wrap myself away and never know such shame again. Last night was the stuff of tavern women, not wives. My mind, my very skin crawled like a beggar immigrant in a strange land where nothing fit as it should.

A loud scraping sound pulled my attention to the stairwell, someone screeching a kettle across the fire grate. Pier snorted at the noise, but remained asleep. I felt relieved for whoever was downstairs for I recoiled at the thought of a single moment alone with this beast now. I threw a coverlet over my nightgown and moved to the stairs.

Uncle Freddy stood by a round oak table near the fireplace, arranging plates.

"Ah, the bride." He walked over to take my hand. "Rested and ready for a hearty breakfast?"

His eyes searched my face. Could he tell?

"You've a long day ahead of you."

"Tiring for sure." I brushed the peppered whiskers on his cheek with a tiny kiss. A dear man. Why had it seemed natural to me that his nephew would have his placid manner, his kind ways?

"Uncle Freddy, everything looks tempting. And fruit as well." How to sound normal when I wanted to shriek profanities? "Were you the first shopper abroad this morning?" I tightened every muscle to keep my voice light, mask the tremor.

A peat fire glowed in the hearth; the room mercifully warm. Even in the pleasant months, the morning dampness in these old stone houses iced your bones. I was grateful to see that water warmed for our morning wash up. I longed to clean myself, though no amount of scrubbing would erase the stain now indelible in my mind.

"Here, Maagda, try one of these." He offered me a plate of figs. "Off the boat this morning."

I bit into the plump brown fig, seeds moist and sweet on my tongue. In spite of my pain, the fruit soothed me like my wake-up mug of warm milk at home. My body hungered for small comforts. I needed to speak of everyday things, feel everyday things, Papa's quotidian things.

He eyed my nightclothes. "Say, your carriage leaves at ten, yes? Where's that lazy nephew of mine? You must hurry a bit, both of you."

"Why don't you go up and rouse Pier? I'll get myself together back here where I left my bag last night." My clothes lay in a small alcove beside the fireplace. "If you stay up with him while he dresses, I'll call you when I'm finished."

The coverlet hid most of my nightdress and concealed the large spot of damp fluid down the back. I hesitated but a second then threw the nightdress into the peat fire. Sheer gauze, it would be ashes by the time Pier and Freddy came into the room. I watched it burn without a tear. *Ashes to ashes.*

My silk kimono still lay draped over the chair by the fire. No blood would mock its beauty. I rewrapped the gown to send home with Ria. The silk was much too fine for the soiled start of my marriage.

I bathed quickly, sloshed the warm water again and again between my legs, and scoured my already raw bottom until I could no longer bear the pain. My grape muslin day dress hung on the wall peg. Its sun-bleached white collar and cuffs a mockery. I wiggled into it and tied a vivid floral print scarf 'round my shoulders. Just as I tucked the last strands of curls into my cap, I heard voices at the door. Papa, Miekke, and Ria bounded into the room, a merry group, still boisterous from yesterday's party. They threw their wraps on chairs and circled round Freddy's table of fruits and cheese.

"Another exciting day," Papa boomed in a voice accustomed to shouting against open sea winds. He strode in and hugged me.

I longed to stay in the safety of his embrace, beg him to take me home, but pride and shame sealed my tongue. Papa would be the goat of Hoorn if I ran home now, a maiden in fact, but a bitter woman in mind, and all of my own choosing. I would not put him to further ridicule.

"Where's my son-in-law?"

"Dressing upstairs." I struggled to stem tears and the quake in my voice.

"Come. Share this grand breakfast Freddy laid out for us. There's plenty." I heard myself chattering, empty word upon empty word. "Here, Ria, you must try these figs. They're so ripe the seeds burst on your tongue." "What about you, Miekke, nothing to eat?" A scream choked in my throat. How ridiculous this small talk when I wanted to rage against Pier Veerbeck. Yet I hugged each word. Quotidian. My lifeline.

"I'm not hungry, Maags. I realize now that you leave us." She came and put her cheek next to mine and I felt the warmth of her tears. "I can't bear for you to go."

Today Miekke behaved unlike her dancing, bratty self. But at this moment, I most wanted her normal tart youthfulness, have her rag and torment me as she did most mornings at home.

Papa saved us both from spilling tears. "Of course, you'll miss your sister, Miekke. But you'll be so busy at the Yard, you'll be grateful to come home at night and sleep in a room all to yourself." He patted her arm. "Maagda has trained you well. You'll keep the books, and the orders and the inventory as she showed you."

I was sad to leave the fray, the promise. Such an exciting time at the Yard. Even English merchants now paid to haul their cargo on our fluyts because the vast holds meant lower freight rates. I would trade my marriage for the Yard in a trice.

Pier and Uncle Freddy clattered down the stairs.

"What," Pier joked, "the party goes on?"

His face was drained of color, made the ginger of his beard and hair stand copper against the pewter of his face, his eyes dead like yesterday's fish. I prayed the wine and brandy sickened him still, and almost smiled when he clutched the side of the table to steady himself.

He blanched when I offered him pungent Gouda, waving it under his nose. I avoided his eyes, but knew the cheese did its work. He thrust the plate away, and gulped a tankard of warm ale. Good. Today's coach ride would jostle and throw him about, paining him as it would pain me. My own tortuous ride might be bearable to know he suffered.

"The wagon's here," Papa called from the door. He'd arranged for two of the Yard men to haul our bags to the coach. We'd walk the two blocks. There'd be enough sitting on the ride, anything to delay the coach's lurch along the thirty-odd miles to Amsterdam.

My mind screamed at me, *don't go to that coach.*

Papa and Freddy carried the valises and boxes from the house. My boxes from home were already stowed on the wagon. Pier tried to help, but stumbled about, useless. Amid the bustle no one seemed to notice that we hadn't exchanged the smallest pleasantry.

My legs were wooden, would not allow me to step toward the door. Once over that threshold, it would be too late to turn back. I grabbed at Papa's sleeve, pulled him into the alcove beside the fireplace where I'd dressed earlier. "I can't leave, Papa."

He turned me to face him, braced his hands on my shoulders. "What? Can't go? Of course, you can. You're a married woman now. Your place is with Pier."

"But, Papa... " I stammered. Do I say to my father, my *ijzer mens*, that I'd been buggered? That this new husband had coated me in honeyed words, then set the bear upon me. My mind screamed, *tell him, tell him the truth.* Instead I said in a voice barely above a whisper, "I'll miss you so, you and Miekke."

He folded his arms around me, pulled me to his chest. "My poor girl. Perhaps I've held you too close all of these years." He tried to soothe me, telling me I was merely tired from the fuss of the wedding.

He pulled a cloth from his tunic. " Now, dry your eyes. Can't have your new husband thinking I raised a babyish girl child." He guided me back into the sitting room with a firm hand on my arm.

I burned with shame for begging him to take me away from Pier and marriage. But to act the good wife? I couldn't fathom it though I sensed Papa's thinking and it cramped my belly. By Plutarch's wisdom, a good wife submits to her husband – in all things. A cruel beginning. Guilt and vows locked me in a prison of my own making. My loathing for my own frailty seared my very core.

Pier called from the hall that the wagon was loaded. Freddy shepherded us to the door. "We must go," he urged. "You know old Henrik never holds his coach. You can tell the time by the first flick of his whip."

Pier reached for my hand when I stepped outside. I pretended not to notice and turned to Ria. I avoided his touch by reaching for one of the baskets she carried.

"Your lunch," she said, wiping her hands on her familiar white apron. I feigned to sag under its weight. "For an army? Did you pack an entire goose, stuffing and all?"

She laughed. "There was so much food from the feast yesterday. Besides, you'll need a stock for your larder. There's another larger hamper with your bags. Remember to look for it immediately you get home."

Home? I was leaving home, not going home.

Nearby, Pier heard the conversation about the food. "You take good care of us, And you, Miekke. Is that even more food in your basket?"

She laughed. "Not a bit of it." Folly's head poked up when she pulled the small cover back.

"What? A cat? A cat travels with us?"

I spoke my first words to him that day, "She is not *A Cat.* Folly is a treasured member of the family." I looked him in the eye, challenging a response, and reached in the basket to scratch her head.

The shrill pipe of a ship's horn pierced my ears.

My words to Pier had more frost than I wanted the others to hear, but I prayed the clatter of wagon wheels and the ship's blast muffled my tone.

Pier backed up as though stung, opened his mouth to reply, but stopped. He uttered not a word, merely looked away, my challenge empty in the dirt at his feet.

"How pleasantly do they dote when they frame in their heads innumerable worlds; measure out the sun, the moon, the stars, nay and Heaven itself."

In Praise of Folly by Desiderius Erasmus (Classics Club edition)

CHAPTER 14—LARS

WE FOLLOWED THE COACH AND WATCHED ITS DUST plume long past the turn off Rode Steen Square. Soldiers loitered outside the tavern, sprawled among the benches, ale in hand, a too frequent sight in Hoorn these days. I noticed more than one eyeing my younger daughter and knew it best to send her home.

"Ria, please see Miekke to the house, if you would. I return to the Yard."

"Of course, Lars. Come along, Miekke, we might lend a hand to Sophia and clear away the last of the celebration. We'll have your father's sitting room tidy before he ducks under the transom."

"Oh, all right," Miekke said. She glanced over her shoulder for a wistful last look at the mud-splattered young men. One poor bastard with a missing left arm used his good hand to salute her with his tankard.

"Home, home." I said, seeing where this might lead if she lingered.

Ria took her by the arm and steered her toward our steeg, and I, feeling my daughter out of harm's way, turned east toward the harbor to walk the mile along the water's edge to my work, and time to collect my thoughts. Maagda's tears at leaving this morning bit at the edge of my mind and at my sadness to see her go. What upset her so? No whiner, my daughter. All her life this first born of mine swallowed challenges whole, never feared to try something new. On reflection, she scared me more than once with her audacious indifference to consequence. Was marriage so different for a woman who spent her days around the men in the boat Yard? But, yes, I reminded myself, those men treated her with deference.

"Yo, Lars. Headed for the Yard?"

Freddy caught up with me as I neared the central canal crossing. I slowed, tempered my long gait, and waited, leaning against the bridge cable watching a school of minnows nibble around the rock wall until he stood beside me.

Freddy gave me a good-natured rap on the shoulder. "We're related now, heh Lars?"

"No question, Freddy. Hope that nephew of yours takes good care of my daughter. Wish I knew more of him. You're a good family, but I don't feel I ever got to the core of the man."

"You'll find him solid enough, a man who walks a narrow path through life, knows the right guide posts from the learning he's had. Glad his father let him get schooled. A lot of farmers don't. And I'll tell you this. Pier's a man who watches his pennies, nothing frivolous there, and, he's never been arrested."

Startled, I turned to him. "Arrested?"

"Joshing, Lars, joshing. Your chin's hanging so low, you looked like you were empty for a good laugh."

"You know they seemed a bit strained this morning. First night jitters." He smiled and shrugged. "To be expected, I guess. Pier pestered me for months to meet Maagda. Maybe close up she spooked him. With no mother, he's not used to a woman in his life."

"I noticed, too."

I stopped and considered Freddy a minute. Something was amiss this day, especially that he'd now mentioned an agitation this morning that I couldn't free from my mind. I'd been uncomfortable since I handed Pier the dowry chest at the coach. He reached for it and clutched it under his arm, more protective of it, I thought, than my very own daughter. Damned unsettling. Every part of my common sense shuddered when I thought of the haste of this marriage and all of the things I didn't attend to, things a good father heeded.

"You go ahead to the Yard and set the men to work on those frayed mooring lines back of the hull. Seemed looser than they need be."

I wanted quiet time at home to think more on the morning. My girls and Sophie knew that once my library door closed I was not to be bothered. Sometimes my remedy for a bout of unsettled thought was an hour or two among my treasured books. The richness of their bindings and the trove of ideas they lay at hand steadied me. Damned fortunate we had good printers in Holland to make quality books that all could lay down a stuiver or two to own.

I settled in. My armchair wrapped around me like a winter comforter. I lay my head back, closed me eyes. The past twenty-four hours flashed through my mind in a jumble of pictures, little scenes of guests laughing, my sister Loekke, dancing of all things, and Maagda reigning over all with a smile richer than a harvest moon. But few smiles today. The more I thought about the morning, the more I recalled my daughter looking pallid, a bleached canvas. Many young women found disappointment after a wedding's merry-making. But so soon for my Maagda? Was Pier untutored in the ways of the bed? Come to think on it, he didn't have much to say for himself either. No smiles between them.

Loekke had promised to talk with Maagda, prepare her for the wedding night, certainly not an issue I might broach with my daughter.. Did she excite Maagda about the joy of the wedding, but not the joining that followed? Maagda went to her wedding bed intact. I was sure of it. Pregnant brides were expected in the north, but not in Hoorn. Besides Maagda had spent so much time in the office, little opportunity existed for dallying with a man. And before Pier, who to suspect, only the usual flurry of locals at celebrations in town.

Musings scurried in and out of my head. Damn the pressures of the Yard, I should have gone to Amsterdam to see where Pier took my daughter, even talk to his employer, that Steubing fellow. I feared I put too much weight on Pier being Freddy's family.

A door slammed and glass rattled, reminding me I still hadn't reglazed that front window.

Miekke returned. I heard her hanging her cloak in the closet under the stairs.

Should I mention my concerns about Maagda? Lord, it was one thing to be the father of girls, but ack, to be the father of young women. Who knew what fancies flitted about in their heads? I called down to her. The heavy aroma of yesterday's roasted goose still lingered on the stairs.

"Feel better now that your sister's safely on her way?"

She came and sat at the bottom of the stairwell. "Maagda was too quiet, Papa, even sad, I thought." Miekke looked up at me. "She'd been crying. I'm sure of it."

"To be expected," I said. "This is her first voyage from the home nest." I heard the shake of my own voice.

Miekke picked at yellow flower petals in the corner of the step, left from the wedding party. "Brides should be all pink cheeks and smiles, and that wasn't my Maags this morning." Her blew the petals from her hand. "I'll smile when my day comes."

"And how soon might that day be? Another to flee my nest?"

She giggled. "Not so soon, Papa. Don't worry."

A light rap, the door opened and Ria walked in. She grabbed Miekke's hand.

"Come, no idling about. We've work to do." She waved to me and they turned back toward the scullery.

So, Miekke had noticed. I returned to my library and leaned against the door to shut out their noisy chatter and the remaining sights and sounds of yesterday. This damnable hasty wedding. No time to shine a candle into the corners as a father ought. Never did see the place Pier takes her. My time always taken. I leaned too heavily on my family's need and Pier's word. Bites of shame nibbled at my conscience, made me squirm.

A wedge of sunlight drew my eye across the room to the shelves that lined the west wall. Motes of light sprayed along the glossy hull of my grandfather's model ship, *Count of Hoorn*. I walked over to lift the hand-carved model from its teak cradle, and blew the dust from its fragile riggings. A proud ship, even in miniature.

I carried the replica across the room to the windows and held it up to the light, turning it bow to stern. Every detail perfect: canvass, pennants, wheel. I traced the steep hull fore and aft, the narrow high stern transom with its crescent moon common to boats of that earlier time. She'd take the sea without a groan. On either side of the cabin, the ship bore shields displaying the lion of our United Provinces. Pray god we wouldn't need the lions roar at the Spanish again, or the Germans, for that matter.

The wooden hull, baked from the morning sun, warmed me and eased the earlier pricks of conscience that had begun to nip at me. I returned to my chair, the vessel secure in my palms, and pressed both sides of the bow to release the split hull. The wood fit so square, no one would know the hull was not of a single piece. It had been years since I'd opened the ship, and now the rabbet joints squealed in protest when I slid them apart to separate the sections. Later I'd get soap from the scullery to smear both joint grooves.

I placed one half on the side table, and lifted the first of two rolled parchments stowed in the hull. I didn't intend to open the scrolls. I knew the words from memory. But my unsettled head begged to see them again, measure their meaning. The parchment crackled when I unrolled it, my eyes drawn immediately to the bottom with its seal of red wax and the signature, *Philip de Montmorency, Count of Hoorn,* the nobleman who had dedicated one hundred and ninety-nine seaside acres along with Hoorn's boat yard to my family so long as a blooded Boscher remained an owner.

The words scrolled before my eyes...*bounded by the north wall of the village of Hoorn and north to...from this day forward...honoring the valor of Jan Boscher... in perpetuity.* But it was the final sentence that held my gaze: *In the event no Boscher heir remains to inherit this estate, all property and the rights and privileges thereof, revert in full, to the States General.*

We'd some dim connection to the Egmont side of the Montmorency family. I seemed to recall that the Count's wife was an Egmont. My grandfather liked to remind us as children that we carried this distant strand of Egmont/Montmorency in us, but with a warning not to think ourselves grand. That slim thread was enough though for the Count to reward my ancestor, Jan, for his bravery in the '47 Schmalkaldic War. Every school child knew the Count of Egmont knelt beside our Count Hoorn when the axman cleaved heads from both bodies back in '68. No, the Boschers weren't noble, but we came from stock that valued loyalty above all.

When my grandfather passed the legacy on to me, he swore, "Still sets my blood aboil, them being executed so cruelly." He roundly cursed every Spaniard, living and dead.

These noblemen of ours had set themselves to oppose the Spanish Inquisition. Soured me on religion ever since, but planted the notion of loyalty deep in my blood. I taught my girls from childhood that loyalty to home and family ranked first among virtues.

When my father was killed at the Battle of Antwerp, my grandfather made me swear to protect the Hoorn Trust and the town's future that depended on that deed. My father had confessed to a dalliance with an Antwerp woman who might have been with child. He begged Grandfather's forgiveness. Father's death gored Grandfather like a saber blow that wept and bled 'til the devil's rattle of dying echoed in his own throat.

To this day, I see his white hair hanging in a thick mat, almost covered his eyes, green, the color of deep water. The burrowed crags in his forehead relaxed in the flickering candlelight. We watched the life seep out of him, but his face that night begged a place in my memory.

"Your oath, Lars, your most sacred oath," his voice little more than a hoarse rasp. He clasped my right hand between fingers too calloused to close. "You must seed the trust with Boschers, only Hoorn-bred Boschers." Those last words didn't strike me until later when I read both scrolls myself. Grandfather wanted assurance that no Antwerp bastard might plunder the inheritance.

Now I sat, a white-haired man near his sixtieth year, a pair of daughters, and one, please heaven's gallery of gods, on the verge of motherhood. No matter how difficult the bud of her marriage, I knew my Maagda held the legacy in her heart.

"Like horse leeches, they appear to be double-tongued..."

In Praise of Folly by Desiderius Erasmus (Classics Club edition)

CHAPTER 15—PIER

THE RIDE TO AMSTERDAM PROMISED LITTLE JOY.
Maagda avoided me like pus-filled boils oozed from my skin. Not
that I was hearty. My stomach flapped and tossed. I gagged at the
stench from the canal behind the coach. Anything for the smell of
fresh-scythed clover. To stand in my own fields. At least there I'd
puke in peace.

I was grateful when Cousin Willem arrived to ride with us as far
as Edam. Talk with him might warm the woman. I'd not meant such
a rough start for us. But damn, she was a wife now and she'd better
start learning the ways of men and women. Her shouts last night of
filthy animal still rang in my ears, pinched my breathing. Did I not
own her now, body and soul?

"Mind those seats," Henrik called back from the driver's station.
"Brought a load of soldiers in with me. A muddy lot they were."

I stood to the side to avoid Maagda's searing gaze, the dowry
chest safe safe under my arm. "Soldiers in Hoorn? Why so?" I'd seen
them aplenty in Amsterdam, but didn't think them up here.

"Come back from the fighting in Germany." Henrik fastened the harness. "Had enough of the killing. They asked for the Dutch East India Company, the VOC. Talked about signing on with some long haul trading ships."

"We forget our good fortune," Willem said. "Not that we didn't have our share of fighting to get this Union going." He climbed into the coach. "Our own peace is fragile enough. Let's hope Prince Frederick and our allies keep the Spanish wolf at bay. Makes a difference for trade. And I've no soldiering in me."

Maagda placed her hand over Willem's. "Pray you'll not need the test." The first she had spoken since leaving Freddy's. "My grandfather died at Antwerp for our Provinces." She sighed and leaned back against the wooden seat. "Placed a heavy burden on my father. He took over the Yard before his twentieth year."

Willem shook his head, seemed genuinely touched.

What could I say? I had merely passed time when I asked Henrik about the soldiers, knowing well enough the men came from the fighting. Hadn't the German princes gnawed and pummeled each other for months?

I couldn't imagine me or Willem in that lunacy. More a thinker than a fighter, this cousin of mine. Today he looked the lawyer in a gray travel coat and polished boots. Made me feel ragged in my rumpled tunic and loose breeches. But his eyes were red and watery, his face a grayish paste. The pair of us vulture leavings at best. "How're you feeling this morning, cousin?"

"Better imagined than described. "Willem put his fingers to his temples.

I smirked, but cringed inside at Maagda's sour glance toward me. How long must I pay for last night, for my rights as a husband? Made me wonder if an innocent bride was worth the price. I shrugged and looked away from her.

Henrik had arranged us in the middle seat with our baggage balancing the load front and back. The coach could carry nine, but with our extra cargo, he carried the three of us and one stranger. The man looked tattered, shoddy and only went as far as Edam where Willem would leave us. Once we dropped them off, I'd be alone with Maagda, maybe a chance to right her thinking.

Henrik was about to snap his whip when a trio of soldiers strolled toward the coach, their uniforms mud-caked. I laid the dowry chest on the floor of the coach, clamped between my feet. I'd feel better once I hid it away under the floorboards at home.

"Your VOC's closed. Today a holiday?" one of the young men asked the driver. He saw Maagda in the middle seat. The soldier draped his arm over the door and looked right at her. "Perhaps this pretty lady might know."

Before I said anything, Willem lifted the soldier's arm off the door. "Madam Verbeek is not the town clerk." He scowled at the man.

Henrik called back, "They mightn't open 'til noon. With ships coming in on different tides, they mighta had a late arrival last night. Then again, might be nothing at all. Arrivals' been slow of late."

"We'll stay anyway," the soldier said. "Where can we get some food and drink around here? It's been a long road."

Henrik directed them to a tavern on the northwest corner of Rode Steen Square, a block further back from the water. "You won't get lost," he told them. "It's the only patch in Hoorn, one block north, one block west."

The soldiers started to walk away. Willem called to the young blond man who'd lounged on the coach near Maagda. "Here," he said, "I was rude. Treat yourself and your friends to a drink." He gave the soldier two stuivers.

The soldier looked at Willem for a moment like he thought it a trick. Then he whistled in appreciation, his eyes on the gold signet ring Willem wore on his right hand.

"Where you from?" Willem asked.

"Denmark."

"Long in the war?"

"Long enough to learn I stuck my neck out for god knows what. First you charge and kill the others because one week they're Catholics or the next week, because they're not. I got fed up. Me and my friends, we took our money and bolted." He waved thanks and ran grinning to join the soldiers on their way to Rode Steen and warm ale.

A strong breeze blew in a good whiff of salt air. Cleared my head some, but my stomach tossed when Henrik finally snapped his leather over the team and we lurched off.

Willem tapped my arm. "Pier, is there much talk of the war in Amsterdam?"

"Mighty god, yes. The taverns are full of it. People down many a tankard swapping stories they've heard from troops straggling through. Men like those paid foreigners we saw today. Amsterdam's clogged with them." I spread my arms across the seat behind Maagda. She shrugged into herself. "From what I hear, the German states take a beating. Bohemia, too, and we've supported them. The East gets the worst of it, and now there's talk that Sweden'll send troops, too."

The stranger behind us leaned forward. "Couldn't help hearing," he said. "I'm just back myself. The land sours in blood; whole villages ransacked and burned."

We yelled to each other over the clatter of the road, the rattle of the baggage, and Henrik's shouts to the horses. The wind snatched at our voices.

I turned in my seat to face the soldier. "Did you come back with those men we met at the depot?"

"No, I got here two days ago. Like them, I thought to sign on with your East India Company. But can't do it." He thumped his right thigh. "Caught a musket ball in the top of my leg here. Oh, pardon me, ma'am," he nodded toward Maagda. "Your VOC people said I'd never be able to work in the riggings or haul cargo with a game leg. I'll try my luck with some of the cheese makers around Edam. If that doesn't work, I'll move on to Amsterdam."

Maagda's blank stare sprang to life. He caught her sympathies. "Have you no home to go to, no family?"

"No. Like a lot of these men, I fought for whoever paid me. There's no other work to be had. And what you've heard about Sweden is true. Their king, Gustav Adolphus, sent men to scout the battlefields. I met some of their officers when we fought near the outskirts of Bohemia."

"That'll only prolong the fighting." Willem looked sour. "If the Swedish king takes it into his head to support the German Protestants, he could sink our prosperity. Gustav wants the northern German provinces so he can grab Baltic ports for Sweden. He needs those trade routes."

Maagda looked at Willem, her mouth dropping. "If Gustav blocks the trade routes, he'll hurt the Yard and the VOC. All of Hoorn will suffer."

Willem nodded to her, then turned to the soldier. "Look here. I live near Edam. Let's talk when the coach gets in. I might be able to help you find work." He reached back to shake the stranger's hand.

"Willem, how kind you are." Maagda smiled. First one of those I'd seen today.

"And if you move on to Amsterdam, look me up at the gem center," I added. "I cut and polish in the Steubing rooms, the biggest diamond merchant in Amsterdam." I wouldn't be outdone by Willem when I could see Maagda warmed to his offer. But I did mean to help. I could at least take the soldier to the tavern and introduce him around.

We rode in silence until we met a snarl of road traffic near Edam. Henrik maneuvered the team around carts, big coaches like his own and draymen crowding the cobbles while they unloaded wagons. Wheels of cheese stood stacked against warehouse fronts ready to be taken aboard the empty drays.

Two boys chased our coach, and tried to poke long sticks into the wheel spokes. Henrik flicked his whip over their heads to warn them off.

"They think I'm mean," he yelled back at us. "They never give a thought to what'll come if the stick snaps and flies back in their faces."

Maagda rummaged in the food hampers Ria had sent along. She rearranged meat pies and fruit and bread.

The coach jerked to a halt at Edam's Creamery Tavern. Many a night me and Willem filled our bellies in the tavern's smoky rooms. Henrik asked if we needed time in the tavern. But, we had Ria's food, and I was anxious for him to push on.

Maagda stood up.

"I'd like to stop a moment." She called to the stranger who gathered his pack and a stray bag.

Maagda handed him one of our baskets. "We have more than enough for the rest of our journey," she said. "Please take this." She pulled back the cover. "There's some fine goose, cold ham and cheese, and don't let those flaky prune pastries get old." A dark stain from the butter in the pastry crust spread over half the cloth cover.

The soldier started to refuse. But you could see the hunger in the poor bastard's eyes. Still, I thought that food would be better in our own larder. Might feed us another day. I could've eaten one of those rich pastries right now, but held back, not to dampen Maagda's kindness, but I could see I'd have to watch how Maagda spent my stuivers in the markets.

The soldier thanked Maagda and left the coach, but turned to throw us a formal salute before limping away.

Willem grasped my hand in farwell and put his arm around Maagda. "Cousin Pier, may I kiss your bride farewell?"

"If she bades you."

"You must promise me, Maagda, that you'll never travel between Hoorn and Amsterdam unless you stop at my home to refresh yourself. Bring Pier, if you must, but if he gives you any trouble, let your new lawyer cousin know and we'll haul him to the justices." He gave me a fond thump on the back and called to the soldier to wait for him.

Within fifteen minutes we were on the road south to Amsterdam.

Maagda returned to her former seat on the far side of the coach. She lifted the cat from its basket to her lap and stroked its head.

"You comfortable, Maagda? There's a cushion here from Willem's seat."

She took it from me and almost looked grateful.

I moved into Willem's seat and reached across her for the food hamper. "Maybe we should eat. There'll still be plenty for a supper when we get home."

She drew back when I picked up the basket.

"Perhaps one of the cold eggs," she said. "And a small biscuit for Folly."

I passed her the food and a cloth and picked out a goose leg the size of a big fist for myself. Settled now, my belly growled with hunger. I could almost taste the pastry she gave away, but I ate the goose in its stead and relished the fat that matted its joint.

"Good food. I don't remember tasting this yesterday."

"No," Maagda said, "I don't imagine you would."

A North Sea iceberg, this woman. She pulled the coach rug up to cover her dress against the dirt from the road. Probably thought I shed dirt as well.

We finished our food in silence, a silence that bored into a spot just above where the goose lodged in my belly. Everything rushed past us, trees, the long poles of canal boats in the water that ran in a line beside our road, a trio of windmills where a polder drained. Time rushed by, too, time I thought I had to settle her down.

"Maagda, we need to speak of this breach between us. Henrik can't hear us over the road noise."

The coach lurched from rut to rut, and Maagda jolted with it, a look of pain drawing her lips tight.

"Do you have explanations, Pier, for a bitch of the streets? That is how I feel. Like I'd been taken by a frenzied cur in a back lane." She looked toward the front of the coach at Henrik's back.

Stinking cow shit. Her venom stung me, as had her words last night. Me a filthy animal? I wanted to shout at her, *I'm a husband, your husband*. I thought of the soldiers' talk of the war. I had my own private battle here, and I was losing.

"Last night was the wine, the brandy."

She turned to me again. "If last night is a picture of what is to come, I wonder how our vows might be called a marriage."

"When we reach Amsterdam, we can start new. Can you see that?" She had me groveling. A mere woman yet.

"I won't spoil my father's wedding gift by sleeping in it with you if that's what you have in your head. I'll never allow this to happen again."

Ah, Papa Lars' wedding gift, the great new bed where he said our children would be born. I'd never meet his measure in my wife's eyes.

"How then do you think to be a wife?"

"...they utter many things that do not hang together."

In Praise of Folly by Desiderius Erasmus (Classics Club edition)

CHAPTER 16—MAAGDA

I KEPT MY MIND ON THE SCENES RACING PAST
Henrik's coach...the isolated farm with horse and share plowing a
late field, children rolling in the hay mounds, wagons maneuvering
for advantage on the road. Each glance from the carriage was a little
slice of comfort to chew on, everyday life, ordinary, or quotidian to
refrain Papa's new word.

The spray of sea lavender I had picked yesterday before the wedding would be the first thing I placed in Pier's rooms. I had walked
to the water before the wedding, a farewell, to hear a last time the
sea's shallow slap against the beach, and to look back at the roofs of
Hoorn, to etch the image of home in my mind. I called the memory
up as we jostled among carts heading into the city, anything to keep
at bay what awaited me in this strange place with this strange man.

By now the sun cast its light to our backs from over the North
Sea to the west. The air cooled. I huddled in my coat, snugged the
carriage's dust cover closer to my neck, as much to avoid Pier as to
shield my dress and scarf.

Pier's earlier question, "How do you think to be a wife," flitted round in my head. How indeed? My duty lay like a lead cloak over me. I shrank in humiliation to think of running home. I'd make a Papa a fool for allowing me to select my own husband. And what of the other young women in Hoorn who now thought to do the same? Who flees a marriage of twenty-four hours? I could not, just could not bring myself to tell anyone, certainly not Papa. To him, my marriage cradled the future. I tried to settle myself, but the slower the coach moved in gathering traffic, the faster my nerves jumped until I realized my feet were tapping the floor boards.

When we cleared the outskirts of Amsterdam, Pier sprang to life, the torpor of yesterday's toasts as distant as the setting sun. He pointed out landmarks near swallowed in dusk.

"Just there, up the canal, see the tip of Nieuw Kerk?" He looked to me for a response, but I said nothing. "I don't know why it should be called new. That old pile of stone's been around for two centuries or more.

"And there, down the Damrak, that's where the trading's done. Burghers bargain for shiploads --fabric, spices, timber—anything the ships bring home."

Pier tried to impress me that he was a city man now. He spoke like I'd never seen Amsterdam. Admittedly, such trips were rare for me.

"Listen, Maagda. Hear the hollow sound of the hooves? This plaza is a dam, *the* Dam, like its name. The Amstel flows under our coach!"

Pier rambled on about city sights. But new or old. I saw little of distant surroundings as night crowded the last bits of light from the sky. There was more to catch the eye closer to our coach. Cart traffic stood wheel to wheel. Strollers dodged the horses and stepped over their steaming piles among the cobbles. Many of the people still aboutwere workmen ready for home and a hearty hutsepot. The crowds dwindled to individuals, men in turbans, and a little fellow with a long braid of hair down his back. Exotic to me, even the babble of words I caught. Untamed, chaotic music with words that held no meaning for me. I smiled to think of Papa and his passion for language.

In Hoorn we talked about the flood of new people in the city. The war drained money from battle-weary towns while our Provinces promised work and wages. Few went hungry now. Amsterdam boomed. Even the lowest paid workers had stuivers in their pocket for the occasional frill or trip to the tavern.

We'd seen the crowds when we came into the city last month on a hurried visit to buy the material for my wedding dress, no time that day for wandering or gaping at new construction. Papa feared Amsterdam might soon overshadow Hoorn, and lure our anchorage and shipbuilding. Our little seaport would be in for hard times. In our house the need to maintain a Boscher Yard lurked like a thick layer of dust coating the surface of our lives.

Papa often said, "I'm a builder, Maagda, not a commercial man. I don't know how to compete. Never had to."

His buyers sought him out. How soon would that change? The question was no mere trifle. I mulled it on many of my daily walks. I liked the drafting and copy work I did for Papa, but where our boats went, how they were used, that's what I burned to know, where I felt certain our future and Hoorn's lay. And now the worry of that Swedish King and his plans for the Baltic was another bone to gnaw on. Somehow I knew trade was the answer, but it spun in my mind a mere puzzle at present.

Pier nudged me and pointed to the left, a canal street lined with large houses so new no soot darkened their brick fronts. "Here's the Herengracht. Amsterdam's money lives behind those doors."

Henrik called to us that he might need a detour.

"Them rich burghers don't want common cart traffic." He slowed the carriage to turn.

By now, the tall gables of homes in each block loomed as mere outlines against remnants of fading light, yet a quiet elegance radiated from shining windows and massive doors. Here and there a beautiful stone relief was still visible over a lintel. I thought to see the designs in daylight. I'd heard how families decorated their entrances to show their trade or a favorite myth.

Pier edged closer to me. I moved nearer the door to look outside. He dropped from my thoughts when one dwelling pulled the breath from me. The front, a honey cream and ochre, glowed with the remnants of twilight, and drew my gaze upward to a bell-shaped gable such as I'd never seen before. And a pair of them at that. Then I realized it was a double house with three glazed windows across each floor. The soft flaring bell-like curve lent a grace its neighbors didn't have with their sharp angles. Most of the homes in the block were topped with the newer stepped gable, though one or two retained the old triangle slant like our house in Hoorn.

But even here in the best of Amsterdam's quarters, the reek of garbage and night refuse in the canals forced me to turn away. So unlike home where a tang of sea salt and a constant breeze kept the air fresh except in humid summer.

"You must be tired, Maagda, but we're close now." Pier nodded toward a small street off to the left, blocks after we'd crossed the Vijzelstraat Bridge, the last landmark I recognized.

I stole a glance at him. Last night's terror gripped me anew. We'd be alone soon in his house, and then… I pulled the coach robe higher, suddenly afraid because I'd lost myself in the feast the city spread for my eyes, had even let some of the protective tension drain from me.

"This is a good spot for me," Pier said. "Close to my work and near cheap markets."

Cheap markets by the elegant Herengracht? Odd. The truth unfolded quickly enough.

"Here. Turn right, Henrik."

"I don't know, Pier," the driver shouted over his shoulder. "These lanes get more like foot paths, almost too narrow for the coach."

He swerved to avoid three men who staggered from a tavern, and women who milled about on their own.

Pier grinned. "Business ladies."

By now I was no longer sure how many turns we'd made since we left the Herengracht, but the change shouted at me. Streets narrowed. Homes seemed dwarfed after the four and five storied houses in the wealthier sections. Everything was cramped, squeezed close.

"Ack, how do you stand the stench here?" Gutters ran with slops where there was no canal to dump night buckets. I hid my nose in the coach cover.

"You don't notice it after a while." Pier answered and then called to the driver. "The next bend, Henrik. See the door with the open arch at the side?"

Black everywhere now. No moon. Just pitch dark night. An occasional lantern in small windows threw a small glimmer on the cobbles. Revelers carried a torch round the corner and cast a faint light to the house Pier pointed out. I followed his gaze to a narrow gabled brick building that squatted at the end of a cobblestone alley. Its first floor windows were shuttered tight. Atop the shuttered floor another row of four windows with tiny leaded panes looked back on the street. One more tier, like a cake, sat at the top with a pair of double leaded windows.

Pier rattled on. "From the outside it looks like a house with three floors, Maagda. But it's not. The shuttered windows and the ones just over them are all one room with a high ceiling. Up there, those double windows, that's the bedchamber. The house used to be a printing plant. That's why the first floor's so high."

My god, I thought. He takes me to a factory for my new home. I burrowed deeper into the travel robe, willed it to seal me in the coach, never to step down into this dismal unknown. Why had I rushed this marriage, accepting Pier's word for the home he would take me to? What a foolish woman I've been. I chafed for not making time to see the place on my visit last month. Was I so dazzled by my coming wedding?

Pier directed Henrik to stop by a small arched entry. Whitewash or stucco, impossible to know in the dim light, peeled from gaping dark spots across the lower wall.

"There's another door just inside the garden," Pier said to Henrik. "It leads to a storage area where we can stow the bags and boxes for tonight. We'll take the food hampers inside. My wife'll want them in the kitchen."

My wife? I shuddered.

Henrik's lamp guided us through the arch. What Pier called a garden was a strip of hard packed dirt less than two feet wide. The earthen area was strung along a wall that adjoined another house. Next to it, a walkway of uneven cobbles stretched to the storage room door.

Pier started to help Henrik unlash our packages when a booming voice called, "Ho, Veerbeck. That you, returned? And your bride?"

"Ho, yourself, Pieter. Yes, she's here. Come meet her."

A square chunk of a man lumbered over to the coach. His mass of hair and beard were so black they blended with the night.

"Maagda, this is Pieter Bol. Pieter and Colinda and their three boys live in the house on the other side of the garden wall. Where's Colinda?" Pier asked.

"Oh, she took the boys to her mother's in Utrecht for a few days. The old lady's ailing again. Here, Madam Veerbeck. Let me take those packages, and welcome."

"Please call me Maagda." I shrank from Pier's name.

He smiled. "Maagda it is."

Pieter helped the driver move our belongings into the storage area, while Pier ushered me into the downstairs room and a tiny scullery off to the side of the fireplace. When Pier lit a candle, a startled mouse skittered across the floor. Folly heard the squeak and leaped from her basket to give chase. The candle caught and light flickered across the room. I drew my breath. Spines of shock needled every inch of me. I'd kept my expectations low, but never so low as this.

After last night's horror and today's long, draining journey with a bruised body, the sight of the room came like a blow. This house held no secrets, no door to open to a sudden burst of freshness or beauty. It spoke a language with a single word. Grime. The walls had been whitewashed at one time, but now they peeled from dampness, and grayed with soot from the fire and oil lamps. Nothing softened their dinginess, not a picture, a figure, nothing. In one lone spot, a few Delft tiles hung askew, and nearby, a single shelf held a pair of pewter plates and a mug. One charred pot dangled from the two hooks in the beam above the fireplace, while to the right, a soiled tattered drape older than Pier and me together, hid a cramped sleeping couch.

Sweet, sweet figs, a peasant's hovel.

I'd begged Papa to let me leave my comfortable home, my beautiful Hoorn for something no better than a foul factory? Tears stung my eyes, but I squeezed my lids tight to staunch their flow. I could not, would not allow Pier to know one more weakness in me. But Pier read my face when he walked back into the room.

"We'll live simply, but you'll see, Maagda. It'll be worth it in the end. I haven't owned this long. When we clean this room, give it a coat of whitewash like I did up in the bedchamber, it won't be bad. You must know all kinds of woman's tricks to brighten the place."

The driver shouted for Pier. "Okay, Henrik, coming. Maagda, Pieter will bring water in for you and get a fire started. I keep a supply of peat."

A new enemy gnawed at me. *Time.* Henrik and Pieter were finished, ready to leave. Pier and I would be left to dawdle over a meal, to talk, to face the question of the bedchamber.

I ran through the door. "Henrik, Pieter. Come. You must share our cold supper. You've been so kind to us." Both men looked startled.

"Pieter, you said your wife and children are away and you'll need to eat. And you, Henrik, you have a long trip back."

"Oh, no, Madam Veerbeck. I stay in Amsterdam tonight. My sister lives nearby. She holds supper for me." His graying beard moved up and down when he licked his lips in anticipation of this sister's meal.

Pier frowned, almost scowled. Pieter looked from me to Pier. He, too, was about to refuse when I slipped my arm through his and started to walk back inside. I turned to thank Henrik and said good-bye. Pier stared after us.

I grabbed my largest hamper and snatched out clean dishes and a cloth to cover the small oak table in the corner. I asked Pier to light more candles while I arranged cold goose and ham, Edam cheese and the remaining pastries.

"Hold a minute," Pieter said. "I have something for our meal. I'll be back."

Pier was about to corner me with questions, when Pieter walked through the door with a covered pail brimming with foamy ale. "This was for you anyway, Pier. A welcome home. Colinda knows you like warm ale in the morning, but I think a good swallow is in order with this feast."

Pier and I picked at the cold leftovers, but Pieter ate his full while he talked of his boys and their antics, and tidbits of gossip about the area. "Little Hans loves new people. He'll follow you around and pepper you with questions until Colinda rescues you." Pieter laughed, waving a goose wing in his hand. "And it's not society around here." Our neighbor stuck his nose in the air. "But you'll find us all friendly, and ready with help any time you need it. Heh, Pier?"

Pier merely nodded. The red on his cheeks and brow warned me his temper simmered beneath the surface.

I feigned interest to have Pieter linger and talk. Pier contributed nothing. He was quiet, agitated. He ran his thumb up and down his tankard's sloping side. His face darkened by the minute. He turned to Pieter.

"It's been a long trip, my friend. I think we should call it a night and let Maagda get some rest."

"Oh, right." Pieter rose immediately. "Thanks for the food, Maagda. Call on us anytime. I know Colinda'll want to show you her favorite markets."

Pieter walked to the door. "Pier, I put the bed together as you asked." He turned his great mass of black hair and beard toward me. "That's some wedding present your father had made for you, Maagda." He whistled, and jumped his caterpillar brows.

I'd all but forgotten Papa had sent the hand carved bed ahead on one of our small boats.

Pieter closed the door and Pier let out a great sigh. "Finally."

To busy myself, I cleared off the table and stacked the plates in the pail of water that warmed by the hearth.

Pier reached for my arm. I shrugged it off.

"Maagda, come sit with me." He moved me back toward the table. "We've got to talk about this marriage. How to put things right between us."

I brushed his hand away. "Don't touch me."

He flinched, stood silent for a moment. "Maagda, I will give us a better life than what you see here. Listen. You'll learn maybe I'm not bad like you think." He ran his fingers along the edge of the table.

"Pier, a man and a woman can't know each other in a day. It's a gradual learning of the good and the bad. But when the bad and ugly come so quickly... it's hopeless, like trying to stop a rain drop."

He reached for my hand again. I caught my breath, but forced myself not to pull away.

"Look at me. Look *at* me. Last night was sudden, I know. But it was my right."

My eyes flew open, and I shrank back in the chair.

"Damn you, woman. Has no one told you what goes on in the marriage bed?"

"Not that, not that," I whispered. "Yesterday we took vows to honor and protect each other. Within hours you ripped those vows and my body like so much paper."

He recoiled as if I'd struck him. "Yes, yes. Our vows. Yes, I honor them, but you must as well. And that means you honor my rights. And they are not the rights of an animal. They are the rights of a man, a husband."

I cringed at his words. I sank into the seat, trembling, trapped and exhausted. "I can fathom nothing more this day. We both need rest."

He hesitated. "Yes, we're both tired. I'll take you up to the bedchamber."

I tensed. "No. I sleep alone, either in Papa's bed or there, on the sleeping couch." Even if it crawled with vermin, it would be better than Pier's body next to mine.

He dropped my hands. "We'll do it your way. For tonight. You go upstairs; I'll take the sleeping couch." His hands curled into tight fists.

I mustered a small nod. His tense, pulsing jaw muscles told me I'd pushed him as far as I might dare.

Mounting the stairs, I noticed a pulley and rope by the side. "What's this?"

"In the old factory days there was machinery bolted to the floor. The ropes pulled the steps up to the ceiling, out of the way. The owner probably lived up there." He looked straight into my eyes, testing my next move.

I hesitated. My wits told me to pull the stairs. I fingered the rope, felt every strand, then let it drop…a gamble on his word.

"...with so much loss of sleep, such pain and travail have the most foolish men thought to purchase themselves fame?"

In Praise of Folly by Desiderius Erasmus (Classics Club edition)

CHAPTER 17—PIER

THE SLEEPING CLOSET LEFT ME CRAMPED, SCRATCH-
ing. I untangled my arms and legs to get moving, to throw fresh peat
on the grate, shuffling around the room in my bare feet. If Maagda
slept, I didn't want to rouse her. The damp room chilled me. I didn't
care about it myself, I wore as little cloth as I might in the house, but
I figured I could at least warm the place for the woman. Be damned
if I'd walk up those steps. She'd think I was about to climb in bed with
her, not that I didn't consider her body more than once last night.
Took care of it myself like I usually did when a whore couldn't be
bought. Wrong, by god, wrong. I held a husband's rights now.

Did Maagda think marriage was a celebration every day, like the
wedding party? *She would listen to me.* I didn't have to work at the
shop 'til noon. Steubing gave me my first morning back as free time.
A wedding gift, he said.

I sat at the small oak table to sip my ale and lay out the day in
my head. I'd take Maagda to the markets; let her select whatever she
wanted to stock the larder. Maybe purchase some whitewash for this

room. Then we'd talk. When I left for Steubing's, I wanted to know what pillow my head hit tonight. This war with Maagda cracked and muddled a man's thoughts worse than those battles in Germany.

Haste wouldn't do with her. Maagda needed some gentling from me. But I couldn't let every day become a skirmish. Still I didn't want to break her spirit. Wouldn't want a sniveler on my hands. I married her for the strengths I saw. We'd need every sinew in both our backs and every stuiver in our purse when we moved to the New World.

"Morning...."

She caught me off guard. My thoughts had muffled my ears.

"You kept your word last night. I'm grateful."

Was that a smile playing round the corners of her mouth?

"If you're ready to eat this food from Hoorn, after I'll,

I'll take you to the market."

I explained about Steubing, that I had the morning free. She looked around the room, peered out the grimy windows. I followed her gaze. Made me realize how shabby I lived. Guess I should've prepared her. What with work and meals in the tavern, I'd spent little time here. A man alone had few needs except to sleep. I only bought to grow the money from the farm. With all the war people flowing in here, anything with four walls would turn your stuivers into good silver florins and fast.

"Maybe we can find a bit to brighten up the room. Some white-wash for in here." Maagda glanced around again, but said nothing.

She came and sat across from me at the table, but nibbled bits like she had no taste for the food. We pecked like simple wrens at thick sausages and the last slices of hard cheese.

"I don't know much about the markets, Maagda. I usually keep a cut of cheese and some ale around for the morning. At night, after work, I sup in the tavern. "

Maagda's eyes measured me. "Yes, for today, maybe just enough to get a meal started, a hutsepot, perhaps. A good stew will last awhile...with some fresh vegetables added in a day or so."

"Be nice to smell food on the fire. And I wouldn't mind some Leiden cheese with cumin."

" You like Leiden cheese? So much I don't know about you."

A crack in the ice or a barb at me? "I'll point out when I like something at the market." I gave her my broadest smile. A crack in the ice, but a start. Maybe soon, common husband and wife talk, but she said no more. I wondered if no one prepared Maagda for marriage. If she was that innocent, it'd be easier for me to make sure there'd be no babies unless I wanted them. This legacy thing was so much rubbish, just a way to keep Maagda tied to that conniving father of hers.

The new market sprawled along the Dam, maybe twenty minutes from the house if you took long strides. Maagda'd find any food or woman things she needed: meats, fowl, cheeses, vegetables, breads, even brooms and cloth. Some growers hawked from pushcarts; others had regular stalls with old sailcloth shade above. Made a man's stomach growl to see the sides of beef, red and marbled, dangling from hooks. Always the aroma of spiced sausage sizzling over a small fire. Maagda moved ahead of me, picking through potatoes and cabbages. Nothing with a blemish suited her. She threw more back than she kept.

"We'll need mutton and vegetables to start the stew," Maagda said. At least she asked if I liked mutton. She piled prunes, turnips, greens and ginger into her basket. "Do you keep vinegar? A good hutsepot needs vinegar and spices."

"Maagda, you see how plain I've lived."

She glanced at me. "Plain you call it."

I told Maagda to buy what she needed, but winced as stuivers flew from my purse like fleas from a dead dog.

"You know, Pier, your downstairs windows could use curtains after they're cleaned." Maagda fingered fabric at a cloth merchant's stall. She smiled at me. "I like to sew. Soon as we tackle the walls, I'll make curtains."

Her smile warmed me. By god, except for the way she spent money, the morning looked better. Stuivers for cloth would be worth it. If Maagda talked of curtains, she thought to make a home.

I guided Maagda toward a cart yellow as a noon sun with daffodils. Biggest I'd ever seen. Oh, be damned, a coin more. I pulled a bunch and handed it to my wife.

"Fresh blooms, fresh life." I said.

"Why, Pier..." She flushed, but took my arm as we walked away.

Both market baskets groaned. I suggested a different route home. If I talked of the years ahead while we were here on the streets, it might cut the chances she'd flare into a rage.

Shoppers jammed the narrow passages between stalls. We skirted women who gaped and squeezed and sniffed for freshness, and sidestepped merchants who whacked the hands of boys who tried to pinch an orange here, a plum there. Loaded wagons jostled past, pressing us into the other buyers. I kept hold of Maagda as haulers shouted for right of way, pushing us back against a tub of plucked hens.

"Maagda, are you pleased with the shopping?" We had shaken loose from the crowds. "We spent almost a florin."

"Hmm, that much. So unusual?" She tucked a cloth over the cabbages she carried.

"Well, yes. I watch my stuivers and save for the future."

Maagda stopped in the middle of the bridge and turned. She was a handsome woman with sun glinting off the strands of golden hair that feathered round her cap. Even the strain of the past two days seemed less marked around her lips and eyes.

"This future, this is the plan you spoke of yesterday?"

"Yes. Like I've told you many times, I dream of good land, at least a hundred acres, maybe two hundred. A place where we can support ourselves, give our family a good life." Her eyes sparked when I mentioned family.

We set our hampers on the bridge rail and backed against the cool stone. Garbage floated on the water below.

"What of your work as a gem cutter, Pier? Surely, you earn enough for us to live and still save."

"I do. And when my apprenticeship ends, I'll belong to the new diamond guild." Two boys ran between us, whooping a German war chant. "I'll earn more stuivers, perhaps even florins over a year."

"We'd be comfortable then?"

The breeze from the Amstel pulled at her cap. She tucked a loose strand of hair back into its fold.

"It is good work, but I'm not meant to spend sunlight hours like a pet mouse in a dark corner. My life is in the open."

"Just so, Pier, but where in our province would you find so much land?"

"I look to new lands, wife. A place where there's plenty of ground to buy, cheap but good acreage. Another thing, we have peace now, but bloodshed next door. How soon before we're pulled into that war?

"Sweet figs, Pier! You speak in riddles." She stepped away from the rail. "You want drained polder acres safe from the war. Where in Holland might that be?"

Her words heated with that touch of fire I'd come to recognize, could almost smell the smoke in the air around her.

"Maagda, move over here out of the way." I guided her to a niche at the end of the bridge. "There are places beside Holland, bigger than Holland, that would give us all the land we need. Don't you see? If we live simply, if we put off starting a family, we can earn and save enough to buy good land…anywhere."

She made a sharp turn, her face looked like whitewash.

"Pier, what do you mean? Anywhere? And no children? You'd have us leave Holland?" She pulled her wrap tight and backed away from me.

I stroked her arm, but my patience thinned. "Calm yourself, Maagda. Let me finish, damn it. Just listen."

Maagda's tone and her quick movements attracted curious glances from passersby. I turned us toward the water, our backs to the street. I had to shout over the traffic and the yelps of boys throwing stones at the ducks in the canal.

"I told you yesterday you'd understand about the wedding night when I explained my plan. Well, part of it means no costs for children until we become settled in a new place." I paused, squeezed her hand. "I've watched how Pieter and Colinda struggle to feed and clothe that brood of theirs, and him with a decent job. Weights a man down." She stood, a tree rooted to the spot. "I was drunk two nights ago, soused, so I took you in a way that wasted my seed. So now it is out and said. I must speak plain. There's no other way to put this away from us."

She grabbed the bridge rail. "No seed? That's what you muttered in the night."

I moved behind her to block any move away from me. *She'll bolt, Pier. She'll bolt.*

Maagda sagged against the rail. "Is there more?"

I strained to catch her words.

"Yes. Listen to me."

She crossed her arms in front of her, a hand clasping each elbow, so tense the knuckles turned white, and her back pressed against the stone.

"When I was a small boy my father took me to Leiden to my grandfather who lay dying. We stayed and buried him." I looked down the long canal, remembering that time years ago, willing her to hear me out. "We sold his house, his furniture and on the last night in the city, we slept at an inn where a small group stayed. We fell in with them and listened to their tales around the supper table. They planned to cross the Atlantic to Nieuw Amsterdam. They told us of a land so vast it would take hundreds of years to explore its corners. Can you believe it?"

She stared at me, her mouth open, waiting for words to come.

"Across the sea, Pier? "My god, you don't think to move us across the sea."

She froze, then suddenly whirled round, hurled the flowers into the canal and lunged at me, her fists beating against my chest. "You bastard. You married me with a lie. You told me you wanted a family. How could keep such insanity from me, from my father?" She shrieked and clawed at my face, shoved me back to the rail. I reeled at her angry strength.

Shoppers stared at us. A burly mason shouldering a hod of bricks stepped toward me, the pole from its v-shaped trough aimed at my face. I reached for her wrists, but quickly dropped them, afraid he thought I attacked some strange woman.

In that instant, Maagda pulled away and rushed into the crowd. She ran back toward the market. I grabbed the baskets and hurried to follow, rushing past the mason, calling her name, plunging ahead, searching for her white cap and paisley shawl. Gone, dammit, gone that fast.

I raced to the market, sped through each aisle, each stall. The crowds swallowed her, hid her in a sea of faces, skirts, and long, marbled carcasses swinging from curved hooks. Damn the woman. And she had no idea how to get home, didn't even know the street name. I froze. Would she even try to come back?

"What authority was in their Holy Writ that commands heretics to be convinced by fire rather than reclaimed by argument?"

In Praise of Folly by Desiderius Erasmus (Classics Club edition)

CHAPTER 18—MAAGDA

I RIPPED AWAY FROM PIER AND RAN AMONG THE shoppers streaming from the market. People looked at me, tears streaking from my face, bunches of shawl tight in my clenched fingers. Eyes blurred, I ran into a woman and knocked her market basket from her hands. Oh god. She cursed me even as I mumbled an apology, but it forced me to slow down, to gather my wits. The market lay ahead and to the left. Best there I thought. How could I return to that house, Pier's house, with such hurt and anger flaming in me?

He would search for me. But the morning lanes seethed with traffic. I might remain unseen in the crowds. Pier wouldn't leave the food baskets behind...too many stuivers spent on them. He'd lose time while he gathered them up.

People milled about the stalls. It seemed all of Amsterdam shopped today. Women stood shoulder to shoulder and haggled over sturgeon, potatoes, eggs. They lined up ten, twelve deep at the stalls, bent to smell the fish, squeeze their thumbs into wheat loaves, heft legs of lamb. Much more crowded than when Pier and I bought here earlier.

Pier! My head throbbed in a beat to his phrases, *no children... across the sea,* Words that filled me with despair, words that I must never repeat to my father. How could Pier hold back such a life-rending plan? He knew my duty to the Trust. Until we talked on the bridge, I'd begun to ease my mind about him, tried to understand his taking of me as a drunkard's act. But to start our lives on such a secret? I hugged my arms round me to quell the angry trembling in my body.

I needed time to think, to sort myself out, so I stepped behind a stall that spilled carrots and cauliflowers over its sides. Reason said that Pier would look for me among the stalls we'd visited earlier. Best not to linger in the food area then. I slipped over to mingle with the women who bargained with cloth merchants. I felt like the sea terns we chased on the dunes when I was a child. Now I sympathized with the frightened birds when we made them scurry and look for a place to hide from our childish torment. Pier's torment was hardly childish. His words clawed at me.

I forced myself to calm down, to feign interest in the bolts of wool and linen, my eyes alert for my husband. Then I saw him two stalls away. I grabbed a swath of blue wool and pulled a length of it across my face. His head swiveled left and right. He skimmed the crowd. Pier passed within ten feet of me; food baskets swung from both his hands, his face twisted in anguish.

Good. I hope he ran with fear of my father's rage.

"How much you need, lady?"

The wool vendor's voice caught me unawares.

"No, no. Seeking color just now." I rewound the nubby fabric and walked as leisurely as my trembling knees would let me to the next aisle to lose myself among women who haggled over twig brooms and bramble scrubbers.

I moved to a spot near a draper's stall where I could sweep my eyes over the length of the market. The street where I entered when I ran from Pier was behind and to my left. I must go in another direction. Then I saw it. The spire of Nieuw Kerk that Pier had pointed out to me last night rose above a lane of gabled homes and shops.

The market behind me, I walked toward the church. Pier wouldn't think to look for me in this direction. I noted landmarks so I might return later to the stalls, the sole place from which I had any sense of where I might be.

Would the church be open? In large cities houses of worship remained locked between days of service. With so many immigrants afoot, the churches tempted nesters on a chill night

I heard voices singing a long amen, the music coming not from the Nieuw Kerk, but a small chapel at the next corner. I quickened my step and saw the carved wooden doors swing open. People trickled into the lane, mostly women, some tying scarves about their shoulders, and a few men, those past a day's work, squaring their brimmed hats over their gray hair.

"Does the church close now?" I spoke to a woman about my own age who walked down the steps near where I stood. A small girl with red ringlets let go of the woman's apron and ran to a flower box on the top step.

"Our church never locks up," she said, turning to pull the child away from the box where the little girl stood on her toes to grasp at a single poppy in bloom. I couldn't help but smile at the little one and wished she had gotten her flower before her mother stopped her. Her small pink lips pushed forward in a pout, but she wiped her hands on her own little apron and took her mother's hand after a final glance back at the flower.

I waited until the worshippers left and the little head with red ringlets had turned the corner before I entered through the side door. The chapel was a miniature of the grand cathedrals I'd seen in pictures, and like them, dim. Candles flickered near a lady statue, and at the front of the center aisle, a red lantern cast a warm glow to soften the gilt trim on the high marble altar. The Calvinist church of my youth stood stark compared to the gilt and color here, even in so small a place. Papa often said he was sure his favorite, Erasmus, was not a gilt and pomp papist like most Catholics. Was a vanity the Roman's idea of a heaven?

I walked to the lady statue with her blue mantle and a bouquet of pale flowers that had perhaps started life as red roses. She held a chubby infant wrapped in a loose swaddle, a boy, one foot kicked high and an arm outstretched toward his mother's face.

I sank into the quiet, let the hush fold me into its calm. Across the aisle an elderly woman bent over the seat in front of her and worked a string of black beads through fingers distorted with swollen red joints, her knees resting on her folded shawl.

Is this a woman's future…alone with little black beads for comfort? Or early death, like my mother. My bleak lot as a wife fell on me like a heavy shroud. How was I to fathom would might lie ahead? I knew now I had a place inside me for pain, for betrayal, a place that had depth, that could be measured in silent wails. But it was a place my spirit refused to dwell, even now.

The lady statue drew me. I found a seat near her altar and sat mesmerized, watching tiny flames from a bank of candles animate her face.

We had neither statues nor candles in my church. Nor incense. Its pungent scent lingered in the background until I stifled a sneeze, shivering at the unfamiliarity around me. I sank into the seat and exhaled slowly, skeins of tension peeling back, and I willed myself to dissolve into this strange, silent void. For these few moments, I wanted only to sit here, to cleanse my head of its thundering ache.

The old lady with her beads coughed, a wracking, deep cough. She wiped her lips on her sleeve. What miseries brought her here… family, ill health? Her weariness showed in the steep curve of her back, the way her crippled fingers moved the beads. Did she really believe those beads would lift the misery she prayed over?

I looked again to the lady statue, a young mother aglow with love for her baby. Yes, the baby. I'd mothered Miekke because our own mother died so young. But it wasn't enough. I wanted the adoration of an infant like the one before me, a baby who depended on me for its very life, just as the life of the Yard, indeed our town, swung on the future of my marriage. I sobbed. I hadn't meant to cry aloud. The old lady looked up and came over to me.

"Are you not well, dear? Can I help?"

I shook my head.

"Would you like me to sit with you a bit? Sometimes it's hard to be alone, even in God's house."

Her gnarled fingers felt warm when her hand clasped mine. Deep crevices lined her forehead and her thin, cracked lips. But her dark eyes sparked with life. I straightened up and thanked her. My hand felt cold when she let go. I sat and twisted my two rings, one of bondage, one of promise.

"This is a good place to bring your woes." She patted my shoulder and moved to the rack of candles at the lady statue. She dropped a coin and lit a small taper. I watched her cross herself and move her lips in prayer and I wondered what words she said to that mother and her infant son and wondered, too, if she heard the response she prayed for.

The woman turned to leave and smiled at me. I must remember her kindness, her caring in my diary, a page to read when I needed a cup of courage. When the chapel door scraped behind her, I walked with hesitant steps toward the rack of candles. I didn't have a coin with me. "I will repay this candle," I whispered to the lady and lit my own taper.

Prayer didn't come easy to me, more a ritual during our holiday visits to church. I knelt for the first time ever, and my knees sank into the soft cushion. I looked up at this radiant mother and whispered my anguish, asking for the strength to think clearly, make a sound decision.

The ancients were wise. They had a god for every need. With just one, if indeed just a single deity existed, why would he have time for my need to understand this mystery, this Pier I'd married. I knelt I don't know how long, the fleeing minutes of no concern. No answers came, but the quiet calmed my thoughts.

A desire to hurt Pier lingered, even in this holy place. Deep in my belly, there rose an urge to flee before I suffered anymore from him. To think how I had softened toward him earlier at the market. Had I been cleaved with a knife, I couldn't feel more torn. I was raised a woman of honor. To walk away from my marriage vows would bring me years of guilt and scorn, and shame for my family. And what of children? I recalled Papa's words when I pleaded with him to take me home yesterday. Perhaps he was right. The reality of a wedding night was so different from my innocent daydreams. Was all of the gaiety of a wedding day nothing but a mask for torment to come? How many brides started marriage so badly?

Thoughts of Papa and the disgrace I might heap upon him cooled the anger that burned in me. I could not go home to cause him more pain. Hadn't I loosed this misery upon myself with my pride, my willfulness? Now, I must solve it myself.

Pier had kindled his vision of the New World since boyhood, yet he was no closer to a move across the sea today than when he was a lad at Leiden. What drove him so? Money? A need to start anew? Did he despair because of the small holding he worked, or because he never had sufficient stuivers or florins to invest? Would anything sway Pier from his hunger for this unkown life across the sea, in this place of savages?

My imagination rioted with possibilities once I pushed myself past the hurt. If work in the open meant so much to Pier, might work at the boat Yard satisfy him? Papa had often talked of my marrying a local man, someone who knew ships, the sea, someone who might relish the promise of the Yard. I had teased, "Papa, you want me to marry a caretaker for your grandsons 'til they inherit?" In the cool dimness of this sanctuary, my question no longer seemed a jest, but rather a sound idea. Papa would teach Pier well. And while Pier wouldn't tolerate learning from me, I might speak here and there about how I ordered our wood from Sweden and Germany, perhaps how we built inventory timed to our vessel orders. Perhaps even my dim ideas about trade with the VOC might fall into place.

Many maybes. But worth the try. My breath quickened to think it.

And didn't time hold promise? Now that we were married, Pier might realize happiness lay close at hand, perhaps prize life here like those displaced souls who flocked to Holland to escape the war.

I know time would be my friend. I'd make it my friend.

The last knot in my stomach loosened. If I could force myself past our vile wedding night, we might yet make this a marriage...in Holland, in Hoorn. Indeed, I could see it like one of our old waterways, a polder that might become green with life when it was drained and dried and seeded. Yes, a life in Hoorn.

Before I left the church, I stopped near the door to tidy myself. I pushed stray strands of hair back under my cap and smoothed my skirt. On a whim, I removed my apron to fold the bib back behind the waist and look a little more dressed. I wished I had rose water to splash over my face. When the chapel door closed behind me, I walked to the street with a lighter step. I hoped to see the old lady who had spoken to me, wishing I could share a warm smile with her, let her know I'd found comfort in her sanctuary.

A male voice boomed at me. "Maagda, Maagda Veerbeck, hello." Our neighbor, Pieter, crossed the cobbles to where I stood. "If you're goin' home, want some company?"

"I'd be pleased to join you," not adding that I was lost, and had no idea where I stood that very moment.

Pieter was jovial, almost bounced along despite his hulk. His Colinda and the boys returned tomorrow. I envied his joy of family.

But a darker thought clouded my vision. I glanced again at his size and thought of his poor Colinda, if he, like Pier, took horrid acts to the bedchamber.

"I've been over beyond the Dam at the Great Fish Market," Pieter said, "picked up fresh cod for the family's homecoming." He held up a package that filled his ham-sized hand. "My Colinda works miracles with a catch like this. When she cooks it up with root vegetables, the boys eat like their mother put a sweet pudding on the board."

Pieter laughed and talked on, while in my mind I reasoned with Pier.

"His net caught a great many fish though he himself was fast asleep."

In Praise of Folly by Desiderius Erasmus (Classics Club edition)

CHAPTER 19—MAAGDA

PIETER, BADE ME A GOODNIGHT AT THE SIDE GATE. A hint of candlelight flickered through the sooty windows. I kicked at bits of old trash and crumbled stucco that littered the walkway and stopped near the door. The peace from church ebbed, left me empty save a skim of anger that still simmered. The grimy house, Pier inside…both brought back fear and hurt.

The door opened. Pier stepped toward me, his arms outstretched. "You've come home, Maagda. I've been worried."

I stepped around him to enter the house.

"Where have you been? I have a right to know."

"What right is that, Pier?" His tone squelched the lightness I felt earlier. "Have I no rights of my own?"

"I am your husband. We're married for god's sake, Maagda."

I hadn't meant to be so cold. The pleasant images I'd conjured for myself at the church vanished at the sight of him.

"We need some understanding, Pier."

I hung my shawl on a hook by the door, then snatched off my cap and shook my hair loose.

Pier hovered close. He grabbed my shoulders and spun me 'round toward him. "Understanding what? Who's been filling your head with nonsense?"

I squirmed at his touch. "You deceived me, Pier. I needed to sit somewhere quiet, to think through this madness of yours. Leave our homeland for a godforsaken wilderness? Live childless?" I clenched my hands into a fist and thumped his chest. "I don't know if I can ever forgive you…or myself. I allowed passion to play me for a fool."

Pier let go of my shoulder, but grinned at my admission. He sat down at the oak table near the hearth where a low peat fire nibbled at the chill in the room.

"I didn't lie. I said I wanted to be a father. But not now. Did we speak of months and years?"

"Don't mock me with cunning phrases. You knew what you wanted from the start. Do you think I would have wed you? That my father would have agreed to this marriage, despite his long acquaintance with Freddy, if he knew you would take me away?" I slammed the table, stinging my hand. His ale tankard jumped and spilled into his lap. Then I sat down, the table a welcome barrier. I'd no place to go. I dared not attempt the dark streets of a strange city.

Pier whisked his hand at the ale. "So you want war? Is that it?" He grabbed a cloth to blot the wet spot. "Maybe you weren't meant to be a wife, Maagda. Maybe you should go back to Hoorn and play Papa's little girl all your life."

I grabbed the edges of the table; bile scalded my throat.

"If I go, the dowry goes too."

This wasn't the scene I promised myself when I left the church. I'd came back to make some sort of peace, but I made battle instead.

"This gets us nowhere, Pier. I am your wife now, but I won't be treated like chattel. That's what I meant about an understanding."

Pier stared at me. "And…?"

"And I'll work beside you to make a life. But you must promise me at least three years in Holland before any move." I had to seal him to a promise of time, a few years to change his mind, to work round him, to bear a child.

"Three? I see five years of hard work to save enough florins for the life I see ahead."

"Pier, The money must be part of the understanding, as well."

"What money?"

"The dowry. It ennobles the legacy, a trust for our children, as Papa said. You can not count it in your plan. You must promise me." I had to use the dowry as a weapon, an assurance there would be children.

Pier shot up from the table. "A dowry is a gift for the marriage, not something to bargain with."

I sucked in my breath, astonished at his gall. "You think my father, the biggest employer in Hoorn, had to pay for my marriage? Am I so unattractive and dull-witted that I must be sold to a husband?"

He grabbed my wrist and pulled me to him. "Judge for yourself."

I jerked out of his grip and slapped him. "You bastard. You didn't marry me, you married the shipbuilder's dowry. Is that it?"

Pier rubbed his cheek. It flamed from the force of my blow.

"Good, Maagda, good. I need a spirited woman for the years ahead."

I stared at him, hardly believing what I heard. My own words trapped me and now he let me stew in that scalding pot I had set to fire. "You accepted Papa's 5,000 florins, knowing its purpose," I hurled back at him.

Pier threw up his hands and walked to the hearth where he jabbed at the embers.

"Take it however you like, Maagda." He stood silent a moment, his back to me. "I'll promise the three years in Holland you ask for, but during that time we stay in this house, together, settle into a real married life."

I burned from the slur over the dowry, still uncertain of Pier's intention. But he appeared unruffled. His calm baffled me. I fidgeted with the tankard on the table, rolling it back and forth between my palms.

"What do you mean, real married life?"

"That I am your husband and have a husband's rights."

"And those would be?"

"The marriage bed, of course."

"Pier, first you insult me, then you ask me to join you for more savagery like our wedding night. What do you take me for?"

"No more buggery, Maagda. I made that promise to you last night and I meant it. I am not proud of my drunken start with you." He looked at me his eyes clear and solemn, and then he reached across the table and laid his palm on my arm.

At that moment he was again the handsome, ginger-haired suitor who asked Papa for my hand. I didn't pull away, thinking of my resolve at the church hours earlier, willing it back, until he added, "and no babies for those three years."

PART TWO

Amsterdam & Hoorn

1630

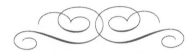

"And now ye shall hear from me a plain
extemporary speech, but so much the truer."

In Praise of Folly by Desiderius Erasmus (Classics Club edition)

CHAPTER 20—PIER & MAAGDA

"SO, YOUR FATHER SUMMONS YOU TO HOORN AND you race along like a horse to its oats. What if I summon you, Maagda? Do you run so quickly? Heh?

She raised her eyebrows and with the slightest shake of that damned creamy hair of hers turned away. I followed her up to the bedchamber and stretched across the bed to watch her pack. She moved about in a loose-fitting night dress while she picked slips and knickerbockers from the wardrobe, some with bits of ribbon and lace. Funny how a touch of frill stirred a man, at least this man.

"Now, this with the ribbons," I said, picking up a chemise and letting my fingers twirl through the bows near the narrow shoulder straps, "should stay here."

"Do you make jokes, Pier?"

I reached for the knickerbockers in her hand and ran the ruffled border round its leg through my thumbs. Soft as the inside of a woman's thigh. I sucked in my breath.

"Put these on. Let me see them from the back. No top, or maybe just the chemise."

"Stop your foolishness." She moved away, closer to the window on the pretense of checking a seam in the slip she held. "You've seen me dress often enough."

"No, not so often. You undress in the dark, and in the morning you hurry out of here like a north wind blows through the room."

My face flushed with the heat building in me. Her eyes drop to where my breeches strained across the bulge I wanted her to see.

"Put them on."

"No, Pier." She put her hand to her mouth. "Not tonight. I won't do that tonight."

I threw the knickerbockers to the floor and stepped toward her, meant to grab for her and throw her face down on the bed, but I stopped when I saw the flash of fear in her eyes. Instead, I put my face so close to hers she had to feel my spittle when I hissed, "how many 'no's' do you think I'll stand for?" I spun away, thumped down the stairs and slammed the door behind me. Better the back privy than nothing. But inside I boiled. I wanted her to bear the taste of me to Hoorn and her father.

When I got her on that ship to the New World, she wouldn't have choices, who came first, wife or daughter. Or business woman. Ha. She fancies herself a business woman with that sewing she does. She knows nothing. Her wits scatter, either running off to Hoorn, or tending that squalling infant next door. Leave the child to its mother, for god's sake. No, she says, Colinda needs time to heal. Maagda thinks having that baby here will tempt me to fatherhood.

No thanks. I see it, hear it and I can smell it. That's enough for me.

I bolted the privy door behind me.

The clop of Henrik's team on the alley outside bade me hurry. I showed Pier what I had cooked and stored in the larder for him.

"How long this time?"

"I can't say. It might be only a few days, longer if there's an emergency." Fear of the latter gnawed at me. I kissed Pier's cheek. He brushed away my small attempt at affection, but picked up my small bag to take to the coach. I carried Folly in her basket.

"You don't take much other than this fool cat." He tossed the light bag into the coach.

"I left a change of clothes in Hoorn last time and I can always borrow something from Miekke." A joke really. Miekke could wear all of Mama's dresses, but I was larger-boned like my father. More than likely it would be one of his tunics I'd throw over me. And I certainly wouldn't leave Folly behind. Pier was none too fond of her and I feared that she'd not be here when I returned.

Papa wouldn't send for me on a whim. I tortured myself with thoughts of broken limbs, fire, a breakdown at the Yard, Miekke's failing health.

With so much to worry over, I had hoped to leave home this morning without a verbal scuffle. Pier still smarted over my refusing him in the bedchamber last night. He nagged that I left sewing orders unfilled even though I assured him all was in hand. I knew Colinda would keep our ladies supplied with fabrics and measurements. She enjoyed these little escapes from her family routine, and better still, she was skilled at dodging guild drapers who feared we stole their custom, which we did and not without a certain glee. Without Colinda my little band of seamstresses, my Copper Thimble, might have never reached reality. Now I had ten women sewing Copper Thimble labels into dresses and on the hems of finished orders. Pier knew of my sewing, that Colinda worked with me, but I kept my dealings with the other women from him. I didn't trust him, knowing extra funds were about. He'd have us boat bound in a trice.

I waved as Henrik pulled around the corner. Pier stood at the garden entrance, a scowl etched on his face, no wave, no kiss thrown.

The patch of earth where he stood was a real garden now. I saved vegetable scraps to make compost and was delighted with every steaming gift Henrik's horses left behind to build rich soil. We needed the space for vegetables, but I permitted myself one fancy, a clump of sweet violets no wider than the span of my hand. I'd brought it from our garden in Hoorn. I loved the cheer of the tiny blooms. Some women picked the flowers for a tea or wine, or to brew a cough remedy, but for me they brought the sweet promise of warm days and nights. How could I have guessed that I'd reach a time in my life when the smallest clump of earth given over to flowers was luxury?

We were almost to the turn at the end of the lane when I realized Colinda stood by her door to wave a farewell, Breeda in her arms. The baby clutched a soft white lamb I had sewn from scraps and stuffed with goose down. She held the little creature by its left ear, yanking it from side to side then stuffing it between her pink lips. I blinked back my longing.

Pieter was in the lane, too. He rolled a hoop along with a short stick, giving lessons to his oldest son. He hailed my husband to join them. Pier waved him off.

Foot and dray traffic engorged the city's twist of canals and cobbles, slowing our escape, lanes teeming with strange voices, strange dress. These wanderers knocked on doors to look for rooms, wandered with bags on their backs, or pulled carts groaning with dresses and tunics and mattresses and chairs poking out between the sideboards. At night, many were said to bed down along the canals, nesting in empty boats. Poor souls.

The traffic trapped us until we crossed the Damrak and saw open country ahead on the North Road. My trips back and forth to Hoorn had become so frequent of late that I knew every trickle of water by the road, every tree, every bend in the canals. When we passed my landmarks, I sighed to myself: *25 miles more, 10 miles more.* At one fork, where the road branched off toward Edam, a lone windmill stood in decay on a low hill. One of its sails had torn away; another hung in tatters, to move only when a gale swept across the open waters beyond. Its sloping sides curved inward, reminding me of a woman's skirts, perhaps a wife looking to the sea for her mate's return. But to me, this ghost of a mill seemed a lighted window candle ...*thirty minutes to home.*

I saw Ria first. She knelt scrubbing her front steps, head lowered, her gray skirt pulled up to her knees and her apron padded beneath her as a cushion, a pail foamed with suds at her side.

Henrik stopped the team. Ria looked round and ran to the coach.

"Maagda, what a surprise." She flung her arms around me. Her warm hug of welcome eased my mind. If something were amiss here, Ria would know. "I didn't expect to see you back so soon." She brushed a stray lock of auburn hair behind her ear, trying to tuck it into the tight bun she wore at her nape.

I caught her quick glance toward the coach. "No Pier?"

I just shook my head, surprised that she still asked since Pier hadn't been near Hoorn since the day we married.

She told me Papa and Miekke were not yet back from the Yard, and invited me into her kitchen for treacle cakes she had baked that morning, and offered some to take to my *skin and bones sister,* when I said I must hurry to the boat yard.

I caught her glance at my waist. "Eating for two yet, Maagda dear?"

I blushed and turned my eyes from her. Ria knew me too well to try to hide truth from her. "No...no, not yet."

"Well, don't worry." She patted my hand. "For some women, it takes more time." Her voice was low. She, too, was childless.

Words fought to spill out of me... *Oh Ria, it takes a husband, not merely time.*

"Oh, and there is news." Ria arched her eyebrows. "Willie van Pelt is to marry in the Spring. A cod heiress from the north." She shrugged her shoulder as if the words meant little, and to me that was their exact worth. My sympathies lay with the heiress.

I took the sweets she offered for Papa and Miekke, kissed her cheek, and walked toward the canal bridge, hurrying my steps and churning to know why Papa sent for me.

"For this is the Thunderbolt with which they fright those whom they are resolv'd not to favour."

In Praise of Folly by Desiderius Erasmus (Classics Club edition)

CHAPTER 21—MAAGDA

THE YARD WAS LESS THAN A MILE AWAY. AT A BRISK pace I might walk there in fifteen minutes. I wished I had worn other shoes. But I had to make the short walk clad as I'd alighted from Henrik's coach moments earlier in my plum dress and pale gray apron. Miekke would delight in the vivid pink scarf I wore around my shoulders. She liked my touches of color. I had two in my bag for her, a surprise. She always looked so pale of late. I thought a touch of color might brighten her spirits. I thought Ria right, too. Miekke looked brittle, like she'd snap in two if you hugged her.

Crossing Grote Noord, I encountered Anna Pelter coming from the direction of the boys' school, her own youngster tagging behind her with a ball he bounced against the stoop of each home along the way. "Ho, Maagda. Visiting? Where's that diamond man of yours?"

"Busy, Anna, always working," I called over my shoulder, no desire to stop and talk or to quench her obvious thirst for Pier. I swung to the right and the gravel lane that skirted the shoreline.

I walked at a good pace, twisting a stalk of salt grass in my fingers. All the while I pictured dreadful images of accident, even though Ria's calm had eased my mind.

Papa had built the tiny office at the boat Yard on stilts to cover a large dry area where we stored our lumber. From this high perch he saw each work area, from the blocks where the timbers were planed to the cradles where journeymen pounded pegs into a ship's skeleton. And I knew he enjoyed the vantage point to watch seabirds, too.

My Papa was a dreamer and I often thought his flights of fancy from his reading found wing on the odd tern or gull.

I climbed the steps. Miekke cried out when she saw me. By the time I reached the landing, she and Papa both rushed through the door, vying to see who would hug me first. We fell into each other's arms, laughing.

"I didn't expect you so soon," Papa said.

"You knew she was coming?" Miekke's pursed her lips in pique.

Ria was right. Miekke's bones strained against her skin. The fabric of her bodice lay slack.

Papa put his arm around her. "I have something to pick over with both of you, a family matter" he said, "and you're already here. No need for a special notice. Besides, you'd drag Maagda to chase bargains in the stalls before I ever spoke to her."

I winked at Miekke, but turned immediately to Papa. "Do we have trouble at the Yard, something I should know?"

"We fare decently here," Papa said, "but it is about the Yard, the business that takes my mind these days."

He pointed to his latest fluytship. The mellow afternoon sun painted a soft golden light over the lacquered hull rising from its cradle of crossed beams some ten yards in from the water's edge. "News of our light ship stirs interest in Germany and England," he said, not without a note of pride in his voice.

My patience wasn't what it used to be. These months of tension with Pier had eaten the edges off my nerves. I wanted to scream at

Papa: "*Please get to the point!*" But I knew better than utter such words to Lars Boscher.

Miekke nudged my arm. "Willie van Pelt's about to…"

"I know. God help the woman."

Papa removed the leather apron he wore during his workday. "Come, let's walk along the dunes to home like the old days." At the shoreline, Papa stooped to pick up oyster shells the gulls had left empty and skipped them over small, rippling wavelets. He seemed in a good turn of mind. I, on the other hand, suffered a pounding headache. I had little patience these days for games or delays. Papa was not one to deceive or cozen, the latter, his latest word from Erasmus, but I stretched too taut for amusement or anything beyond a forthright reason why I'd been called to Hoorn.

"Let's sit and watch the sunset." Papa pointed to a small sand hill with a greenish yellow covering of sea grass. The Zuider Zee lay to the East. The sun warmed our backs, casting rose and mauve bands across the sky and over the gabled roofs of Hoorn to our south.

"Sometimes I come here to sit and think back on the grand times we've shared along this stretch of beach," Papa said. "Remember the first time I brought you girls up here to teach you to fly your kites? Why in a thrice Maagda took on the windmills like that splendid Don Quixote fellow in the book we read together."

"Oh, Papa, 'twas the gale whipped the kite right out of my hands. My line got all tangled."

"I am tangled at this moment," he said, the smile faded, his jawline hard.

"I've had an offer for the Yard."

"To sell?"

"Yes."

I sucked in my breath. "Papa, what of…of grandfather… the Trust?"

"I'm not so nimble as I used to be. I have to think about what the years ahead bring. That Yard is your inheritance, yours and Miekke's.

I think to pass on something worthwhile to you and Hoorn as my grandfather passed it on to me. Perhaps he would see the wisdom of such a move in these times..." Papa turned his eyes to the sea, "and forgive me."

Miekke didn't say a word. She stared at Papa, eyes wide, mouth slack.

My head buzzed. Papa renounce an oath? His health? And what of the States General?

"What do you mean, Papa, no longer nimble? What do you hide from us?"

He exhaled slowly, and looked from one to the other. "We must be honest here, take stock of our positions as a family. To start, I must look at my age. He tilted his head toward me. "A body is like a ship. It gets older and the parts wear, the sails get holes, the wood rots. Like me. I get short of breath of late. Feel the odd pain here." He rubbed his chest.

"What is it?" My voice little more than a whisper. "How long have you had the pain, Papa? You've seen the doctor?"

"Yes, yes. I've talked with Doctor Rooper, just back from his exciting trip to England."

"I don't care a fig for the doctor's travels. What of you?"

"Doctor Rooper's trip to England is important. He learned something that might explain my chest pain."

"Papa, for god's sake, what is this about?" Miekke shouted. She stood up with fists bunching her work apron in tight balls. "Is this why Klemp from the VOC's been around the Yard so much of late?"

Papa tried to soothe her. "Calm yourself, Miekke. You know you mustn't get overwrought. And no, this has nothing to do with Klemp. He spends time here because his own office is not busy enough these days. Money flows to mainland trade and those mysterious tulips."

On some elusive day or hour in the past months, my sister had traded her tart tongue for a perpetual whine. I'd been so caught up in my own woes, I'd failed to notice that Miekke had become an ailing autocrat.

He put his arm round her shoulder. "I can't give you a name for the problem. Remember when you were younger; we saw those wonderful drawings by that sketcher, DaVinci? He cut into cadavers to learn how they worked."

"Disgusting," Miekke said.

"Not so. DaVinci drew a human map that helps our physicians. Think of him as a body explorer like our Hoorn navigator, Schouten. Didn't Schouten discover Cape Horn and named it after our town? If not for him, we wouldn't have such good trade routes today and no need for our fluyts. Just so, if DaVinci hadn't explored the body, maybe Doctor Rooper would be at a loss to help me."

I grew more agitated, but I knew this was Papa being Papa.

Finally to the point, Papa said DaVinci had seen mounds of fat that clogged tiny channels in the body where blood should flow. A few years ago an English doctor, wrote a book that showed how this flow of blood worked. A circulation system, this William Harvey called it. He reasoned, Papa said, fat that piled up and dammed the flow of blood to cause pain.

"Think of it," Papa said, "like our ship channels. If they fill with silt, nothing sails through. Doctor Rooper took a month in England to study with this Harvey fellow. When he examined me, he thought I might have these *dam* deposits." He laughed at his play on words.

I couldn't smile.

He picked up a razor clam shell and drew a picture in the sand to show us what he meant. "Dr. Rooper sketched the circulation path for me like this."

I watched him draw and realized my father would not have told us in such detail if not already convinced he had something to worry about. Exhausted from tension, the trip, and now this foray into a world of medical talk so strange to me, my sole reality was my beloved Papa's sudden vulnerability.

I mangled blades of sea oat in my nervous fingers. "What's to be done for it?"

"No one knows. Doctor Rooper proposed that I eat fewer greasy foods, since grease seems to be the villain."

"There's no medicine?"

"Of a sort. The doctor dries hawthorn berries and crushes them into capsules that I swallow after every meal." Papa took a small packet from his vest pocket and showed us the thin sleeves of brownish grains.

I flung my arms around his neck almost knocking him back into the sand. Dear god, would my Papa die soon? He lifted my apron to dry my eyes. Miekke sobbed. I squeezed her hand. Both needed me.

"Ladies," Papa looked at us. "I'm not about to vanish. I merely need to slow down. Lars Boscher intends to watch out for you a good long time. The very least I can do is to be here for my grandchildren." His eyes bored holes through my guilt.

I felt the flush creep up from my neck.

"So this is why you intend to sell the boat Yard?"

"I didn't say that I intended to sell the Yard, Maagda. You leap too far ahead." He patted my arm. "The offer came from a Bremen shipbuilder who wants to enlarge his business in a westerly coastal port. Wants safety from the war."

Miekke asked, "Why doesn't he start his own Yard?"

"Prime land's too expensive to start from scratch," Papa said. "Better to buy someone else's property and build from a known base. I must think on it, persuade myself it's the best move for us, for Hoorn. As it now stands, our Trust reverts to the government, the States General. Who knows what the State might approve and what would be left for us. That's my knot."

I hadn't thought much about the government's stake in our legacy, and I had no idea how to deal with it. But I did know another boat builder would hurt us. "If this Bremen buyers started his own place, he'd be our competitor," I said. "Doesn't this man know Amsterdam is now building a larger yard and even now we worry about Hoorn's future? Even the VOC treads a perilous path these days."

Papa nodded. "He's a wise merchant. With the war in Germany at high pitch, no one knows when another mercenary general like Wallenstein will come back to burn and plunder. He leaves nothing but charred village bones behind him." Papa threw up his arms. "Who would invest in such chaos when there's safety here?"

I perked up. "But Papa, how does he expect to do better when we worry now that the bigger builders here will hurt our own fortunes?"

"Come, Maagda. Do you think he's about to tell me? And what would I do if I knew? I'm getting too old for new ventures." Papa bit his lower lip.

My inner voice wanted to scream ...*Papa, Papa, I will run the Yard for you, honor the legacy. Who knows what the States General might decide? I have thoughts how we might thrive. I think we must trade. Yes, trade.*

He rose, brushed sand from his stockings, and turned to me. "You should tell that Pier of yours he better find his land soon. Yesterday, I heard a parcel sold for 2,000 florins an acre. And that was twenty miles north of Hoorn. Such good business chances move quickly in these times. For every beggar immigrant that the German war chases to Holland, there's another fellow with a fat purse looking for opportunity. Perhaps Pier should settle here at the Yard. He has a head for business."

My legs trembled.

Papa reached for my arm. "What is it, Maagda? You're whiter than a bleached sail."

Dear god, what was I to do? Papa needed me here and I felt sure the germs of thought I nurtured about trade would sustain the Yard, yet he talks of Pier. How to make Papa stop thinking of me as a child. Here I stand with years of learning in the Yard and he speaks only of Pier.

And, too, there was Pier's threatened move, his mad burning to emigrate. If Papa prepared to disavow the legacy, he must be told. Pier had not been honest with me, but I sinned, too, by holding the truth from my family.

"To work miracles is old and antiquated, and not in fashion now."

In Praise of Folly by Desiderius Erasmus (Classics Club edition)

CHAPTER 22—MAAGDA

WHEN PAPA REGAINED HIS COMPOSURE AFTER I confessed the news of Pier's emigration plan, he took me to his study. He put hands on my shoulders. "We must keep Pier here at all costs." Then he pulled the model ship, *Count of Hoorn,* from its perch and had me read the papers concealed inside. I had some vague memory of the contents, but the threat failed to penetrate until I finished reading, may fingers shaking.

The papers acknowledging that an heir, a bastard heir, might exist as nearby as Antwerp shook me, but I didn't dwell on the possibility. I was much more agitated that he considered giving the Yard to Pier to anchor him here, rather than sell to the Bremen buyer. An alarm sounded inside me, and I knew it urgent to take precautions about our inheritance now, because I didn't trust Pier. If Papa even thought him worthy of the Yard after keeping him at arm's length these two years, I needed help, and I could think of but one person who might guide me.

Yesterday, planning my return to Amsterdam, I gave the coachman, Henrik. a note for Pier's cousin Willem in Edam. I asked if I might stop on the way, a business visit. I'd accepted his hospitality several times before, usually on the road to Amsterdam. These had been casual visits. A bit of cheese and bread, good conversation, then I was off.

I found much to talk of with Willem, a commercial attorney. He took interest in our boat Yard and the variety of woods, spices, cloths and minerals the VOC ships brought back from Batavia, or the ores and lumber Baltic runners unloaded from the hulls of our fast boats. Did he dabble as a middleman when exceptional goods came on the block? I toyed with such an idea, that it might be the financial future of the Yard. I had much to learn about trading before I expressed my thoughts to Papa. The more my mind worked on what happened to the VOC when burghers put their money in speculative ventures, tulips for god's sake, the more I reasoned there had to be a link we might forge between the VOC's and our fluyts.

Today I visited for more immediate reasons. I would not speak of an Antwerp claim. Who might be sure if he or she even existed, but I knew the strength of Pier's threat. Much as it broke my heart to think of Papa's leaving us, I had to learn if Miekke's and my inheritance might be protected from Pier under the law. The future depended on it.

Willem stood on the front steps when my coach rattled up the cobbled drive. I caught a glimpse of the spacious gardens, a sea of flowers in sunny yellows and oranges along the side, a burst of color to brighten the somber ochre of his stone home.

Willem extended his hand to help me step down. He looked warm, but magisterial, standing amid his splendid surroundings. I thought him a dashing man and wondered that no woman had snared him.

Willem invited Henrik to go to the kitchen, and ushered me into a bright room at the back of the house, a small glass conservatory flooded with midday sunlight. Boxes of seedlings that would find their way into his summer gardens sat on shelves where they caught the sun's warmer rays from the south. The flowerbeds behind the conservatory spread at least two hundred feet to the edge of a canal where a windmill's sails caught the breeze. I could just see the mast of the small skiff berthed at his dock there.

Willem took my wrap and folded it neatly over a corner chair, his movements carrying a graciousness, some melding of the robust with the serene, that soothed me when near him. He poured a ruby-colored wine into delicately etched goblets, each rimmed with a fine band of gold. I sank back into the chair, as much into the comfort of its plush cushions as into the snug aura of his friendship and his home. I'd no taste for wine, but I took a small sip to be polite, and set the glass back on the marble-topped side table.

"You come to talk again of your sewing business? I trust the guild gives you no trouble."

I laughed. "The *Copper Thimble* thrives, thank you. And we manage to outwit the guild lackeys. Since our ladies are scattered around our quarter, there's no one house or shop where custom is so obvious."

His housekeeper, Voonda, appeared with a tray of cheese and cold meats. She'd served in Willem's home since before his wife died eight years earlier. She greeted me with a suspicious smile that showed gaps where, she had months earlier confided, a sledding accident claimed her front teeth. She seldom let them show, giving her normal expression a pinched look. I caught her sideways glance, almost a sneer, when she placed the tray on the table before us. Could I fault what she must question… me a lone woman making visits to her handsome, widowed employer, yet what could be further from my thoughts.

Willem asked after Pier. I brushed the polite inquiry away and said I would speak of him soon, but today I had more urgent business, and launched into Papa's thoughts about selling the Yard

Willem sat forward in his chair and leaned toward me. "A big step. Does he merely toy with the idea or has he signed papers?"

"No papers. It would be complicated. The States General has first claim on our business and the property. Now, Papa's more concerned about protecting what he holds of value, the profits over the years, for Miekke and me. And Pier, of course. Papa worries whether to sell or to find a new manager."

I explained to Willem that many of Hoorn's men, perhaps three in ten, worked at the boat Yard. The wrong move might mean hard times for many families...and the town. "What we need to do for the sake of all is to expand our business," I said.

"You're against these moves?"

I held back, not yet prepared to explain the legacy or Papa's thoughts of Pier taking over. "I want to run the Yard."

He grabbed the cloth from his lap, and choked a spray of ruby wine onto the white linen.

"What of your marriage, your home with Pier...your, your life in Amsterdam?"

"We will manage these things. The possible crisis in Hoorn matters most." I sighed. "At least you didn't mention that I'm merely a woman."

He looked at me, his face still red.

"Maagda, I don't know what to say. You trip me into a rabbit hole." He refilled his wine glass.

"I believe there is opportunity just over the horizon and we must be ready to take part in it. I don't say I fathom it yet, but my instincts tell me we must add a trading arm to our shipbuilding enterprise."

Willem's head snapped up. "Trade? What sort of trade?"

I smoothed the cloth on my lap. "I'm not sure, but I've spoken with Klemp from the VOC and watched how their investors fall away. I sense there's a way we can use that void to our advantage, but the fine details elude me. I'm without experience in these matters."

Willem sucked in his breath. "I know something of trading."

"You will be a help later, I'm sure, but now I must concentrate on keeping the business."

I stemmed the volume of words that wanted to flood from me, forced myself to temper what I might say.

"Understand I do not ask you to make a decision for me. I come to you for your wisdom. For now I need a legal opinion about these assets in light of my marriage. I...I..."

"What?"

"I don't trust Pier with such temptation. Not now."

"He's your husband for god's sake."

"I don't mean that Pier would steal, nothing so base. But he's desperate for money. I fear if Papa willed the business to me or gave it to Pier as he's already suggested, Pier would sell it out from under me for the cash."

"Maagda, to even consider such a possibility. What in satan's inferno? This is my cousin you speak of." His jaw muscles quivered.

"You've been close to Pier for years. Hasn't he ever spoken of his wish to emigrate?"

"He's talked of buying land, but never said to emigrate."

"Pier told me that since childhood he wanted to emigrate to Nieuw Amsterdam."

"How ridiculous. It was only in '09 that Hudson landed in the place. We know nothing of it yet. And there are scant reports back from recent voyagers. Most men sent by the VOC to colonize these hinterlands sail to satisfy a penalty. They're guilty of crimes, ready to eke out a living in rough circumstances in a wilderness rather than prison here."

I told him that Pier believed the New World so vast he would find all the land he lusted for at little or not cost. I toyed with my food. "And now he says we must leave within six months. You see how many ways I am torn here?"

Willem held up his palms to me. "Slow, please. My wits scatter. These matters beg deep consideration when family is at stake."

"Your wits take flight no more so than my own. On his wages Pier will never save the florins to sail. He'll push that rock up the hill 'til he's withered. And now so many possible temptations."

I sagged back, let the cushions catch me, and watched the muscles in Willem's lean face pull from grimace to grimace. His graceful fingers twisted around each other as he mulled my tale.

"These worries eat at me. If my father offers Pier our business outright to keep us here, and he's said as much, then what's to keep Pier from selling it at first chance. The thought chills me. I must go back to my father with a sound idea to keep the boat yard." I blushed to say such things of his cousin, but I saw no recourse. I didn't think this the time to tell Willem I must fulfill the family oath. Enough for him to understand my immediate dilemma.

I lifted my chin and looked him in the eye. "I'll stay in Hoorn… alone, if I must."

He whistled. "You've pondered this, haven't you?"

I nodded, my lips tight.

"You would seek a separation?"

"I'm not ready to speak of such arrangements. For now I must know what legal rights I have if Papa turns the business over to me or to Pier, or should there be an outright inheritance. One step at a time." I ran my finger along the arm of the chair. Mama's ring caught my eye. "Some mornings I wake up and wonder who am I, what my first duty must be, wife or daughter."

Willem took another sip from his wine goblet. "And what of your duty to yourself?"

I turned my head away, could not answer, but relieved he thought of me in friendly terms after what I'd confessed about his own cousin.

" Maagda. You realize I specialize in commercial, merchant law, so I can't quote word for word on joint property rights. I'll look into that."

"I understand."

"But I can tell you this much. Any Dutch woman may inherit and bequeath property on her own. And if there were a dowry involved at the time of your marriage, the courts would side with the wife to recover a full portion if a husband is proven to have squandered the asset."

"Yes, my father provided a dowry, but I'm not concerned about that money. Pier knows it's dedicated to our children. I want to protect the value of the Yard and have Papa realize how strong my own intention to grow the business."

"Perhaps I speak too soon, Maagda. I'm sure you haven't told me everything, but keep in mind that our legal system casts a blanket of protection over women who file claims against males, say one who mistreats them or who squanders funds with prostitutes."

I lowered my eyes, thinking, Willem, how close to the mark. I wondered if the courts considered strange carnal acts abuse. I knew I'd never be able to relate those scenes in public. The prostitutes were another matter. I felt sure Pier used them regularly, but how to prove it? Did I want to?

Willem reached for my hands.

I squeezed his warm hands in gratitude.

"I've never understood Pier," Willem said, "always thought him more Calvinist than Catholic. Too sober, no spontaneity. I find him dry. The rest of us Dutchmen still like our games and music, a quenching brew. But this, this plan to emigrate astounds me, some shade of him I never saw. Perhaps it's what attracted you?"

His calling Pier a Calvinist made me laugh aloud and broke the tension that stretched in a tight band across my chest.

"Pier's a handsome man. He turned my head, Willem, and he had that bit of mystery, a freshness about him. When you grow up in a small town, the young men never become more than the little boys you went to school with. Pier came along…new, attractive, a puzzle to unravel." I drew tiny circles on the plate with the tip of my knife. "Father was concerned because Pier urged a hurried wedding.

But Papa trusted my judgment and his long friendship with Pier's Uncle Freddy. And I admit I was besotted. His talk of an exciting future whetted my curiosity, easy to do with a twenty-four year old who knew little more than Hoorn. I learned too late he held such a dream."

"Too late?"

" I was terribly naïve. I thought a warm, loving home would divert Pier. Now this obsession of his could hurt too many people I love. I can't allow that, no matter the cost."

A loud thumping interrupted me.

Voonda poked her head 'round the conservatory door. "Your coach, Madam Veerbeck." Voonda grinned at me, lips pressed tight and what I caught as the merest hint of jealousy in her eyes.

We walked to the door. Willem held my arm.

"Must you always fly away so quickly, Maagda? Your visits are more a bee's hasty sip of a rose."

I kissed him quickly on the cheek, Vonda watching from the door, and stepped up to my seat.

Henrik flicked a light whip above the horses and the coach moved toward the road.

I looked back. Willem stood fixed on the step, his hand shading his eyes. He watched 'til we rounded the drive onto the dusty road-bed south. I'd return. Today's visit was but the first step on the path to my new future. My breath came in easier passage now. Willem calmed me.

"Just like some men who are so hard to please and withal so ready to do mischief, that 'tis better be a stranger than have an familiarity with 'em."

In Praise of Folly by Desiderius Erasmus (Classics Club edition)

CHAPTER 23—PIER

STEUBING LEANED OVER THE SHOWCASE ON THE other side of the shop and counted coins into a small leather bag. "I must leave early, Pier. Be sure to lock up, will you? That's a good fellow." Steubing trusted me to close up, lock the safe, bolt the shop. This new duty began about six months ago when he planned a fresh series of buying trips.

I listened for the chimes from Nieuw Kerk, and flicked the hourglass with my finger. Maybe an hour left of my twelve-hour day. Why not leave? It was too early for many burghers at the tavern. I could stop home to see if Maagda had returned, maybe take her a little treat. I've been rough with her of late. I'd walk home through the market.

I set Steubing's precious March diamonds back in their plush tray, each in its own exact spot. The old man fussed over the position of the stones. I swung the heavy door until I heard the click, then locked the safe and left.

Maagda looked up in surprise when I walked in. "I didn't expect you so soon."

I handed her a small pot of the yellow daffodils she liked so much. Her face flushed.

"Pier...what?" She looked at me like I was a stranger and then placed the flowers on the oak table near the hearth, turning the pot 'til the yellow heads faced her.

"Good trip?" I asked. "All well in Hoorn?"

Maagda looked from me to the flowers.

"So much has happened, Pier. I don't know where to begin." She sat down at the little oak table and touched the yellow petals as she talked. "Come sit with me and I'll tell you about my father." She lifted her cap off and shook loose her hair.

I shrugged, said I couldn't stay, had to return for business. A stretch of the truth, but it might be good business in the end.

"Oh." Her voice went flat and she pulled her hand away from the plant.

A bit of guilt tugged at me.

"Maybe Sunday we'll have a good walk down by the docks and treat ourselves to a meal at the inn there." We'd never had a meal away from the house before, but I felt fortune about to befriend me.

Maagda looked up, her mouth open. "Why, Pier, that would be... nice."

"Well, don't wait up for me. I could be late. I'll wake you. We'll talk then."

She picked up her cat and held it on her lap. "Oh, by the way, I ran into your admirer, Anna Pelter, while I was in Hoorn. She asked after you."

Good. Maybe my wife would value me more if she knew other women found me to their liking.

I brushed her forehead with my lips, and cautioned myself not to start something I didn't have time to enjoy. She excited me when her hair splayed around her shoulders. Her loose hair tempted me, golden in the late sun. An invitation. *No.* I reminded myself that I had other business. Today my gold lay elsewhere.

When I got to The Black Lamb, most of the tables were empty. Three burghers sat in the corner next to the fire dealing faro cards. I laughed. Their Calvinist predicants thundered from the pulpit against card playing in the home so the righteous burghers ran to an alehouse for their gambling. Hid from their children's eyes. So much for the power of the pulpit.

The tavern owner set out pewter tankards for the night's business. He wiped and arranged them in rows like a troop of soldiers by the big casks of ale .

"Tasty partridge you had last night," I said, to get his attention. His face, pinched at the forehead, drooped into wide jowls. Had narrow shoulders that sloped into a barrel of hips. Built like he drank and ate his profits.

"Enjoyed it, eh? Stay around, then. There's a fat goose roasting. And we got cheese in from Leiden today."

I cut a slab and ordered a tankard of ale.

"Last night in here three men sat at a table next to mine. Over there under that lantern. The burghers called one of the men an artist. Not a big man, kind of ruddy, small pointed beard. Talked a lot about plants. Onions and tulips. Know who I mean?"

"Hmm. Oh, onions and tulips." Then he laughed. "Of course. Van Goyen. Comes in here regular. Probably see 'im in the next half hour or so. What d'ya want with him?" He wiped his fat hands on a greasy apron.

"I'm interested in those onions and tulips you laugh about."

"Getting the fever, heh? Bet every man in Amsterdam with a spare stuiver wants them little devils." The barkeep shook his head. "Can't see anything in it myself."

I hacked off another slab of the cheese and took my tankard over to a table. The artist seemed jovial enough to me last night when I overheard his talk with his friends. How would he feel about a stranger who asked questions? I drummed my fingers on the table and waited.

I heard the scrape of the door opening, and turned. But the tall burgher who strolled up to the bar was a stranger. Quarter of an hour later, van Goyen walked in, alone. The tavern owner greeted him. "Hey, Jan. That fellow over there asked for you." He pointed me out even though there were few people at other tables.

Van Goyen walked to my table. "And what can I do for you, my good fellow? If it's a painting you're after, I don't do portraits. I'm a landscape man."

I introduced myself. "No. No portraits. Hardly worth preserving." I laughed, and pointed to my face.

"Pity. I have friends who'd enjoy a commission or two right now."

I motioned to the other chair, and invited him to sit. "If they're in need of cash, why not tulips?"

"Tulips?" Van Goyen's head jerked up. His eyes widened. "What do you know of tulips?"

"To be honest, nothing. But I was in here last night with a friend. You sat at the next table. Couldn't help but hear you talk, something about onions, tulips. Said you turned stuivers into florins with them."

The artist eyed me for a minute. No doubt he looked at my workman's smock to judge my purse.

"You look for investments?" Van Goyen tilted his chair back and clicked his unlit pipe against his teeth.

"A good place to put my future, yes." My heart flicked like a cow tail.

Van Goyen asked if I worked in the area. When I told him I cut and polished at Stuebings, he perked up.

"A diamond man, heh? A store of those icy treasures, have you?" He leaned closer.

The tavern filled with hungry merchants and burghers who pushed their way to the ale kegs. One of the faro players saw van Goyen and called him to join their game.

I decided to stop playing cat and mouse before he lost interest and moved away to the card players. "I have florins to invest. It's a matter of where and how."

"Why tulips?" Van Goyen hoisted his tankard of ale and drained it. His finger bore colored pigment stains, like mine with their black carbon.

I signaled the barkeep for refills and turned back to him. "I heard what you said last night. I plan to leave this area in six months and I mean for my pocket to be full with enough florins to buy at least a hundred acres of good land."

Van Goyen whistled. "Damned ambitious, don't you think? I move to The Hague myself, but probably to a small studio. A hundred acres. That'd take a mighty big stack of florins."

I nodded. To speak of my plan aloud made my stomach lurch. The ale bubbled around in it, fizzing and popping. My flesh crawled now that words put bone and blood on my thought.

Van Goyen waved off the card players again. "What's a diamond cutter want with land?"

I told him about my old dairy farm, how I wanted good land and a fine herd. I didn't mention that my future farm lay across the sea in the New World.

Van Goyen eyed me. I could almost hear the questions he asked himself about how serious I might be, how many florins I could manage. Then he warmed up and talked again of the tulips. The artist told me there was more than one way to make big money with the plants.

"Since you'll leave in six months, you don't want the actual bulbs. You don't intend to plant them yourself, gather offshoots, the multipliers, to sell on the market."

He befuddled me. "How could I buy tulip bulbs, yet not have them?"

"It's all paper, my friend, all paper." Van Goyen smiled. "That's the wonder of this new kind of market. You buy paper, then sell the paper for a profit."

Van Goyen launched into the details of a scheme the likes of which I'd never conjure. I would buy a paper contract that said I would own a specified number of bulbs from a prize tulip when the grower lifted the bulbs from the ground, perhaps next June. But, as June got closer, I would sell my paper to someone else who wanted those same bulbs. Since the time was shorter then until the bulbs were lifted, I got paid more money for my contract than I bought it for. A profit. Usually a very handsome profit. Easy. I knew I had to bite this apple.

Questions in my head bubbled more than my ale. How could it be so easy? How would I know which tulip to buy? When to sell? Where were the buyers who'd buy my contract?

My qualms must have shown because van Goyen said, "Calm down man. It's Pier, right?"

I nodded.

"Listen, Pier," van Goyen said. "I've made a small fortune when I buy and sell these contracts. It's a new financial deal, not widely used yet, but trust me, it'll catch on big once people realize how easy it is."

I began to interrupt with another question, but the artist raised his hand to stop me.

"Right now many investors still buy the actual bulbs. That's the joke about the onions. Tulip bulbs look like onion bulbs."

He told me the story of a friend of his whose manservant saw the bulbs in a sack and sliced them as onions to eat on bread.

"They were Viceroys, worth 2,500 florins each. My friend was ready to throw his servant bound and gagged into a canal. That worthless lout of his shat a treasure away the next morning."

I choked on my ale. 2,500 florins for a single bulb. Where could I get that kind of money? "These bulbs cost so much?"

"Not all of them," the artist explained. "They grow in value as their color or size makes them more rare. A lot of buyers start with small contracts, then buy and sell 'til they can afford the best tulips."

People guarded their bulbs and their contracts fiercely, van Goyen told me. "I have an artist friend up in Hoorn, name of Baburen. He wanted to grow bulbs, then sell. Had a trip wire rigged around his garden with bells so he'd be alerted to intruders. You'd be amazed at what folks do to protect those little sweetmeats."

Baburen? Baburen? I knew I'd heard that name before. Then it came to me. The militia painting in Uncle Fredrik's house by Baburen, the artist who'd switched to bawdy scenes from the taverns.

I got so excited listening to van Goyen's stories a flight of bees buzzed in my belly. My ale sat untouched in front of me. I hated myself for the time I'd wasted working for piddling savings when such easy money waited for the asking.

"How do I get started?" I asked the artist. who'd been urged once again to join the faro game.

"Look," van Goyen said. "You seem like a good enough fellow. But think about it. If you want to make a move, I'll be here Thursday night. One of the tulip colleges meets in the back room. I'll take you in, introduce you. You'll see for yourself how it works."

"Tulip college?"

"That's what they call these buyer meets," van Goyen said. "Sort of an informal guild."

He slapped me on the back, and moved over to the faro table where a heavy screen of smoke all but hid the players by now.

My palms ran wet at the thought of it all. Where could I get the cash to invest? My savings would buy only a smirk in such a market.

Remember you want to sail before the year is out, Pier. There must be a way.

A voice jarred me out of my thoughts. "Mind if I take this chair?" A tall blond man in a mud and blood stained military uniform hovered where the artist had sat. I'd been so caught up with van Goyen and the tulips I hadn't noticed The Lamb was now packed. Drinkers spilled out the tavern door, tankards in hand.

"Help yourself. In fact, sit here if you like. I'll be leaving."

He thanked me and placed his tankard and a plate of sliced goose on the table. Spoke like a gentleman, this soldier.

"I'll just leave this and go back for bread." He motioned to the plate of meat, steaming, covered in thick gravy, boiled turnips in butter on the side.

The rich smell of the soldier's food moved up to my nose and sent licks of hunger through my belly. I'd had nothing to eat since breakfast except that bit of Leiden cheese when I got here earlier.

The stranger returned with a half loaf of dark bread. "I've been on the road all day," he said. "I could eat two meals this size."

"So could I now that I see your food. Mind if I sit and join you in dinner?"

"Don't know about sharing, stranger. I've had a long ride with no meal."

"Oh, I mean to get my own." I scraped my chair back and left to fill a plate.

He introduced himself as Bjorn Kristiansson, a Swede from outside the city of Gotesberg.

"A military man. What brings you to Amsterdam?"

"Got mustered out of the army when a musket ball caught me in Germany."

"So Sweden fights now?"

"Not openly. I was an officer in King Gustav Adolphus's ranks. We scouted action to report back to our commanders, a reconnoiter party. Got too close to a skirmish near Mecklenburg and took a ball in the shoulder." He patted the top of his left arm. "Not much good to the army like this."

"Bad luck. On your way home now?"

He chewed a mouthful of the meat. I gnawed at mine as well; the goose more tender than I expected. I sopped up the gravy with a thick slice of the dark bread and helped it all slide down with another gulp of ale. The smoke in the tavern got heavy enough to make me choke. The burghers worked at their pipes. I could barely see the stranger's face.

He stopped chewing. "No home to go to. No real family. Never had a job other than my king's army."

The Swede wiped his plate clean. "I thought I'd stay in Holland and look into places to use my mustering-out money. Heard your VOC had good prospects. I plan to find a place to billet here, and then I'll make short trips to some of the port cities to see what opportunities lie about."

"You've no place to stay?"

"No. Just arrived in your city. A bit after dark. The coach dropped me close by. I saw the tavern lights so I figured I'd eat, then look for a place to sleep."

"Might be a problem," I said. "The city's mobbed. People pour in here every day like a flood on the Amstel. That damned war in Germany and Bohemia chases people out of their homes. They want to get away from the battles so they come here."

"I feel the same," the stranger said. "I've seen enough blood spilled to last a century. King Gustav's interest won't help. He means to march from the Baltic down through the German States to claim land. Wants to ring the Baltic in Swedish-controlled port towns." He took a good swallow of his ale. "We're a poor country you know. Gustav wants commerce."

I remembered my cousin, Willem, saying much the same thing the day after the wedding when we rode to Edam with another solider back from the war.

Before I'd even thought the thought, I heard myself say, "I might be able to help you with a room."

"Some desire to be accounted wealthy abroad,
and are yet ready to starve at home."

In Praise of Folly by Desiderius Erasmus (Classics Club edition)

CHAPTER 24—MAAGDA

SHADOWS FROM THE LANTERN DANCED ACROSS
the pages scattered on the table in front of me, while schemes for the
boat Yard skittered like fireflies through my mind. My eyes drooped,
wanting sleep, but I couldn't leave the warmth of the kitchen fire for
bed without some plan however slim. I didn't intend to let Papa and
Miekke worry through the future of the Yard alone. We would seek
solutions…new designs, new buyers, or better, trade. Yes trade. But
no matter the plan, Hoorn must keep its Boscher Boat Yard, that
much I pledged to myself.

What would Papa think of a second dry dock with two hulls in
the works? How to vary the supplies, the crews? I guessed at numbers and wrote them on the paper. I'd heard that Amsterdam was
building such twin cradles in the yards that lay north of the city.
They were meant for large, long voyage ships, far different from our
light, shallow draft fluytships. Would there be commerce enough?
I would walk to the Amsterdam Yards and see for myself what the

complexities might be. Papa would insist on facts. I listed the questions I must find answers for.

Ideas whirled one around the other, but somehow the thought of cargo trades pushed all other ideas over the horizon in my mind.. Such trades meant investing, not building, an avenue we'd never trod before. Was it such a leap from building the boats that carried shipments to owning the shipments?

I'd no doubt that Willem's stories of his cargo profits swayed me. Yet, there seemed a soundness to cargo, a natural link with our boats, the transfer of cargo from the VOC's long haul galleons to our shallow draft fluyts. The war-stricken inland states to our East hungered for goods. I wouldn't traffic in munitions, but Willem told me that merchants snapped up foodstuffs and medicinals as quickly as ships unloaded. My remembrance of past conversations at home suggested Klemp and his VOC were ripe for a new venture. Why should such a venture not begin with the Boscher boat yard?

Best to sleep on it, but I needed to quiet my mind. I let my thoughts drift to my afternoon of sewing with Colinda. God gave my dear friend a rich singing voice, a mellow contralto that rang in notes so robust they seemed too big for her small frame. She's at least a half head shorter than me and much more narrow in the waist. Colinda sang when she stitched. Soothing. Made me feel like a babe in its cradle, gently rocking. We spoke of it earlier today as we stitched.

"Small wonder your children sleep so well, Colinda. Sometimes I hear your songs in the afternoon when you put them down for their nap."

She smiled and continued her tune. I hummed along, the most I could offer in the way of talent. Sometimes I teased her. "You do these last three pleats in the drape and I promise not to sing."

Colinda laughed. "Your voice is not so bad as you tell yourself. Besides, my mother always told me never stop another from singing no matter their voice. A song on the lips means happiness in the heart." I frequently left our stitiching sessions with a dancing step that stayed with me from her music, but the happiness part was nowhere near the truth.

Not willing to fight my need for sleep any longer, I mounted the stairs with Colinda's pleasantries in my head, hummed her song and danced quick steps while I undressed. I bent to snuff the bedside candle when I heard the door open. Pier came home later than I expected. His voice and a strange male voice echoed up the stairs, the second, a gentle, refined tone. I knew that voice didn't belong to our neighbor, Pieter. Who in the world...?

"Maagda, you awake?" Pier clomped up the steps.

"Yes. Not to bed yet." I knew he couldn't see me in the dark. "Who's downstairs?"

"A guest. Come down to meet him. Then change the bed linens."

A guest? Bed linens? At this time of night? I lit the candle and started to pull the linen off the bed when I realized it hadn't been slept in. The bed was unrumpled. Pier must have spent the nights I was away on the sleeping couch, or... Not worth the thought.

I gathered a cloak over my nightgown and walked downstairs. A tall, slender stranger rose from a chair by the table, a soldier of some sort, tarnished gold braid on his shoulders and sleeves, his uniform road and battle weary.

"Maagda, greet Captain Bjorn Kristiansson of Sweden. He returns today from the war in Germany. Wounded, too."

The Swede extended his hand. I took it, but my eyes shot questions at Pier. He brought me downstairs this late, in a nightdress yet, to meet a stranger?

"Captain Kristiansson will stay with us for a few weeks," Pier said.

"Bjorn." The man smiled.

With the fireplace behind him, I saw little of his face, but caught glints of gold on his tangled blond hair, thickly matted as if his cap had lived on it for weeks at a time.

Before I could utter a word, and it would have been a sharp one, Pier took my arm and guided me back toward the stairs. "Let's gather a few things and bring them down here. Then I'll shown Bjorn where he's to sleep."

"And where might that be?" I hissed the words at Pier.

He pulled me toward the back of the bedchamber. "In this room, of course. We're getting a good price for it."

My jaw dropped.

"You've rented our bedchamber to a stranger? Is there no end to your greed?"

"With all the immigrants mulling round the city, there isn't a vacant bed in Amsterdam. We can earn a few extra stuivers here. All this man needs is a place to sleep and a little breakfast."

"We run a house for lodgers now?" How could Pier even consider a stranger in our tiny place?

"No, no." Pier grabbed my wrist. "It won't be for long. The fellow looks to deal with the East India Company. He's got money to invest there and he wants to travel."

"What do you know of this man? You want a total stranger in our home, in the very bed Papa made for us?"

"Sssh, Maagda. He'll hear you. Don't be so damned fussy. It's just a bed. Not a shrine. With as much time as you spend in Hoorn these days, you'll hardly notice him. Now, gather whatever you need for tonight and we'll sort the rest out in the morning."

This husband still had the power to stun me. Had I learned nothing in these long months of marriage?

"You're so crazed for money, I wonder you didn't sell me to the stranger in the bargain?" He laughed aloud and turned away, leaving me to stand shaking in anger by the bed. The candle trembled in my hand.

I snatched up a frock, petticoats, and an apron for the morning, wondering how I'd find a bit of privacy to dress on the morrow. I heard them on the steps.

"Goodnight, Madam Veerbeck. Thank you for taking in a stranger. I am grateful."

I nodded. Fury locked my tongue. The Swede's polite manners didn't cool my anger.

The lumpy sleeping couch sat tucked into a wall niche across from the fireplace just to the left of the front door. The short bed lay hemmed in by wall on three sides, leaving a man or woman to curl up to make themselves fit. Neither Pier nor I could lie perfectly flat. When he came downstairs, Pier would crawl in first because he'd expect me to get out to fix his morning meal. He was tall, so he'd have to sleep with his legs sprawled at an angle, leaving me little space. It made no difference. My ire banished sleep to some remote corner of possibility. As for breakfast, he could forget that. If he wanted to run a boardinghouse, let him arrange a meal.

The men talked above in the bedchamber, snatches of their words tumbled down the stairs. *VOC...Batavia...North Shore...Board of Governors...fellow investors.* I sat on the edge of the couch to wait for Pier, fuming about this crippled marriage that stumbled through a debris of conflict. I'd tried to show him gentle fondness, but Pier had dug a hole that sucked me in, made me a convenience, squelched the passion that might have lay in me.

Pier accused me of spending too much time in Hoorn. Why not? There I could call my soul my own. Papa valued me for what I thought, for what I brought to our days from my mind and heart. Willem treated me that way, too, a woman who harbored her own mind. Pier had reduced me to a vessel to relieve his basest needs, or a talent to stitch for coins to fill his coffer. I loathed myself for giving way these many months. When would I accept the truth that I would change him, that childish dream in the church with the lady and her child, the dream that I would make him see the value of a family life? Silly as a little school girl I'd been.

And now a lodger, yet another insult.

Perhaps I should go back to Hoorn now to shoulder some of Papa's burden, let Pier take his money and leave. He could find a woman for his needs anywhere. Early in our courtship Pier claimed a fondness, said he found me attractive; he liked my companionship, said I'd be the perfect helpmate for the future. Was that enough for him? Surely, not for me. The slim bond between us was not reason enough to put an ocean between my body and my heart. To think of never seeing my Papa, my Miekke again tore the very breath out of me.

Folly strolled out from under a bench, stretched, then leapt into my lap. I stroked her head, her back, long leisurely sweeps of my hand. She purred. How I envied her. Would I not treasure such loving caresses? A fleeting memory of the Swede's hand as he held mine in greeting. Fingers long and clean, firm yet gentle. Pier's fingers were black from his work that ground carbon into them twelve hours each day. Those fingers never attempted to bring me pleasure in the soft, tender strokes I craved. When his hands did touch me, it was but a response to the final thrust of his own pleasure.

He came down the stairs. "Maagda, no more talk about the Swede. We will sleep now."

He fell fully clothed on the coverlet. "We'll make provisions in the morning. But you'll be happy to know I have a new means for getting all the money we need, and soon. It won't be long, Maagda. It won't be long. I picture it…my…our march aboard ship to the New World."

Fear gnawed anew, chewing at me deep within my breast. I slipped into what was left of the couch, shifted the last bit of duvet to cover my shivering limbs. I shook not from cold, but from fury, from fear and a resentment that flared and rose from my belly.

My thumb reached to twist the small ring, my mother's garnet that I wore on my little finger. You were right, Papa. Marriage does consume a woman, if she lets it.

Pier slept at once. His rasping snores seemed to bounce and echo from the three walls that enclosed us. I slid from the couch and moved to the table, wrapping an extra cover around me.

To hell with Pier's limits on peat. I added a new clump to the last embers in the grate to warm the room. Folly brushed my legs in greeting, and jumped again into my lap when I sat. This was new for her, having a snug place to roost in the cold of the night. Pier always chased her from the bed upstairs. She purred a sweet rhythm while I cuddled her close and tickled a favorite spot, an arc of bleach white fur between her ebony ears.

I had drawn the curtain across the opening where Pier slept. I could not make out forms as my eyes became accustomed to the dark, lit only by the glow from the grate. Yet I saw that one of his feet pushed against the curtain, created a bulge in the flowered fabric. Good that I left the couch. I'd be shoved to the floor by now.

I laid my head on the table, rested on my crossed arms. Weary though I was, I found enough iron of spirit to whisper to the dark walls. I played again in my head the talk I'd had with Willem. I'd be damned in hell before I'd leave Holland, Pier or no. The road to Hoorn was my only road.

Of a sudden a laugh shook me. A boarder, heh? So much for Pier's wont to walk around the house with little covering. Except his hose. He never removed his hose. I'd never seen Pier's feet. He'd roll his workman's cotton stockings down to his ankles on warmish days, but never remove the things, never let his bare feet touch the floor.

I giggled in spite of my bad humor. A sudden curiosity piqued at my thoughts. I wondered what his toes looked like. Were they straight or hooked and gnarled from some childhood illness. At the moment, I wanted desperately to see Pier's feet, examine his toes. Did he have the required ten?

"...and another for a small and uncertain gain exposes his life to the casualties of seas and winds, which yet no money can restore."

In Praise of Folly by Desiderius Erasmus (Classics Club edition)

CHAPTER 25—PIER

A YEASTY AROMA BIT AT MY HUNGER EVEN BEFORE I opened my eyes. Maagda must be warming the morning bread.

By god, Thursday. Van Goyen and the tulip college tonight. Excitement stirred the pit of my stomach before I turned the covers back. I was hellishly anxious, my thoughts straining for the end of the day. A good thing Steubing was away on one of his long buying trips, meant I'd hurry to The Black Lamb early. I wanted to hear every word, learn how I'd dip into this new wealth. A nip of caution made me wonder if they'd expect me to invest tonight.

Maagda was still icy around the edges because I brought Bjorn home to board. She'd spoken little since Monday night. Deep down, Maagda's a good woman. A shame she's so damned tied up in her family. Her father did me little service filling her head with all his learning and book twaddle. A wife should know to follow her man's direction, that's all she needs in life. I needed a strong woman beside me in the New World. Women were scarce there, I've heard, only the odd widow. But I'd take no petticoat direction in my house, here or over the ocean.

"Good morning, wife," I greeted her with a playful slap on her ass. She gave me a scathing glance then moved away to pour my ale. "Bjorn up yet?"

"Up and gone. He said he might see you later today at Steubing's. He was to meet with someone at the VOC."

"See, I told you he wouldn't be under foot for long. Already he begins to make plans. Why don't you show him around the markets on Saturday while I'm at work? A nice gesture. He's paying well to stay here."

Maagda said nothing. Merely shot me a frosty flick of the eyes. Oh well, who cared? By Saturday our lives might stand on the verge of big change, if all went well tonight.

Maagda told me about her father's chest pains. Didn't sound like much to me. She'd have to get over it. If I made a move on the tulip market, we'd be on a boat for Nieuw Amsterdam before she knew it. Her duty was to me now, not her father. I couldn't suppress my chuckle. Nothing, but nothing would interfere with my good mood, my prospects after tonight.

Lars must be at least sixty. My father didn't make fifty, and my mother dead little more than a girl at my birth. Better to go while you're still upright. Seen too many of those old men feeble as babies and befuddled to boot. Hell, we should all be in such decent shape at Lars' age. Look at the man. Still building boats.

I gulped my bread and ale to leave and called a quick goodbye to Maagda.

Bone-rattling cold gripped me in the wet streets. I crossed my arms to pull my tunic close. November here always seeped chill into a man's bones. Almost as cold as my wife. I laughed aloud. Today I didn't care. The New World would teach her something about being a strong man's woman. When a thought like that crept into my head, I wondered about my own mother. Was she the strength and comfort my father expected when he married her? How strong could she have been, going and dying to bring me into the world? Women were a disappointing lot.

A stray cat hunched over its catch by the edge of the road. I tried to give it a swipe into the canal with my boot, but missed. *Eat hearty, you little bastard. Next time I won't miss.* That's where that cat of Maagda's was headed. A nice long swim in the canal with the other garbage. Damned if that animal would get on the boat with us.

Better think of what I must do today. I'd work on the five March stones, the cream of Steubing's horde. He'd overseen the rough cuts before he left.

Steubing reckoned those bits of clear ice would bring more than 6,000 florins when they were ready for sale. I knew in Amsterdam some wealthy merchants might invest as much as 9,000 florins in personal jewels, sometimes more than they had in merchant shares. Could be the gems I worked on today would be made into a single necklace. A lady would grow dizzy with happiness that her husband thought so much of her, and a man would have his investment in sight. The rich prized hard assets.

What would a rich man think of a piece of paper that said he would own flower bulbs in six months? A piece of paper for something that looked like onions? Did the papers carry the weight of a hard asset like Steubing's diamonds? A lot of *ifs* in this new tulip market.

I cut and buffed the stones an hour or more when the bell jangled. Bjorn strode in rubbing his hands together. He had a small blanket wrapped over his light military jacket that he'd brushed almost clean. A light stain still colored one shoulder, probably old blood from his wound.

"So you found me. Cold enough out there to shrivel a man's balls, eh Bjorn?

"Ah," Bjorn said, "I'm used to the cold, but the dampness here makes the chill bite deep." He looked at the wheel where I worked and the tray of stones at the side, and whistled appreciatively. "You spend your time in extravagant company."

I laughed him off. "When you're around this stuff so much you're no longer awed by it. To me these are another job to finish. Speaking of jobs, any luck with the East India Company?"

"I'm not looking for a job. Oh, I want to work, but at my own investments."

I jumped at his words like a sparrow to suet. "What kind of investment?" Such talk was my sole thinking of late. It came at me from all sides. Bjorn had told me earlier that when he resigned his army commission after his wound, he got a sizeable lump of florins as mustering out pay. Enough to get him started in civilian life.

"What I think," Bjorn said, "is to invest in a cargo venture on one of the VOC ships, then work that ship as it travels to Batavia and back."

"Batavia? What a journey." I whistled. "That's half way 'round the world."

He told me he wanted introductions to a group of investors who pooled their money. They would buy into a shipload of silks and spices to be sold for enormous profits when the ship returned to Amsterdam.

"You have to wait for gains," Bjorn said. "And there's always the possibility that a storm might wreck the ship, or a pirate raid take everything. But the rewards," he took a deep breath. "The rewards could be so vast they might set a man for life." He grinned, lips tight. "I wouldn't mind owning a vessel one day."

He nailed my ears with his talk. The more I considered the tulip market, the more I came to believe its rewards outweighed the wait and the risk. I'd worried it was too dangerous to own an article of trade with only a piece of paper. Yet here was a man willing to throw his money in with people he didn't know, to travel to the other side of the world to buy goods, and then chance it might be lost on the voyage home. The tulips looked better all the time.

I told Bjorn about my conversation with the artist, van Goyen. "I'm to have my first look at how the market operates tonight. Want to come along?" I regretted the words right off. Would the others frown on a complete stranger? Someone uninvited?

"No, but thanks. I laid down my florins at the VOC. I'm committed. Should have an investor group to join within the next couple of days and a ship in a matter of months. I can't afford to gamble now." Bjorn paced. "They explained how the VOC's Governing Board of Seventeen worked to bring men with assets together. Only way to keep their ships moving. They welcomed me. Seems cash is lured elsewhere in these times."

He started to leave.

"Bjorn, I asked Maagda to show you around the markets on Saturday. Might be a good idea, especially if you plan to invest in merchandise for sale here in Holland. You'll see what they open their purses for."

"And she agreed?"

I nodded.

"She didn't seem too pleased to have me around." Bjorn pulled the blanket around his shoulders. "I've tried to stay out of her way."

"Don't worry. Maagda's got a lot on her mind with her father sick. She doesn't mean anything by it where you're concerned."

"Fine then. Saturday it is." He tossed off a friendly salute and left.

The hours limped along. I began to wonder if old Steubing put a stopper in the hourglass. I flicked the top half in frustration, but the grains still dropped one at a time. It seemed a full growing season passed before the last grain fell.

"...measuring how far a flea could leap, and admiring that so small a creature as a Flye should make so great a buzz."

In Praise of Folly by Desiderius Erasmus (Classics Club edition)

CHAPTER 26—MAAGDA

LIKE MOST FANCIFUL THOUGHTS, ONCE IT GRABBED me, it wouldn't let go. I flung off my paisley shawl and pulled open buttons as I raced up the stairs so swiftly my petticoats tripped me, my heart pounded, but I was happy that neither Pier nor his Swede were in the house. Maybe Maagda Boscher wasn't welcome beyond the Bourse portico where I was to meet Willem in an hour, but what of Marteen Boscher, a male trade agent of Willem's from... from Antwerp perhaps.

Our future lay within the Bourse's pillared entrance, the very heart of commerce, trading. I was sure of it. Willem gave me vivid accounts of the frenzied atmosphere, the hectic bidding, the posturing that scored trades. For all our freedoms, women were not permitted inside. He asked me to await him in the shadow of the Bourse walls, to listen yet again to a second hand account of how money and goods changed hands.

But why? I wanted to feel the tension, to taste the sweet victory of a sealed deal, to see with my own eyes the eyes of my fellow trader.

How else might I understand the new course I must take to Papa? I recoiled at forming such judgments from another's words. Not that I didn't trust Willem's view. I held him in the highest esteem. But Papa would demand to know how I formed my judgment, not what someone else, almost a stranger, proposed we might do.

Pier owned but a single pair of dress breeches to wear with stockings, the breeches he had worn on our wedding day and had not donned since. With cinching at the waist, garters at the knee and a loose-fitting tunic, I might remake myself in minutes. Rummaging through the cupboard, I found the old soft velvet hat he had worn on our walks together in Hoorn. I nipped away the thread that held his guild medallion, knowing I could stitch it back when I returned, tied up my locks and stuffed them inside the hat.

I looked in the glass beside my cherrywood cupboard and smiled in spite of the gale wind that was my heartbeat this moment. It was Willie van Pelt and the breeches all over again. When I was twelve, I'd finished my six years of schooling, all that girls received then, and vowed to find my way to further learning at the boys' school. I borrowed Willie's breeches from the clothesline behind his house, cut my hair and slithered through back alleys to climb through a low window into the last seat in the boys' schoolroom. I remember hiding my face in a new Atlas from Bleau's of Amsterdam. Of course, I was found out instantly, shaming my father, and making me the butt of jokes and catcalls from every boy in the school. When Papa pulled off my cap, one of his, and saw what remained of my golden curls, something akin to the dying stalks of an autumn grain field, he turned purple with rage and called me the most defiant child in Hoorn...in all of Holland. His words thumped heavy as the clang of the smithy's anvil in a shop just behind the school. I don't pass a smithy's shop to this day without thinking of Papa's cadenced condemnation, or Willie's breeches and my pitifully shorn locks. But that was then and this was now and Willem wasn't my father, and my need gnawed at me hour on hour. I saw no other course.

I took another turn, looked again at the glass. What *would* Willem make of my masquerade?

I stepped with caution up the garden walk, peered round the open gate and with no one about, sped up the street and round the corner certain I'd not been seen.

Willem was not in sight when I posted myself at the foot of the bridge over the Bourse's water entrance. A clutch of boys ran beside the water, chanting *stroke, glide, stroke, hide.* I walked nearer them to watch a small boat with wares from one of ships in the harbor row toward the Bourse. A pair of wooden panels under the building pulled back and the boat, mast lowered, flowed into a tunnel built beneath the stone bridge where I'd been waiting.

I walked back toward the bridge where I was to meet Willem when I spotted him rounding the corner from the direction of the Weigh-House. He walked with a tall, dark man, Willem's hands punctuating his words like a flailing windmill, the other man's arms locked across a chest heavy with gold chains. They stopped, shook hands, and Willem pointed toward the Bourse wall where I waited in the shadows. He walked my way, his eyes searching the crowd. I strolled up behind him and tapped him on the shoulder. "Which first, food or business? I understand the Bourse is only open for two hours."

He whirled around, blinked and lowered the brim of his hat to shade his eyes. "What?" He squinted. "Lord above. It's you. It is you?"

I grinned. "Marteen Boscher, trader's agent, ready to serve you." I couldn't resist the playful moment, knowing what serious business lay ahead.

He shook his head and grinned. "You are quite a woman, *Sir*. But why?"

Keeping my back to passersby, I explained to him that I must enter the courtyard and visit the alcoves and the second floor shops to hear the trading for myself. My father would accept nothing less, he tells me constantly to think first, then act. "That, Willem, is what I do this moment."

My eyes roved over the clusters of men gathered near the entrance, awaiting the strike of noon and their assault on profit or loss. A cacophony of numbers, laughter and blasphemy filled the air. Willem pursed his lips, some discomfort I suspected, at my woman's ears hearing such words.

I touched his arm. "I know you bring me news of the boat yard inheritance, but…"

"The news is good, in your favor."

My shoulders sagged. "Such a relief. There is more to discuss, but later, before we part today."

He was about to speak, to ask me, I'm sure, what else might be so important. But the great clock tower above us struck noon, and the groups surged forward, a helter-skelter confusion of pushing and shoving, further talk impossible. I began to understand why women were excluded. Amsterdam's middle class of merchants left gentility under the entrance arch, each man now for himself. When we gained entrance, Willem pulled me to the side away from the fray.

"We'll mingle after this crush finds the punters they want. You'll see them settle here in the courtyard." He pointed to the glassed enclosures above a colonnaded arcade. "Those are just shops, the real business is done right here in the open."

I nodded, my head pivoting right, left, then back again, breathing in the aroma of pickled herring, tar and beer from the stalls on the Dam behind us. So much to take in, so much money changing hands and not a piece of goods to be seen, a market of men and money only, no merchandise. Papa would see it as a riot of risk, adventurous greed. My picture to him must be painted in far different tones.

"Willem, look at that poor soul." I nodded toward a man standing just off from a cluster of burghers. He gnawed on the knuckles of both hands, tears on his cheeks, and a fidget in his step like a child in need of the pot.

Willem laughed and turned his back so the man couldn't see his mirth.

"A charade. He wants the merchants to see he's at his wits end, that he's ready to take any deal. You'll see many such bits here."

We moved through the crowd. When I caught a fragment of interest, I'd touch Willem's arm so we might stop near enough to listen.

A burgher, black from hat and cape to the boots that shod his feet, pounded the chest of a roughly dressed punter. "Five hundred florins. Not a piece of silver more."

"I can get six."

"Then take it."

"You'll lose your place for this load. This is the final share."

The burgher, face flaming, fingered the small knife sheathed at his side. "You push me to the wall." He handed the punter a small leather sack. "Six, damn you."

I stood tense during the brief transaction between the men, and moved closer to Willem. "Is it always so dramatic?'

"Mostly. The coin here is information. That's where you get the edge in any deal." He pointed to man reading from one of the state courants about ship movement, and then to another man pulling the latest courant page from a punter's hand. "See how they joust for the latest bulletin?"

My head spun dizzily, trying to sort out and relate to what I'd seen along the city's docks, how it might change the future of our Hoorn boat yard. An undertow of change swept along our seaboard, keenly real to me each time I visited the dock area. River traffic sailing in from the sea swelled by the week, and so did the yards that maintained these trading fleets. The reason swirled before my eyes at this very moment, every merchant, every burgher with a florin to spare dealing to buy or sell a ship's cargo.

Papa suggested as much on my last trip home. "Klemp told me yesterday that the VOC thinks to close its main office here...move everything to Amsterdam." He rubbed the back of his neck, stiff I thought from worry. "Even grandfather might kneel to the weight of that shift." He carried the burden of the legacy, a constant stone on his back.

Like everyone whose life was wed to the sea, my father set store by the VOC. Growing up in a port town, we learned young that the East India Company's moves foretold how well we might live in the months to come.

"But Papa," I tried to reason that day, "even if the VOC and its long haul ships leave here, we'd still have the Baltic and Mediterrean traffic. Klemp looks to rethink the VOC's future. Should we not look in new directions as well? Trade, perhaps?"

Papa took my hand, looked me full in the face. "No sophistry, Maagda, no tricky words. Thought, not haste."

I knew now Papa was wrong. Yes, think it through, but with haste. What else did I see around me at this very hour, in this foment that was the Bourse. My head cleared. I knew now I could not remain in Amsterdam. The boat yard's future taunted me. I had to be there. This adventure, or misadventure of mine today with Willem sealed my course for the future.

Willem had wandered a few yards away, speaking with a punter. He caught my eye and returned to my side.

"I must speak to you of my marriage, of ending my marriage."

His eyes widened, and he shook his head as if to dust old thoughts away.

"I'm not overly surprised, certainly not after you had told me before you were ready to stay in Hoorn, alone."

I nodded affirmation. It would embarrass me to speak the truth of my marriage to Willem, but I was without choice now. I had not realized when I dressed to masquerade my way into the Bourse, and it may be nothing but my own trivial fancy, but my costume made it easier to bear the shame of such a conversation with Pier's own cousin.

We were like a chess game now, Pier and me. Who might check and how soon? I must depend upon Willem and the law to clear the board.

*"For what is more foolish than for a man to study
nothing more than how to please himself?"*

In Praise of Folly by Desiderius Erasmus (Classics Club edition)

CHAPTER 27—PIER

THE LAMB FILLED EARLY. A CLOUDBANK OF PIPE
smoke layered down from the ceiling, a mix of tobaccos flavored
with everything from aniseed and thyme to lavender and nutmeg. It
gagged me and made it hard to search out van Goyen. I recognized
one of the burghers he drank with earlier in the week. I edged over
to a row of musk-smelling barrels along the sidewall where I could
watch the door. No ale for me tonight. Just cider. Couldn't afford to
muddle my thinking.

Van Goyen's cronies spied him before I did. They hailed him
when he pushed through the heavy oak door. I sagged in relief, but
fought the urge to buck the crowd to where he stood. Let him greet
his cronies first, settle in.

After the artist took a second healthy pull at his ale, I walked
toward him. I wanted to approach him full face, give him every
chance to remember me.

"Ho, Pier," he called. "You made it. Good. Come meet my friends."

I waved to him, so relieved I tightened my grip on my tankard for fear of dropping it. .

Van Goyen introduced me as his jeweler friend. Old Steubing should hear that!

The men greeted me and went on with their talk of the meeting ahead, speculating on which bulbs might sell tonight. One of the burghers poked another and asked if his herd soiled the street outside. All doubled in laughter. I was lost.

Van Goyen saw my puzzled look and said, "Pier, last week a pound of White Crown tulips sold for 600 florins to be paid when the bulbs were delivered. But the buyer had to add four cows to the deal to be delivered the morning after the meeting."

His story stirred another round of guffaws. They laughed, but my throat tightened. I was beyond my reach here. Couldn't back out now though. I'd make van Goyen look a fool to have brought me.

"What's a man like me to do when he doesn't own a bit of livestock?"

"Diamonds 'ill do," a short burgher in the corner shot at me. Again everyone rolled in laughter.

There was a heavy thump, thump at the back of the tavern. "It's time, gentlemen," someone shouted over the din.

Chairs scraped as the men gathered hats and tankards to move to the college. I sensed a change in the buzz of the tavern. Laughter leveled off to a mood of attention. Amsterdam's monied burghers filed into a large room. They pointed out sellers and murmured the names of bulbs. I heard Viceroy, Centen, Semper Augustus. Such high flown names for a flower.

Van Goyen pushed next to me. "Pier," he said, "unless you're prepared for your first plunge into the market, you might merely watch and listen tonight. Pay attention to which bulbs fetch the highest prices. The delivery dates. How much is expected to be paid tonight, how much on delivery."

"I'll watch." The action moved fast. There was a system, but I couldn't follow it.

Van Goyen was a skilled guide. "Some of the sellers auction their bulbs. They begin with a high price and lower it until someone makes a reasonable bid," he said. "Everyone bets that when these bulbs are lifted in June, they'll triple, maybe quadruple what someone paid tonight."

I felt like a cat cornered in a dog's domain. But I soon realized the buyers were a mix – burghers, commercial men, growers, landowners, even farmers. One man bid coinage along with a suit of clothes in payment. Another bid wheat and rye and still another, a team of oxen. One burgher offered a track of land, and another, a thousand pounds of aged cheese.

Van Goyen told me he'd used his own paintings to pay, along with two gold drinking vessels, family heirlooms.

"Was it worth it?"

His face creased into a grin.

The pace in the room picked up, became feverish. Wooden discs passed hand to hand with numbers chalked as a possible bid. When a price was struck, buyer and seller disappeared into the smoky haze at the back of the room to haggle the final details. Van Goyen whispered that if the pair didn't reach agreement, the chalked bid was wiped out, another put in its place. Then the disc moved back through the buyers for another go.

"Do you buy tonight?"

"Can't. I've got more tulip paper than assets to back it," he said. "I'm holding tight for at least a month, then I'll put some of my paper into the action. I need one or two good returns so I can cover myself."

Van Goyen's paper might be my entrance into the market. I'd rather buy from him than try to enter this fray. I asked if he'd sell to me.

"No thanks, Pier. I learned early on not to deal privately. If a bulb turns out sour, the buyer holds you responsible even though you're not the grower. No, I want to sell on the open market. And that's how you should buy if you intend to trade. Listen close to which bulbs fetch the best prices tonight, then decide what you want and how much you're willing to put on the line. Think assets, not all cash."

The frenzy ebbed. Wooden discs were wiped clean. Pairs moved away from the crowd to sign papers, their bargains struck.

The flurry, the pace, the sheer nerve of these trades left me drained. Never had I seen so much of value change hands so fast. All for something that lay under common dirt that just might become the most sought after flower in Holland. I shook my head and thought of the merchant who put his shop on the line tonight. That was balls, or stupidity. Made me wonder what kind of streak ran in us Dutchmen to make us such willing gamblers.

Van Goyen invited me to join his group for another drink. I said no. Told him I had too much to think about.

"There'll be another meeting two weeks from tonight," he reminded me. "Maybe you'll take your chance then." He turned back to his burgher friends.

When I stepped outside The Lamb, the day's cold drizzle had stopped. A chill north wind blew the sky clear. Stars looked like some of Steubing's best cut stones. A good sign, I told myself, whistling down the alleys toward home.

Now to find the assets that would buy me into this quicksilver market. What can I put on the line? What can I sell? If I used the dowry money, I could return it from my profits with neither Maagda nor Lars the wiser. A thought.

Damned if the excitement didn't arouse me. I felt myself harden and thought of crawling into the warm bed with Maagda.

"Let Folly be her own trumpet…"

In Praise of Folly by Desiderius Erasmus (Classics Club edition)

CHAPTER 28—MAAGDA

"PIER, LOOK, LOOK HERE." I STOOD BY THE OAK TABLE and waved the paper as Pier came in the side door. Maintaining civility with him these days took every shred of patience I possessed, and there was little enough to go round, but I had to play the wife until Willem had my questions to him answered beyond doubt.

"What do you go on about, woman?"

"Papa comes. He wants us to meet him at the docks, down beyond the Dam. He promises a surprise for us. How exciting that he visits." My father had little enthusiasm for Amsterdam and rarely set foot in the city. As buoyed as I was by his surprise visit, another part of me twitched with an uncomfortable curiosity and foreboding about what his visit brought. My father was a dreamer, hardly a man of mercurial turns, but events of late, his health, the truth of Pier's plan, were enough to send the strongest among us into uncharted waters.

Pier tossed his coat to a hook beside the door. "Too bad. Tell him I bid him well, but I don't have time for morning dallies. I work, you know."

"Mr. Steubing is away." It was an expected response from Pier. I jollied him for my father's sake. "You put in long hours. Surely for one day you can open the business an hour late. Besides, Papa says this surprise is for you."

"The only surprise Lars has for me is a kick in the arse. Now that you've told him I mean to move us abroad, I'm as much in his favor as a trot to the privy."

I bloodied my lip in an effort not to smile. "Aren't you curious?"

He looked at me, a long measured look, his jaw off center. "Is this something you and your father hatched?"

These days he was suspicious of everything.

"Who knows what his visit means?" I shoved the notepaper across the table to him. Henrik had left the message under the door late last night. I found it just before Pier came home late and pushed me to the sleeping couch. There was to be no more of that. He scoffed at my *no,* but knew I would not create a scene with Bjorn in the house. It was quick. I spit him out like a dose of curdled cream.

Pier took the note from me and read it aloud.

Dearest Children. I'll embark at the main quay in Amsterdam tomorrow morning about nine. Sorry for the short notice. Ship finished sooner than expected. Important Pier be there. I have a great surprise for him. I'll wait for you at the chandler's shop. Please go right there. With deep affection, your Papa.

"Children, indeed." Pier sniffed and reached for his warm morning ale. He asked why I hadn't told him about the visit when he came home last night.

My face flamed. "You hardly gave me time for talk."

He smirked. "Okay, I'll go to the dock, but only an hour, mind you. Steubing might as well be here the way his cronies follow my comings and goings. I think they send pigeons to tell him what I do."

Our chatter awakened Bjorn, who came down the steps rubbing sleep from his eyes. "What's all the excitement?"

"An adventure, old man. Grab your coat and join us. Maagda's father sails to town this morning with a surprise. We're to meet him at the quay."

Bjorn hesitated. "Sounds like a family outing to me. Maybe I should wait and find out about the adventure later."

Bjorn's sensitivity took me by surprise. I'd grown accustomed to Pier's blunt rejoinders. Why could my husband not realize that some of life's most treasured moments, like today, should be shared by a precious few

Pier couldn't contain his cynicism. "Nonsense, Bjorn." He handed the Swede a tankard of heavy, dark ale topped by creamy foam. "If my father-in-law comes to town, it's an event. We must greet him with our full army, all trumpets blaring."

Not attuned to Pier's mockery, Bjorn's eyes appealed to me for guidance.

My father was the most important issue here, and I needed time alone with him. I must tell Papa about my scheme for the Yard, for trading, my talks with Willem. I'd best keep Pier in a good humor, and maybe Bjorn would distract him enough for me to speak with Papa.

"You're welcome to join us, Bjorn. I'm sure my father will be pleased to meet you. He follows the war. He'll want to hear of your exploits."

Pier had brought home some of his favorite Leiden cheese laced with cumin. Folly wrapped herself around my legs, hoping for a tidbit. I broke off a morsel, which she ate from my palm, purring in gratitude. I placed the cheese plate on the table along with thick, dark bread for Pier and Bjorn, and moved away to tidy the room.

Would Papa come back to the house? He would expect a bright, clean home. I didn't want to disappoint him. Papa always joked that cleanliness was bred into Dutch women. I wouldn't mind Papa seeing our place now.

The room had a small charm about it now. I'd cleaned and polished the old wooden floor and Pier laid an entry of black and white tile squares at the door. The atmosphere welcomed, warm and homey, with walls whitewashed and bright flowered curtains at the casements. In my wanderings through the marked I found the odd bit of colored glass. These bottles and jugs sat in the windows to catch the sun and reflect their reds, greens and ambers on the clean walls.

To keep a touch of my real home, I'd hung a stormy seascape of Hoorn harbor. The painting caught the eye as soon as you walked into the room. I'd placed it on the wall directly opposite the door. The artist had painted the scene as if he sat in a skiff on the sea looking across a fleet of galleys and small fishing boats, all with sails unfurled to catch a breeze that would carry them into the quay. The waters roiled, flags and pennants atop the sails waved outstretched to show the westward path of the wind. Sometimes when I was lonely for Hoorn, I'd stare at the picture and could almost hear the ship's bells ring and the pennants snap.

"Let's go."

Pier jarred my reverie. I didn't need a second invitation. I longed to see Papa. Had Miekke come with him? I needed time with her, too. She must be part of anything we planned for the Yard, and it was none too early to plant the seeds of change. Over the years I'd come to realize that the longer people mulled a thought, the more they came to accept it as their own.

We walked the short distance in a brisk twenty minutes, and as we turned the last corner to the wharf area, I recognized my father's tall frame bent over rolls of cables near the first of the dockside shops, a shorter man at his side.

"Pier, look. Isn't that's your Uncle Freddy there with Papa." The two men in the distance waved to a short figure of a man walking inland from the dock.

Pier followed to where I pointed. "Damned if it isn't." He whistled. "That old dog. So that's the surprise." Pier laughed and ran ahead to wrap Freddy in a bear hug. The startled man stumbled backward.

Freddy's broad-brimmed hat fell off and rolled close to the water. Bjorn scooped it up before it sailed over the side.

Papa clutched me in a warm embrace and kissed my forehead.

"Papa," I stepped back. "Let me look at you."

"I think you'll find me fully assembled, every part accounted for." He laughed, and I could detect no difference from my last visit to Hoorn. Perhaps his hawthorn berries worked.

I looked around. "Where's Miekke? I thought she might be with you."

Papa said he and Uncle Freddy traveled to Amsterdam only for the morning. The Yard needed rigging and couldn't wait for it to be sent up to Hoorn. "Would delay our promised delivery of the new ship," Papa said.

I held his arm. "Was that Klemp walking off just now?"

"Yes," Papa said. "He sailed in with us. Looking for space here in Amsterdam."

A tinge of fear swept me. Already the VOC prepared for change. I wanted to say something about my meetings with Willem, but Papa looked to Bjorn who stood quietly in the background. Pier made the introductions.

"From the war, heh? We must talk. I want to know more about what that Swedish king of yours thinks to do."

Pier turned to my father. "Lars, it was good of you to bring Uncle Freddy. We haven't seen each other in years. A fine surprise."

Papa laughed. "I thought you and Maagda might be happy to see this fellow." He reached for Pier's shoulder. "But Freddy is not *the* surprise." My father grinned like a schoolboy caught with a forbidden sweet. Papa put his arm around Pier's shoulders and started to guide him away. "Come."

Papa's arm around Pier's shoulders? Did an alchemist throw a spell over my vision? I shook my head in disbelief, expecting to hear a rattle of something loose within. I couldn't fathom what to expect.

We walked away from the shops and skirted the rim of the quay. Every berth was packed with cargo ships. I wanted to point these out to Papa, mention the cargo, the future trades, but with so much activity, we had to watch every step and I couldn't move far enough from the others to speak privately. Men wheeled barrels to and from the vessels; huge nets swung cargo from the decks quayside; workers shouted guidance to the hands above. We stepped around coils of rope, stacks of boxes and barrows of goods waiting to be moved. I walked this way many afternoons of late to learn what the ships hauled. So much to discover.

Papa took notice. "A busy place, eh? We could use more of this in Hoorn."

A hundred yards upstream, a three-mast schooner lay on her side atop smaller boats that kept her afloat. A crew of fitters scrambled around the ship's bottom to scrape barnacles and replace rotten planks. One man fanned a flame pot where pitch heated to coat and reseal the hull. Good money in that, too, I'd heard. Every ship returning from a long voyage needed a complete overhaul. So many new ways to think of keeping work in Hoorn.

When we reached a small clearing amid the ruckus of the dock, Papa stopped. Pier stood with his back to the water. Papa asked him to turn around.

"Son," he said, "the real surprise is here."

Son? Papa called Pier son? Not in these two years had I heard such a thing. I was stunned. Pier gasped. The morning raced beyond my comprehension.

We followed Papa's gaze to a fluytship, its barrel-shaped hull moored directly in front of us to run parallel along more than a hundred feet of the quay. Harbor water slapped the boat to rock it in a gentle sway.

"Step back," Papa urged and pointed forward to the bow. There on the top of the hull, just below the deck in ornate gold letters, the word *Veerbeck*. Our collective breaths escaped in a great whoosh of air. Pier blanched. I stood rooted in disbelief; I grabbed his arm for support. He trembled under my grip.

Uncle Freddy later confessed he knew the secret, but still, he seemed ecstatic. He slapped Pier on the back. "Oh, you most fortunate of men." He beamed.

Papa studied our faces. He glowed, clearly satisfied with our stunned reactions.

My eyes fogged like I waked dazed after a sleeping potion, that I watched a pantomime played with strange actors. Only weeks ago in Hoorn Papa shouted and railed against Pier's plan to emigrate. Now, suddenly, Pier was son? Papa's newest ship to bear the Veerbeck name? Had the hawthorn scattered his wits?

"Come. You must inspect your ship, Pier." Papa stepped toward the gangplank.

Pier hung back, yet to find his voice.

"Come, come," Papa said. "We haven't much time. We run too close to the tide."

We followed Papa up the narrow walkway and clung to the thick rope railing. He pointed out the design changes on board the *Veerbeck* that made our fluytships unique. Three masts carried sails to power the fluyt. Papa's hand swept the hull, showing its extraordinary length. A vast storage hold lay below the deck.

"See there, the low prow? This design reduces wind exposure." Pride swelled in Papa's voice.

Pier had yet to utter a word. His head turned fore and aft, taking the measure of the boat, his face gray as peat ash.

"What kind of voyage is the ship designed for?" Bjorn asked. I had forgotten his interest in maritime commerce.

"The fluyt has a shallow draft," Papa said. "We can maneuver in tricky harbors like this, but they're mostly used for Baltic and Mediterranean ports. Takes a small crew, maybe 20 to 30 men at the most. Depends on the cargo."

Pier gripped the rail as if tarred to the wood. I stood numb between him and Papa, unsure what words to utter.

But Bjorn seemed intrigued, asking questions about the ship's structure and what it hauled.

"Mostly grain from the East. See these bulging sides? Plenty of storage. The buyers here warehouse the grain until prices go up, then put it on the market for huge profits."

Yes, Papa, I thought. And we should be garnering some of those profits.

Bjorn whistled.

"Some laugh and call the fluyts big tubs. But that tub design saves substantial taxes."

Bjorn stepped closer to Papa, listening. Pier drifted away toward the rail.

"We have to pay to use the straits between Scandinavia and Denmark. The tax is figured on the ship's deck space. With this new design, the deck's small. The big portion of the cargo stows in the hold below." Papa stomped on the deck.

Pier had yet to say a word. I tried to read his face. Shock or rage, I could not fathom which. Nor could I harness my own senses. I was as stunned as I knew Pier must be.

Papa ushered us into his cabin for ale to celebrate the new ship.

"To the *Veerbeck*." Papa raised his roemer in toast. "And its new owner."

We all followed his gesture toward Pier, our glasses clinked.

I'd begun to think this was another dream.

Papa turned to my husband. "So, Pier, what do you think?"

Pier stammered. "I... I don't know what to make of all this."

We emptied our roemers, and Papa turned again to Pier. "Let's you and me talk." Bjorn moved to leave, but Papa waved him back to the table. "You all stay here. Pier and I will walk on deck."

"Uncle Freddy, what goes on here?" I said.

He flushed, apparently embarrassed. "Maagda, dear, Lars explained it to me as we sailed over this morning. But I don't see it my place to say a word."

While my father and Pier talked privately on deck, I chaffed that Papa didn't tell me of his plan. What hope had I now of my thoughts to trade? My talks with Willem about the inheritance, the future of the Yard, suddenly as empty as the roemers on the table.

The cabin door flew open and Pier slammed it with gale force fury. "You. It's your fault," he shook his fist at me. "You connived with him, put him up to this."

Papa stood behind him at the door, gray as harbor fog. Uncle Freddy's head snapped up.

"I won't have it," Pier shouted. "I won't be trapped here." He bounded from the cabin and I heard his feet pound down the gangplank. I called after him, but he'd fled.

"Papa. What happened? Are you all right? I've never seen Pier like this."

"I failed," Papa uttered. " I did try to trap him, with generosity. Instead, Pier caught me at my own dissembling." He groped for a seat. Whatever was exchanged between them left my father crumpled in a breathless heap.

He reached for my hand. "My darling girl. I thought I did something good for you. But I think I've made matters worse. Foiled by my own selfishness." His effort to speak made him cough, gasp for air.

From the corner of my eye, I caught a glimpse of Bjorn slipping out the door.

I squeezed Papa's hand. "Catch your breath. Then for God's sake, please tell me what this is about."

"Lars," Uncle Freddy asked. "Want me to leave?"

"No, no Fredrick. You may as well understand the whole of it as well. I told you only part of the story."

Papa, his hand trembling, poured more ale in the three roemers and told of the scheme he'd hatched to keep Pier and me in Holland, in Hoorn. When he learned that Uncle Freddy knew nothing of Pier's plan to emigrate, Papa related what I had told him during my last visit.

"He wants to leave us? I can't believe Pier would think such a thing." Freddy got up from his chair. "For years he talked of nothing but buying land to farm. I always...we all thought...good god, that he meant here, here in Holland."

Papa's eyes brimmed. "I thought if I turned the Yard over to Pier, gave him ownership with a trust for Miekke, he'd jump at the chance to be his own boss. Earn a fine living for you both. I was dead wrong. Pier wants land and he wants freedom and he sees the New World as the only place he'll have both."

He took both my hands in his. "This fluyt was to be called the Maagda. But I thought that once Pier saw the name *Veerbeck* on the bow, he'd grasp what his future could be. I used it as bait. The ship was meant to honor you both and keep you here."

"You offered him ownership?"

He covered his face. "I've made a horrible mistake, Maagda. Yes, ownership, but with the proviso that the boat yard must stay in the family. Only god knows to what extreme I've pushed the man now."

I panicked. My stomach cramped. Pier would never budge from his plan to leave after this.

"Papa, we must talk." I gripped the chair. "I've thought of nothing but you and the Yard since my last visit. I have a notion..."

The door opened. "We have to leave, sir," a seaman called in. "The tide pulls fast. We've got to cast off to beat the ebb."

Papa jumped up. "Come, Maagda. Run for the quay. We'll talk another time."

I moved quickly, but my thoughts raced into a corner where I'd be trapped between what my father might do and what I knew I must do. Willem's papers. I had to place them in my father's hands. But they needed explanation. I couldn't merely pass them on and run from the ship.

If only… Papa pushed me toward the gangplank. Too late now. I ran down to the dock.

"Maagda, over here."

Bjorn lounged against a dockside stanchion near the stern of the boat. The sight of him, hatless, his thick tangles of blond hair ablaze in the sun, sent unexpected warmth through my trembling limbs. When he reached out his hand, I took it like a drowning sailor. I tripped on a hawser and sagged against him for a moment, but got hold of myself and stepped back. His warmth steadied me.

"For what is there at all done among men that is not
full of Folly, and that too, from fools to fools?"

In Praise of Folly by Desiderius Erasmus (Classics Club edition)

CHAPTER 29—PIER

MY RUN FROM MAAGDA AND HER FATHER COOLED
my rage, but I was winded and needed a drink. I slumped into The
Black Lamb, dropped into a chair and sank my head down onto my
arms. I moved only to pull a draught from my tankard of ale, glad for
the morning quiet of the place. The tavern barely stirred this early in
the day, the only sound the rustle of the barkeep's broom on the oak-
planked floor. I rested for about ten minutes, my head coming clear.
A footfall approached.

"Ah, I hoped I might find you here."

Bjorn stood over me. I motioned for him to take the other chair.

"What in Augustus' name happened back there?" Bjorn sat. "I've
never seen a morning fly from celebration to chaos so fast."

"I'll tell you what happened." I straightened and looked at him.
"My father-in-law just tried to buy me. No, make that *tie* me, tie me
to his little fiefdom in Hoorn. And my beloved wife stood by to egg
him on. Probably schemed with him all along."

Bjorn put his hand on my shoulder. "I think not, Pier. When you left the cabin with Lars, Maagda looked puzzled. She questioned your uncle. Freddy said Lars had confided in him, but he wouldn't tell her. Thought you'd want to give her the good news. He was happy about it. But, I think Maagda felt shut out because her father hadn't brought her into his plan."

"I'll tell you what that old buzzard had in mind. Tried to lash me to his Yard with a mess of legal knots. Sure, he gives me the business. But I must sign a paper that said I wouldn't sell it for twenty years and that I'd set aside thirty percent of all profits for my sister-in-law and the rest must go to my children. He thinks she's too frail to ever marry, so her future has to be tied to the boats. And this is after the Stats General gets the bulk."

"You think his offer unreasonable?"

"Damned unreasonable. But worse, he tries to make small of me with those strange words of his. Told me to think of the encomium I'd leave behind. Whatever the hell that is."

Bjorn hesitated, then said, "Means praise or a eulogy I think."

"Worries about when I'll die, does he? The bastard probably can't wait." I crossed my throat with my hand like a knife slicing me. "But here's the real kick in the balls. If I left Holland, the business had to remain with my children who were to live in Hoorn…no matter where I went. And you tell me Maagda didn't put her father up to that?"

Bjorn whistled. "That's a tight bind, Pier. But I say again, Maagda looked as puzzled as the rest of us."

I had no reason not to believe the Swede, but my mind wouldn't settle on it. Ever since Lars dumped that shit on me this morning, calling me son, I smelled something rotten. Son, my ass! He merely greased the skids. Thought he could launch me into the water as easily as one of his ship. I have to admit Maagda did look shocked.

"Did Maagda stay with her father?"

"No, your uncle and Lars had to leave fast. The crew warned them about the tide. They had to catch the surge or be stuck in Amsterdam for another twelve hours."

"What did Lars do after I left?"

"I don't know. I got out of the cabin right after you burst in. Not my place to be there. But in a matter of minutes they were back on deck. The crew threw the hawsers free even as Maagda ran down the gangplank."

"What of my wife? What did she have to say of all this?"

"She watched from the quay until the fluyt sailed out of the channel. She was quiet. I walked her home and came to look for you."

"You're a good man, Bjorn. I can use a friend right now. Have a tankard with me."

Talk with the Swede drained some of the poison in my mind. Though I rankled still that Freddy took me aside on the boat to chide me for not visiting Hoorn since the marriage.

The pounding in my ears, the throb in my chest calmed, but my work called even as I tried to shut all thought out of my head. I should be across the canal at the shop. But I had to get some of this venom out of my gut. I told Bjorn how my dream for a future to own a large parcel of land had started when I was a boy back in Leiden…how I'd plotted and planned to save enough florins to make my move…how I hung around the quay when ships returned to hear tales of life in the new land.

The Swede listened. He nodded now and then, but asked few questions. He let me talk it out.

"Lars' offer of your own business doesn't tempt you at all?"

"Hell, no. His deal ties me in legal knots, and there's too much I don't like here. It gets more expensive to live. And it's crowded. We're a tiny Union, a fragment compared to the countries around us. With that damn war, people pour in every minute. You know what that means? They'll work for a few stuivers to get started. Hurts wages for the rest of us and it'll get worse."

I stopped. "I don't mean people like you, Bjorn. You're here to invest. That's healthy."

He tipped his tankard to mine. "I understand."

It was too late at this point to worry about family privacy, so I told Bjorn we had to sail soon or I'd never get Maagda untethered from her father.

"I know it's not my place to question, but your venture sounds like it'll take a stout bag of silver."

"I don't have enough in my pocket now," I said. "But I think I've found something that will change that."

The Swede's eyes narrowed. I knew there had to be questions in them, but I was not ready to talk about van Goyen and the tulip option however much it heated my blood.

I emptied my tankard. "Got to open the shop. Steubing's spies probably count each grain of sand that I'm not at my bench." I laughed.

I left Bjorn at the tavern and walked across the canal bridge to the diamond shop. For the first time, I noticed that it was a nice day. Good sunshine. No wind. Even the canal didn't stink. The morning had been a blur; I couldn't remember what the weather was when we started for the docks. My gut lurched when I thought of it. Launched a good, loud belch.

When I strolled through the hall at the gem center, I made it a point to wave and say *"Goodday"* to as many of Steubing's fellow merchants as I saw. *Log me in, you old bastards. Let the boss know I'm here to earn my bite and board.*

I set up my work area, then unlocked the safe and brought out the tray with the five March diamonds. Damn, those stones did draw your wind. I'd wager they'd bring more than the 6,000 florins that Steubing expected. More like 8,000 or 9,000 florins. My mouth juiced.

Cold as ice on a January canal these stones, yet they heated my palm. My heart pounded against my ribs. The idea sparkled, clear as the stones themselves. I blew out slowly. Could I pull if off?

Pier, what are you, a sissy-skirt? This might be your last chance. Do it. Now. Steubing'll be none the wiser.

*"What not worse than Divorce would daily happen, were
not the converse between a man and his wife supported and
cherished by flattery, apishness, ignorance and dissembling?"*

In Praise of Folly by Desiderius Erasmus (Classics Club edition)

CHAPTER 30—MAAGDA

AFTER THE SORRY SCENE WITH PAPA AT THE QUAY, I
expected Pier to burst through the door last night still streaming
fury. I was stunned when I heard him whistling a pleasant tune on
the garden walk.

When he entered the house, he kissed me on the forehead and
told me he knew I had nothing to do with Papa's offer. Relief swept
me, but not the relief Pier might read in me. He'd gotten over his
rage, but my senses pulled along different courses. Should I go ahead
with my own ideas, rough though they were, or push Pier to accept
Papa's plan for the present knowing that path fraught with danger.
Which the better to save Papa and the Yard? I feared I'd be unable
to prevent Pier from selling the business before I was ready to make
a decision about a trading venture. Dare I chance it? This was no
time for interminable yeas or nays. The Yard must belong to me in
the end.

Pier seemed excited, fidgety, poking around the room, looking in shelves, lifting lids from pots. After wiping his finger along the edge of the hutsepot and licking the juices, he said, "I'm ready to make a big deal in florins. I'll make that boat yard look like a child's pastime,"

Child's pastime? Geese on a gale a speck beside my flock of questions, but I checked myself. Pier must consider thousands of florins if he thought the Yard so trifling. I said as much.

"I couldn't cut a stone any finer than this deal cuts. We'll be sailing for the New World in six months, maybe sooner."

His face bloomed in a rare smile. He ranted on, salivating over all the acreage we would have, with tales of streams so full the fished jumped into your hand, and enough game in the forests to feed a table year 'round. He threw three cups in the air, tried to juggle them while he spoke, his mood so jovial. One crashed to the floor, scattering pottery shards to the far wall. He glanced at the stairs, uncertain whether the noise had awakened Bjorn asleep in our bed. "No matter. Less to stow." He shrugged and kicked the fragments into a pile.

Afraid to betray my fright, I lowered my eys and reached for Folly who purred around my legs, and I asked him, the merest tremor in my tone, what might provide such grand returns and so quickly.

"Stop fiddling with the damned cat." Pier shoved Folly away. "I've been introduced to a new guild of sorts. Wealthy burghers, landowers. Their trades hold your money only a few months at most, and you sell in your own time. Even weeks."

His words didn't ring true of the Pier I'd seen of late, hording stuivers, secretive about his savings pot. Would he dare risk it? Beads of perspiration tacked down my spine.

"Some kind of trade from the East?"

"You simple woman." He laughed.. "Ships, the only thought that finds space in your head. There's a bigger world, you know." He turned his back to me, saying nothing more.

But frightened as I was, a small smile creased my face. A bigger world than trade, imports? Shipping brought the world to our docks, our markets. I was about to remark on it and to ask more questions, when he shushed me, pointing toward the upper chamber where Bjorn slept. "No more tonight," he said, and left me to gnaw on these meager crumbs.

I dashed off a note for Henrik to take to Hoorn. Considering Papa's declining health now, I didn't want him to worry about me. Pier's anger had ebbed like the tide, I told Papa. He was already harnessed to a new plot. I wrote a second note for Willem in Edam... *Must see you soonest. When are you next in Amsterdam?* I willed an immediate reply.

The questions I considered earlier in the evening about the future of Yard now smoke up the chimney. Pier hastened my decision.

Next morning when Pier slid onto the bench at the oak table for breakfast, I tried to ease talk back to our savings. He waved me off.

"It's too new for you to know, but it's nothing to do with boats." He missed no opportunity to scoff.

"But where's the money to come from to invest, Pier? Our savings?"

"Don't get a bee under your skirts. I'll not use a single florin from the savings pot, or your precious dowry. I have other means."

Where might he find other florins? I started to ask, but Bjorn came down the stairs and Pier cut me off.

"Bjorn, good friend. A fine morning to you. Ready for your grand tour?"

Bjorn reached for the cheese platter. "Grand tour?"

"This is the day Maagda's to show you 'round Amsterdam,"

"Of course." Bjorn turned to me. "How could I forget such a kind offer?"

Sweet figs. Between yesterday at the quay with Papa and now this new money puzzle, I had forgotten Pier volunteered my day to the

Swede. I needed no distractions now. Better I should prepare myself to face Papa, to speak with Willem. But, if I refused to go with the Swede, Pier would press me. Rather than deal with his doggedness this day, I accepted what must be.

Bjorn, sitting with his back to the coals, sliced into the cheese, a hard Edam. Folly left my side and strolled over to purr at his feet. He found a crumb that he placed on the edge of his finger for her to lick. He smiled up at me. "She's a friendly little creature."

"Folly's been a conniving nuzzler since she was a tiny kitten. She craves kind treatment." I shot Pier a reproving glance.

"Folly? Prone to foolishness, is she?" Bjorn tickled Folly in her favorite spots, under her throat and behind her ears.

I tried not to like this man. We were not meant to have a third person in such a tiny house, in such a brittle marriage. For me a lodger meant yet another rift between Pier and me. But I could not help warming to someone who took time for my Folly.

I picked her up and cuddled her, explaining that she was named from my father's favorite book. Folly would have none of it. She leaped down, confident of yet another crumb from her new patron. I laughed at her little disloyalty. She rubbed her head against his boot.

"A book? Don't tell me." Bjorn jumped up; Folly leaped away. "*In Praise of Folly*, yes?"

"Why yes."

"I've read it...many times," He said, excitement glowing in his smile, his eyes. "It's upstairs in my pack. That clever Erasmus goes everywhere with me. His satire forces a knowing nod on every page, reminds me how foolish we are most of the time. And your father reads him?"

I nodded. A comfort akin to home spread across my breast. There was more to this man than an intrusion into our lives. It might not be a chore at all, perhaps even grand to spend a day with a person who read, who might share thoughts about his books. Papa said reading

Erasmus was like a conversation with a well-tuned friend. I missed our Sunday readings. A day of fine talk might not be a trial after all.

Pier sneered. "Ack, even the cat's name comes from your father."

The ice in his voice bade me turn the conversation elsewhere. Pier thought books a waste of time, filling people's heads with ideas that had nothing to do with real life.

I described placed we might visit, telling of markets and guilds akin to the business he planned. He winced when he tugged on his old army coat. I guessed his shoulder was still stiff from his wound. He'd cobbled together street wear from remnants of his uniforms with a few civilian blouses and it seemed one non-military pair of breeches.

He turned to Pier. "With your permission, I'd like to thank Maagda for her time today with a noon meal. Perhaps one of the inns."

Pier agreed so readily, I thought he'd shoo us out the door that moment, eager for us to be off so he might count his coins, his pieces of silver.

I hadn't intended to change clothes, but now that Bjorn mentioned a meal at an inn, I ran upstairs to slip out of my apron and dust cap. Wouldn't it be nice to look like more than a housekeeper for a day? I rummaged through my cupboard for my best cap, a delicate white eyelet, trimmed with a cluster of sunset mauve ribbons that fluttered down the back. I tied it on, felt decidedly brighter. Excitement bubbled through me, tamping down the nagging thoughts of Pier and Papa. I missed being merry, to while away hours with no more intent than a joyous idling of time. When I came down again, Bjorn looked at me and smiled. He noticed.

*"I am no counterfeit, nor do I carry one thing in
my looks and another in my breast."*

In Praise of Folly by Desiderius Erasmus (Classics Club edition)

CHAPTER 31—MAAGDA

A BRIGHT MORNING, SUNNY AND CLEAR, PERFECT
for an outing, perfect for a lightness of spirit after so much inner
gloom.

We sauntered through the market stalls jammed cheek by jowl
so we couldn't determine where one seller ended and another began.
Bjorn hunted out the exotic spices, the gingers, cinnamons and pep-
pers from the East Indies. He picked up a small packet and wrinkled
his nose at the pungent odor of coriander, and marveled that it had
been grown half a world away.

I tipped a tiny bit of the dried seeds onto my thumb and rolled
them between my fingers. "Ack, don't bring so much from your
voyages. A terrible smell, though I know many women favor it for
their pot."

"Now that you say it," a hearty laugh rumbled up from his chest,
"these seeds smell like my old camp roll."

His laughter broke through the fragile edges of our strangeness.

We navigated six aisles of stalls to reach the back of the market where a variety of imports spilled from vendors' stalls, mostly cloth from the Mediterranean and wood from Norway. We wove through a throng of monied matrons, trailed by housemaids carrying their market baskets. The holders of the purse fingered squash and turnips, poked apples and searched through the fresh catch to bypass cod or fluke with the cloudy eyes of yesterday's net.

"Lord, you'd think they bought fine lace instead of bits for the pot." Bjorn raised his eyebrows and smiled, and reached for my elbow to guide me around a barrel of a man trundling a wicker basket of beets through the narrow aisle. A soft touch, and welcome.

I picked up a perfect sweet onion and showed him the surface. "Only a lazy or feeble woman trusts her maid to make choices. For a fine meal food should be unblemished, like this onion, when it reaches the fire." I was tempted to buy the onion, its skin golden, perfect to add deep, rich color to my soups and stews, but this was not a day for onions.

"*Cod cold from this morning's sea... tangy oysters...mutton here... new Goudas...fresh duck eggs.*"

Bjorn bought a pair of apples and a small sack of my favorite treacle cakes, and we found a sheltered bench to sit on and refresh ourselves. He polished the fruit on his tunic before he passed it to me. With my first bite, sweet juices sprayed over my chin and cheeks. We both laughed. He was about to wipe the fruity nectar away with his pocket cloth, but pulled his hand back. He muttered a red-faced aplogy. I dabbed with my own cloth, and he shifted talk to the VOC, telling me that he had pledged funds in a cargo venture and expected a handsome profit.

I thought of Klemp. "The VOC must welcome your investment. They face competition for the flow of florins now."

He nodded, and his excitement stirred me. I yearned for more than my life of cooking and needles. The thrill of commerce nibbled at me almost daily, satisfied only in Hoorn or my conversations with

Willem or Klemp. Even though my *Copper Thimble* kept me agile, trying to outmaneuver the guilds at every turn, such trivial feats hardly inspired the pleasure I read in Bjorn's face. What, I wondered, would this man think of a woman in commerce? We had spoken briefly of my work in Hoorn.

"I yearn to go," he said, "but first I'd like to spend some time with your father."

"My father?"

"Yes. I mean to learn about ships, how they're built, what to look for in a long haul vessel. If my returns build the way I see the future, I intend to own a boat, either alone or with another investor."

He looked around for a place to throw his apple core.

"Here by the lindens. The birds will eat it down to its seeds. If you like, I'll write father to ask if he'll meet with you." My mind conjured a picture of them together in warm, animated conversation, and the image was pleasant.

He agreed, and his eyes sparked with the talk of adventure, and something else I noticed as well. They were blue as the morning sea, but clear, honest and he looked at me with, with…what? A tinge of heat coursed through me, and it was good.

Bjorn tossed the apple cores, wiped his hands and sat down again. "Okay. Where to next?"

The shouts from the hawkers ebbed. Now near noon, shoppers left the market, baskets full, purses empty. Within minutes the great clock on Niew Kerk struck twelve bells. I suggested an Inn on the quay I'd heard of, looking forward to something more enticing than the hutsepot that hung over my own grate. No matter what I added, stew was stew. The palate not only dulled, it shriveled and died.

He jumped from his seat all smiles, all energy and took my arm to avoid a dray wagon that hauled turnips and potatoes out of the market.

The busy middle quay lulled to a bare hum at the noon hour, the only sound the squawk of the gulls fighting for crumbs from the workers lounging to eat in empty barrows or on bales stacked along the dock. Many sat with slabs of hard cheese and dark bread spread in their laps, a tankard of ale close by. No ship horns sounded. No shouting back and forth among the workers. We threaded our way among them, careful to avoid coils of rope, snakes of anchor chain or the splintered wood that fell from dropped crates. The inn, the Galleon, lay ahead to our left. Pier had spoken of taking a meal there weeks ago. I hadn't been away from home for a meal since Papa bought us supper on our visit to Amsterdam to buy material for my wedding garment, a day so hurried there was little time to enjoy the growing town.

When Bjorn pushed the barrel shaped door open, the piquant steam of shellfish in vinegar and spices wrapped round us, quickly firing my appetite. The inn buzzed, oak benches crowded. Serving women in rolled sleeves and aprons darted around, platters heaped high with oysters and steamed fish, faces glistening with heat below caps that tamed damp hair into place. At the rear of the room, vapor rolled from an iron grate where pots big enough for a trap's lobster catch sent steam to the ceiling. We found vacant seats at a table near the windows.

Bjorn ordered a double platter of fresh oysters, and he opened them like he'd been born to the blade. He ran the edge through the bivalve muscle to pop the shell, careful not to spill the tangy liquid. He held the first one opened to my lips and I sucked the oyster and its juices in one sweet and salty swoop. He smiled at my appetite. We attacked the platter like greedy children with a tray of cakes, hoisting the shells to our mouths, sliding the cold meat with its juices onto our hungry tongues. I sucked in my cheeks and pursed my lips. The salty sweetness danced on my dulled palate.

I watched Bjorn guide an oyster onto his tongue. The shape of his mouth, the tip of pink that slipped the oyster from its shell, stung my senses to life. I caught my breath in surprise.

"A piece of shell, Maagda?"

"Yes. Yes. Too many oysters too fast." I sensed a deep pink colored my cheeks.

He rolled another plump oyster onto his tongue, and licked a bit of juice from his own plump lips.

Visions of his mouth on mine, his tongue darting, searching for the silk in my body's hidden places startled me. My hands trembled so I had to put the shell down.

I pointed to our mountain of pearl-lined shells. "Perhaps three dozen?"

"Easily." Bjorn licked his lips to capture the last bit of juice. "Have you eaten oysters roasted over an open fire on the beach? Back in Sweden when we camped by the sea on maneuvers, we'd rake for oysters, clams, too, then build a great fire and let the wood and sea kelp simmer down to hot embers to steam our catch open."

With the mention of his early army days, Bjorn told me about his life in Sweden, how after his parents' death from one of those sudden diseases that sweep over the land, he'd been given a home with an older couple near Goteborg.

"They doted on me and even though I was still a mere child, Aunt and Uncle Teckle treated me like another adult in the house. Never asked me to call them Mama and Papa.

"I think I was wild when I first came to them, frightened and wanting my family. Uncle Teckle read aloud to quiet me. But even better, he gave me a sense of possibility in a world that at best lacked reason for me. That's how I learned to appreciate your Erasmas. He's known well outside of Holland."

I realized but for a stroke of fate, he might have died along with his mother and father and not be seated across from me today. The thought troubled me. I barely knew this man, yet his words, his kindness, the grace of his body, stirred me. I thought again of how I flamed to watch his mouth suck the oysters from their shells. Could this be the same stranger, the intruder, I resented scant weeks ago even yesterday?

I toyed with the cut of sturgeon Bjorn had sliced and served me, large enough to cover half my pewter dish. He devoured the fish as he had the oysters, talking between swallows of his army life.

"Yet you resigned your commission."

"Yes, but remember, Maagda, I was a peacetime soldier. I won't draw a lurid picture, but the carnage I saw sickened me. He slid his knife through another portion of the fish. "One soldier can't make the peace, but I could be one less to do the killing."

"I'm surprised they let you go."

"A wounded soldier's no good to his comrades. Besides, we Swedes weren't officially in the war. But anyone with a whit of political sense would see through our King's scheme. He travels through the countryside, using the name Captain Gars to learn first hand where to strike."

"A strange name for a king."

"It's said he conjured it from the initials of *Gustavus Adolphus Rex Sueciae*, Latin for *Gustav Adolf King of Sweden*. He wanted to fight in the real battles. No hide-behind-the-throne monarch, our Gustav."

Bjorn's color rose. He pushed the sturgeon aside. "No more talk of war. Why taint a fine meal and an agreeable day with such conversation? A man doesn't discuss such waste with a lady. Remember what Erasmus said of war: he called it "A savage thing, more fit for beasts than men, so outrageous it came from the Furies."

At the moment my own furies battled, and he, the center of my storm.

"A prince who, like a fatal comet, is sent to bring mischief and destruction.

In Praise of Folly by Desiderius Erasmus (Classics Club edition)

CHAPTER 32—MAAGDA

"LADIES, PLEASE. YOU MUST HURRY. HE'LL BE HERE any minute."

"Just one or two small tucks." I tried to speak clearly through the pins I held between my teeth.

Madam Janssen's twittering nerves didn't bother me. I still glowed from my happy outing with Bjorn a few days ago. Each sunrise brought a lightness of heart I'd almost forgotten.

"Hurry. Hurry." She bustled from the room, one hand on the cameo brooch at her neck, the other waving a scented cloth in the air.

I giggled.

"Colinda, she'll never make it. That frantic woman'll collapse before the Prince walks through the door."

Colinda laughed and threw up her hands.

"Why'd she get us back here for these changes, knowing the Prince of Orange would arrive at four? She should have sent for us days ago. Here I thought we'd ended our work with these draperies."

"Me, too. My arms ache from all of the hauling and pining and hanging."

Madam Janssen refused to visit Jacob, our cloth merchant, to select a material.

"I don't go the markets, my dear," she informed us. "A task for my girl."

Colinda and I lugged heavy bolts of fabric back and forth from the Damrak to her home, one of the new fashionable houses on the Herengracht. It took three trips before the woman decided on a blue satin with a sheer silk over-curtain. She insisted we find tapestry straps the shade of the drapery blue, even though I'd warned that dyes took different tones from fabric to fabric.

"It would have been so much easier," Colinda said, "if she'd let us do the finishing work here instead of carrying these back and forth every day."

I laughed. "My dear," I drawled with my best Madam Janssen imitation, "It wouldn't do to have this room untidy when my banker husband arrived home to relax of an evening."

Colinda grinned. "What's gotten into you, Maagda? You're full of fun of late. But you'd better hush up. She'll hear you."

I'd been like a tittering schoolgirl after a first kiss since my excursion with Bjorn. But I didn't want to break the spell by talking of that splendid day even to my good friend. I kept to the job. "Madam Janssen's in her own world today, royalty visiting and all. Just look at that crystal and silver."

I pointed to a polished oak sideboard behind an arrangement of stuffed chairs near the fire. Trays of pear quarters layered with Gouda cheese, dainty slices of dark bread and sweet powdered jellies sat before a pair of crystal decanters. She had arranged porcelain plates trimmed in silver along with matching engraved silver knives and delicate white linen hand cloths. Quite grand. I smiled, amused at Madam Janssen's display of finery. If the prince was coming to beg money, the lady made it clear the Janssen's were awash in florins.

"Those silver roemers alone would keep my family in food and ale for a full year," Colinda said. "Imagine drinking from something so rich."

Colinda and her family managed well enough on Pieter's wages at the Elsiver printing house, but she'd made me understand they still needed the extra coins we brought in from our *Copper Thimble* sewing.

I lifted one of the roemers and turned it in the light.

"Do you have silver like that at your home in Hoorn?"

"Lord, no." I laughed. "We lived comfortably. But in that one respect my father is a good Calvinist. Nothing fancy for us. He preferred to put his florins into our future. That's why he paid private tutors for Miekke and me after our six years at the town school."

"Pieter and me want that for our boys. Breeda, too. Have to keep sewing to make that happen though." Colinda waved her thimble clad finger at me. "Wonder why Prince Frederick's coming here. He's not so welcome in this part of the Union."

I rubbed my fingers together. "Money. He needs florins to supply his troops should Spain's Phillip take a hungry look at our southern border again. Papa spoke of it last time I was in Hoorn."

I climbed down from my stool and looked at the drapes. "Colinda, a small tuck there, to your left." She gathered the silk in a few quick stitches. "Perfect. I think we're finished."

We picked up our scissors, thread and the extra material that lay about the floor.

"I wouldn't mind having a glimpse of the Prince." I said. "Madam Janssen said there'd only be two or three in the party."

Colinda beamed. "Wouldn't that be something to tell at home? Maybe we could wait across the canal and see him step down from his coach."

A smile spread across my lips and my cheeks. "I mean close up. Right here, in the same room."

Colinda waved her hand and tapped her finger on my forehead. "I think your stitches have come undone. She'll shoo us out well before Prince Frederick arrives, unless you mean to hide behind the stuffed chairs."

Madam Janssen swept back into the room. She had changed into a billowing white skirt held away from her hips with layers of petticoats, all topped by a scalloped blue overskirt that matched our drapes.

"How lovely, Madam Janssen. The Prince will be dazzled."

"Thank you, thank you, Maagda. Now, away, both of you. We've not a minute to spare."

"We'll be gone in a flick," I said. "We have another order to finish yet today."

Now that the thought of meeting the Prince took my head, it wouldn't let go.

A foolish impulse seized me. The lady turned to leave and I tucked my sewing basket behind the rose covered chair near the fire.

"Maagda, what…?" Colinda was about to retrieve the basket.

"No, no." I shook my head at her, grabbed her hand and started for the door.

"You wouldn't dare."

"Oh, come, Colinda. Where's your spirit?"

We said our goodbyes and crossed the bridge to the other side of the canal to await the arrival. Since this was a private meeting, no onlookers had gathered in the area, and it was mere minutes before the sleek black coach rounded the Prinzenstraat. The House of Orange seal with its trio of rearing lions blazed on the carriage door. The royal Dordrecht coach slowed to a halt just beyond the marble steps of the Janssen house. A pair of perfectly matched black horses knickered, their muscles atwitch after a hard trot. I nudged Colinda and pointed to the white and orange ribbons that fluttered from halters just behind their eyes.

"Oh figs, Colinda. The coach will block our view."

All I could see now were three white plumes moving from the carriage. A pair of tall black hats worn by burghers floated up the steps on either side of the white feathers.

A crowd of youngsters turned the corner chanting "Orange… Orange."

"We followed 'im round the whole horseshoe of the outer canal," one boy boasted. Sweat trickled through the dirt on his grinning face. "Yea, all the way down from the Amstel," another tattered youth said.

"How my boys would love to see this," Colinda whispered. "So sorry we couldn't get a look at him."

"Come with me."

I near dragged her to the Janssen's door and gave the great bronze knocker a solid rap. Madam Janssen's girl swung the door wide.

"Oh, oh, you mustn't come in now."

"I must. We hurried away without our sewing kit and we're to be at another client's immediately."

Still pulling Colina, I shoved past the startled girl toward the loud voices in the reception room to the right of the hall, nearly knocking a bronze horse from its perch on a side table of inlaid marble.

I pushed open the door, my belly fluttering. Madam Janssen's head jerked up, and she darted toward us. "Ladies, ladies. This won't do. You must go. Shoo. Go on."

The Prince, splendid in his fitted black suit and white lace collar, glanced at us. He had removed his soft velvet hat with its white plumes, and his chestnut hair, a mane really, tumbled in long waves around his face. When he looked full at us, his eyes danced with little sparks of light. He smiled at each of us in turn and gave a slight nod of his head.

When Madam Janssen moved again to usher us away, the two men on Prince Frederick's right turned.

"Maagda Boscher?"

Good lord, Klemp from the VOC.

"Maagda?"

"Willem."

My face flamed. Why in a thousand stitches were Klemp and Willem here?

The Prince looked at Willem. "And the lady is?"

"May I present Maagda Veerbeck, my cousin's wife."

I lowered my head and curtsied, but looked up in time to see Klemp grin and shake his finger at me as if to say, *naughty, naughty* to a child.

Willem took my hand and looked at the Prince.

"You'll excuse us, sir?" He ushered me out to the hall, Colinda still in tow, Madam Janssen beside the prince, faning herself, in relief no doubt.

"Maagda, why on earth did you barge in like that? What are you doing here?"

"Colinda and I just finished the drapes in that room. I purposely left my sewing basket behind so I could meet the Prince. Just a lark, Willem."

I thought he'd be angry. Instead, he covered his mouth to stifle a merry laugh.

"What a woman. That is too delicious. I don't know what's gotten into you of late, but I must tell Prince Frederick. He'll be pleased that two charming women created a ruse to meet him."

I introduced Willem to Colinda. Each knew of the other, but had never met.

"May I ask, Willem, why you and Klemp are here. I thought the Prince not so welcome in these quarters."

He told me Klemp represented the VOC, of course, and that the merchant's guild and city regents retained his own legal services. He was to protect their interests when the Prince made appeals for funds. As Stadholder and Chief Magistrate, the Prince had the right to raise money, but the merchants worried he put too much pressure on them, perhaps too eager to cross the border into the German fray. They didn't want the Prince rushing to equip an army.

"Klemp says the Prince pressues the VOC. Their monies to the State have slowed by the month," Willem told us. "This worthless tulip trading."

The VOC again. How tied our little Republic was to the forturnes of its ships and the sea, and my own conversations with Klemp over the past two years fresh in my head.

"Now I must return to my work." Willem smiled. "But I tell you, your little prank brightened a dull day. One more call and one more sweet and I'll swear off food. This is our fifth stop. The Prince means to leave Amsterdam with groaning coffers."

He took Colinda's hand, and then kissed my cheek, saying quietly, "I'll have some news for you in a week. Meet me Tuesday next at noon outside the Bourse…as Maagda."

I hiccupped shallow breaths, but managed to nod; still embarrassed that Willem caught me in a prank for a second time. Though I considered my disguise at our earlier Bourse meeting more necessity than prank.

"I'll fetch your sewing basket and send for a coach to take you home."

Outside, Colinda turned to me. "Now there's a man."

"The Prince is rather grand."

"Goose. Not the Prince. I speak of Willem."

"Willem?"

"If you don't see it, Maagda, so much sewing dulls that needle in your mind."

"I'll be hanged if ye find one half-witted fellow, nay or so much as one quarter of a Wise man amongst 'em all."

In Praise of Folly by Desiderius Erasmus (Classics Club edition)

CHAPTER 33—PIER

THE HOUSE RANG HOLLOW WITH THE SWEDE GONE to Hoorn. Maagda sat in the far corner near the window, layers of cloth scattered round, her face hidden 'neath the tumble of her hair, uncapped for once. She bent over some pearly fabric, pulling a needle and long thread through its folds. She worked hard. I'll give her that.

She didn't look up, kept her eyes on the cloth in, but hummed some merry tune. How long since I seen her so? Surely, not since the Swede arrived. To have the stranger out of the house restored her good humor. Come to think of it, she'd been more relaxed for weeks. And she wears those colorful scarves again.

It occurred to me that we'd be alone here tonight. I warmed at the thought.

Bjorn's trip to Hoorn to shop the boat yard surprised me. That Swede must have one helluva pile of silver if he thought to roll a single trip's profits into a ship. Damn, wouldn't I like to have a bag of silver like that for my own stake.

Everyone's full of surprises. Even Maagda, and more than her recent good humor. She came home the other day excited about meeting Prince Frederick. The Prince yet. All the same, he doesn't amount to much in these quarters. After that pirate admiral, Heyn, relieved the Spanish fleet of its silver shipment in '28, you'd think our treasury would be full to bursting. Ha. I'd show them how to use it. Never anything in it for minnows like me.

"Maagda, I leave for the shop."

"So early?"

"Steubing's still away and the work doubles. I've got special pieces to cut for a London buyer, too." She nodded, picked up her humming and started stitching again before I'd passed the door.

I walked along the canal and glanced at my empty hands. I could feel those five perfect diamonds clenched in my fist. Even the sun played diamond tricks on the waters below me, the ripples a sparkling flock of silver birds...or Steuben's stones. Those March stones would shorten my wait for florins to mere weeks. The thought itched like a flea in my breeches. I kept telling myself there was no point letting good barter lay idle any more than letting a fertile field lay fallow.

Steubing's buying trip was meant to keep him on the road another ten weeks. If I borrowed the diamonds to back my tulip contract, I could have the stones back behind lock and key in short order. He'd never know the stones been at work building my fortune.

My knees wobbled some, thinking of all that could go wrong? The seller might take the stones and sell them himself. What if I picked a bad set of bulbs and the price dropped, though van Goyen said there hadn't been a falling price since he started trading last year.

"Dumkopf. Move. Move," a drayman shouted at me as I stepped away from the canal. I jumped back. My heart hammered and I shook my fist after him. The bastard's left wagon wheel barely missed my foot. These crazy foreigners pushed their loads through the crowds like us citizens were long dead shades. I had to get off the streets, go to the shop, hold those stones in my hand, then my mind would be firm.

The usual two guards stood at the front entrance to the building. The merchants pooled stuivers to pay for round the clock duty. Safety was worth the cash. I nodded to the pair at the door. They never spoke. The old guard, Roop, sat half asleep in a wooden armchair near the back stairs.

His head jerked up when he heard my footfall. "Mornin', Pier. Must be later than I thought."

"No, Roop. I'm early. Got a heavy day."

"You're a good worker, Pier." His head slumped back to rest on his drum of a chest.

Yeah, be sure to tell Steubing, I muttered, and pulled out the key for the shop door. I glanced again at the guards near the front, the building's only entrance. More than once I pondered what might happen if we ever had a fire here.

I'd bought a cold sausage from a cart near the shop. I unwrapped it, perched on my stool and nibbled. A spice seed caught in my teeth. I used my gem pincers to pick it out, all the time staring at the safe across the room where the stones were locked. Four of the five diamonds were finished. I had cut and polished them to a depth that made Steubing catch his breath when he saw the first cuts.

"Pier, you've a talent for this," he said. "You'll soon be the best in the business."

Best in the business. Hah! A pat on the back, but it still took half a stuiver to buy ale. *Save the praise; give me florins.* There wasn't a job in the gem center that paid the wages I needed if I was ever to get off my ass and move.

I looked again at the safe and laughed at myself. I sat like a schoolboy ready to peek at his first naked woman beyond the window, yet afraid to open his eyes.

I wiped my greasy fingers on my shop apron, moved across the floor to the safe, and slid the curved key into the lock. I pulled back the heavy door, breathing in short jerks, and checked that the gems were in place before I lifted the top velvet tray. The five March diamonds looked like North Sea icebergs caught in torchlight.

What am I doing? Pier Veerbeck is not a thief. Easy, easy, Pier. This is not a theft. You don't steal…just borrow. Remember. Just a loan.

I shook my head to clear it and bumped against the safe, and my trembling hands jarred the tray. Oh shit. The tray jumped from my grip, hit the bare plank floor and bounced. The diamonds scattered.

My stomach lurched.

The sausage rose in my throat. I stumbled blindly, my eyes watering so bad from gagging that I couldn't spot a single stone. I clutched the counter and heaved a sour muck. I could feel one hard stone through my soft boots. I cleared the sweat from my eyes. I dropped back, to sit and shiver against the grinding table.

The stones. I had to find the stones. I fell to my knees and used my calipers to push away the remnants of meat, now rancid in the stew of my puke. One. Another. And another. A fourth. Ack. Ack. Where was that last stone? I crawled around the cold shop floor, splinters lodging in my damp palms. Finally, I lit a candle and moved it around inch by inch to light the spaces under furniture. There, under the leg of the safe, the fifth stone. My stomach moved in and out like a bellows.

I wiped the stones clean and returned them to the safe before I went outside to pump water to clean myself. Roop was asleep and the two guards stood at the corner jabbing each other with their long clay pipe stems, arguing over whose turn it was to take a piss. I shook my head and hurried back inside. I locked the shop, took off my breeches and tunic to sponge them. I started a peat fire in the grate, willing the cloth to dry fast. After I washed the stones two, three times, I threw the water over the floor to mop up my mess. The old planks, rough and splintered, soaked up some of the putrid stuff. The shop would stink like a shit hole for days.

I stayed on the floor, the air around me astink with sour meat, an omen for certain, one that stung the hairs on my neck.

"Nor is it to be believed what stir, what broil this little creature raiseth, and yet in how short a time it comes to nothing."

In Praise of Folly by Desiderius Erasmus (Classics Club edition)

CHAPTER 34—MAAGDA

THE LIGHT FROM THE WINDOW WANED. MY NEEDLE and thread lay limp in my hand, the quiet of late afternoon lulling me to half sleep. Stories a sailor returning from a VOC voyage drifted in and out of my half wake, half sleep. He had told Miekke and me of people in the East who kept small, colorful pet birds in cages. In fine weather they'd hang the cages outdoors so the birds might sing. Often, they strolled the streets and parks with their caged pets

The sailor told us he would visit an outdoor café and see caged birds sitting on the tables where their owners sipped tea. In my imagination the birds created wonderful rainbows with feathers in reds, yellows, oranges, bright green, even deep purple, plumage we never saw. Sometimes, he said, the birds' owners would dab a finger with sugar and hold it through the bars so their pets could taste the sweet.

In my innocence, I conjured images of small creatures that reveled in loving care until it came to me that the birds had everything but flight, freedom.

My marriage was no less a cage. Pier tried to hem me inside the walls of his dream. I was a thing to be owned, a pet to kiss the hand that gave me an occasional treat. No more.

My meal with Bjorn at the quay, our talk afterwards, fed more than my palate. He appreciated me as a woman with thoughts of my own. Each time I relived those moments, I'd strain against the cage of Pier's dream. For that one free day, time didn't matter. No Pier, no anger—only the joy of living. And then this morning I awakened from a dream so vivid, the place between my legs throbbed. I couldn't see the man who made it so, but I knew it not Pier.

In a way I pitied my husband. He was tethered to his obsession and couldn't let go. We tilted on a seesaw, Pier and me. Did he never think the ride would end?

"Madam Veerbeck? It's Henrik here." He rapped so lightly, and me so lost in my recollections, I barely heard his knock. I went to the side door to see the carriage driver waiting with a folded paper in his outstretched hand.

"From your father."

"Henrik, can you wait? Papa may expect a reply."

"Sorry, can't do that. I'm not going back to Hoorn right away."

"Tomorrow?"

"No, Ma'am. Town's closed."

"Closed? What do you mean closed?"

"There's a bad sickness. Seems to be spreading. Won't let anyone in or out of Hoorn 'til they know what it is." He turned to his team.

Henrik's words snapped me fully awake. I groped for the chair so I might sit and read Papa's words.

Dearest Maagda, we're quarantined here, but I wanted you to be informed. There's a new illness spreading from the East. One of our seamen returned from a Baltic trip gravely ill. The doctors fear he brought disease back with him. As a precaution, the Mayor has asked that we all remain confined to our homes. The Magistrate has redirected shipping to other ports. You'll see them at your harbor in Amsterdam.

Miekke suffers again, too. We don't know if her malaise comes from this new sickness or her continued frailty. She is fevered and won't take food. The doctor sees her, and Ria tends to her.

Bjorn's been a great help. He, too, must stay until the quarantine is lifted. A good man. He's made many friends here, and I will tell you, he's what I'd want in a son.

Daughter, I know your heart will be with us, but don't try to come here. One ill child is enough. You must stay away; protect yourself.

With deep affection, Papa.

The words blurred through my tears. Not go to them? I must.

I remembered when a plague struck in 1623. Hoorn was spared. Shipping was diverted to Hoorn as Papa wrote it now would be to Amsterdam. Maybe a ship was my answer. Papa knew many of these captains. Surely his name might prompt one kind soul to help me. If I caught a ship going from here north on the Zuider Zee, I might even row ashore at Hoorn.

Maagda, you're being ridiculous.

It was true. A worthless, impractical thought. But I could visit the docks in Amsterdam, hear news from inbound ships. Perhaps scant, but better than no news.

I sat upright with the sudden awareness that my worry focused on a trio of faces…Papa, Miekke and Bjorn. The threat of tragedy forced me put into words a heat that lapped close to the surface of my days now. This stranger, this Swede, claimed more from me than tender sentiment. From the message, I see he's claimed Papa's affection, as well.

I caught Henrik as he jockeyed his coach around to leave.

"What of Edam? Is Edam closed as well?

"No. No sickness there I heard of."

"Can you take me to Edam and back early tomorrow?"

"Why, yes. Not much traffic for me with Hoorn closed up."

I would see Willem and return before Pier came home from work. With the sickness in Hoorn, there was too much at stake now. I must have Willem's papers, a clear legal opinion to guard Miekke's and my inheritance. I prayed also that Willem might have the law's answer for this hopeless marriage.

"...if Men would but refrain from all commerce with wisdom."

In Praise of Folly by Desiderius Erasmus (Classics Club edition)

CHAPTER 35—PIER

WORSE THAN A TEMPEST MAAGDA AND ME, WHAT with the bad news from Hoorn and the town bolted down. With her worries about family, and mine about the diamonds, we snipe at each other every time we cross through the same room.

After today that'll change. The tulip buyers meet tonight. I'd already talked with van Goyen. He'll be there. I'll need a friendly face to pump up my courage, point out tulips worth a bid.

With Steubing away for at least two more months, I had time to make a short trade. Even if I kept a contract for as few as five or six weeks, I'd make enough profit to start trading with my own money. Or so van Goyen tells me.

"Pier, I go to the Damrak. Would you like fresh fish for tonight, a change from our hutsepot?" Maagda waited by the door in cap and apron, a straw market basket slung over her arm. At least she asked what I wanted, a decent sign.

"No. I won't eat here tonight. I have business." I was ready to add that fish was pricey right now. Let her have her little luxury. Once I put Steubing's diamonds in my pocket, could I worry about an extra half stuiver for a cod?

Maagda nodded. I reminded her that I'd leave for the shop before she returned.

When she closed the door, the sudden quiet roared in my ears. I'd like a band of drummers to march through, to beat their skins hard and loud. Maybe drive the silence out through the walls. I needed to leave the house.

I dawdled along the way, poked among the street fruit vendors, stared over the bridge at the canal waters and spat into the filth floating by.

Anything to pass time. I didn't want to be at the shop any sooner than I must, and I didn't care a stuiver what Steubing's cronies thought. If I put those diamonds in my hands before the end of the day, I'd not get another thought into my head.

I passed the sausage vendor. No. Not after last time. I really believed it was the sausages that made me sick. A stroopwaffle instead. A little sweet caramel and sugar never hurt anybody. With my first bite, the white powdered sweet sprinkled down the front of my green tunic, the one Maagda made for me as a marriage gift. It began to wear thin and fray.

At our building Steubing's good friend, Alexander, unlocked his shop door at the bottom of the stairs. He and Steubing played faro with two other gem dealers every Thursday night. I could only guess how many stuivers, even florins, passed in those games.

"Hello, Pier. How're you today? Good news from the north, heh? Guess your wife's pleased. She's from up that way if I remember."

"She is. Hoorn. What good news?"

"They've opened up the town. Haven't had a new case of the sickness in two days."

"Where'd you hear that?"

"Down at the quay. Ran into van Kerk, his first trip from Hoorn since the quarantine. Knows your father-in-law, by the way."

I waved my thanks and ran up the thirteen steps. Might be good to urge Maagda to go to Hoorn. Get her away from the house. I knew my mind would be wrapped around tulips, and I didn't want questions from her.

The shop door swung open. I pocketed my key. The squat metal safe waited for me, baited me. Usually, I paid it no mind. But today the dull box grew like a giant in my eyes, some ogre from a childish tale. It smothered the room.

I stood by the window to finish my sweet cake and watch the gem merchants stream in and out of the building. We had ten dealers in the Center. Each one specialized in either a different stone or a unique cut. Steubing had done business here for at least fifteen years that I knew of. Learned the trade from a family in Belgium. With the war drying up cash buyers, there weren't many foreigners with florins to spare for gems. Most of our custom was local, with a few exceptions from England. The war hadn't touched them. If a buyer did come from a warring province, Steubing insisted they come with a letter of introduction in hand. While he knew they tried to hide their money in gems, he insisted they pay cash, no vouchers. He was a sound businessman. I looked up to him for that. He didn't dance around a deal. He knew what he wanted, and he'd settle for nothing else.

Well, Pier Veerbeck knew what he wanted. Today he would get it.

I dusted the last of the sugar from my vest, wiped my hands clean, then moved across the canted wooden floor. Years of customer traffic cut grooves into the wide oak boards. The day's early sun slanted through the window and hit the pegged planks at an angle. Made the floor look like ripples in a canal, or maybe it was my belly that bubbled.

It's time, Pier.

One quick glance at the shop door to make sure the bolt was in place and I slid the key to open the safe. The black trays sat like militia columns, each part of a troop that marched across the shelves. A regiment of diamonds Bjorn said the day he'd stopped by the shop. I lifted the tray with my five March stones and carried it like fragile glass to the workbench where I examined each stone yet again with my loupe and then placed the stone in the small leather pouch that I'd concealed under my vest. Only one person would see these diamonds this day. That would be the man who sold me a contract on the finest tulips 6,000 florins might buy. My gut quaked.

Fl. 6,000! Pier, how could you forget?

Who would believe the value of the stones without paper to prove the worth? I had to find Steubing's records. His cluttered wooden desk in the back of the shop held enough piled paper and dust to hide a dinghy. For a man so particular about how his diamonds were stored, he paid scant heed to his records. I found a small wooden box in the bottom drawer with his appraisals and receipts. I hadn't thought of the receipt. What would proof of value be without proof of ownership? I took the receipt, dated March a year ago. So that's why Steubing called them the March diamonds.

I stuffed the papers into my vest when I heard voices outside the door. A knock. I threw the bolt and van Goyen and another man I'd never seen before waited in the hall.

"Ah, Pier. Good day to you. This is my friend, Klees, this town's most knowledgable tulip man. Dare we enter your holy of holies?"

First I pushed the safe door closed, then I ushered them to the few chairs we kept in the shop.

"I brought Klees along because he's told me about a very special bulb that might come on the market tonight. Right Klees?"

The other man, shorter and darker than the artist, nodded. His hands looked grimy, as though they were never out of the soil.

"I'm not buying tonight," van Goyen said. "Neither is Klees, but I thought you would be interested."

"I'm a virgin in this market, Klees." I laughed. "I need all the help I can get." I studied his face and asked, "But why are you willing to tell me this?"

"A reasonable question. I don't have florins to buy right now. Maybe in three or four weeks." He leaned with his elbows on the counter. "Van Goyen told me you wanted a short trade. I figured if you took the contract on this new variety, I'd know who had it when I'm ready to buy later in the month. I want these bulbs."

"Ah. And then I have a ready buyer when I need to sell." I was staking all my faith on van Goyen's experience. What else did I have to go on?

"What's so special about this bulb?"

Van Goyen didn't miss a beat. "Color, Pier, color. Hasn't been a thing like it. The flower is so deep a shade of wine, it's almost black. Like an eggplant. It's called the Admiral of Hague."

"A haughty name." But it rolled on my tongue, bitter and sweet, like the tang of new herring and a bit of stroopwaffle.

"It should be haughty," Klees said. "This flower'll pull bids out of a Calvinist preacher. Almost worth as much as one of the broken bulbs that bring color out on a white or yellow background. Any contract on the Admiral 'll turn more valuable by the hour."

By the hour. My mouth swam in its own juices.

"Can you close up early, Pier?" van Goyen said. "We want to get to The Lamb ahead of time. It'll be crowded tonight."

Why not? My time here was worthless now.

The artist knew his market, by god. Burghers, farmers, local merchants, all hurried in twos and threes toward the tavern. It would be hard to find a table. I didn't care. I'd no room for food in my thinking. Klees and van Goyen greeted several men by name, waved to others. The air crackled, a storm inside four walls. I looked around. Burghers usually calm and full of laughter wore flushed faces, their lips knotted tight.

"Look, there's Horder." Klees pointed to a shaggy-bearded man wearing a tattered broad brim, the center of a group of well dressed burghers near the back of tavern. This fellow, Horder, towered over the others.

Van Goyen whispered, "He grows the tulips we're after. Has fields on the south side by the river."

My gut tightened. Buyers surrounded him. They paid court to Horder like he was the Orange himself.

"The word's out," Klees said.

Van Goyen brushed Klees aside. "It's all talk now. The important thing is what happens when the bids open."

Small clusters of three or four moved to the back room. Tables emptied. Chairs were kicked out of the way or clattered to the floor. Men lifted their tankards for a final gulp of ale. No drink allowed in the college.

Buyers talked in the low, steady hum of bees draining honey. Van Goyen told me to grab a stick of chalk from a box by the entrance, then we took seats midway up the room. I searched the crowd for any of the gem dealers from Steubing's place. Couldn't chance one of Steubing's cronies seeing me with gems. But not a face that I recognized. The grower, Horder, wasn't to be seen either.

"Maybe, he won't sell tonight after all," I whispered to van Goyen. If Horder didn't offer the bulbs, I'd have to wait another two weeks to buy and that would cut my deal a whisker's breadth from Steubing's return. I'd miss my chance.

"More likely," Klees answered, "Horder doesn't want to play his hand too early. If he's smart, he'll wait until the small lots of common bulbs are bid and gone. That'll leave the serious buyers for the big plays."

Serious buyers? If I wasn't so damned nervous, I'd laugh. I'd never spent a stuiver in this market and now I was to be a serious bidder?

I twitched like a dog in a briar patch. Bids opened and closed. Twenty-two lots of bulbs passed hands. The buyers who used up their funds moved to the back of the room where they stood and spewed their foul pipe smoke into the air.

"They're up to the Viceroys. It'll be soon," van Goyen said. He pointed to Horder leaning against the smoke smudged wall in the seller's corner. The grower marked his plate to pass among the bidders.

I knew from what van Goyen had explained earlier that Horder would mark a high price on the plate and expect it to be bid down. I could either move to the back and be among the final bidders or mark a price so high that Horder had to consider it.

Horder made his move. He put up a half pound of Admiral of Hague bulbs to be lifted the following June.

Bidders grabbed for the slate, but once in their hands, the action stopped. An sweat of minutes crawled by. Each took his time to study the last bid on the slate, to fathom Horder's price. My fingers twitched so I shoved them in my pockets.

The action stopped when two growers passed the plate back and forth to strike out their bids and enter new numbers. Horder grabbed the plate. "You play here," he hissed. He spit on the plate and wiped it with his palm, chalked in numbers and passed it on. Then the slate sat in my quaking hands. A single number showed.

Van Goyen snatched it from me. "Christ, Pier. You shake so bad, I can't read it." He held the plate at an angle to see it clearly. "Fl. 4,800. Whew. Can you best that?"

"Do you think 5,000 florins?" I whispered.

"An extra two hundred won't stop the bidding. Can you go higher?"

I stalled. Sweat oozed from my back, my arms, my balls. My hands were so wet the chalk slipped in my fingers.

Because the plate had been wiped clean after earlier bids, I had no idea now what Horder wrote as his asking price. According to van Goyen, the bid prices should move down. If the grower scoffed at 4,800 florins , what was his first number? My thoughts froze.

If I risked the entire 6,000 florins' worth of the diamonds, I boxed myself into a corner, because if Horder turned thumbs down, I'd have nothing more to bid.

"5,500 florins?" Both van Goyen and Klees nodded.

I wrote the number. My wet hand left its print on the slate.

Horder looked at the plate. He took a devil's hell of time to follow each stroke of the number with his eyes. Finally, he pointed to the back of the room. I had to will my leaden ass up from the chair.

"Go on," van Goyen urged. "We'll wait in the tavern. You're on your own now."

Horder moved to a dimly lit corner near the door that went to the Tavern's main room. "Let's hear your deal," he said right off. "Ain't seen ya before. Who are ya?"

I told him I was Steubing's man from the Gem Center. Horder's lifted his chin, eyeing me, and nodded. Steubing had a reputation I could trade on. My voice was low and I faced the corner so only my back showed to the other bidders in the room. I pulled the leather pouch from inside my vest and emptied the five March diamonds onto a small square of black velvet in my palm. Horder sucked in his breath, but he hesitated, cautious.

"How do I know they're any good? Might be glass."

"I have provenance." I showed him the papers. Horder held the documents to the lantern. "What's this fl. 6,000?"

"That was the price paid for them before they were cut and polished. Worth another three or four thousand florins now, I suspect."

"Then why do you bid them for less?"

"Because I want them back," I said.

"You what? Want them back? You got a monkey up your sleeve?"

My tunic stuck to my shoulders. Every inch of me was soggy with sweat. *Don't bungle this.*

Horder turned away. "You waste my time," he said.

I grabbed his arm.

"Hear me. I have a buyer who will take my contract in six weeks at the price on your bulbs that day. Then, I'll give you the 5,500 florins and you return the diamonds to me. It's a straightforward, simple deal."

Horder rubbed his neck, stared at me, his eyes narrowed. "Never heard of such before."

"Look at it this way, Horder. During the next six weeks, you hold hard value worth much more than our deal. What's to lose?"

The grower tilted his hat back and scratched the front of his head with the stem of his pipe. "I don't know," he mumbled. "Still sounds like a monkey's in there somewhere."

The deal hung by threads.

"Horder, think." I willed myself to speak like I knew this life of real traders. "You hold the diamonds for the contract, and when I buy them back, I'll add another 100 florins to the price. You get 5,600 florins instead of 5,500."

He pulled his hat back to a spot low on his brow and pushed the paper to me. "Done."

"...in the fortunate Islands, where all things grow without plowing or sowing; where neither Labor nor Old-Age was ever heard of..."

In Praise of Folly by Desiderius Erasmus (Classics Club edition)

CHAPTER 36—MAAGDA

I HEARD A SOFT RAP AT THE DOOR. THE DRIVER, Henrik stood with cap in one hand and a white folded paper in the other. "A note for you Madam Veerbeck. I'll wait."

I poured him a tankard of ale and went to the table to open the paper with its unfamiliar script of large letters carefully crafted.

Dear, dear Maagda. Such sad news to write. Your father died this afternoon. He passed to his Maker in quiet dignity. The doctor said the widespread sickness here had touched him mildly, mild enough for him to get well again. But his weakened heart couldn't survive the burden. I know this is an unbearably sad, tormented time for you. I am so very sorry. Miekke had rallied from her illness, but this blow has returned her to bed. Ria cares for her.

I will wait here to do whatever is required until you and Pier arrive.

These words ring hollow with me, but my heart is full for the sadness that they lay on you.

Lars was a fine man, Maagda. I'm so enriched and grateful to have had these last weeks to know him. Bjorn

A moan tore from a place so deep inside, I thought my body might splinter.

Henrik put his gloved hand on my shoulder. "Sad, sad, Madam Veerbeck. I'm sorry to bring you such news."

Henrik had tears in his eyes. Of course, he'd known what the note said. Bjorn surely had told him. Probably all of Hoorn knew. Papa was loved. So many owed their very living to him.

I gathered my wits and asked Henrik to fetch us in the morning for his first run back to Hoorn. Then I seemed to step through some invisible door where I felt both numb and raw at the same time. Papa's leaving took the shape of my world away. Now, without my old boundaries, my fondest boundaries, I foundered, drained empty. I looked down at my empty hands like they held some trace of my life that had slipped through them.

I was still at the table with Bjorn's note in my hand when Pier returned last night. A piece of stone, I couldn't move back into the world where we, the quick, walked and laughed and sipped each breath of life.

"You sick or something?"

I handed him the paper, my eyes unable to focus through my tears. He came and put his hands on my quaking shoulders.

"Maagda, I am sorry. But this is nature's way. It was his time. Be grateful your father had no long pain."

Yes. Papa would not want to linger, a stranger to himself in illness and a burden to us. I looked up at Pier. "Henrik will call for us in the morning for his early trip to Hoorn."

My husband lifted his hand from shoulder and walked to the fireplace..

"I can't leave here. You know Steubing's gone. It's to me alone to keep the business open."

"You mean you won't close the shop even for my father's death?" I grabbed the table for support. "You can't put a sign on the door, have people return later?"

"It isn't so easy. Besides, there are contracts here that change day by day. On a minute's notice I might need to make choices that involve thousands of florins. I regret it. But I must stay."

"Regret? That is all you can say? You piss on my grief; you are one heartless imitation of a man."

His head jerked round. "I've never heard such talk from you."

"I've never lost my father before."

He threw his hands in the air and walked toward the staircase.

"Come. You're upset. You need sleep." He beckoned toward the bedchamber. "After you rest, you'll see this for the natural way life is, that I am not being unfair."

Did nothing reach or hold this man's heart? My fingers reached for the butter crock on the table. I itched to hurl it at his head. The unfeeling bastard! But I pulled my hand back. Papa would have demanded better of me. Must passion and reason be such strangers?

"Come to bed."

I didn't answer. I had taken the mattress from the sleeping couch to beat it fresh in the small field behind the house. I planned to sleep alone until I had news from Willem and could leave for good, but yesterday's rain had soaked the mattress and I had to go upstairs. We used the bed, each on our own side. The last time to be near him, I promised myself.

I read Bjorn's note once more, and pressed his gentle words to my breast, wishing the paper might be the warmth of his hand.

*If a Man could look down from the Moon and behold
those innumerable ruffings of Mankind, he would think
he saw a swarm of Flies and Gnats…snatching, playing,
wantoning, growing up, falling and dying."*

In Praise of Folly by Desiderius Erasmus (Classics Club edition)

CHAPTER 37—MAAGDA

OUR SMALL GROUP OF FAMILY AND CLOSE FRIENDS
left the ship at the boat yard dock after the brief ceremony that buried Papa in the brine of the Zuider Zee. Mourners who had awaited
our return came forth with embraces and kind words, and walked in
two and threes to their coaches, Ria and me to the mocking silence
of home to tuck Miekke back into her sick bed. Then I told everyone
I would like to be alone, perhaps wonder along the shore. I knew
friends would call at home later, but I needed time to myself.

We had already agreed that we would have food and drink for
visitors, but rather than the late, traditional meal, we would send
most of them on their way with a coin to toast Papa in the tavern.
Bjorn, known to so many in Hoorn now as the fine tenor voice that
joined Papa's rich baritone in tavern singing, would dispense the
coins. I'd been surprised to learn that our neighbors came to regard

Bjorn as family, a cousin or nephew from abroad. I said nothing to dissuade them.

But for the moment, there were sounds to be placed in my memory, sounds that I must hear again in the silence of my own company, sounds I would never forget. The scrape of chains that bound Papa's body to an oaken plank. The grate of wood on wood when his burial board tilted and rocked on the teak rail. The screech of gulls overhead carrying a dirge of their own on a stiff westerly wind. Then, the splash of the sea when the weighted bag split the surface of the water. The words of Klemp's eulogy touched my heart, but the raw sounds of wood and wind etched themselves in my innermost self.

"When I die take these bones to the sea," Papa had told us during his lifetime. He'd no taste for a pit of earth in the local churchyard. Who could know we'd give him to the waters from the deck of a ship bearing my name. Freddy told me Papa had scraped the name *Veerbeck* off the bow the morning after that ugly scene with Pier in Amsterdam. *Maagda* was lettered in. Papa never mentioned the change. I touched Freddy cheek. I know he loved Papa and I don't think I shed a single tear more than he for the loss he felt. He bristled still because his own nephew stayed behind in Amsterdam, an insult to both my father and to me, and confessed that to his mind Pier never deserved the ship or Papa's tendering of the business

Bjorn remained at the Yard in my stead when we left the boat. He looked after Aunt Loeke until the last of the mourners departed. They understood how ill Miekke had been, that I must take her home. Ria's husband carried her from the coach to her bed and helped us settle her under the duvet. Miekke flushed with a fever so hot her eyes watered.

"I'll sit with her," Ria said. "You go."

When Miekke fell asleep, I slipped from the house.

I pulled my cap tight, kept my head down, and walked an empty back lane toward the beach. A stray cat brushed at my skirt, but I paid it little attention. My own dear Folly slept snug on a pillow of my old slips in her wicker basket beside Miekke's bed.

My tears had shed themselves dry. I trudged through the soft sand, brushing my hands over the tasseled heads of sea oat, a growing thing, alive. Even the scent of bramble roses along the fence posts meant little today. Living things in any form, flower or bramble, mocked my loss. Never had I felt such nothingness, or so alone, so pressed by the weight of loss and what lay ahead.

I paused by a shallow fresh water pond behind the sand hills. A swirl of pollen scummed the surface, forming and reforming into arcs and circles, spirals and curves. I dipped my finger into the water and scribed *Papa* into the yellow coating, only to watch the word pulled shapeless in the water's subtle motion. Here one moment, gone the next. I shuddered.

Klemp's words replayed in my head. His eulogy and the others who shared memories spoke of Papa's stewardship of the Yard, the Hoorn Trust, his kindness to the men, but nothing of the scholar, the man who escaped his world of duty to a world of words, the dreams of others.

Walking back toward the sea, I found a hollow in the lee of the wind and spread my faded paisley wrap on the damp earth. I sat, letting my mind drift, to become a tuft of thistledown to float on the air. I recalled the morning I left Amsterdam. Henrik had little to say. He whipped the horses to top speed along the open road to Hoorn, kind enough to leave me to my grief. I sat alone in the coach, immobile, empty of words. Never had a silent armor so shielded me from the real world of dray and farm and people as during that ride.

I pushed Papa's death to the outer reaches of my mind, refusing to let the thought find a shape, and spent much of the early trip stoking anger over Pier's refusal to leave Amsterdam. He protested that it wasn't only Steubing's absence that kept him at the shop, but a pending diamond contract that might change in a trice. Resentment at Pier's bewildering lack of feeling kept my grief at arm's length.

It did occur to me that Pier shunned the burial because of his bitter rejection of Papa's offer. Would I ever know or care? Pier and I stood so far apart now, the gap between us wider than the sea before my eyes.

I knew no one, especially Pier, would feel Papa's death as I did. I accepted that. But Pier gave less care about my wrenching loss than strangers on the road. My very husband lacked the warmth of friends and neighbors. He shared my body these last years, but nothing that reached heart or head, his or mine.

When I had arrived and people asked after him, I embroidered excuses. He seemed forgotten after that. Small wonder. He hadn't returned to Hoorn for a single visit since the wedding. Even Ria, ever alert to all that concerned me, asked but once. "Pier doesn't join you?" Her eyes smoldered when I shook my head.

Papa's death sobered my thinking about so many things, but most especially Pier and our marriage. A more clear measure of myself slipped over me with the ease of a new dress, and while part of me longed to rage at him, this new awareness told me that rage would grant me no peace. I saw now that what I craved beyond all else was home. I knew, too, that my every breath would be ragged with Papa's loss, and I knew that tongues would wag with no husband by my side. But I belonged in Hoorn. Every decision I faced in the days and months ahead would bring me here, here to the solace of my home. No matter the Anna Pelters with jealousies, or the Widow van Pelts with venom in their veins, for each of these, few though there were, there were a dozen Rias and Freddys and yes, Klemp.

The warm sun lulled me. I sat and stared at the sea. Finally, I shook off my cap and ran my fingers through my hair to loosen the matted strands. I pulled up my knees, folded my elbows, and lowered my head to my arms, closing my eyes to the real world and allowing my thoughts to ease and drift to the rhythm of the water that lapped the shore. The sun baked my shoulders. I willed its warmth into my spirit.

"Maagda? Is that you?"

I looked up at the tall figure silhouetted in the sun.

Bjorn smiled. "I wasn't sure. I've never seen you with your hair loose."

"You startled me. Has everyone left the Yard?"

"Yes. Mayor Jessel took your aunt home in his coach. I'll look in on her later if you like. Might I sit?"

I shifted and made room for him on my shawl. "I don't know how to thank you for being here. You've been the strong arm for me."

"It's been a long time since I've felt needed."

His hand reached to stroke the soft beads of moisture on the grass. Starting at the bottom of a blade, he used his index finger to run gently to the top. He seemed to delight in the tiny cataract of water that flowed down. So simple, so natural an act. At that moment with him on the sand, my world shifted, a gauze I hadn't known existed lifted from my eyes. Had I noticed before that a blade of grass had a delicate fringe of red along its edge? That bayberry perfumed and softened the sharp tang of sea air?

"Are you chilled?" Bjorn said. I thought he might put his arm around my trembling shoulders.

I shook my head and looked away. He didn't move toward me.

Since Bjorn had spent the last weeks in Hoorn with my father, neighbors thought him an old family friend. Not that I was uneasy about our sitting together here. It consoled me to see how easily he meshed with family and neighbors. He appeared to take everyone, every event in stride.

"Will Pier make it here at all?"

"He says not. There's a business contract that might change quickly. Pier feels he must be on hand to make a decision."

Bjorn's drew his cheeks in.

"Do you know what he speaks of?"

"No. No. I know nothing of the diamond business. But look, Maagda, I have weeks before my VOC ship sails." He shifted to look me full in the eyes, keeping a small space between us. "I can stay on here as long as you need me. I'm sure there is much to be done. Like the Yard. What's to become of it?"

"I'll be forthright. I plan to remain in Hoorn, keep the Yard open. I've taken the legal steps."

I thought him about to reach for my hand, but he stopped. His hand hovered just above the sand.

"You can't mean it, Maagda. How? What of your home with Pier?"

"Pier set the mode for our living: first business, then a life. It's the touchstone I mean to hold here." I pushed my hair back from my shoulder. "My father worked a lifetime to make the words *Boscher-built* mean something in the maritime trade. I will keep the tradition alive. Besides, look at the men who would be out of work if Miekke and I closed the Yard. Too many families would suffer as would the States General."

"Maagda, I assumed you might stay on a while to nurse Miekke, but the other, the Yard..."

I admitted that, of course, Miekke came first. With my aunt and Ria close by, my sister would be well cared for. But the boat yard was another matter. There was no one else. I knew the finances, the contracts, the inventory. I gripped the edge of my shawl. . "I have good help. Freddy has acted as a general manager. I trust what he knows, and I'm secure in his honesty. And the other men, too, have been with us a long time."

Bjorn listened, but said nothing. He lifted handful after handful of sand, and let the grains sift slowly through his fingers. I don't think he was even aware of the act. I pointed to his little sand pile.

"You've become an hourglass."

He looked at the mound. "Nothing so predictable. Maagda, you have a will of iron."

"You're not the first to suggest that I might not be so easily bent at times." I realized that Bjorn danced a light step in a fragile area. "Do you wonder how Pier will respond to my decision?"

He looked away, but not before I saw the red touch his cheeks.

"It is not my place to know."

"Don't be embarrassed," I said. "Others will have the same question. I must become accustomed to it." I spoke more bravely than I felt. "I don't know how much Pier has told you of his plans. He's involved in an investment and expects to reap a quick fortune, then emigrate across the Atlanic Ocean to his Promised Land."

Not a muscle on Bjorn's face twitched, nor did his eyes flicker. I couldn't fathom what of this might be new to him.

"So your father offered Pier the business to keep him here?"

"Yes. Like me, poor Papa misunderstood what drove Pier. He thought Pier sought only money, but his passion is more grand. It must be vast acreage or nothing. The burning eats at him every waking minute."

Bjorn eyed my clenched hands. "You have much anger."

"Not anger. Perhaps one sadness layered with another. My father's death crushes me and I have failed him."

"You? Failed your father? Nonsense. He spoke of you with tenderness and pride."

I bit my lip. No salt from my eyes would cleanse my guilt of not giving Papa his grandchild.

Bjorn lay back on the shawl, cupping his hands beneath his head, pulling taut shoulder muscles that strained 'neath his tunic.

"Lars and I spent evenings by the fire in his library, boots by the grate, a good pipe in hand."

In spite of my sadness, I smiled.

"He was a sound man, Maagda, good values. He spoke of how Erasmus thought a man might lead a moral life, and I would talk of Petrach, who said much the same, that ethics brought a man more worth than a church."

I listened to Bjorn and pictured them, their legs stretched out, their stockinged feet close to the warm flames. A syrup of comfort wound through me, that image of Bjorn and my father together.

I told Bjorn cherished family stories about how my father and grandfather had worked through holidays, festivals, even weddings, and how my grandfather took a ship out to sea for testing and missed my father's birth.

Bjorn sat up. "Oh that must have set well with your grandmother."

"She found a way to mark the affront, unintended though it was. She named Papa Lars after the man she would have married had my grandfather waited much longer to ask for her hand."

He laughed. "By god, Maagda, you carry her blood."

"I trust so. Papa planned for me to marry a man who would take over the business and produce sons for the future. He tried with Pier. I must step into the void."

"We all have our dreams."

"But, must they drive us? Pier calls his ambition. I call it obsession."

Bjorn said nothing, toyed with a shell in the sand. I was sure some male loyalty to Pier held his tongue.

"And you, Bjorn, what of your dreams? You'll realize them with your VOC voyage." I heard the slight tremor in my voice. In that instant I understood that his leaving in three months would be yet another fierce blow.

His cheeks flushed a deep scarlet. "The best dreams are shared dreams."

Heat rippled through me, starting a tremor so deep in me I thought the sand beneath would give way. I forced my hand, palm down, into the sand to restrain myself from reaching to touch the strands of golden hair that fell over his eyes.

Too much. Too close.

I stood abruptly and brushed the sand from my skirt. "I must see how Miekke fares."

My tone tore us from what lay so near the surface. Our hands had almost touched that last moment, but the tiny space between our fingers never closed.

I did not trust myself to look at him. He rose as though from a faraway place, and we walked home in silence.

"How pleasantly do they dote when they frame in their heads innumerable worlds; measure out the sun, the moon, the stars, nay and Heaven itself.

In Praise of Folly by Desiderius Erasmus (Classics Club edition)

CHAPTER 38—MAAGDA

BJORN AND I HAD FEW ENCOUNTERS, NONE ALONE, after our return from the dunes that afternoon. Friends gathered at home to sit with our grieving household. I spent what time I could bear with our visitors, but I couldn't bring myself to touch the meats and fishes and cakes they brought.

Poor Freddy couldn't seem to tear himself from the house. I'd catch him looking from staircase to door in expectation that the Lars he knew would walk back into his world. And his disappointment at Pier ate at him like a raw wound. Each time he took my hand and whispered, "I'm so sorry," I sensed he meant sadness as much about Pier's absence as Papa's death. I had explained about Pier's business, but Freddy called it a beggar's shame. I felt the same, but said nothing.

And Anna Pelter, Pier's admirer of our courting days, asked after him, too, one of the few who did. "Your Amsterdam diamond man not here?" her eyes darting among the guests.

"Business," I murmured and moved on, but not before I heard her exclaim over the wax candles throughout the rooms instead of the less costly oil lamps.

No husband in sight, no swollen belly. I knew what Hoorn thought. I'd been abandoned. Well, let the least among them whisper and wonder over their hutsepots and pipes. It would become real soon enough. And who would care if I had done the abandoning? I looked into the faces of my neighbors, honest burghers, honest working people, and knew them here out of love and respect for my father. My time would come.

After greeting the last of the new arrivals, I ran upstairs to Miekke's side, not to let her grieve alone. My concern over her illness dulled my own pain. And for Miekke's part, intermittent tears gave way to her favorite stories of the man who'd held our lives together. Then she would sleep again.

Before she drifted off, she remembered the exciting day Papa returned from the Yard with our treasured silk kimonos. I ran my fingers over the softness of her blue kimono draped over the bedpost. I hadn't seen my kimono since the night of my wedding.

When Miekke seemed settled for the night, I slipped down the passageway to my bedchamber. The house had drifted into its nighttime quiet, save a creaking board here or there, and a faint stir from Bjorn's room, a soft humming to a quiet melody. I stopped to listen for a moment, admiring the peace of mind that allowed him these tranquil notes.

I entered my bedchamber and crossed to my rosewood cupboard to search among its lacquered shelves for the tissue-wrapped package I'd sent home on my wedding night. My hand found the crinkly paper before I saw the package. I pulled it out, removed the tissue and shook the kimono loose from its years of concealment. Folds and creases melted away from the silk. My kimono shimmered in the low light from the candle's flame.

I undressed slowly. Candlelight flicked along the folds of the gown. An invitation. I imagined its touch on my body. I slipped my arms through the wide sleeves and the silk sent pleasant caressing fingers over my thighs, my breasts. Such must be the delight of a lover's touch. A vision of that earlier moment on the sand with Bjorn heated my flesh again. I tried to shake the urgency from me. I picked up and folded the clothes I'd tossed on the bed. I took a cloth and water and wiped my teeth. I brushed my hair in rapid, wild strokes to that point where pain verged on pleasure until I could stand it no longer, and I pitched the brush far across the room. Then I paced.

My breathing grew labored. I felt each passage of air inch its way down to my belly. I needed but one small move, a single step. An instant of truth flashed in my head. Had I not, in some niche among my thoughts, conjured this moment, planned each step, savored its juices in my mind?

I held fast to the door knob and then turned it, slowly. Another deep breath.

I crossed the passage and rapped lightly on Bjorn's door. Part of me wanted him not to hear. But in my soul I knew I could not turn back. I heard a chair scuff. The knob moved, and the door opened in one swift motion. A lick of candle flame lighted him, standing there, my father's gray blanket wrapped around him.

He took a step back when he saw me, and he pulled the blanket tight around his waist.

"Maagda. What…?"

I moved inside and closed the door behind me with one hand, and used the other to unleash the sash that tied my silk kimono high, under my breasts. The silken folds parted, a slight rush of air brushed my skin.

His eyes widened, astonished. "You would do this?"

I nodded and pulled his hand to me.

The walls, paintings, candles, shadows…nothing existed. We seemed to float above the pillows. I willed the moment to be unending.

Later we nestled under the duvet, front to back, bare nested spoons. Bjorn's arms encircled me, his lips so close that his breath warmed my ear. He whispered. "You are like a bride." I told him why.

"But let it be said in defense of Erasmus that he had boldly inscribed his name upon his little package of combustibles, that he had not hidden it in some obscure cellar, but had placed it in full view for all those who had eyes to see."

In Praise of Folly by Desiderius Erasmus (Classics Club edition)

CHAPTER 39—MAAGDA

I'D SPENT MUCH OF THE NIGHT TOSSING, SLEEPLESS, my body overjoyed at my lovemaking with Bjorn, but my mind knotted, knowing I had to make a firm move at the Yard, and that I must make that move quickly. I'd sifted one gesture after another through my thoughts, but none bespoke the ringing finality this day demanded.

In the morning Bjorn walked with me toward the Yard. We crossed the narrow planked path cut through the sandy hummock leading to the Yard's south gate. On either side, sprays of rimed seagrass glistened from sun now pulling higher over the distant eastern shore of the Zuider Zee. I stopped and listened. The piercing ring of metal smashing metal told me the forge plunged into its day, and plumes of black smoke from the char fires layered the lingering mist. My heart hammered with the anvil's beat. I turned to smile at Bjorn, overjoyed that the men were at their jobs.

We crossed into the Yard, and I looked for Freddy.

"What's that hissing sound?" Bjorn pointed to the right of the forge where six men with cloths tied round their heads pushed and tugged a plank into position.

"Papa's steam box. Once the plank is hewn to shape, we steam it for one hour for each inch of thickness. Then it's carried aloft still hot so it might be shaped to the hull and clamped."

"Looks a nasty job to me. I didn't see that when I came through with your father."

"It's not fired every day. But it is the worst of jobs, and most of the men have burns to show for it."

Freddy saw us and broke free from a knot of workers planing oak timber for bitts and chocks.

He hugged me. "I didn't expect you so soon." His eyes misted, still rimmed in raw red ovals. These last days lay open the depth of Freddy's affection for my father. I never realized before quite how strong his bond, but I bore him no foul thought. How could I? Hadn't he showered a large measure of his heart on me? I lingered in his embrace, our mutual sadness seeping one to the other. I caught his quick glance at Bjorn and knew he thought Pier should be at my side.

"Not fair to keep them," I nodded toward the staring men, "wondering about their futures. The longer the question hangs in the air, the more time for rumor to take hold."

Bjorn nodded. "After the burial yesterday, a town woman standing near me cried to her neighbor that they'd have to move to Amsterdam now to find work."

So it had started already.

Papa's office beckoned. More than one man stole a glance at us as I followed the path to the stairs. I dreaded the sight of his empty chair and knew the weeks and months ahead would hold many such moments, places where Papa should be, but would fill only in my grief.

The lumber storage area caught my eye before I stepped onto the first tread.

"Freddy what's this?" I pointed to the right side of staircase. The entire north end of the timber storage area beneath the office lay bare as a beggar's cupboard. "Where's the shipment of larch? Isn't that to be cut into knee braces for the hull by month's end?"

Freddy raised his hands and shrugged. "Bad weather. Nothing's to be done about it. I'll go over the log with you in Lars'…in the office."

I wondered what else might be behind schedule, what other surprises awaited me, and knew that much as I couldn't bear separation from Bjorn today, hours would stretch into early evening here. I was relieved yesterday when Klemp offered his help. Klemp and Freddy would be the crutches that held me up in the weeks ahead. I must try to see Klemp today.

Bjorn took my arm when I started again for the stairs. I held back. "You best go back to town." I pressed my mouth hard to lock more tender words inside. "I'll be here until supper, or later. Better, too, that the men see me at work."

He held fast to my arm. "It's so soon."

"This moment will come no matter how long I delay." I looked into his eyes longer than I meant to. "Perhaps you'll spend some time with Miekke? Try to cheer her?"

He hesitated, but dropped his hand. "Of course. Go to your work. I'll wait with Miekke to share supper with you."

Bjorn bade Freddy and me farewell, then trudged back toward the wooden path. I realized an emptiness in my chest the moment he stepped away. Part of me wished to walk with him, last night a flame that still burned. Yet an even heavier part pulled me toward the challenge that lay here. I knew I'd be tested day by day, indeed, hour by hour, each turn, each direction, measured in the men's heads against *what would Lars do.*

When we reached the landing outside the office door, I stopped before going in and raised my fingers to touch the inscription painted there…*L.Boscher, proprietor.*

I forced my eyes, my lips, my chin into composure. I felt the men's eyes on me, and sensed it would be fatal to let a tear cross my cheek. To the world beyond my own grief the time for crying had passed. They, the workers, might mourn, but they were ready to move on, to ensure they had earnings. I turned to speak to Freddy, standing so my face might be seen by every man who looked up.

"Please ask the painter to come."

When word spread round the Yard that the door now read *M. Boscher* under Papa's name, none would question that we meant to go on.

"Nor do I esteem those Wise men rash that call it a foolish and insolent thing to praise one's self."

In Praise of Folly by Desiderius Erasmus (Classics Club edition)

CHAPTER 40—PIER

NOT A WORD. NOT ONE. DAMN THAT WOMAN. NO doubt she thought to punish me since I didn't travel to Hoorn for Lars' burial. All these weeks? Nothing. Less and less a wife to me.

When Pieter from next door stopped in, I unloaded my anger.

"You'd think she might at least send a note with Henrik. My Uncle Freddy found time to write, though it was nothing more than a good dressing down for dodging Lars's burial. Oh, shit, Pieter, maybe I'm in a black mood because of this dreary, never-ending rain. Can't keep the place warm. Feels like the wet seeps through the walls."

I'd just finished mopping up the tiles inside the garden entrance. Water seeped under the door from the flooded path. Woman's work!

Pieter let me spew all of my venom before he spoke.

"Come now, Pier, I'm sure Maagda has her hands full in Hoorn. You told me yourself that her sister's bad sick. When my wife's mother did poorly, Colinda was gone for weeks."

I remembered the time.

"And what about her father's business?" Pieter turned his palms up. "She's probably over her head trying to get his affairs in order, close up the boat yard."

"Lars probably has that Yard so tied in legal knots, there won't be a coin coming to my door."

His mentioning the Yard brought Freddy's letter fresh to my mind. Who did he think he was to tell me he was ashamed of me, that he regretted introducing me into the Boscher family? Wouldn't doubt he had an eye for the old man himself.

Pieter said nothing. Instead, he placed his hand on my shoulder and spoke only of Maagda. "Look, friend, you wouldn't want her on the roads in this storm, would you?"

Pieter had a good point, but still my blood boiled that Maagda forgot my existence. She had duties here in Amsterdam. I'd fix her memory soon enough. Once we boarded that ship for the New World, she'd have no Hoorn to run to. I'd be the piper who called her steps.

And Freddy...he could damn well go to hell. I didn't need family where I was headed. Said I shamed him as well as Maagda. Well, wouldn't she be shocked at how soon we were to leave Holland and her shame. My tulip contract grew by the minute. I heard last night that Admiral of Hague bulbs sold for 1,000 florins over my contract. Fl. 6,500! I whistled. A 1,000 florin profit in a mere three weeks. How many months of hard work in that boat yard matched such a windfall?

I was tempted to put my contract on the market this Thursday when the college met again, take the profits and return Steubing's March diamonds to the safe. But I'd promised Klees I'd wait until he had enough florins to buy my paper. And always the niggling doubt in the back of my head, would Horder surrender the stones?

My stomach churned constantly. The pull of bigger profits, florin piling on florin, by god, it fueled a bonfire in a man's gut. Now I understood the charged air, the shouts, the rages among the traders when I passed near the Bourse. You might win or lose, but always the chance of the big win.

I bade Pieter a good night, itching to leave the house and slosh through the sodden streets to The Lamb. Needed to be near the stir and excitement of other traders, men who shared my excitement. My boots clomped like hooves in lanes that gushed streams of rain, the gutters so full the waters met in the middle, no cobbles to be seen. The canals ran high, too. They roared in torrents toward the river. In two spots the waters leaped up to the very bridge rails. God help anything that got in the way of that water. A damned ugly night. I was a fool to slog through these streets, but there was a pit deep in me that needed the stir of my cronies.

I spotted van Goyen as soon as I entered The Lamb's smoky rooms. He stood near a table and counted stuivers for a faro game with his burgher friends. They reserved the last table in the corner near the fireplace. A light steam curled up from their wet tunics where the fire warmed and dried them, sitting there under the lantern to deal and place their wagers. Damp beads dotted their faces. One or two removed their hats and stood with damp, matted hair.

I was tempted to join them, to stand near the heat of the grate. With the storm and the cold, my bones chattered like ice.

"How about I sit in on a few hands, van Goyen?"

"Ah, Pier. Feeling lucky with the way your contract moves?"

"Perhaps. I still have a few spare stuivers."

"Take my advice. Save your money. These players are sharks, cunning. Anyway, I should think that to watch your tulip profits mount gives excitement enough."

"Plenty, and I smack my lips with the taste of it."

He slapped my back and laughed. Was he amused that tulip fever caught me in its vise or that I sounded the rank trader that I was?

"Van Goyen, I must know something." We moved away from the faro table. "Why have you taken such trouble with me? You explained the tulip market. You introduced me to Klees, and you offered me advice on Horder's bulbs, and all moving toward riches. Why?"

Van Goyen's usual smile switched to a dark, somber grimace with cheeks drawn and nostrils quivering above his mustache.

"You suspect me of something underhanded, is that it?" Van Goyen looked stung. He moved to walk away.

I grabbed his elbow. "Wouldn't you think it odd if a stranger did this for you?"

"A stranger did. That's how I got into the market." He sneered. "I tried to return a kindness by doing the same for you."

Regret covered me like the rain. "Go ahead," I said and pointed to my chin.

Van Goyen bit his lip, then grinned and gave me a light punch on the arm.

"Think about it, Pier. Markets need buyers and sellers. The more action in the market, the greater your chance of traders to bid up prices. You had the interest, the assets. Why not help you along?"

"Look, I rue what I said. I've never made such a risky investment and between us, I'm brittle on the edges.." I put out my hand.

Before van Goyen returned the grip, the tavern door burst open in a gust of wind. A slanting rain swept through the door, slamming the heavy oaken panel back against the wall and knocking three chairs down along the way. Two men pushed in, flinging sprays of water from their waxed coats. "Volunteers. Now! The Amstel's burst. Breached to the south. Flooding everywhere. Hurry. We need every one of you." Burghers scurried from their seats, grabbing for hats and coats, rushing for the door. "Come. Quickly, come," they shouted.

Through the opening I heard church bells toll the alarm. The devil take me if I didn't know this would be an evil night.

Van Goyen turned to me, his florid face drained white, no trace of a smile now.

"You better be on good terms with your god, Pier. Pray hard. Horder's plot sits a quarter mile behind the south dike."

Who knows not but a man's infancy is the merriest part
of life to himself and most acceptable to others?

In Praise of Folly by Desiderius Erasmus (Classics Club edition)

CHAPTER 41—PIER

THE RIVER ROARED AROUND ME LIKE ONE LONG
cannon blast. Water crashed against what remained of the dike,
cracking through any weak spot. The river surged, stomping our
puny efforts. On this godforsaken morning, every able-bodied man
in Amsterdam humped his muscles to shore up what remained of
the dike. I willed to end it, drop into the mud, never to draw another
wisp of air.

"Pier, come. We need help over here," Pieter signaled to me, his
words swallowed by the howling storm. We'd all grown hoarse from
our shouts over the bellowing waters and roar of the wind.

Rain funneled down my back, squished from my boots and
blurred my eyes. Storm waters pelted me with the force of musket
shot. Damn this westerly gale that pounded a drum roll in my ears. I
was wet to the marrow, certain some devil stood on the clouds piss-
ing himself empty.

My muscles ached, back, shoulders, legs, every inch of me thick with weariness. When I tried to lift the shovel, my hands and arms shook like a palsied old man. Men barked orders along the line.

"Move in here…Shore up that wall" and how many times, "Oh, god, another break. Catch it. Heave the bags. Dam it, dam it."

Our bodies snaked like a writhing chain from danger to danger.

So numb. God I was numb. I couldn't force another step from my weakened legs. We'd packed sand since alarm bells jolted the city after nine last night. Suddenly, I could see the figures of others around me and realized morning had broken. I looked at the sky. Night faded, but the clouds hovered, black as a cannon barrel, the rain so thick is swallowed any sight of the city to the north. Sent shivers through me. And the rain. Sheet after sheet of solid water. The river swollen like a pus-filled wound. The higher we barricaded the leaks, the higher the water churned, the wider the gash cut in the fragile barrier. We whipped ourselves in hopeless, foolish work.

I slammed my shovel into the soggy earth and backed against a dray to watch the Amstel's muddy waters sluice around me toward the flat plots where Horder's tulips lay buried. I heard worried growers rant about mold, rot, about slim chances for bulbs to survive. Maybe the water on their faces wasn't all rain. One man choked on his words, remembering an earlier fight against floodwaters. "Mud heaved them bulbs, roots and all, right out the ground. Looked like little bleached skulls spewed." His words spawned a stew of maggots in my belly.

Tulips gone. What the hell would I do? Steubing would send the law hounds for sure. God that I had the balls to throw myself into the Amstel's torrent, to wash away. Better to rot on some far away field, food for some other man's crop.

I'd caught glimpses of Horder along the line. He shoveled and stacked barriers like a maniac, a man with a mission. Burghers I recognized from the tavern moved trance-like, waist deep in the water, at their sides draymen who slogged back and forth with sacks of sand.

"Here, more here."

"Hurry. Another furrow. Be quick, faster, you heathens."

The rain-fat river roared, cracked like thunder, all but drowned the barked orders, the pleas for help, the hopeless directions.

I beat my fists into a wagon board, shouted my rage to the wind. Probably not a man here who didn't feel the same.

My tired bones counted little next to my fear. The diamonds, Steubing's March diamonds. Ack. I might just as easily toss them to the storm. The thought caromed around my head.

An arm thumped my shoulder. "Bent out, are ya? There's warm ale over there. It'll pick you up. We need you back on the line." An unknown voice, an unknown face. Who was it who spoke? We all looked alike by now. A slime of mud covered our sodden clothes, masked our faces. I'd long since lost my hat. My hands were raw from the shovel, blistered to bleeding.

Pier, why stay? To what end?

Horder. He walked my way. Water from the storm cut gorges in his mud-smeared face. His slumping gait told the losses that walked with him.

"How bad is it?" I grabbed his mud slick sleeve.

"Gone. It's all gone." His voice ragged, hoarse.

"Oh my god. My contract."

He froze an instant and wheeled on me.

"You snivel about a miserable half pound of bulbs, you sodden bastard?" He lunged. "I've lost everything. You hear? Everything."

He swung his shovel at my head. I ducked. Mud sucked at his boots, made him swing wild, else he would have bashed me with the wide scoop. His near miss threw me off balance and I plunged into the muck. He lunged again, but I rolled out of reach.

His missed thrusts seemed to reel Horder back to his senses. He dropped the shovel. I'd slammed against a wagon wheel, pinned between him and the dray. Horder looked down at me, his face twisted in his own private agony.

"Forget your lousy contract, you worthless pile of shit." He scowled and spit in my face before he turned away.

CHAPTER 42—MAAGDA

THE LOVELIEST OF DAYS MELTED INTO THE MOST
bittersweet of weeks. I ached for my father. His loss hung like a dark
curtain across each hour of my day. But my moments with Bjorn
lifted the shroud to let small rays of sunlight enter, chasing every
thought save Papa from my head. A spring-like air swept through
me, a promise of rare happiness.

Since that first night, we celebrated the end of day in each other's
embrace, touching, exploring, sharing pleasures I had only known in
my fancies, awed as awareness, one of the other, spread through us
and stoked the heat in our bodies.

"Remember our first night?" I sat in Mama's rocker in my bedroom, Bjorn on a cushion by my feet. "Would you have taken that
step? Come to me?"

He stood and pulled me up; his arms circled my waist. "I think
so, yes." I felt his grip tighten. "There was a moment on the beach
that afternoon when I had to hold back from sweeping you onto
the sand."

I laughed and a lick of pleasure lapped through me, recalling the unbidden current that had passed between us that day.

"To think I would know a woman who brought ideas and passion and humor to my life," Bjorn whispered. He stroked my throat and let his fingers trace light touches around me face, then leaned over me to kiss my eyes. He propped himself on his elbow and studied the length of my body, the duvet thrown off to the side. His finger traced a path along my right shoulder and curved in gentle strokes to my breast.

We tried to be discreet, particularly now that Miekke grew a bit stronger and moved about the house. I believed my staying in Hoorn hastened her recovery. To amuse her, I told story after story, but her favorite tale was my conniving to meet Prince Frederick. "So like my devilish Maags of old," she would laugh.

She almost caught Bjorn last Monday, the first morning she'd left her room. It was only minutes after he'd slipped out that she knocked and entered, overjoyed to be up and on the mend. I wondered that she hadn't been overwhelmed by the scent of our lovemaking, lusty as it was, and I hoped that after so long an illness, she was lost to all but the magic of leaving her bed and walking about. This sister of mine became more like our Mama each day, frail, and almost child-like in her delight at the smallest physical accomplishment.

She noticed the pot of wildflowers on my bedside table. "Why, Maags, you never kept flowers by your bed before. Something your Amsterdam ladies taught you?"

I merely smiled. On fine days, Bjorn would walk out to pick a bouquet of wildflowers that he placed there, a delight to find when I returned from my hours at the Yard. And if I found some treasure from the sea, perhaps an odd or especially lovely shell on my walks home, I would slip into his hand when we first embraced in the evening.

Miekke chattered while I dressed and happy as I was to see her, I was eager to leave for my work.

Klemp was to come from his VOC office early and sort out bills with me. Despite his size, he was always on time and this morning he awaited me when I walked up the wooden path from the sea. I had concerns about payments to a new hemp supplier Papa had taken on days before he died. I thought Klemp would know if the bill was honest.

"Somewhere Lars sits smiling at you," he said. "You make him proud. Wish I had your kind of ambition in my VOC camp." He stood, hands clasped behind his back, gazing through the window to a cradle where a work crew crawled over a new keel stuffing oakum into a hull's seams. "It gets tighter each day, Maagda. Unlike your father's Swedish friend, Bjorn, who invests with us, too many of our burghers chase those tulip profits."

I walked to the window and stood beside him to survey the Yard, smiling to myself to hear that Bjorn was now Papa's friend. "I know nothing of these tulip ventures, but it sounds like fools' florins to me. We have more future in our fluyts and trade."

"Well, my dear, trade's been our fortune, but will we ever see it again?"

"Do you recall," I asked, "when you came to dinner before my marriage and we talked of tulips and diamonds?" He nodded. "Perhaps it's time to speak again of our ships and the VOC's trade."

Klemp looked at me, shaking his head. "There are no spare florins about for diversion." He flicked his finger at a fly on the ledge. "The Gentlemen XVII are locked within a pennigen to every contract we have afloat between here and Batavia."

"Soon I will come to you with a plan to shake such contracts from your mind."

He slapped his thigh and laughed. "You do that, Maagda. You do that. The Gentlemen need a good shaking."

It cut me that he didn't take my talk seriously. But I was in no position to add more until Willem and I reached an agreement. I had been taken with the idea since the day I masqueraded my way into the

Bourse and witnessed the frantic buying and selling for myself. Any business that caused such stir of excitement, such rapid exchange of silver was destined to make us prosperous. The VOC suffered, I thought, because the burghers with money lacked patience to wait a year or more for returns. But they were willing enough to trade once the goods reached our ports. If my budding idea blossomed... If, if, if. So many questions to resolve.

After dinner that evening I told Bjorn about my talk with Klemp, how I saw a time when we might take the VOC's entire shipload to ports along the Mediterranean and the Baltic, no Bourse, no middlemen. A single piece of the puzzle eluded me, but when I found it, I would convince Klemp and his Gentlemen XVII. I knew I could.

"Better you think about the present, Maagda."

We'd been so afraid of losing our happiness that neither Bjorn nor I spoke of what awaited us, the many-headed Hydra that held our future. The thought of a meeting with Pier ate at the underside of my happiness. Not a single word between us since I left Amsterdam.

Conscience nagged Bjorn as well. "Let me face, Pier. He befriended me and now I've taken his wife from him." He locked his jaw tight. "I can never make that right with him, but at the least he is due my honesty. I'll take the coach to Amsterdam and be back in a day."

"Please, no. Understand that I must be the one to confront him. I owe Pier that. He remains my husband in the eyes of the law."

He placed his hand over my lips to quiet me, but I pulled his hand away. "You know that in my heart my marriage ended long before I came to you. Now I must make that ending true. Willem says I have grounds to seek an annulment in the civil courts."

He wound his arms round my waist. "It could be an ugly scene. What kind of man would I be to let you go through the courts alone?"

Willem urged me to seek an annulment because my marriage to Pier was never consummated in *the legal sense*. I left his bed a virgin. There were no children and I didn't feel Pier would lie about his intentions, particularly if I offered him a settlement. My future balanced on Pier's greed, a wrenching knowledge. But, if I could not buy Pier, I must call myself adulteress and allow Pier to file against me if he chose to.

I didn't tell Bjorn that I'd sent a note to Willem to meet the Wednesday coach in Edam with the final papers, the papers that would free me...if Pier would sign.

If not... I couldn't bear to think that now. The law wouldn't take my word alone. Without Pier's name on that paper, I would be bound to offer myself for a doctor's examination. That was no longer possible.

Bjorn's ship to Batavia sailed in two days. No delays now. He swore he'd not go, but I insisted that he must, not let this opportunity leave him in its wake. We lay together in my bed, a single candle burning on the side table. Its glow danced along the strong lines of his forehead and jaw, drew out the traces of gold in his brows and cast giant shadows of us on the walls. How I wanted us to be so large, so towering we might sweep aside all of the problems in our path.

"You expect me to leave, to allow you to face Pier and a legal action? My heart won't let me. Six months? A year? It's as though you ask me not to draw a breath for so long."

I kissed him to stem his tide of words and tears that threatened at the thought of parting. I must make the way myself. I'd chased Pier, was there any other word, as an impetuous, foolish young woman. Hadn't Papa tried to stop me? I would not deserve a love such as Bjorn offered unless I faced my mistakes and set them to right.

"We know so little of each other." I stroked the lines of his jaw. "A deep passion, yes. But what of the bare bones of everyday living that build a lifetime?"

"Maagda, do you tell me these weeks have been no more than a burning passion for you?

"Wait, please. Hear me. If we're to have a life together, let's make it fresh, sure of what we seek. You have your dream. You must see it through. And I must shepherd mine to its rightful place."

"But…"

"I've wasted years living another's vision…a bitter learning."

I lay on top of him, our arms outstretched, hands and fingers locked, my words whispered into his ear.

He struggled to free himself from my weight, to sit up.

He locked my fingers tight in his. "Maagda, don't let yourself believe our time together is no more than our bodies, passion that sweeps away reason. I know what I do here. I've come to you with my reason whole."

I slid from the bed at first light. A gray morning, but at least the heavy rains of the past few days had stopped. Bjorn's head was burrowed in the pillow. He snored quietly, small gentle puffs of air blew from his lips. I drew his features in my mind aware this dim picture must sustain me for months or forever.

I touched my lips to his forehead, softly, not to wake him. *Bjorn*, I whispered to his unhearing ear, *you are to be a father.*

*"And yet it should happen that there was a
mutual good will between them..."*

In Praise of Folly by Desiderius Erasmus (Classics Club edition)

CHAPTER 43—MAAGDA

THE COACH LURCHED FROM RUT TO RUT ON THE
road to Edam. I spoke little to Henrik or the other passengers. Last
week's heavy rains had etched gullies into the roadbed, each mile a
torment as Henrik labored to keep the wheels from slipping into the
furrowed earth. I fretted about the child growing within me, each
lurch of the coach rocking me against the hard sideboards.

Familiar scenes of waterways and farmland flashed before my
eyes, but in my mind, only fragmented thoughts of the last days,
the last weeks. Bjorn's face loomed a constant vision there, the thick
flaxen brows and wavelets of white gold hair on his forehead, hair
that begged for my hand to brush it back. I'd plowed the depths of
my soul for the will to leave him this morning, nor could I stay and
watch his ship heave off from its anchorage. Had he awakened, spoken my name, touched me, my resolve would have melted like an
April frost.

I twirled my mother's garnet ring, circle after circle.

Was he awake now? Had he read the letter I left on the bed-side table?

Would I ever see him again, feel his warmth cradle me?

When I learned I was with child, I wanted to run to his arms. Now I was grateful to have waited. Bjorn and I lived in the moment, awed by the sudden happiness of finding each other, loving each other. The next hour, the next day lay an eternity from the vividness of *now*. Now, with a child growing in me, the present moment sped to a future counted in months. Bjorn must seize his chance, not wait with me to spend a lifetime regretting what might have been had he sailed.

When our coach rolled away from Hoorn earlier, I scanned the ships moored in the harbor. Several fishing boats, a few three-masted galleys and big tonnage galleons dotted anchor points. Which was the *Prince of Orange*, the galleon that would take Bjorn to the East Indies? How mocking that it should be the *Prince of Orange* after my silly escapade to meet our own Prince Frederick of Orange. It was impossible to read the names on the ship's bows. The rising sun threw the hulls into shadow, even as the glare from the windows along Grote Oost reflected light across the waters. My spirits fell, but I was grateful for the sunlight that heated my shoulders.

"See those travelers?" Henrik tipped his whip toward a group of some three dozen men huddled near a quayside dinghy. "They're on their way to the New World. That's their ship." He pointed to a large galleon, the *DeWalvis*, The Whale. Ironic that thirty of Hoorn's men sailed today for Pier's dreamland.

"They've already named the colony they plan to build," Henrick said. "It's to be called Swanendael."

Valley of the Swans! I wondered did they think there'd be swans in the New World? Perhaps a mere hope they'd find a place of tranquility and beauty.

"Look, there's Captain DeVries," Henrik said. "He's to lead the new colony."

DeVries was all bone and sinew, a man with sharp features and a pointed goatee. "Heard a lot of talk about him in the tavern last night. A good commander, they say." Henrik snapped his whip to spur the horses on, but his head turned to follow DeVries.

I wished these adventurers well, but Bjorn stood foremost in my mind, and it was thoughts of him, of us, that engaged me as we struggled along the cratered road.

My heart carried a heavy ring of sadness that Papa hadn't lived to see the grandchild Bjorn and I would give him. What new word, I wondered, would he dredge up from Erasmus to tell his joy at the birth? What thanks would he offer for the gift of a child to seal his family oath? Or, might he damn my baby as a bastard. This pregnancy, my heart's desire, sliced through me with twin edges of joy and pain, one thought flowing with elation, the next plowing a furrow of despair, turmoil my constant companion, and so many decisions to make. I wanted our child, Bjorn's child, but with it came a torrent of doubt – threats to the annulment from Pier, Miekke's response, indeed, the Yard and the town. I trembled to the bottom of my boots.

"Madam Veerbeck. Madam Veerbeck."

My head snapped up. Since I'd conceived the child, I found myself nodding off at the oddest moments. Or, had I so completely wiped Pier's name away that Henrik's call from the driver's seat fell on closed ears? The coach had emptied. We'd stopped at the tavern in Edam and I was the only passenger still aboard. "Would you like to refresh yourself?" the driver asked in his kind manner. After so many years, so many trips back and forth, Henrik was a time-honored friend. Surely, my many trips between Amsterdam and Hoorn added callouses to his hands. "You must be anxious to get home to your husband." He came to the side of the coach with steps for me.

I nodded. *This was an ugly duty trip.*

"Maagda. Over here."

I looked up to see Willem at the tavern. Henrik handed me down. "We have an hour," the driver said. "Plenty of time for a nice meal." My gorge strangled my throat at the mere hint of food. I struggled against the urge and turned to wave at Willem who stood in a finely tailored suit of gray soft as morning mist, a crisp white blouse, and oh my, a red vest. The touch of color made his hair and beard jump out in a sheen black as wet peat. Had the somber lawyer broken free from his somber business?

"You look splendid, Willem." I smiled despite my heavy heart.

"Ah, do you approve? A touch of color appeals to me of late, not unlike those bright scarves and shawls you wear."

"You do take the eye. Is there a lady in your life to enjoy such gay plumage?"

He colored and hurried me through the door.

Willem had secured one of the tavern's small, private rooms for our meal. A leaded window high on the far wall and a candle lantern on the rough wooden table gave the only light. It was enough. No need for Willem to see my watery eyes or any pallor that remained from my morning ills. And I was relieved to be away from the smoke filled main room. So many small irritations of late, things that I never minded before.

He motioned the waiter to leave.

"Maagda, I must inquire one last time. It is my duty. You've given this great consideration? You understand what you ask here?"

I nodded. "There's no turning back, Willem. This is my final trip to Pier. Nothing will change my mind."

"Then here is what must be done."

He read the papers to me, all the while rubbing the band on the small oval signet ring he always wore. "You sign here and this line is for Pier's signature. After both of you place your full legal names on the document, I will take it to the magistrate to be recorded. No need for you or Pier to be present. Understand?"

"Yes, yes, I do. Then what happens? How soon before the annulment becomes legal?"

He no longer seemed uncomfortable to confront such a delicate family situation. We'd discussed it often enough, though he'd yet to voice any reaction to his very own cousin's role in so visceral a drama.

"Immediately. Once the magistrate stamps the papers and enters them into the municipal record, your marriage no longer exists. Unlike a divorce where testimony may be required, an annulment on valid grounds that you each attest to is all that the law demands. And your issue of non-consummation is about as valid as any I know." He hesitated and looked directly into my eyes. "Rare, but valid."

I sighed and exhaled to allow my anxiety an escape in measured drafts. A move forward this, but the ordeal was far from over. There was still the matter of Pier's signature.

"If Pier refuses?"

"Then, as I told you in the beginning, you present yourself for examination."

I shuddered, clasped my arms, my bones cracked cold.

"Are you chilled, Maagda?"

He knew nothing of Bjorn, the child, only my despair at all that lay ahead.

"No, not cold. Relieved, perhaps, finally to take a firm step." No matter what it takes, I whispered to myself.

The waiter knocked.

Willem took me hand. "Ready for some lunch?"

Suddenly, the decision behind me, I was ravenous. "Yes." I smiled. "Oysters. Sweet, juicy oysters."

*"For there are two main obstacles to the knowledge of things,
Modesty that casts a mist before the understanding, and Fear
that, having fancied a danger, dissuades us from the attempt."*

In Praise of Folly by Desiderius Erasmus (Classics Club edition)

CHAPTER 44—MAAGDA

HENRIK HELPED ME REBOARD AND WE SET OUT TO
pitch and bump along the final stretch to Amsterdam. When
we neared the city, I noticed the vast pools of rainwater that lay
about, that splashed high along the sides of the coach at every rut.
Nearby fields were awash with salt water from the Zuider Zee, with
geese and gulls hunting food in meadows, clear signs that the past
week's storm left remnants here much greater than the storms that
drenched Hoorn.

I thought again of Henrik's earlier suggestion of an eager return
to Amsterdam, to Pier. Between Papa's death and Bjorn's leaving, my
husband claimed little of my thoughts these past ten weeks. He might
well be a stranger. *He was a stranger.* Pier had wrapped himself in a
cloak of secrecy since the first day of our marriage. He told me nothing. Even now he keeps his new money scheme locked in his head.

All these thoughts spilled easily enough, but how to put them
into the words I must speak to tell Pier our marriage was over, that

I must have his name on annulment papers before I returned to Hoorn. What would he want of me? The Pier I knew would demand florins, silver, to settle as I asked. The thought repulsed me, but whatever the cost, my freedom was worth the price. There would be nothing Veerbeck about this baby that grew within me. This was Bjorn's child.

The other question that taunted me throughout this trip was what story would I tell my baby about her father should Bjorn not return? The thought danced down my spine like the cold tap of a dead man's fingers. My vision of the years ahead, the vision that set my compass, centered upon Bjorn's coming home, coming to his daughter and me.

Curious, I knew the baby would be a girl, and the thought made me recall a favorite chant from my childhood that said girls were found in the garden among the rosemary plants while boy babies hid under the cabbages. I smiled and recalled what Mama told me before Miekke was born.

"Mama, am I to have a brother or a sister? Can I have one of each?"

For days I poked among the rosemary and cabbages to find our new baby.

Finally mama said, "A baby's garden is in the mama's belly." She took my hand and patted the swollen bulge above her lap. "Papas plant the seeds there and the mamas tend the garden until the baby is a sweet flower in her family."

Strange the tidbits that etched themselves in memory. What would my mother think of me now, a married woman who carried a lover's baby? And Papa, had any of his reading prepared him for such an event? I flinched to think what words might come from him, a flood of joy for the grandchild he sorely wanted, or a curse for my adultery.

Too late for that now. But I was sure the rosemary garden would reward me with a daughter. I believed so strongly that I could feel her in my arms, but I looked down and realized I cradled the green woolen throw Henrik had given me for warmth. So lost in reverie. Perhaps she'd favor Bjorn's Swedish heritage with white blond hair and intense blue eyes. And perhaps she might dream like me, dream of making a mark in her world.

Making a mark…making a mark. The phrase beat to the rhythm of the turning coach wheels. What mark would I leave, and what marks from my past must be wiped clean?

Bjorn was about to make his mark, to sail on a grand adventure aboard the *Prince of Orange.* Had the ship weighed anchor yet? I envisioned him, excited, but slightly sad scanning the dock side as the boat slipped from its mooring. His galleon to the sea.

His galleon!

By god, the word, the vision, swept across my mind, a zephyr gliding over my confusion. How could I have missed the obvious truth these past months while I fretted about the Yard, the future?

"You say something, Madam Veerbeck? Hard to hear up here with the wind."

"No, no, Henrik. I'm quite all right." I must have shouted aloud, unaware and lost in my thoughts.

Bjorn had spoken so often of owning a ship, a big tonnage, long-haul galleon.

His galleon and my fluytship. A shipping marriage so perfect, I became dizzy with excitement to think it.

How could I have been so blind to the until this very moment. We would own the entire chain of trade. No Bourse, no middleman, all the profits in one company. His large vessel would bring home the spices, the cloths, the wonders of the Far East. In Hoorn we would load them aboard my swift cargo ships for the shorter runs to buyers in Baltic and Mediterrean ports. Such was business done now, but with our arrangement, we would have one smooth river of ownership and profit. And might this not be the answer to the VOC's investor problem as well, their galleon cargo to our ships?

If only Papa might share such excitement, look for holes in my thinking.

"You comfortable back there? Need a stop?" Henrik asked. "You seem astir, Madam Veerbeck."

Please don't use that name!

"I'm fine, Henrik. An uneasy journey today."

The sudden clarity of a sound idea soothed like an alchemist's potion. It pressed the rutted road to a path of silk. My agitation rose from a different place. I gripped the coach rail. A perfect picture, save one piece. Would Bjorn return?

"For to what purpose is it to say anything of the common people, who without dispute are wholly mine? They abound everywhere with so many several sorts of Folly, and everyday abustle inventing new..."

In Praise of Folly by Desiderius Erasmus (Classics Club edition)

CHAPTER 45—MAAGDA

WE CROSSED THE HERENGRACHT CANAL BEFORE I realized we'd reached Amsterdam. My eyes usually feasted on the homes of the rich with their ornate facades and draped windows. But today I grew tense, uneasy when we neared the area. A sourness that had nothing to do with my condition made me keep swallowing the saliva that drowned my tongue. I clung to the coach rail. Henrik guided the team round the last narrow corner, Pier's house loomed larger to my anxious eyes than I knew it to be.

Henrik helped me down from the coach. "Not much baggage."

"No, a brief trip. Much to be done back in Hoorn. I return quickly."

He touched his cap and was about to turn the team to leave.

"Wait, Henrik, please."

I scribbled a quick note for Henrik to deliver to Willem when he drove back to Hoorn this afternoon. I asked Willem for an urgent meeting at the Traders' Café near the Bourse. Even with Bjorn gone and no possibility to include his cargo now, I had other means to move my scheme ahead. My heart ached for this venture to be a joining with Bjorn's, but I couldn't afford a year's wait for his return. The Yard called for me now. Willem's would be the crucial role, if he agreed. Together we must convince Klemp that such a seamless joining as I envisioned was the VOC's future.

Two problems spurred me to think as never before. I must persuade Pier to place his signature on the annulment papers, then I must put a cargo trade in motion through Willem. I shook in my slippers, frightened, excited. I prayed Miekke had faith that I used our inheritance wisely. I thought to gamble all here, all. Did I have the steel for it?

Please, Papa, pour your instincts upon me... let me make a good decision.

Henrik backed the coach away and I walked to the house. Litter everywhere on the path. Pier never touched a broom while I was gone. I almost laughed. Had I expected he would?

The garden door to the house was unlocked and yielded easily with my light push. The dimness inside on a sunny day startled me. Pier had all of the windows covered with old sheets of paper that the printing company had left stored in our shed. How odd. My eyes blinked to adjust to our dark sitting room. Oh, sweet Jesus. I caught at my throat choking on my own gulps of air. The cozy room I had left was a jumble of papers, Pier's shirts and breeches tossed on chairs, in corners, my frocks draped from door hook and handle. Pots, dishes thrown helter skelter. Clothes hung from chairs, across the table, even into the pots at the fireplace. My favorite paisley scarf lay part ashes by the cold fire. Everything we owned thrown about the room like so many tattered rags. Terror wrapped 'round me. Shaking, I backed toward the door, calling out for Pier, thinking he might lie under some heap, the victim of this ransacking. Only my echo answered

With a shiver of fear about to paralyze my steps, I dropped my bag and ran to Pieter and Colinda next door.

Pieter answered my frantic knock. "Maagda, thank god you've returned. We were ready to send for you."

"Where's Pier? We've been robbed, the house a shambles."

"Maagda, Pier's in trouble. I can't fathom what kind."

I was dazed… my shock at the house and now the sight of Pieter's face screwed in anguish. He reached for my hand to calm me.

"Pier hasn't been home much that we've seen. Then, night before last, we heard crashes, one loud bang after the other, then curses, curses."

"And, and…?"

"I ran over," Pieter said. "The door was open and Pier stood in the middle of the room, not a stitch of clothes on his body. He dashed about like a man possessed… emptied drawers, cupboards, threw everything he got his hands on." Pieter breathed in short puffs, drawing the scene. "I thought him drunk. But when I called to him and he turned, I knew he was sober as a predicant."

I grabbed Pieter's arm.

He told me Pier stood among the shards of his smashed savings pot and begged him for every florin, every stuiver he could yield.

If Pier has shattered his sacred pot, he had to be in danger, real danger. A stab of guilt pierced me. *How little I've thought or cared.*

Pieter offered to go back to the house with me, but I declined, feeling safe, knowing the chaos Pier's work.

At my own door I hesitated hardly sure which way to walk. Clutter left not a single path through the room. Pier spared no cupboard, no drawer, even knives and spoons and dishes scattered among our clothes. Did he think he'd discover coins in the cutlery box?

Suddenly, Pieter's words came back to me: *He looked for anything of value he could sell.* My hands flew to my ears. Papa's sapphires! In my distress over Papa's death, I packed no jewelry when I left for Hoorn. I had worn only my wedding ring and my mother's garnet that day, and I'd removed the wedding ring before my father's funeral.

I raced up the steps, tripping on my petticoats. Sweet figs! The bedchamber more a shambles than the lower room. The duvet lay in a heap on the floor. He'd ripped the mattress from the bed. Goose down everywhere, the pillows rent, laying. sagged, shredded at the foot of the bed. *God, how desperate he must be.*

Every stitch from my cupboard, petticoats, bloomers, had been flung across the room. I crawled round on my hands and knees, searching through the piles for my small ebony jewel case. I found it beneath one of Pier's shirts, jammed behind the leg of the bed. I lifted it. No jangle of brooches and earrings. I slid back the lid. Empty. My throat tightened.

The bastard. He'd left nothing of my few cherished pieces.

Oh, and there, under the edge of the duvet. The floorboard! Ripped away. I didn't have to look to know Papa's dowry money was gone. Pier stripped us bare.

I sank into the jumble of bedding on the floor, feeling the heat of frustration swell to fill my eyes. I had so little of personal value. But my wedding earrings, the lovely sapphires Papa had given me. Gone. *Oh, Pier, you suck the life from me.* I flung the box against the wall, venting the anger that beat so wildly in my chest.

I didn't try to clean up the mess. Instead, I picked through the shambles and gathered a few of my dresses. There was little else, a few blouses, two skirts and an apron, a petticoat and scattered linens. I stuffed them into my bag and fought off an urge to toss a live coal into the debris.

Nothing would mark the passing of my time here. So different from when I moved from Hoorn to marry Pier. Then, I left small tokens of my life in my bedchamber at home—a looking glass, my favorite brush, and yes, my silk kimono. Now I wanted all traces of my time with Pier to vanish. No one would enter these rooms and see any remnant that said, *oh yes, the woman, Maagda, lived here.*

I walked through the cluttered rooms, dragging the corpse of my rotting marriage, cursing Pier, but even more, the headstrong Maagda of old.

My one desire was to find Pier and somehow get his name on the annulment papers. But this rage of his, this derangement, gave little hope of his letting me go. Now, amid this despair, my thoughts, so wounded, so fragile, yielded to a certain truth. I'd been a fool to think my pregnancy a time of joy. What right had I to become a mother? The town would scorn me, mock my father's memory. The old wags would warn their daughters away. *Oh, yes, there's that Boscher woman. Had to defy tradition and name her own man. Look what it got her. Alone with another man's baby in her belly. Shame. Shame. Now the town'll go to ruin with no proper heir.* The Widow van Pelt would lead the bray. In a small town like Hoorn no hideaway promised shelter.

Might Aunt Loekke and Miekke and Ria turn away, too? Would they shut their hearts to my baby?

I looked at my fingers, the small finger where my mother's ring was barely visible in the dim light. Papa put it there with such trust in my future. I cried out, and beat my fists against the chair arms. *Papa, Papa, how I've betrayed you. How I've betrayed myself, jumping from an ill-thought marriage to ill-thought comfort in another's embrace.*

A groan rose so deep from inside me, I clutched my belly in fear. I could not bring an innocent life into such a world as I'd made for myself. But where or how might I muster the courage to trade my brew of stinging nettle that had readied me for motherhood for this wild carrot, this bishop's lace that would bleed the small life from me?

"But tell me, by Jupiter, what part of a man's life is that that is not sad, crabbed, unpleasant, insipid, troublesome, unless it is seasoned with Pleasure, that is to say, Folly?"

In Praise of Folly by Desiderius Erasmus (Classics Club edition)

CHAPTER 46—PIER

"MY GOD, MAN, HAVE YOU BATHED SINCE LAST week's flood?" Van Goyen shifted to the side when I neared him at the faro table. "I've smelled sweeter canal slops."

"Stuff it up your nose, van Goyen. Looks don't get a man into this game." My eyes shifted to each of the burghers, the punters, who sat around the table. "All that counts here is money."

He waved me away.

"I can buy in."

"You've never played before. Go home and sleep it off."

"I'm not drunk, and I've got cash." I threw my small leather bag onto the table. Must have been at least 1,500 florins in it, every coin left from my savings, the dowry and the trinkets I'd managed to peddle in the market. I'd lost most of the dowry money quick, in flimsy deals near the Bourse. The traders knew a green sucker when they saw one. Florins gone on bales of moldy cotton that I gambled to trade, but couldn't unload, now tossed to the bottom of the Amstel. A bitter way to learn I'd no talent for the Bourse.

One of van Goyen's cronies eyed the bag and urged me to take a seat.

My nerves were raw as boned fish. A big win at faro was my last chance. Steubing returned this week. If I couldn't pay off Horder and get the diamonds back…no, I couldn't think it.

I'd had little sleep or food since the flood. I'd spent my waking hours trying to beg or borrow florins. The tulip contract was worthless. I'd an urge to shred that damnable piece of paper, bite into it and tear it to scraps with my own teeth, but it was the only link I had to the diamonds.

Klees chortled when I reminded him of his promise to buy my contract.

I shook my fist after him.. But it was the same everywhere. I'd hunted out moneylenders. I offered my bag of florins and the deed to my house as security. My prospects for repaying 5,500 florins and interest on my wages was too rank a deal for any of them. I'd scoured the Damrak and the Jewish quarter. Not even the lowest among the street lenders would take a chance on me.

I watched a few more turns of the game. The burgher who dealt as banker said he'd quit after the current deck. Deal the cards, that was the best way to win. You needed a big stake to bid for the dealer's spot, but I was sure my bag of florins would do it. I had to chance it.

What to do? If I played as a punter, my best chance for a big win was to call the last three cards in the right order. If I won the auction to bank and deal, I raked in all the loser bets each turn.

Van Goyen whooped, a big win and the dealer went broke. His seat opened to bids. One punter shouted fifty; another one hundred florins.

"Five hundred." My bid was barely audible. There was a murmur around the table.

"We haven't gone higher than 100 florins," one of the burghers, the player beside van Goyen, said. He rapped the table with his ale tankard, his face flushed, but his eyes never left my money bag.

"Then maybe it's time for higher stakes." I couldn't believe such words came from me, my speech no kin to my tongue.

"Too rich for me," the burgher sighed and left the table.

A magistrate who'd hovered in the background grabbed the vacant seat, his medallion and chain of office clanging against the table.

"No more bids?" The retiring dealer's eyes swept the punters. "Looks like it's yours," he said and handed me the deck

I willed my hands not to shake while I shuffled the cards and passed them to the man on my right to cut.

"Will you keep the case?" I asked when he returned the deck to me. I knew I couldn't watch the deal and keep track of the cards at this point. He agreed and pulled the box to his side of the table. He would move a small tile on a connecting rod each deal to show which card had been played, giving the bettors better chance to place their money where a win might be expected. Now that I held the dealer's seat, it seemed unfair to me that they got even that chance.

I steadied my voice. "Place your bets." The words of a stranger.

A blur of hands stacked coins on the thirteen spades on the game board. The players bet across the suit. Any card was a possible winner on the first deal. Van Goyen's marker was engraved with an artist's brush. He bet on the ace, an eight and the king.

A thousand ants crawled under my skin. I couldn't keep myself still.

Then, my virgin deal. The first card, always a throw away; the second, the dealer takes bets on whatever money comes up, but the third card was the money card. I drew and flipped the eight of diamonds.

"Good man," van Goyen shouted. He had five florins on number eight. I had to take coins from my own money to cover his win, five florins from my own stake.

Damn his luck. A mere glance from him now made me twitch.

The bastard won again when I turned up an eight of clubs. Only two more left in my deck, the eight of hearts and the eight of spades. His luck couldn't hold with those eights. No man's luck was that good.

"Barman, ale all around." Van Goyen grinned and shared his win with the table. The other players seemed infected by the artist's fortune, and the remaining heft of my bag. Bets got heavier. Not a common stuiver on the board. They all bet florins now.

I licked at the sweat around my mouth and watched the players put their money down. Four of them rode on van Goyen's charm with the eight. They pulled hard on their pipes. Faces blurred in the smoke. I turned the cards over. Holy satan's hell! Another winning eight, the spade. Van Goyen pounded the table.

"A great dealer, Pier. You're a great dealer," he shouted over the roar of the winners.

Five bettors, among them, had fifty florins on the eight. I sucked in my breath and pulled fifty florins from my bank to cover their wins. I gnawed at my lip. There was only one more eight in the deck. This bastard's luck had to run out. Nobody could count on four straight wins.

The rumble of excitement among the players sent tremors through the oak floor, and the tremor seeped up through my boots. I watched round the table. That last high payoff loosened purse strings. Faces around me ran with sweat. Some of the men pulled off their hats and threw them on the floor behind the chairs. Burghers stuffed their pipes and lighted anew. Players and watchers alike drained their tankards of ale. Refills were ordered all around, but not me. I couldn't drink. The air hung heavy with the smell of men looking for a kill. Onlookers crowded behind the players. I was wedged into my corner sure I'd sink under the table if the crowd hadn't been there to prop me up, hide my shakes.

"Deal, man, deal. The cards glued or something?" They pushed me to move on.

The magistrate counted a stack of 50 florins and eyed the eight on the board. He glanced at the case keeper to weigh the possibility of eight coming up so soon again. I bit into my lip. The magistrate's chain of office rattled when he reached to pull the stack of coins back. I began to breathe easier.

Sweet Jesus, no! He's not pulling his bet. The magistrate built a second stack of florins to match the first. One hundred florins. He looked at me with a grin, then pushed the two piles of florins on to the eight. I was about to say no, but I remembered that I had not set wager limits when I won the deal auction. A murmur ran through the crowd. Then a gasp. I choked. Van Goyen slid two hundred florins across the board and onto the eight.

"Crowding my luck, your honor?" The artist laughed.

I needed no glass to know my face was white as cold ash. I reached to turn the cards.

"Wait. Wait," one of the burghers called. "This is too good to miss." He added another two hundred florins to the mountain of silver on the eight.

Five hundred florins on the turn of a card! My heart all but stopped, my throat so tight, I couldn't swallow.

My fingers tapped on the table. Van Goyen stared at my hands. I clutched the side of the table with my left hand to steady myself and slid the cards from the top of the deck. Sweat trickled under my arms, along my spine. First the discard. Then the dealer's win card, a queen. A single florin sat on the queen of spades. Not another bet on the table, nothing covered but the eight. I pulled the lone coin to my stack and reached for the final card. My hand trembled. The crowd hushed. I squeezed my eyelids tight, willed my hand to flip the card and show its face. A roar erupted that shook the timbered walls of the tavern. I didn't have to look to known I'd pulled the eight of hearts.

I slumped back against the wall, sweat oozed from every port in my body, my pathetic moan lost in the frenzy. The tavern exploded in raucous shouts, applause. The walls rang. Back were slapped. Cries of "Who would believe?" "Wait until I tell this at home." Van Goyen shouted over the din. "Drinks for the house." He looked at me, shaking his head with an *I told you so* glimpse of pity.

"Rue, Angelica, Buglosse, Marjoram, Trefoiles,
Roses, Violets, Lilies, and all the Gardens of Adonis,
invite both your sight and your smelling."

In Praise of Folly by Desiderius Erasmus (Classics Club edition)

CHAPTER 47—MAAGDA

WILLEM SENT A MESSAGE, ASKING ME TO MEET HIM
at the Bourse. I donned a warm wrap and fought a chill wind walking across the open Damrak. In spite of the bite in the air, Willem
lounged on a bench waiting, and waved away a companion when he
saw me approach.

"What's so urgent?" My voice taut, cold as the wind sweeping
bits of leaf and paper around my feet. I was still raw awaiting news
of Pier, the packet of bishop's lace smoldering in my pocket, and the
question of my baby burning in my mind. I braced now, expecting
yet another blow.

Catching my mood, Willem offered no pleasantries. Right to
business. "If you're serious about VOC trades, Maagda, I think we've
caught a good wind." He took my arm guided me to the Bourse visitors' tavern.

The trade. Of course, why else would Willem ask me to meet him?
I let my shoulders sag, the knot in my throat fall loose. I expected

him to tell me he was wrong about the annulment. I allowed myself to fall loose and slumped against the brick wall behind at my back. My self-possession was unraveling a day at a time and I needed a direction, anything, to knit myself to one piece again.

"The VOC's spring voyage has been sighted near the mouth of the Mediterranean. Should be in port the early part of next month, barring storms or pirates." Willem's eyes danced, his cheeks a high color, more visible now that, like many local men in the new fashion, he'd shaved his beard.

"And that means...?" Dare I set foot in this new venture with so much of my life at stake?

He explained each step, the need for agents, for advance information from paid scouts along the way, all the turns that meant a difference between profit and loss. He knew seasoned scouts who would report when a ship had taken water in her hold, how good a grade the carge, whether barrels and bales were measured to full weight. They bartered such news for their living.

"And? And?" I clutched my knife, poised with sharp dip in the air like a weapon.

Willem laughed and reached for my hand to pull the knife flat. "It's a standard cargo. Spices, mostly coriander, pepper, cinnamon. Crates of china, too, and bolts of silk. Here. Take a look at the manifest."

I pulled the small table lantern across the scratched oak table and unfolded the paper, mouthing the scribbled words, each line of the inventory that Willem had reeled off.

"This is it, yes? Puts us in the cargo business?"

"The first step. This is what we might bid on if you agree...and have the florins." He narrowed his eyes. "And remember the dangers, remember 1629."

Willem reminded me of the VOC ship, *Batavia*, that ran into coral reefs off the western coast of Australia in that fateful year. All lives lost. Wreckers salvaged some of the load, but several burghers went bankrupt. And to make matters more perilous in this day, some of our neighboring governments, especially Spain, encouraged their crews to raid our ships at will.

I'd weighed such costs during the long months I puzzled through this cargo venture. Now my head told me to seize the opportunity, to keep our business alive. But my heart was too heavy with another dread to let me think clearly. Miekke had agreed early on that we would put money from my father's estate into the business. We also had fifty percent of the proceeds from the new fluytship on the Yard books to keep us afloat, along with substantial cash. Buying into the VOC cargo would all but drain us. I'd thought all along she would need more assurance, and now I was the one to hold back, weighed down by the more tormenting decision of my baby, this tiny form taking root in my belly.

Willem studied me. "You look pale today."

I brushed his comment aside. We could lose everything here, destroy my father's long years of toil and those of his father before him. I worried that my sister didn't understand that risk. My head spun with such worries and the child, always the child, and be damned, yes, Pier. But might there be another chance?

"When must I put money on the table?" My voice fell to a whisper. "...and how much?"

Willem poured himself more ale from the pitcher he'd ordered, leaving a trail of droplets down the side of his pewter tankard that he swept away with the finger that bore his oval signet ring.

"It depends on what portion of the shipment we bid for. We need a letter of credit with an open amount over the VOC's published minimum. Could be as much as 14,000 florins, but it won't be made public for another week or two."

I tried to keep my mind on his reasoning, guilty to the quick that I might yet pull away from this trade after all of his work, and guilty that the vision I conjured of a VOC alliance that would mean so much to so many might die aborning. "Doesn't the amount we buy depend on where we plan to sell?

"Just so," he said, and spread his hands on the table. "That's the gist of such commerce." Once we knew our markets, he'd have to locate buyers through his string of agents in those ports. "It takes time and we don't have much of that right now. We should make decisions within the next seven days."

Yet another deadline, another fall of the calendar that might crush me. I had only days, I knew, to decide about the fatal herbs I carried.

I twisted Mama's ring, Miekke's shadow, her possible denial, lurking just behind my eyes. Yet, Willem's excitement seduced me, rode like a warm current over the turmoil in my head.

The new fluytship at the Yard was almost ready for delivery to a port north of Rome. If I put a second crew of men to work on the final rub down, we might launch the boat before the VOC ship docked in Amsterdam, ample time to buy the VOC cargo and load it on this new boat bound for the buyer in Italy. I tested the idea in my head while Willem sipped his ale, his eyes on the manifest in my hands.

"What do you think of this, Willem? We stow the VOC cargo on the newly built ship we're ready to launch, sail the cargo to the buyer you find, then deliver the fluytship to its owner north of Rome. We might even offer the owner a small payment for use of the ship to carry our goods." In my heart I wanted to buy the VOC's entire cargo, move to an alliance immediately. I knew that impossible with my cache of silver. We'd need the profits from our first trade to make any further move, to convince Klemp of the bold scheme that had brewed so long in my head.

"Ah, now you think like a merchant." Willem scribbled numbers on his papers. "Here's another thought. Maybe your new ship owner would want to buy the entire cargo to resell himself." Willem spread a small map on the table and drew a circle around Rome on Italy's west coast.

I scanned the colors on the map and traced a line with my finger south and east of Italy's heel. "He told me he had plans to carry goods, here, through the Bosporus into the Black Sea. This might be the perfect move."

Vitali, the buyer, said he wanted a Boscher fluytship to carry Italy's olives and cereals to Odessa and ports in the Crimea and return, his hold filled with the region's store of minerals.

Miekke, Miekke. Would you desert me when so much is possible here, when I've yet to lose my child?

Willem grabbed the manifest and rapped it against the table. "If we wrote a contract like that with your buyer, we would have a second option that might launch our new venture on a grand scale." He flushed with an enthusiasm that sent tingles of energy across the table.

"Might you raise enough florins to fill the holds of two boats, have two fluytships deliver commodities that you own?"

"Two?"

"Certainly. Think a moment. You have one fluytship for your buyer in Italy and you have your company fluyt docked in Hoorn. If your own boat's schedule is free, why not fill it with VOC goods and send it off to another port? All we have to decide is where. I'll find an agent to scout buyers."

I fanned myself, frightened, but elated by such a prospect.. What would Papa think of this daring plunge? In my heart he whispered, *try.* Papa believed life was a ladder where the new generation moved a step higher than the old. Would I fancy less for my own child? That hand at my throat again. Would there be a child?

"Maagda, what is it? You ill?"

"Sorry. No. You think there are so many possible buyers out there?" I did a quick calculation in my head of how much silver I might pull together. Not enough, I knew, to take the risk Willem proposed. I'd bankrupt us.

"I'd stake my property on finding buyers. Our neighboring countries fight a long war. Their stores grow short by the battle, and it's foolhardy to deliver cargo over land routes, even some sea routes. Sweden's Gustavus eyes our own Dutch maritime commerce in the Baltic. Better we look to Mediterranean buyers." He hesitated, thinking, clicking his ring against the side of the tankard. "Such thoughts make me feel like a vulture feasting on carrion, but the war exists. The misfortune of our neighbors is good fortune for Holland's shippers. Why not us?"

When he mentioned the war, Bjorn's face flashed in my mind. I had seen the wound high on his shoulder, had traced the ragged scar with my fingers.

"You didn't flinch when I said *why not us.*"

"Sorry. My mind took a different turn."

"What I suggest is that rather than take the commission you've offered me, I invest with you, become a partner, for some reasonable percentage we agree on."

Stunned, I sat forward in my chair to look more closely into his face through the dim tavern llight. Willem's eyes didn't waver. They widened and held my gaze.

"I hadn't thought of a partnership…at least now…perhaps in a year or so."

I stammered, hesitant to tell him my hope that Bjorn would return for a joint venture with his galleon and my fluytships.

"At least then you have thought of taking on a partner?"

"Perhaps…nothing so definite."

He frowned and his heavy black eyebrows merged at the bridge of his nose. "Look at this way. As your partner, I'll join my cash to yours. Makes buying most of the VOC's cargo from this voyage possible."

Willem's willingness to invest as a partner assured me he thought highly of our prospects, yet I hesitated to take such a commitment from him.

"Maagda, I have the funds and the contacts, and some experience with trades. You have the funds and the ships. And perhaps, most important, we trust and respect one another. A natural alliance."

"My instincts tell me yes. But there's such turmoil in my life now. One moment I see it clearly, the next I'm muddled." Still in the back of my mind lay a different *natural alliance,* and the child?

"You muddled?" He leaned forward. The lantern glow accentuated his immaculate white collar, the gentle curve of his brow and cheeks. His eyes, luminous, honest as a schoolboy's. " It was you who conceived this entire plan, who dared to take over a venerable business, who at this very moment holds papers that will free you from your husband. Do you call these the acts of a muddled woman?"

His words, his concern so touching, they cracked the dam that held my emotions. I'd not told Willem about Pier, about the ransacked house or his theft of my small bits of jewelry and the dowry money. The story rushed out of me now, a swipe of words that painted his kin as villain.

He reached across the table and took both my hands in his. "What in the god's name had Pier gotten himself into?" Willem shook his head and shuddered. "And you sat here thrashing out plans for a new venture like there was no other consequence in your life."

"I am anything but calm. There's more at stake here than I can say. Before any decision, I must return to Hoorn and speak with my sister. This is her venture, too."

"I've no wish to press you, Maagda, but with so little time, it is you who must call our next move." He sat at ease now, his head bent. Willem's mass of blue-black hair fringed his forehead and shoulders as if arranged for an artist's canvass. Would that I enjoyed his composure.

"First I must go to Miekke, then find Pier. But don't feel today has been to no avail." I hesitated, my hands balled into tight fists. "I will have my answer to you by sundown, day after next."

"You appreciate timing is tight?"

"Yes, of course. Our fluytship buyer comes in tomorrow for his final inspection of the boat."

"And the partnership?"

"If we go ahead, might we work it out on a venture by venture basis, nothing formal?"

"Is that what you wish?"

"At least for the first year while we build a history to guide us."

He reached over and covered my hands with his.

"Perhaps by then with the annulment a thing of the past and our good business relationship growing, we might..." He stopped.

"Might what, Willem?"

"Nothing. Nothing. A fleeting thought." He pulled back his hands and turned his head away, but not before I caught a glimpse of crimson rise up his cheeks.

He pulled his lips tight. "Much too soon to talk of events a year away. Let's think of today. We both have letters of credit to produce."

> *"And yet they are so bold, that you'll scarce believe how*
> *they not only assure themselves of immortality and a*
> *life like the gods, but promise it to others, too."*

In Praise of Folly by Desiderius Erasmus (Classics Club edition)

CHAPTER 48—MAAGDA

INSTEAD OF RETURNING TO SEARCH FOR PIER, though I needed to find him, I left Willem and boarded the coach to Hoorn. I had to prepare for my meeting with the fluyt buyer, and speak with Miekke, and deal with the bishop's lace in my pocket. Miekke could well refuse to yield her share of the inheritance when she learned of the child.

I knew the trip to be a selfish one. I felt trapped in some spinning cage where cargo trades, annulments, Bjorn's leaving and my baby, all swirled 'round me. Above it all, the specter of bishop's lace and the loss of my child, a torment that robbed my soul of rest, day or night. I grasped at wisps of air. Perhaps to sit quietly and talk with Miekke, away from the tumult, I might strengthen my own faith in these choices that I faced.

In some small pocket of my mind, I fretted about Pier. I had no idea where he spent his days, or where and how to approach him. I'd checked at Steubing's shop, but no one was there. Bile rose and scalded my tongue at any thought of crawling to him. So much depended on today and Miekke.

While the coach wheeled north, I fought to take in ordinary pleasures, tiny roadside bramble roses that trembled in the coach's draft. Beyond the dust of the road trees in new leaf shimmered in a soft lemon shade, while the pines in a woodland thicket beyond stood black as peat. The tones as varied as my mood.

When I got home, Sophie told me Miekke took fresh air in the back garden. I found her there, a light throw around her shoulders, her eyes closed and her face up to the sun. I stood silently for a moment and relished this moment of serenity and innocence. Had I the right to splash my dark worries over such peace?

"Miekke." I called softly.

She opened her eyes, blinked and rose to throw her arms around me. She was warm from the sun and smelled of the fresh earth and young blooms of the garden.

"Maagda, home so soon? I didn't expect you for at least another day or two."

We linked arms and walked back to the bench where she left her wrap.

"Well, little sister, I've missed you, and I have much to tell you." I halted. "And, to ask of you."

"Oh, Maagda, you're so serious of late. What's happened to you?" She didn't look at me, but picked at the fringe on the russet shawl she wore. "You've been no fun since you married. Except for your little frolic with the prince." She pinched my arm.

I took her hands. "Please listen, Miekke. We round a turn in the road now and there may be no way back."

"Turns in the road, indeed. I haven't the spirit to move from this spot."

Lord, she tried me. My reserve of patience stretched thin from the friction of these past weeks. How to reach her?

"Remember how Papa told us the story of that ancient Greek who warned that you may never step in the same water twice? Life flows past in a changing current, the moment, like the water, never stays still. This day is not the same as yesterday, nor will it be like tomorrow."

While I spoke, Miekke picked up a brittle hawthorn leaf, a remnant of seasons past, and twirled it in her fingers, an absent motion; I prayed not from an absent mind. I required her attention, but thought to select my words with care. I learned well Papa's lesson: words may persuade or poison. I'd had my fill of poison.

"I've spoken with Willem about our inheritance, Miekke. We share many ideas about the future, where best to seek our fortunes."

"Why do we need Willem? What does he know of Papa's business, the Yard?"

"He's traveled beyond Grote Noord. He sees the world in its larger scale. We must, as well."

She held the leaf in the palm of her hand and blew it softly into the light breeze that stirred the bog sedges near the wall. I watched its lazy, undulating path and sensed it reflected my sister's mindless bent this day. My eye caught the sprouting garden border where I'd planted a bed of jonquils in Mother's memory. I thought to balance it with these new tulips everyone spoke of to honor Papa. Better to think of new spring blossoms each year than the sea lapping him away.

Miekke turned to me. "You worry too much. The Boschers have lived off the Hoorn Yard for generations back. Why should it change now?"

Frustration bubbled in me, almost broke the surface. I fought to keep my voice soft, even.

"That is what we must understand. Hoorn's commerce no longer moves in that reliable current as it did in grandfather or father's day. You should come to Amsterdam, see the new shipyard that keeps two boats in production at the same time. We can't compete, Miekke."

Her brow creased in a frown and she snugged the shawl closer to her chest. My words reached her. "And Willem has a plan?"

"Yes, I…Willem and I think to invest in a trading venture. We would buy cargo that VOC ships carry back from the Spice Islands in the Pacific and resell it, might even use our own fluyt to transport the stock to other ports."

I let my words float on the air before I added, "and when Bjorn returns and buys his own galleon, we might import the cargo from his ship, no middleman."

Miekke looked at me as though I spoke through my ears. "What do you know of trading? What of Pier, your home with him in Amsterdam?"

The moment thundered in my head. I closed my eyes and breathed slowly.

I pulled her into my arms and whispered, "What if there is no Pier, no marriage?"

She jerked away from me, grabbed the arm of the bench. "Maagda, has town living in Amsterdam scrambled your head? You speak like a mad woman."

I waited, let her settle.

"No, Miekke, not mad. I see life more clearly than I have since the day of my betrothal."

She knew of Pier's planned emigration, but none of the sordid beginnings of my marriage or his refusal to give me children. I told her now in as little detail as I deemed fitting about how this might be the means of my annulment. Miekke's usual pallor drained to a white so devoid of life I feared she might faint. I held her close to me again. The salt from her tears spilled to my cheek.

"Did Papa know?"

"None of this. Only that Pier wanted to leave Holland."

I rubbed her back, cooed as to a child. Her frailty so vivid, I felt every bone in her back.

"Hush, hush, Miekke. We'll manage. I promise to always be here to care for you."

A pair of gulls swooped in from the harbor, screeching while they circled close to the old heap of kitchen scraps near the back garden wall. I pointed to the birds, tried to jolly her.

"See, the birds mock our tears. Like them we must fly to new prospects, put yesterday in the dust bin."

Miekke turned her head up to the birds and managed a weak smile.

I gave her time to dab at her wet eyes, but I had to go on. When she returned the cloth to her pocket, I took her hand again.

"There's more." I pulled my lips tight before I went on. "I'm with child. Bjorn's child."

I feared to breathe, awaiting her stricken shriek. Instead she leaped from the bench and threw her hands into the air, a dizzying feat for one so frail.

"Maagda, Maagda. A baby. Our own baby. How joyous." She urged me up and whirled me in a little dance down the garden path, more energy than I'd seen from her in weeks.

"Then you must forget new business," she said. You must rest, lots of rest."

Suddenly, she froze. "Oh my lord. What am I saying? If you're with Bjorn's child…my own sister. Why, you're, you're…"

"An adulterer," I finished for her. I took her hand. "It tears at me, but I think to let the child go."

She jumped away, but moved again toward me, her hand open. "Let the child go?" She slapped me hard. Stunned, I felt the heat in my face. She turned from me and clutched the bench. "That's killing."

I reached for her, but she pushed me away.

"You're vile, Maagda, absolutely vile. You don't deserve what Papa left. He would suffer a second death knowing this." She spit the words at me, and fled into the house, slamming the door.

I heard the bolt bang home. She locked me in the garden.

I slumped against the frame, knew it useless to pound for her to open, so I dragged myself back to the bench and collapsed into a frenzy of bizarre images – Papa, Bjorn, a baby girl -- my hand clenched around the packet of bishop's lace. Never in our lives together had we quarreled like this. Nor in my life had there been so many knives pointing to my quick.

Miekke locked the house against me, her heart as well. While years of business had taught me to see the many shades of gray in life, my sister saw only black and white. Her comment about Papa struck like a blow to my belly, but her rejection of me, a blow to my soul. I'd prayed for Miekke's acceptance, now a mere trickle of water on hell's hot stones.

Through the next hours, I moved like a limp creature with some unknown hand to pull the string that kept me afoot. Sophie had opened the door for me shortly after Miekke had bolted it, but my sister hid herself whenever I neared the house.

I went to Papa's study to sit and think, the packet of bishop's lace still in my hand. The agony of decision left me shaken, my head a mass of thunder, and my body wet with a storm of its own making. To divert myself, I looked round the room where Papa had spent so much of his time. My eyes were drawn to the bookshelf where *The Count of Hoorn* rested. When I lifted it, the sense of Papa, my family heritage, flowed to my core. I let my fingers trace the miniature ropes, the sails, the wheel. The warmth of Papa's hand seemed to linger about the ship, though reason told me it was nothing more than sun from the window.

The joints gave more easily than I expected. Papa must have waxed it soon before his death, perhaps the afternoon he told me of the rolled parchments that rested in the ship's hull. I unfolded each carefully, read the words. Though my eyes misted, the meaning burned into my bones. I bolted from the chair. What if a bastard lived, someone who claimed our legacy? Was it not possible my grandfather and this Anna Fletten he took up with in the fright and loneliness of war created a child together. Never once since the day Papa told me of the letter did its meaning cut through with such clarity...until this reading, this frame of mind. But now, by god, it sliced through me hot, like a shaft of molten metal.

I went to the window and looked north toward the Yard. Though I couldn't see a bit of it, its presence reached back to me across the sand. I clutched the sill, and the room closed in on me, the walls squeezing the breath from my body.

Trembling with weakness, I felt for the Papa's chair and collapsed into it, my head a thumping mass. How had I not realized a threat before? Had I been so buried in my miseries with Pier, that all else bounced away? I read the letter once again, the words scorching. Might there be a man or woman in Antwerp, someone near my age, to claim our Trust? It took my unborn child, the baby just moments ago I thought to lose, to make me understand the stakes here. How low I'd fallen these few days. What right had I to crawl away from this future, my Hoorn-bred child's rightful heritage.

I took several deep breaths, my chest rising and falling, straining against my dress. I walked to the window and pushed up the sash. No faltering now. I opened the packet of bishop's lace and emptied it to the seaborne wind, praying Papa would guide me, strengthen the resolve I'd need for the decisions ahead.

I sent word to Willem, and a note to Klemp at the VOC to ask for a meeting. With the sudden clarity of a blue horizon after a storm, I saw what had to be done, how to win the VOC. If only Miekke could see it as well. And what of Pier?

My new ship owner from Italy arrived as planned to accept the launched fluyt. All that remained for his business was to paint the ship's name, *Pot di Oro,* on the bow so he might see it before he left on a Baltic buying trip. Normally, our woodworkers carved each letter, but Signore Vitali, hadn't decided on *Pot of Gold,* until the morning he inspected his craft. He was so pleased with his choice that he accepted my idea of transferring our cargo onboard when I promised to send a woodcarver along to have his letters ready for the hull when we delivered the boat to his dock.

How I wished I might barter so simply with my sister. I'd tap softly on her bedroom door, but she'd steeled herself against me and I'd be greeted by a silence so shrill, it pierced my soul.

On the morning of my return to Amsterdam, I stood in the narrow alcove near Miekke's door still shaky from the convulsions in my mind these past days. I rapped and rapped again. I called to her, beseeching her to let me enter.

"Miekke, Miekke, you tear at my heart with your silence." I sank to my knees and pleaded, so lonely my bones chilled in the frozen silence. I clutched a letter I'd written and slid it under the door. I wrote that I returned to the city to find Pier and to close my life there, all the while begging her understanding and love for the child to come. I knew all too well Miekke could yet make a move to foil the plans I set in motion. But the worry that my unborn child would have no family to welcome her weighed heavier on me than any thought of Pier or the new business I pursued for all our sakes.

CHAPTER 49—MAAGDA & PIER

"HELP YA, MA'M?"

"Steubing's."

"Second floor front. Stairs at the rear."

I knew the way, but thanked the guard and stepped through the massive carved door into a dimly lit corridor. I had no idea what I might learn here. My thoughts were divided between the urgency of finding Pier, and my crucial meeting with Klemp when I left the diamond shop.

Idle merchants sat puffing at long-stemmed pipes outside small shops that lined either side of the hall. I made my way toward the stairs, and several men nodded or touched the brims of their black hats. A guard slept in a chair near the back. I moved around his bulk, and a dwarfish, stooped man beckoned an invitation from the last shop on the left. I shook my head and walked to the staircase where years of wear had polished the oak treads to a sheen. At the top landing, a single door loomed with a muted light flickering through the small leaded glass in the transom. It had been dark when I stopped here days ago in search of Pier. I rapped, jiggled the handle and tensed at what lay ahead.

A muffled voice called through the door, "No business today."

"Maagda...Verbeck. You sent for me." Steubing had delivered a note asking me to come to the shop this morning. My neighbor, Pieter, brought it to me the instant I returned from Hoorn.

Seconds passed, then a key turned, a bolt slammed to its stop, and the door opened a crack. A gray-haired man with veined cheeks prized the door slightly ajar, holding it with fat, stubby fingers.

He motioned me inside the empty quarters. "Where is Pier? I thought to find him here." My eyes roved over the work area, the magnifying glass and scraps of blue velvet on the counter, the hulking black safe, its door open. Cobwebs, choking dust everywhere. No hand or foot had disturbed this place in weeks, certainly not Pier.

"My March diamonds, my five best stones. They're gone. And I have a buyer from Antwerp who comes tonight with cash, good florins, to take them." He gulped ale from a tankard on the counter. "Your husband was the only one who had keys to the door or the safe. Is there any sign of break in or damage?" He swept his right hand around the shop and paced the short distance between the door and the safe. "The diamonds had to leave here with Veerbeck."

I sank into a nearby chair so hard it jarred my backbone. A puff of dust scattered around me. "Pier sought florins, silver, but not as a thief. He is not a common thief."

Steubing's eyes burned back at me. Anger poured from every taut muscle, the rigid set of his mouth, the eyebrows knit tight across his forehead, raised to brush the whitish strands above.

He sneered. "My empty vault speaks for itself."

"Is this why you sent for me today? You seek payment for your stones?" My blood slowed to an icy trickle. The annulment...the VOC trades. Was my future, my child's future at stake because of some fool business of Pier's?

"I want my diamonds." Steubing slammed his tankard to the counter, sloping a puddle of ale on the counter.

Whether or not Pier was guilty of Steubing's accusation, I saw our inheritance about to vanish. I had no idea what the stones were worth, indeed, whether or not I had responsibility here, thinking perhaps Steubing tried to trick me for silver. I needed Willem. Must a wife repay a husband's crime? Was there a crime here? Some ruse of Steubing's, perhaps twice selling the stones for delivery and using Pier's absence to blame him? The winds of my mind blew hot and cold, struggling to believe Pier not capable of such low dealing, yet afraid the future that would cost me dearly might slip away this very morning.

"Someone will pay, either in silver or in prison. We'll know soon enough. The constables bring the bastard to face me this hour."

Stunned that he was to be here now, I went rigid in my chair. I told Steubing I hadn't seen Pier since my father's funeral, these many weeks past.

"He was with you in Hoorn?"

"No, he stayed to tend..." a noisy stomping on the stairs stopped me.

The door was thrown open, and the beefy hands of a constable shoved Pier into the shop. He was filthy, his clothing rags, the green tunic I had sewn for him torn down the front, blood stains running through its left side, probably from the bruise that darkened that side of his face near his eye. His hair was matted with dried blood above his forehead, and oh lord, his hands tied behind his back. In my worst thoughts of him missing never did I expect to find him in so sorry a state. An anxious bubbling rippled in my chest. I didn't know whether to reach out to him or add my own blows.

Nailed Jesus, what's she doing here? I tried to turn away but the constable pushed me toward Steubing. Maagda took a sharp breath, her hand flying up to her mouth.

"Here's your man."

My left eye was swollen shut from the pounding Horder gave me when he caught me in his one good field yesterday. Bastard broke my right thumb, too, before he turned me over to the magistrate.

Steubing lunged at me, breathing hard, guttural rasps, but he checked himself at the counter. "I'll see you in the worst hell the law has." He spit in my face, and part of the yellowish glob ran down my sleeve.

Maagda rose from her chair, moved toward me.

"Don't," Steubing ordered, "go to your chair. I trusted your man, took him in when he knew nothing. Then he steals from me, steals the most valuable property I own. He's less than a cockroach to squash under my boot."

He kicked at my ankle. Maagda cried *stop*, me bending in pain, though a new truth ran up my leg with the hurt: this was but a taste of what the coming weeks would bring.

"I'll finish you where Horder stopped." Steubing moved toward me again, his right arm up and ready to strike.

The constable grabbed his arm and pushed him back. "None of that. Better to let the law have 'em."

"Where are my diamonds, you bag of offal?" He pointed to the safe.

It gaped at me like a condemning eye. I hated Steubing for making me face him with Maagda in the shop. Why did he have to bring her here? For that I'd give him no satisfaction, tell him nothing. Let him ferret it out.

I cocked my swollen eye to catch a quick glimpse of Maagda. She'd gone white where she sat now, her arms tight across her breast, hands clamped in tight fists on her elbows. Did a tear roll on her cheek? For an instant, an odd feeling coursed through me. I wanted her to touch me. Yet, I wanted to hide, not let her see me bloody and tied. I likely smelled like bad fish, too, but I couldn't know. My nose swelled shut just below the battered eye.

I blinked to clear my sight, but the constable tapped my shoulder and pushed me round toward the door. "He's best in my ties." He waved his hand at Steubing. "He'll be in the magistrate's court."

"Pier." Maagda's voice trailed after me to the stairs. The sound came to me like I was under water, still in that river's flood, too muffled to know if there might be a note of kindness in it.

> *"Nay, there is scarce an inn, wagon or ship*
> *into which they intrude not."*

In Praise of Folly by Desiderius Erasmus (Classics Club edition)

CHAPTER 50—MAAGDA

PIER'S BATTERED FACE LEFT ME LOOSE OF LIMB AND wondering which of us carried the greater sin. I was sick that he faced long years of hard labor in some god-forsaken tangle of heat and toil on the other side of the world. Pier's image stayed with me as I walked toward the wharf, wishing I might forego my meeting with Klemp at this moment, but he traveled into Amsterdam especially at my beckoning and we hadn't the comfort of time. We were to meet at the waterfront inn, The Galleon, where Bjorn and I shared our first meal. A biting wind tugged at my cap and swirled my skirt tight, slowing my pace to small steps. I paused before a chandler's window to adjust my cap, pulling the sides closer to my ears and fluffing the lace trim where it had curled back, and I rearranged my skirt into neat folds before I turned the final corner out of the wind onto the dock road.

Willem and I had talked through the details of the meeting earlier in the week. Now as I moved from cobble to cobble, I urged myself to recall our plan, steering my eyes from the fleet of ships anchored in mid-river and quelling my speculations about what each carried. I agreed with Willem that it best for me to see Klemp alone, to first trade on his friendship with my father, before I spread our daring scheme for him.

I stood a moment before the great oaken door, its bronze pull in the shape of a billowing sail frozen in my hand, setting my thoughts to a slow, deliberate course. I threw the Maagda of old, the Maagda who would leap unthinking at flashing glimmers of life, to the water-borne winds back on the river.

Klemp had reserved a table and rose to greet me, brushing my cheek in a kiss that was all whiskers. He was not one to follow the new fashion of shaving beards and mustaches.

"You don't look yourself, Maagda." He pulled out a chair for me. "The business getting too much for you."

"Not at all," I assured him. "I've concerns at home. My sister does not fare well."

The inn was crowded, every seat occupied. Merchants lounged near the door waiting for a table. Klemp hailed a server to order our meal, a baked salmon with roasted beets, turnips and leeks. Then he turned to me.

"So what is this mystery, the meeting that couldn't wait until Hoorn?" Between words small puffs of white smoke burped from the bowl of his clay pipe. "You caught me at the right time. In two days, the Gentlemen XVII gather, and I could not have left Hoorn." Klemp's eyes wandered around the Inn as he spoke, wondering, I supposed, how many investors for his ships might be in the room. His gaze returned to me with no trace of smile. "Only for Lars' daughter would I make this journey."

I thanked him for that courtesy, but took my time to answer his question about why I asked to meet.. The dining room was warm, so much so, I felt uncomfortable in my wrap. I let it slip to the back of my chair. The steam in the air that swirled about the diners settled in my hair, and I knew it curled in tight ringlets around my cap. I brushed the curled wisps back from my face.

"You spoke to Papa and me often of the VOC's difficulty finding investors in these times," I began. "Are many still reluctant to buy into your trips to Batavia?"

Klemp tapped his pipe stem against his lower teeth yellowed from years of smoking to the shade of parched jonquils. "In matter of fact, yes," he said, waving smoke away from his face. "This tulip craze reaches serious magnitude now. Burghers buy and sell with little thought, yet make unheard of profits in weeks. Mere options on paper, you understand. Who wants to wait a year or more for a ship to return with these paper tulip profits close to hand?" He brushed random ash flakes from his tunic. "The situation grows so serious I'm told the States General might step in to halt the trading."

I toyed with my salmon to hide my delight at his words. "Then perhaps there is no better time for us to talk."

"To talk of what, Maagda?" Klemp kept his pipe burning throughout the meal, adding to the layer of smoke that hovered below the blue and white tiled ceiling.

My hands were damp, and the cloth of my dress stuck to my backbone. I swallowed before I spoke.

"I ask your advice on a scheme, an idea, that might, *no, that will,* bring profits for the Dutch East India Company and the Boscher Boat Yard." I let out a great breath, so strong, it felt every breath of the morning had been captive inside me waiting for this moment.

Klemp whipped his pipe from his mouth so fast I feared his teeth might follow. He stared at me… moped his brow with a pocket cloth. "Young woman…"

His voice was hoarse and he coughed. I thought a fishbone choked him. I started to rise, but he waved me back. He cleared his throat.

"Profits, Maagda. You speak of profits." Klemp took my hand. "Do you know our investors have earned as much as one thousand percent profit on several of our trips?" He patted my hand like he might a child. "Most of this Republic's wealth comes from VOC shipping. That is why we worry about losing investors. Even the States General pressures us. Prince Frederick will speak to the Gentlemen XVII this week."

I remembered what Willem said about the low coffers the day we met the Prince. It was schoolboy lore that while a Dutch family might live comfortably on 300 guilders or florins a year, several early investors in the VOC, especially one Jacob Poppen, now the richest man in the Republic, was said to have a worth of 500,000 guilders.

"Yes," I said, "great wealth has returned to many who've invested with you and that's why your board of governors can tell the States General what to do." Klemp let go of my hand. "But we speak of the past. What of now? What of the future?"

Klemp narrowed his eyes at me, and took his pipe from his mouth about to speak, but I gave him no chance. "You say new investors are scarce." I leaned into the table and placed my hands flat, fingers splayed, thoughts fleeting through the long months I'd toyed with pieces of this puzzle. "Suppose you had but a single investor who came to you with florins that meant voyages might sail to catch the Eastern crops at their peak for shipping, that you no longer must rely on joint ventures?"

Klemp turned his palm over and held my hand in a firm grip. "Ah, a sweet dream in these times, dear lady."

I tightened my grip on his hand in return before I let go. I wanted him fully aware of me, that I was serious. "Listen then, while I spin such a dream." I amazed myself as the words started to spill out, spinning my exquisite folly. Surely, Papa was somewhere in the ether filling my head with these words.

I picked up my table knife. "It works like this." I cut two pieces of salmon on my plate, a large one and a smaller one. "That large piece of fish is your galleon returning from Batavia, holds filled with spices, lumber, perhaps a new cargo I've heard talk of, a coffee bean. And this, the minnow fish if you will, is but one Boscher fluyt. Your cargo unloads to our holds for quick voyages to buyers along the Baltic and Mediterranean."

Klemp looked at my plate. "Fanciful, Maagda, but certainly not different from what we do now. Where are the assured profits you speak of?" He tapped his fingers impatiently.

I sat upright and smoothed the lace on my cuffs. "With my plan cargo is bought and paid for *before your voyage,* by..." I spoke the name slowly... "the Boscher Ship and Trading Company."

He blinked and started to repeat the new company name, but I was afraid to stop.

I ran on, telling him that we would buy all of his cargo at an agreed upon price before the voyage. When his galleon docked, we took ownership of the cargo and stowed it on our fluyts for trips to buyers readied by our own agents, the latter, Willem's doing of course, but I held that card a bit longer.

Klemp's brows knit into a solid line of snow. He scraped his chair back, I thought to leave. But he inhaled a huge breath and settled.

"You are telling me that you will guarantee a price for all of our cargo, your company alone? I knew your father ran a successful boat yard, but such funds as this?"

I laughed, a hearty, throat-filling laugh, the first time in weeks, at last some easing of the tensions that bound me. "Yes, we have done well. But there's more to it."

Now was the time to reveal Willem's stake, and, too, the profits we expected from the cargo buy that we had arranged only days before, already guaranteed to give us a handsome return.

"You've worked with Willem, so you are aware that he's a commercial lawyer. But perhaps you did not know that he has agents the breadth of the continent." I brushed my hands across of the table and my knife clattered to the floor. No matter. " Their business is to know where the buyers are and what they require. What we propose with this new arrangement is that you send a smaller courier craft ahead with your cargo manifest as each voyage nears port here, and we ready the buyers." At some point, we planned to order specific cargo before the voyage, but now was not the moment to go so far. We had to learn the seasons in this new climate and how and when crops were ripened and picked.

Klemp's face colored deep as the beet juice on his plate. I feared apoplexy, but he breathed quickly and seemed to recover, and sat, gripping the table. "Do you realize the risks you suggest here? Between storms and pirates from the Spanish crown, some of our cargo never reaches Hoorn or Amsterdam. That's the rub now."

I nodded, and cast my glance around the inn. We had talked for more than an hour. Many of the tables had emptied. Taking up a knife again, I moved the two pieces of salmon on my plate so they moored side by side. His eyes followed my hand.

I spoke slowly. "There's a third stake holder in what I propose, the State. All of Holland knows Prince Frederick badgers the VOC for more income. We mean to have the States General share a percentage of our profits...if the State will send ships to meet your galleons and provide safe passage from the Canaries to home port."

He leaned back in his chair. "I'm stunned, Maagda, stunned. You are Lars Boscher's daughter, no doubts there. But this is a huge scheme, perhaps too ambitious."

He held his pipe just short of his lips.

I smiled at him. "We can do nothing about storms at sea. Too bad we can't have Nature share the profits as well. But we can stop the losses from piracy if Prince Frederick understands how profitable our plan is to the State." I raised my eyebrows. "That would be your job."

I spoke each point yet again, making clear that the State profited doubly in our success, once by the share we gave them and again by its taxes on VOC profits.

"By god, you're a bold one. Still the daring lass who named her own man."

I opened my lips as if to speak, but instead, patted them with my meal cloth. No point in bringing Pier's plight into the conversation.

Klemp tilted back in his chair, and I watched as he ran his tongue over his teeth, fearing to take a breath for what he might say.

"I'll think on it."

I measured my words. "Might I go to my partner and say you entertain our plan?"

Klemp thumped the table and laughed, but turned serious quickly enough. "What I entertain is not so important." He slapped the bowl of his pipe into his palm. "I'll present your scheme to the Gentlemen XVII on Thursday before the Prince joins us. But, be warned, they are slow to change. The Republic's future might well hang on a move such as this."

"Then for what concerns Hell, how exactly do they describe everything as if they had actually been there?"

In Praise of Folly by Desiderius Erasmus (Classics Club edition)

CHAPTER 51—PIER

BEADS OF WATER TRICKLED ALONG THE WALLS OF my cell. Damp everywhere, even the straw mattress in the corner, if you had the guts to call that rag a mattress. The chill bit into my arms and legs and my bare chest, my skin like dead fish to my own touch.

The first few days I paid no attention to the cell, the wet, the vermin, the sour stench of old piss everywhere. Words, brittle as cracking ice, rattled in my head. My sole vision was the magistrate's finger pointing at me while his voice boomed: *You, Pier Veerbeck, guilty as charged. Fifteen years hard labor...* the smash of the gavel, the guard's iron grip on my shoulder, pushing me from the dock to the prisoner's door.

I caught a single glimpse of Maagda. She wiped her eyes. Pieter reached for her arm. Freddy sat, his head bent, refusing to meet my glance. Steubing watched, his lips a tight, sullen line when the guard led me away. He gave me his back when I passed near him. I expected another foul blast of spit. Was the bastard satisfied with my sentence?

To know I'll sweat, pant in a hellish labor pit, should satisfy him for the loss of those miserable stones.

Steubing had fought my contract with Horder in the courts, but the magistrate said Horder took the March diamonds in good faith. Hadn't I showed him provenance. The court said that the grower had no reason to doubt my ownership. Wouldn't mean anything now. I'd heard yesterday that the States General stopped tulip trading, all paper options frozen.

The iron door to my cell rattled. "Veerbeck!"

It was early for the lumps of mash pushed at me twice a day.

"Visitor," the guard rumbled in an ale-soaked grunt.

The door squealed on its rusted hinges, a screech that grated on my ears, sent more chill through me. I heard a step so light, surely, a woman.

"Maagda?"

She walked into the gloom of my cell, no hesitation at the squalor. Her clean gray skirt and white blouse and her rosewater scent, pitched her like a beacon against the squalor. I gulped for air at the sight of her.

"I've brought you clothes and fresh food," she said, her tone dry and matter-of-fact. She uncovered the large wicker hamper she carried, but made no attempt to touch me.

The guard pushed a chair in for her. "Fifteen minutes." He slammed the thick door behind him, and stood there eyeing Maagda through the grill until I shook my fist at him.

Maagda jumped when the bolt rammed back to its iron lock.

"How do you fare, Pier?"

I shrugged. Puny words, and damn few of those, remained between us.

"Would you like to eat something now or should I leave this for later?"

"Later, for me and the rats."

Maagda ignored the self-pity. She put a second, smaller basket down.

"I've brought you some wet cloths so you can clean yourself."

When I looked at the basket, I remembered the day long ago when we left Hoorn and I ridiculed the basket that carried her pet, Folly.

"I thought maybe you brought your cat to round up my cell mates." I swept my hand around the cell with its litter of small black droppings. My sarcasm poured out, unbidden. What did I expect from her?

"Yes, it is horrid. Do they move you soon?"

Useless talk. I wanted to argue with her, push her to curse me, to pound on my chest for the stupidity that put me here. Maagda refused my bait. Her calm bit worse than a bitter root. I hated it, that calm. It put her out of my grasp.

She waited for me to answer.

"I don't know when they'll take me to the wharf. Next week. Next month. Whenever a ship is ready to sail. I am told nothing."

She pushed the food basket toward me, offered a sausage. "I'll ask Willem to call on the Magistrate's office. Perhaps they'll give him information."

I pushed the basket back to her. Something inside me would not let her see my hunger.

Maagda remained steady and put the hamper aside. Had she bathed in ice water for this visit?

"Pier, there are papers that must be signed." She pulled documents from her bag.

"What's this?" I grabbed for them.

"A moment." She pushed away and snatched the papers from my reach. "I must sell the house and all furnishings. You recall the magistrate's order at your trial. The money goes to Mr. Steubing. He tried to get the money from me, but Willem said I am not liable for your crime. Now Steubing's to receive an annual payment from the magistrate's office for every year of your labor."

I winced to think of what that labor would cost me in backbreaking pain. Even my hands. That thumb that Horder snapped still twice its size and throbbing day and night. I listened to the stories from other prisoners here. Nightmares of rotting in some Batavian hole haunted me since the trial. I shit in terror.

Maagda saw me flinch, but carried on with her errand.

"An auction house has offered me 600 florins for the house and the furnishings. Adding the bed, Papa's wedding gift to us, would bring the total to 615 florins. I must have your signature on the deed for the sale."

I nodded to agree, a shred of glee inside that her Papa's bed was to go. When I looked up, I realized she wore no earrings, and when I glanced down at her hand, I saw her wedding sapphire was gone from her finger. So was her mother's garnet, a ring she always wore.

Maagda followed my eyes. "Everything is sold."

"You said you'd never part with your mother's ring."

"I no longer need its reminder."

Did her voice shake a little?

"What did it mean to you? You never told me."

"You never asked." She again offered the paper, a nib and a small, stoppered inkpot she carried in the bag.

Her hands trembled, at my plight I wondered, or some concern I couldn't know. Of a sudden I wanted to reach out and still her hands, but I held back and reached for the paper instead.

In the paltry light of the cell, I could barely read the list, but it seemed to include everything. Uncle Freddy had contributed his militia painting to the sale. My knuckles went white, but I gripped the pen and scratched my name on the page. I knew he did it for her, not for me. More man than I credited him for.

"And that one?" I reached for the other paper she held.

Color rose in her cheeks, and droplets of sweat formed on her face. What's this? Maagda not able to find her voice?

She straightened the bulky pages that had been folded in three, and stiffened herself against the back of the chair.

"This," she said, finally raising her gaze level with mine, "annuls our marriage. Willem prepared the papers. It's quite legal."

I sank against the wall. The words *annul* and *Willem* ricocheted from stone to stone, pounding me with blows I'd not expected. I groped for words, but they came, fueled by a rush of venom. "You divorce me over this with the help of my own cousin?" Anger stiffened my flesh, my bones. "My church does not know divorce, woman."

Maagda sat as rigid as that goddamned bed frame her father had given us.

"Not divorce, Pier. Annulment. Our marriage was never consummated. Even your church says a marriage must be consummated for it to be binding. Its purpose, remember, is to bring children into the world." She held my eye. "Besides, we were not married in your church. We deal with a civil matter here."

I grabbed for the papers, meaning to shred them. I lunged. She leaned back. Her chair tipped over. Maagda sprawled to the floor, catching the bottom hinge of the door. Blood trickled over her hand, and she gasped, but quickly wrapped her apron around the wound and clutched the papers away from the blood.

"Chrissake, what's going on in there?" The guard rattled the door.

"The chair tipped," Maagda called back. "All is well."

"Five minutes, then," he bellowed through the slot, "and keep it quiet."

"Maagda. It was an accident. I didn't try to hurt you."

She righted herself, smoothed her dress, and used her left hand to pat down her hair. Then she replaced her cap. "A scratch only."

I put the chair right side up. She stood behind it, clutching its back. She gritted her teeth, whether in pain or anger I couldn't fathom. She held a fullness about her I hadn't noticed before.

"Pier, there is one thing that must be understood between us. I am appalled that you allowed this obsession of yours to bring you such misery. But the theft has nothing to do with this annulment."

"Oh? You'd be content to sit and wait for a convict's return. Bet your Anna Pelter would wait for me."

She dismissed my words like I was some mute beggar on the Dam.

"I made up my mind to end this farce of a marriage when I traveled to Hoorn for Papa's burial. The decision I made is final. I return to Hoorn permanently."

"To live off the fat of your father's leavings?"

"There is no fat, Pier. But I plan to keep the Yard open, to run the business, to keep the men at work. Your Uncle Freddy will be my general manager."

She had to read the shock on my face. "You think merchants will deal with a woman? Never." I laughed.

"They will deal with the name Boscher, the Hoorn Yard."

Her barb cut deep. My own name was worthless. But what the hell, there was no one to carry it on, tarred or not.

"Still, you're but a woman."

"Yes," a glint of hot coal flashed in her eyes. "And you, Pier, have failed to notice how little being a mere woman means in these times. You asked a moment ago what Mother's ring meant to me. My father gave it to me the day you asked for my hand. He said it would remind me that I must become the person I was meant to be, not someone else's image of me. I am here as such a woman, not as the wife you *acquired*."

Her words knocked the words out of me. She stood back from the chair, eyes level with mine, chin set. Streaks of her strength had reared before in our marriage, but this was something different, something I understood from the set of her jaw that would not be broken.

She tidied her baskets and bag, preparing to leave. "I had hoped you would realize there is nothing left between us. Our marriage has been a ritual of convenience. It's finished."

Her voice held neither anger nor accusation, but her words rattled my gut. Like the night she called me a filthy animal, again this damnable woman laid me low and she hadn't lifted her finger or raised her voice. "What of my return?"

"At the end of your sentence, the government will grant you one passage anywhere a VOC ship sails and ten florins for your pocket, so Willem says. Am I to believe you will come back here when your life's desire has been the New World?"

She held the annulment papers out to me. "Give us both a chance...please." Her eyes glossed, but she turned her face away to hide the plea I caught there.

Still, I wavered, clenching my fingers into fists to mask the shaking. If I signed her paper, I cut every tie I had left to me. I watched a bead of water on the wall break away and slide down the rough stone.

"Two minutes," the guard shouted through the door.

She grasped the chair with both hands, looked me straight in the eye. "I'm prepared to offer 1,000 florins to cut short your sentence if you'll sign the annulment now."

My head jerked back and I laughed. "Where do you hope to get 1,000 florins?" I was ready to taunt her further, but the thought that the money would buy me as much as three years of freedom stopped me.

"Since Miekke is too ill to ever marry, she has agreed that the dowry set aside for her should be returned to Papa's estate. We can manage."

"So, our marriage comes down to money, an exchange for florins?"

"Hasn't it always? Nothing binds us, Pier, nothing save bad memories."

"I didn't intend to steal those diamonds,. It seemed so easy to borrow them for a few weeks."

Did she smile then?

"Your dream, Pier, not mine. Nothing remains of us now. Must we rust through another decade for this truth to reach you?"

I heard the guard's keys rattle. He unlocked the door to usher Maagda away.

She gathered her baskets and turned to leave. I reached for the papers.

"Gimme the pen."

She brushed my hand for a scant second when I returned the inked documents to her. Her warmth spread like hot peat through the chill in my body.

"May the gods go with you, Pier".

The gray of her skirt disappeared around the turn in the hall. I listened to the click of her heels fade down the passageway. The door clanged shut, the bolt slammed. The key turned, and the guard laughed. He'd heard it all. His taunts would come next.

*"A fool changes as the Moon, but a wise
man is permanent as the Sun..."*

In Praise of Folly by Desiderius Erasmus (Classics Club edition)

CHAPTER 52—MAAGDA

THE NEXT WEEKS WERE A RACE THROUGH THE LAST
details of my days in Amsterdam...magistrates to see, papers to reg-
ister, the deed to be presented, the house closed. I'd traveled to Hoorn
for two days each week to deal with the Yard and pay bills and the
men's salaries. Though Miekke no longer locked herself away from
me, she spoke only if I spoke first and then with a frost more bitter
than a dip in winter waters. But it was a beginning, and I welcomed
it, however small. As for neighbors in Hoorn, with Pier gone, there'd
be no need for explanations about my child. I'd give the shame of his
theft nothing more than a shrug. It would be forgotten in time.

I still had no word on when Pier would sail to his remote Pacific
island some 15,000 miles away. My chest tightened thinking of the
scene in his jail cell. So many times I almost broke my hold on myself,
wanting to comfort him in spite of our enmity. Odd to think of him
now as the man who *was* my husband. With Pier's signature, our
annulment had been granted. Willem brought me the final documents yesterday. Such a solid man, Willem. Papa would call him the

helmsman you'd want when you neared the shoals. He'd navigated enough treacherous waters for me of late.

When he arrived yesterday with the annulment decree, Willem said, "You're a free woman now, Maagda...in a way." He handed me the documents with their legal seals affixed. His face looked strange, somewhere between a smile and a leer...devilish.

"What do you mean *in a way?*"

"You've shed that rogue cousin of mine ...but, my good lady, you are up to your handsome brows in debt."

"Willem, what...?"

He grabbed me by the waist, lifted me off my feet and spun me twice around him.

"Stop it. Put me down." I laughed, his joy contagious. "What tavern's had your custom so early?"

"None. But a good wine is in order. It's ours, Maagda. This morning we closed the deal on the ship's cargo. We now own a full third of the stores the VOC brought home. Over thirty percent! Can you believe it?"

Stunned, I bit my lip and drew a deep breath.

"Oh, Willem. So much." Debt indeed and bone-eating panic until every barrel, every bale put florins on our books. And we still had no word from Klemp on the VOC's decision about our future.

"I knew what you went through with Pier, so when you entrusted me with the funds, I stayed in Amsterdam to watch the docks. I didn't want to intrude on your problems here. But it's done. We're a well-yoked team, lady, heh?"

I looked at him. I'd never seen this side of Willem, never noticed before. He was playful, no longer the staid, conservative attorney, the image I'd always carried of him.

My blood pounded, in thrall to the very idea of our successful cargo bid. So many of my dreams finally fell into place. If only Bjorn, Miekke...

"I trust our buyers will stay true to their contracts, Willem." I didn't want to dampen the high spirits of the moment, but I knew a person's word could change. Lord, did I know that.

"This wasn't sealed over a handshake, Maagda. A legal contract protects us...in writing, with signatures. Even if our buyers refused the cargo, the courts would make them pay. Not bad to have a lawyer for a partner, is it?"

On impulse, I grinned and reached up to tug the trim black beard he grew once again. He'd shaved it on some whim or other months back. Surprise to myself, I thought him more handsome with the beard. More finished perhaps.

"I must get word to Hoorn right away so my two fluyts leave the Yard and sail into Amsterdam on schedule."

Willem told me the whole venture, from docking, loading and setting sail for the buyer ports must be ready in five to seven days.

He grabbed my hand.

"Enough of packing and moving chores. Let's go down to the Damrak and admire our crates and barrels and bales. Let's gloat a little. We've earned it." He kissed me on the cheek and pulled me to the door.

I touched my cheek where he kissed it. A good man, Willem.

*"And, as usually happens when the sun begins to show his
Beams, or when after a sharp Winter the spring breathes afresh
on the Earth, all things immediately get a new face, new color,
and recover as it were a certain kind of Youth again."*

In Praise of Folly by Desiderius Erasmus (Classics Club edition)

CHAPTER 53—MAAGDA

PIETER HEAVED THE FEW HEAVY TRUNKS ABOARD. I
'd taken so little that we had Henrik's coach packed with space to
spare. Before I turned the house over to the auctioneer, I gave Pieter
and Colinda their pick of what was left. I cried when Colinda asked
for the embroidered curtains that launched *The Copper Thimble* so
many months ago, curtains that were my first attempt to brighten
Pier's home.

"I'll visit," I promised and wiped a tear from Colinda's cheek.
Pieter turned his head away, but not before I saw the moisture in
his eyes.

I had given Colinda full ownership of the business. The trade
flourished and she deserved the credit and the rewards. Perhaps in
time the drapers' guild would lift its ban on women, and *The Copper
Thimble* might compete as a full-fledged draper rather than a seam-
stress circle. After all, our customers seemed to prefer a woman's

touch. I felt I left something good behind, a thread of independence for Colinda and the ladies who had joined our sewing venture.

"I'll keep your garden watered until the new people move in," Colinda promised. German emigrees, escaping the war, had bought the house. Sad that the garden Colinda would water for them had run to weed in my long absences. Perhaps it would blossom as a play yard for their two small children.

"You won't have long to wait," I told her. "The family's been moving in and out of rented rooms for months. They may be lurking 'round the corner even now, watching for me to turn myself out of here so they might pay off the auctioneer and lay claim to these rooms." We laughed, but I felt it true, and wished them more happiness than I'd ever known within its walls. I harbored no sadness to put it behind me.

Colinda's little Hans clutched her skirts and hid his eyes behind its ecru folds when his mother held Breeda out to me for a farewell kiss. I waved to Hans and smiled at the tiny efforts Colinda and I made of talk for the future. I wanted so much to tell her that I, too, would give birth by year's end. The thought reminded me of another mother, one to whom I made a promise long ago. A final hug and I hurried to the carriage steps.

We loaded my last bag and moved along the lane to turn toward the Damrak. I pulled my shawl close, suddenly cold. I didn't know whether at the air or the leaving.

"Henrik, might we make two slight changes in our route?" I knew I would be his only passenger to Hoorn.

"Certainly, Madam Veerbeck. Tell me where."

"It's Maagda, Henrik. After all these years just Maagda. Please." No need to tell him I had shed Pier's name. He smiled and touched the brim of his hat with two fingers. He knew of Pier's trouble, but in his kindness said nothing.

"By god, almost forgot this." Henrik fumbled in his tunic and turned to hand me a paper. "Klemp over at the VOC sent this along."

My hand trembled when I reached for the note. I unfolded it slowly and closed my eyes before I looked at what might be written there.

The top was blank, but there, there in the middle, a single word, *Yes.*

I cried out and sank back into the seat, tears streaming down my cheeks.

"Madam Veerbeck…er, Maagda, you alright back there?"

"Oh yes, Henrik. So alright. I shed tears of joy. And now we must add a stop in Edam later today." Words of splendid joy would flow into my diary this night.

We moved past the Herrengracht toward the Niew Kerk where I called to him. "There, by that chapel. I'll only be minutes."

The thick door swung back slowly. Inside, candles danced in the muted light. A few scattered souls knelt in prayer. I half expected to see the gnarled old woman who had been so kind to me when I first arrived in Amsterdam. Were her prayers answered?

My eyes moved to the lady statue. She stood serene, her smile fixed on the baby cradled in her arms. I dropped coins in the box near the candles.

"The stuivers are for two," I whispered. *"I pay my debt to you from last time."* I lit a new taper, and looked again into her gentle face. *"And this to ask your blessing and the gift of family love, my sister's love, for the child I will soon hold."*

I held Klemp's paper to the candlelight to read his precious *yes* once again.

Back in the carriage, I directed Henrik to our second stop. We clomped along to the corner of Prins Hendrikkade and Gelderskade, a vantage point for the Oosterdok where ships were hawsered or lay at anchor to await a berth.

"Stop, Henrik. Just here. I don't want to go out along the dock."

Folly lay curled in my lap. I scooped her to my breast for her warmth. She purred with each slow stroke of my fingers.

The berthed ships jammed stern to prow along the wharf. I scanned the length of the dock until I spotted the *Rotterdam,* a three-mast galleon with cargo piled high on two decks. It would set out today for a voyage half way round the world to that remote place in the Pacific Ocean. A group of men in ankle chains lined up along the side, ready to move aboard. Then I saw him, fifth in line, slumped against a large vat, his back to the water lapping the ship's hull.

"Move, now," a heavy voice boomed from the top of the gang-plank. The men in Pier's line trudged up the boards. He lifted a small bag to his shoulder. Its bulk hid his face. He grabbed the rope rail to pull himself each step toward the deck.

"God speed," I murmured. Hardly the voyage he brokered his life for.

"Please, Henrik, home to Hoorn."

Hoorn, Holland — 1658

EPILOGUE

MOURNERS HUDDLED IN SMALL GROUPS ON THE wharf. My mother's ship, the *Maagda,* slipped its mooring and we glided to sea. Many of Hoorn's families waited in a silent farewell near the plum bedecked carriage of the House of Orange until we became a speck on the horizon. Mother would have laughed to know the Prince himself came to pay her tribute. Only our family, a few friends and men from the Yard came on board for this final journey.

I looked back to the town. Morning sun glinted from the polished windows of houses just visible along Grote Oost to our left. The stepped gables of the amber and rose-tinted homes framed the golden glow. How many times had my mother counted that same reflection a good omen when a new Boscher-built fluyt first splashed into the sea? She never missed the first sea trial. Nor shall I.

Uncle Freddy, long retired but still sure of foot on a pitching deck, squeezed my hand. I squeezed back. Together we watched the circular Hoofdtoren on the quay fade from view. The old round weights-and-measures house was a signal of home for seamen grateful to return from long voyages. I remember my mother's stories about how farmers lined up there to weigh their cheeses for sale.

Uncle Freddy put his arm on my shoulder. "She would be proud, don't you think, Maria?" Tears welled in the faded blue of his eyes, tears like my own.

"Perhaps more awed to be remembered like this." It had taken ten years of profitable business with the VOC for the prince and the Gentlemen XVII to bend and recognize Maagda Boscher, the woman. Until then, all custom was between the VOC and the Boscher Ship and Trading Company. Mother had taken it in stride, both the early affront and the later recognition.

"I must see to Aunt Miekke." I kissed Freddy's whiskered cheek and moved away before my tears flowed full. I dabbed my eyes dry with the hem of the dove gray apron I wore over my plum dress. Mother would not have wanted me in anything more somber. I remember her once telling me, "Ill not ripen to lavender until I've had my full of scarlet and plum." She never did advance to a mindset of lavender dresses.

My aunt sat bundled in a blanket against a morning chill carried on a sharp breeze from the North Sea. I had just neared her chair when the sails began to drop. The canvas sagged against the breeze. The ship slowed; I reached for Aunt Miekke's hand. Who would think this frail woman would outlive my mother? Captain Borkke walked toward us.

"It's time." He motioned us to the starboard side. He helped Aunt Miekke from her chair and took my hand. Young Mayor Jessel, Hans, the nephew of the Mayor who performed my mother's marriage thirty-two years ago, stood by the teak rail. The golden chain of his office caught bits of sunlight to soften the austere black of the coat and breeches. My mother's shrouded body lay behind him on a slip board. We had dressed her in her beloved silk kimono. No black this day for her either.

I saw only the back of the figure bent over her. Then his head rose, hatless, and the wind blew his gray hair in a swirl of tangles. A fine sheen of moisture collected on his beard and cheeks. He came to me and gripped my arm when the seamen lifted the board under Mother's now slight body.

"How could three decades fade away like this?" he asked in a quiet voice, almost to himself. He expected no reply, but I caught his glance at the gold signet ring on his right hand. He'd worn it since his twenty-first birthday he once told me, until Mother insisted it be her wedding ring, though too large for anything but her thumb.

My mother married Willem when I was three. They'd been partners in their trading business with the VOC for those three years when she finally consented to become his wife. He slipped into fatherhood as if born to it.

My natural father, Bjorn Kristiansson, had never returned from his voyage to Batavia. His ship, *Prince of Orange,* vanished in a tsunami off the coast of Bantam in the Malacca Straits. Neither survivors nor cargo were ever recovered. I was an infant then, but heard his story one autumn morning when mother and I sat secluded on the dunes. I cozied on her lap, my head on her breasts. She stroked my white blond curls. I felt the warm drop of a tear in my hair.

"My heart splintered like the wreck itself," my mother told me. "I felt the fire of life had been doused to ashes inside me."

She looked at me as though seeing me for the first time. " You are your father's child." Her lips brushed my hair. "You have his eyes, his dimpled chin, his perfect nose. Please grow with his gentle heart and open mind."

I likened her love for Bjorn, as a young girl might, to a comet that burned in a brief streak, while her years with Willem glowed like the calm, even fire that warmed a winter night. It neither leapt nor died away. Bjorn fascinated me, the handsome prince in a fairy tale, but it was Willem who heaved me to his shoulders to watch the militia parade, who taught me the secrets of spiral shells found on the beach, who wiped my tears and slate when schoolwork brought me to despair. All the father I needed.

Years later my mother told me the story of the men in her life. We read her diaries together, small calfskin books I never knew she kept. I marveled that she bore no rancor for the man called Pier. I loathed him in her stead when she filled in details to color the sparely written items she had scrawled in her pages. "Don't hate him," she urged. "He became a man after a hard, bitter childhood. It marked him for life."

"But someday such choices will be yours," my mother had said. "The right person to spend your life with is someone who makes you feel stronger inside than you ever thought you might be."

Another entry described a birthday trip to Amsterdam. She took me to the tiny church of the lady statue. We placed a coin in the small box and lit a taper.

"I had no one to tell but that silent Madonna that I was to be a mother." She hugged me. Even today when I shop in Amsterdam, I sometimes stop at the church to revisit that moment.

Mother lived too vivid a life to confine to dusty books and faded words. Alone with her this morning, I tucked the diaries in her shroud to go with her into the sea. I kept but a single volume, her last. She'd written, "I want you, Maria, to be sure of yourself, to understand there will be times when all that is left for you is to stand alone. And you will. The Legacy is yours now."

Hans Jessel's baritone bid me back to this final farewell. Willem gentled my head to his shoulder.

"Maagda, we commend you to your God, and to the solace of the Deep. Go in peace with the love of your family and of your friends and the gratitude of our Republic. You hold an honored place in our lives."

The soughing of the wind caught the splash and ferried it on high.

THE END

"You will not only with good will accept this small Declamation, but take upon you the defense of it, for as much as being dedicated to you.